THE WOMAN WHO UPPED AND LEFT

Audrey is often seized by the urge to walk out of her house without looking back — but she can't possibly do that. She is a single parent. She is *needed*. She has a job, a home, and responsibilities; not to mention a slothful teenage son's pants to pick up. But nobody likes being taken for granted — Audrey least of all. So the time has come for drastic action. And no one's going to stand in her way . . .

SPECIAL MESSAGE TO READERS

THE WOMAN WHO UPPED AND LEFT

FIONA GIBSON

LARGE
PRINT

First published in Great Britain 2016
by
Avon
a division of HarperCollins*Publishers*

First Isis Edition
published 2017
by arrangement with
HarperCollins*Publishers*

A catalogue record for this book is available
from the British Library.

ISBN 978–1–78541–352–0 (hb)
ISBN 978–1–78541–358–2 (pb)

Published by
F. A. Thorpe (Publishing)
Anstey, Leicestershire

Set by Words & Graphics Ltd.
Anstey, Leicestershire
Printed and bound in Great Britain by
T. J. International Ltd., Padstow, Cornwall

This book is printed on acid-free paper

Huge thanks as ever to my wonderful agent, Caroline Sheldon, and my fantastic editor, Helen Huthwaite, who is always such a joy to work with. Thanks to Jo Marino and Sabah Khan at LightBrigade PR for such great work in publicising my books.

For sixteen years I belonged to an incredibly inspiring and supportive writing group. Tania, Vicki, Amanda, Pauline, Sam and Hilary — you're such great friends, and even though I've moved away I shall still be bothering you from time to time. Thanks as ever to my amazing friends: Jen, Kath, Cathy, Liam, Michelle, Wendy R, Marie, Wendy V, Jane P, Ellie, Jan, John, Jennifer, Mickey and Carolann; to Chris and Sue at Atkinson Pryce Books, and to Kedi for insights on texting with teens.

Thanks too to my dad Keith (who is still sailing the salty seas at 80 years old), his partner Beatrice, and the wonderful staff at McClymont House who look after my mum, Margery, with such kindness (especially Sheila and Ruby).

Finally, to my dear family — Jimmy, Sam, Dexter and Erin, you're my darlings and I love you.

For Susan Walker, with love
and a hug on a chair.

CHAPTER
ONE

Fried Chicken

Pants. There's a lot of them about. Tomato-red boxers are strewn on the sofa, while another specimen — turquoise, emblazoned with cartoon palm trees and pineapples — has come to rest under the coffee table like a snoozing pet. A third pair — in a murky mustard hue — are parked in front of the TV as if waiting for their favourite programme to come on. I'm conducting an experiment to see how long they'll all remain there if I refuse to round them all up. Perhaps, if left for long enough, they'll fossilise and I can donate them to a museum.

Yet more are to be found upstairs, in the bathroom, slung close to — but crucially not *in* — the linen basket. The act of lifting the wicker lid, and dropping them into it, is clearly too arduous a task for a perfectly able-bodied boy of eighteen years old. It's *infuriating*. I've mentioned it so many times, Morgan must have stopped hearing me — like the way you eventually become unaware of a ticking clock. Either that, or he simply doesn't give a stuff. Not for the first time I figure that boys of this age and their mothers are just not designed to live together. But I *won't* pick them up, not this time. We can live in filth — crucially, he'll also run out of clean pants and have to start re-wearing dirty ones, turned inside out — and see if I care . . .

Beside the scattering of worn boxers lies a tiny scrap of pale lemon lace, which on closer inspection appears to be a thong. This would be Jenna's. Morgan's girlfriend is also prone to leaving a scattering of personal effects in her wake.

I stare down at the thong, trying to figure how such a minuscule item can possibly function as pants. I have never worn one myself, being unable to conquer the fear that they could work their way actually *into* your bottom, and require an embarrassing medical procedure to dig them back out. I know they're meant to be sexy — my own sturdy knickers come in multipacks, like loo roll — but all I can think is: *chafing risk*. And what am I supposed to do with it?

Although Morgan has been seeing Jenna for nearly a year, I'm still unsure of the etiquette where her underwear is concerned. Should I pick it up delicately — with eyebrow tweezers, perhaps — and seal it in a clear plastic bag, like evidence from a crime scene? Tentatively, as if it might snap at my ankle, I nudge it into the corner of the bathroom with the toe of my shoe.

Stifled giggles filter through Morgan's closed bedroom door as I march past. He locks it these days, i.e. with a proper bolt, which he nailed on without prior permission, irreparably damaging the original Victorian door in the process. We've just had a Chinese takeaway and now they're . . . well, obviously they're not playing

Scrabble. Having known each other since primary school, they've been inseparable since a barbecue at Jenna's last summer. Favouring our house to hang out in, they are forever draped all over each other in a languid heap, as if suffering from one of those olden-day illnesses: consumption or scarlet fever. They certainly look pretty flushed whenever I happen to walk into the room. "Yes, Mum?" my son is prone to saying, as if I have no right to move from room to room in my own home.

"Morgan, I'm off now, okay?" I call out from the landing.

Silence.

"I'm meeting Stevie tonight. Remember me saying? I'm staying over, I'll be back around lunchtime tomorrow. Remember to lock the front door and shut all the windows and *try* not to leave 700 lights blazing . . ."

More giggles. How amusingly *petty* it must seem, wishing to protect our home from thieves and avoid a £2000 electricity bill . . .

"And can you start putting milk back in the fridge after you've used it? When I came back last week it had actually turned into cottage cheese . . ."

Muffled snorts.

"Morgan! Are you listening? It blobbed out into my cup!"

"*Ruh*," comes the barely audible reply. With my teeth jammed together, I trot downstairs, pull on a black linen jacket over my red and black spotty dress, and pick up my overnight bag.

"Bye, Mum," I call out, facetiously, adding, "Have a lovely time, won't you?" This is the stage I have reached: the point at which you start talking to yourself in the voice of your own child. Where you say things like, "Thanks for the takeaway, Mum, I really enjoyed it."

The spectre of Jenna's lemon thong shimmers in my mind as I climb into my scrappy old Kia and drive away.

My shabby, scrappy *life*. It's not very "Audrey", I reflect as I chug through our small, nondescript town en route to the motorway. Although I don't obsess about her — the real Audrey, I mean — I can't help having these thoughts occasionally.

You see, my name is Audrey too. It *was* Audrey Hepburn; let's get that out of the way. It'll come as no surprise that I am named after Mum's favourite actress, which might sound sweet and romantic until I also explain that she and Dad had had an almighty row on the day she was going to register my birth. She'd threatened to go ahead with the Audrey thing. "Don't you *dare*," he'd yelled (Mum filled me in on all of this as soon as I was old enough to understand). And she'd stormed off to the registrar's and done it, just to get back at him over some silly slight. "What did Dad want to call me?" I asked once.

"Gail," she replied with a shudder, although it sounded perfectly acceptable to me. To be fair, though, I don't imagine Doreen Hepburn anticipated the sniggery comments I'd endure throughout childhood

4

and adolescence. You can imagine: "Ooh, you're so alike! I thought I was in *Breakfast at Tiffany's* for a minute!" In fact our name is the only thing we have in common. I'd bet my life that the real Audrey never picked up a single pair of pants, not even her own exquisite little scanties, and certainly not someone else's unsavoury boxers. Nor did she drive a crappy old car that whiffs of gravy (why *is* this? To my knowledge there has never been any gravy in it). The real Audrey was arguably the most gorgeous creature to ever walk on this earth. Me, I'm five-foot-two (if I stretch myself up a bit) with a well-padded bottom, boobs that require serious under-wired support and over-zealously highlighted hair. I am a shoveller of peas, a disher-outer of sausages and mash. I am a 43-year-old dinner lady and my wedding ring didn't come from Tiffany's; it was on sale at Argos, £69.

While some women feel disgruntled about changing their name when they marry — or, quite reasonably, flatly refuse to do so — I was so eager to become Audrey Pepper that Vince, my ex, teased, "It's the only reason you said yes." I kept it, too, even when I reverted to a "Miss" after our divorce, when our son turned seven. I never tell boyfriends my maiden name — not that there's been many. There was just the very occasional, casual date until I met Stevie nine months ago in a bustling pub in York.

I couldn't believe this charming, rakishly handsome younger man was interested. So intent was he on bestowing me with drinks and flattery, I suspected I'd been unwittingly lured into some kind of social experiment and that a reality TV crew was secretly filming the whole thing. I imagined people sitting at home watching and nudging each other: "My God, she actually thinks he fancies her!" I even glanced around the pub for a bloke with one of those huge zoom lenses. In fact, Stevie turned out not to be an actor tasked with seeing how many middle-aged women he could chat up in one night. He runs a training company, specialising in "mindful time management". I don't fully understand it, and it still strikes me as odd, considering he seems to have virtually *no* time to spare for normal things like going out for drinks or dinner with me. Hence the venue for tonight's date being a two-hour drive from home.

Here's another un-Audrey thing: meeting your boyfriend at a motorway service station on the M6 on a drizzly Wednesday night. Charnock Richard services, to be precise. We are not merely meeting there before heading off to somewhere more glamorous. I mean, that's *it*. We are spending the night at a motorway hotel. We do this a lot, snatching the odd night together when he's "on the road", as he puts it, which happens to be most of the time. However, I suspect it's not just for convenience, and that service station hotels are just his *thing*. His mission seems to be to make passionate love to me at every Welcome Break and Moto in the north of England.

It's just gone 7.30 when I pull into the car park. I turn off the engine and take a moment to assess the situation I've found myself in. I'm parked next to a mud-splattered grey estate with a middle-aged couple inside it; they're chomping on fried chicken and tossing the bones out of the side windows. I watch, amazed that anyone could possibly think it's okay to do this.

A lanky young man with low-slung jeans and a small, wiry-haired dog ambles towards my car. Spotting the scattering of bones, the dog starts straining on its lead and yapping like crazy. Dragging him away, his owner fixes me with a furious glare. "You're disgusting," he snaps.

Before I know what I'm doing I'm out of my car, shouting, "They're not *my* bones, okay? Maybe you should check before accusing people!"

"You're *mental*," the man retorts, hurrying away. The chicken-munching couple laugh as they pull away, and it strikes me, as I stand in the fine rain in my skimpy dress — my jacket's still on the back seat of my car — that I probably *do* look unhinged, and this is all a bit weird. This service station thing, I mean. This thing of Stevie expecting me to jump in my car to meet him with barely any notice.

Yet I do, nearly every time. I picture his teasing greeny-blue eyes — eyes that suggest he's always up for fun — and sense myself weakening. I imagine his hot, urgent kisses and am already mentally packing a bag. Never mind that I have another job, as a carer for elderly Mrs B, on top of pea-shovelling duties. At the prospect of a night with my boyfriend I quickly arrange for someone to cover my shift. Julie usually obliges. She's always keen for more hours.

So here I am, stepping through the flurry of pigeons pecking at the greasy chicken remains. Taking a deep breath, and inhaling a gust of exhaust from a carpet fitter's van, I make my way towards the hotel to meet the most beautiful man I've ever had the pleasure of sleeping with.

CHAPTER
TWO

Meat Feast Slice

Stevie springs up from the sofa in the soulless hotel bar and greets me with a lingering kiss. "Hi, gorgeous! You look lovely, Aud. I love that dress. You smell great too, and — wow — those shoes . . ."

"Thanks." My irritation over the chicken bones melts away instantly. Despite the drive, I opted for vertiginous black patent heels — stockings too, middle-aged cliché that I am (Stevie is a whippersnapper of 34. He was born in the 80s, for God's sake — okay, only just. But *still*).

"G&T, is it?"

"Love one," I say, unable to tear away my gaze as he makes his way to the bar. With his mop of dishevelled muddy blond hair and swaggery walk, he really is ridiculously sexy. He turns and smiles. He has the kind of angelic features — wide, clear eyes, a fine nose and pouty lips — that remind me of the centrefold pin-ups I used to rip out of my teen magazines: the kind you'd collect week by week, desperate for the face bit (which always came last). Whenever we're together, I see women glancing at him in appreciation. Not that there are any other women here now. Apart from us, the place is empty. The barman, who looks no older than Morgan, has already been smirking at us. I guess couples don't often greet each other like this here. The clientele are usually solo travellers — bored salesmen, besuited business types — or couples too tired to drive the whole way home. They're just breaking up the journey. They don't meet here for *dates*.

He returns with my G&T and a large glass of red for himself. "Happy birthday, sweetheart," he says, planting another kiss on my cheek.

I smile. "Well, it's still two days away . . ."

"Yeah, I know. Wish I could see you then but I'm down in the West Country, can't get out of it . . ."

"It's okay, I know how it is. I'm having lunch with the girls — everyone's off on Friday — and I'm sure Morgan'll pull something out of the hat."

"Yeah?" Stevie laughs. "You reckon?"

"Well, I'm not expecting a three-tier birthday cake but he might get it together to bring me a lukewarm coffee in bed." I chuckle as Stevie winds an arm around my shoulders.

"I'd love to be with you." He pauses and sips his wine. "I'm actually thinking of selling the company. Sick of all this travelling, babe."

"Really?" I am genuinely shocked. Stevie has built up his business from scratch and, from what I can gather, has done pretty well for himself. I can only assume he's a workaholic, as he lives in an immaculate one-bedroomed flat above his office in York. Despite it only being a twenty-minute drive away, I've only had the pleasure of going there . . . *once*. He's hardly ever

10

home, he explained. It's just a base, not somewhere he's especially attached to.

"I just want to see more of you," he adds.

"Well, I'd like that too." I sense a flurry of desire as he rests a hand on my thigh.

"The thing is," I add, "we *could* see each other more. I mean, we don't have to stay in hotels so often, do we? Morgan doesn't have a problem with you staying at our place, you know."

"Yeah, yeah, I realise that. He's a good kid." Stevie crooks a brow as his fingers detect the bump of suspenders beneath the flimsy fabric of my dress. "But it's nice to, you know . . . have *privacy*."

The barman squirts a table with disinfectant and gives it a vigorous rub with a yellow cloth. I know what he's thinking: *They're having an affair.* I've already been blamed for the chicken bones and now I'm being labelled as the kind of woman who sleeps with other women's husbands. And I'm *not*. Stevie has never been married, and has no children. Apart from living with a hairdresser in his early twenties — he refers to her as "the lunatic" — he's breezed through life pretty much doing his own thing. "Well," I continue, "there's nothing to stop me coming over to your flat more often."

"That miserable little place?" He shakes his head. "That's another thing, darling. I need to get myself a proper place — a *home* — somewhere that's not just a crash pad . . ."

"I like your flat," I remark.

He looks amazed. "You like it? What on earth is there to like?"

I sip my G&T. "Well . . . it's so pared down and uncluttered. You don't have stuff strewn everywhere. It feels sparse and simple, like a holiday flat."

Stevie smiles. "It's not very homely, babe . . ."

"I don't mind, honestly. I have enough homeliness at home."

He laughs and squeezes my hand. It *is* weird, though, this motorway fixation. I mean, I can understand the motel thing in the movies, in the States. They are tawdry and thrilling and slightly dangerous. Exciting things happen in those places. But this is an ordinary service station in Lancashire, with rain trickling steadily down the windows and a hoover droning away in the foyer. Stevie drains his glass. "Fancy another? Or shall we just head up to the room?"

"It's only just gone eight," I say, laughing.

"Yeah, well . . ." He leans closer and whispers, "Got chilled champagne in my case . . ."

I grin. "Very tempting."

"And proper champagne glasses . . ."

"So you brought your special seduction kit," I tease him, brushing away the tiniest thought that this doesn't feel quite right either — this kit thing — or the fact that we never bother with dinner on our overnighters. But, hell, he is an incredibly sexy man. So I knock back my G&T and grab his hand as he takes my small overnight bag. I've already brushed aside my doubts as we hurry upstairs — there's no lift — and tumble into our room.

We kiss fervently, like teenagers who've just discovered this thrilling act. As we pull apart, I register Stevie's small black leather wheeled case parked beside the bed. I glance around the room, which is pretty standard for a motorway hotel: decorative turquoise cushions arranged diagonally on the bed; coffee- and tea-making facilities crammed onto a small plastic tray on the flimsy desk; a hairdryer on a stand; a notice about fire evacuation procedures and a guide to Interesting Things to See and Do in Lancashire. And that's about it. They're all like this: the four we've stayed at on the M62, and the others we've "enjoyed" — and yes, I have enjoyed them in a bizarre kind of way — on the M6 and M1.

From his case Stevie lifts out a small leather box, in which two cut-glass champagne flutes nestle in an inky blue velvet nest. Not that I need champagne. That sole G&T would have done nicely. Then he's lifting a tissue-wrapped bottle of Krug from the case — it's properly chilled, he must have only just bought it — and popping it expertly open and filling our glasses.

We kick off our shoes and recline side by side on the bed, holding hands, legs stretched out. The bubbles whoosh to my head, and only momentarily do I wonder if Morgan will remember to lock the back door as well as the front.

Stevie kisses me, softly and slowly, and it's so lovely I'm barely aware of the distant hum of traffic outside. Another noise starts up — a fan, or an air conditioning unit — then fades from my consciousness as Stevie peels off my dress, followed by the only decent underwear I possess: a black push-up bra and matching lacy knickers. I can't quite fathom why sex with this man is so thrilling; perhaps because we only see each other around once a week? Or is it his relative youth, his taut, toned body? Or that we mainly do it in hotels? If you add it all up — the weird hotel meet-ups, the fact that I can hardly ever reach him on his mobile — you'd probably say, run a mile, woman, are you a raving idiot? You might even say, would the real Audrey drop everything to rush off and meet her date at a Day's Inn Motel on the M6?

No, of course she wouldn't. But I should also add that, before I met Stevie, I had actually given up on being in any kind of relationship at all. I'd started to wonder if I was emitting distinct dinner lady vibes, even when I was all dressed up for a night out. Perhaps, I'd begun to think, the whiff of school canteen macaroni cheese was emanating from my pores, and *that* was putting men off. For a while, I took to giving my freshly washed outfit a thorough sniff before any night out. Still no luck, until I met Stevie. I know I'm sounding pathetically grateful, finding myself a boyfriend with such obvious lady-pleasing qualities. But we *do* have fun, and it's thrilling to think that, instead of making cups of tea for Mrs B tonight and then coming home to channel-hop on my own, I have hours of pleasure ahead. Okay, I'll have to be up at the crack of dawn to make it home in time for work — pity, as checkout isn't until eleven (I'm familiar with such details) — but at least we'll grab some buffet breakfast. While Stevie's sniffy about the dinner menu, he does enjoy piling his plate high with hash browns and cumberland sausages. Then we'll be off: me back to my small, sleepy town just outside York, and Stevie to his next appointment somewhere in the Manchester area.

"That was amazing," he murmurs, pulling me close. I glance at my phone, which is sitting beside my empty champagne glass: 10.17p.m.

"It really was." My stomach growls as I kiss his delicious-smelling neck.

"You hungry, babe?"

"Yes, I am a bit."

He smiles, and plants a tender kiss on my forehead before swivelling out of bed. "No problem, I'll nip out and get us something . . ." I glance at his lean, taut body as he pulls on his jeans and shirt, wondering — as I always do — how I managed to get so lucky.

In his absence I stretch out in bed, enjoying the coolness of the sheets against my skin. From a laminated card on the bedside cabinet, I learn that the all-you-can-eat breakfast is just £5. I doze a little, then check my phone, to reassure myself that my darling son hasn't plunged his finger into an electrical socket or exploded the TV. No texts, which could signify that he's lying in a fried heap, although I know I'm being ridiculous. No contact from Morgan is completely normal — he tends to message me only when he needs to know where he might find money for late-night chips. And I can't bring myself to text Jenna to ask if he's okay; he'd be *mortified*.

My worries fade as the door opens, signifying that my hunter-gatherer has returned from the service station shop — open 24 hours, another benefit of conducting our sex life on the motorway — with a carrier bag of treats. "Hey," he chuckles, undressing swiftly and clambering back into bed, "imagine finding you here." I laugh as he tips out our provisions, which, I happen to notice, contains one of those Fuzzy Brush toothbrushes that come in a little plastic ball from a dispenser in the loos. "Forgot my toothbrush," he says with a grin.

"Another great thing about service stations," I snigger, which he chooses to ignore. We kiss, and we eat, and then, fuelled by a couple of Ginsters Meat Feast Slices and a tub of Pringles, we fall back into each other's arms.

It's lovely, as always. But I still can't shake off the feeling that this isn't quite right.

CHAPTER
THREE

School Dinners

Thursday, 10.35a.m., and I've just arrived home. The kitchen is littered with empty tuna tins — Morgan is prone to forking canned fish straight into his mouth, but has yet to master the art of depositing the tins in the bin — and an array of crumb-strewn plates. There's a spillage of pink juice (apple and raspberry?) on the table, plus a scattering of shattered Twiglets, like the components of some primitive game. I pick one up and bite it. It lacks freshness. I stare at the mess, dithering over whether or not to lose my rag, and deciding that I can't face a confrontation the minute I'm home.

Anyway, there's no one to be annoyed *at* as the rare nocturnal mating pair has yet to appear. Of course: it's not yet 11a.m. As my darling boy is currently neither in employment nor further education — unless you count a weekend course in beginner's circus skills, foolishly paid for by me, as he fancied "a go at street theatre" — he has no real reason to get up. While Jenna is reputedly studying beauty therapy, the course seems to have an awful lot of leisure time built in. I find it hard to comprehend how two people can do so little with their time.

"I'm off to work now," I call up from the hallway. "You might think about hoovering the stairs, Morgan? And get some shopping in, would you? We need bread, cheese, fruit . . . remember fruit? Does that sound familiar? Apples, pears, stuff like that. They grow on trees, reportedly good for you . . ."

An unintelligible response. At least I know he's alive.

"Or oranges? How about some of those? Full of vitamin C, darling, handy if you want to avoid rickets or scurvy . . ." His bedroom door creaks open and he appears on the landing in his oversized stripy dressing gown. He looks pale — light-starved and faintly sweaty — yet is still handsome in his rather malnourished, hair-untroubled-by-comb sort of way.

"*What* d'you say?"

I muster a brisk smile. "Fruit, darling. Get some, please. There's money in the jar. Oh, and clear up all that mess you left. I don't know who're you're expecting to do it for you. A team of magic elves?"

He peers at me, as if trying to process my incomprehensible request, then shuffles off back to his room.

"Even some canned pineapple would do," I trill, a little manically, as I step out into the street.

My daytime job is at the local primary school. The brisk ten-minute walk is just long enough for me to shake off domestic irritations and slip into the cheery persona required for working in the canteen. Our home town is definitely a proper *town*, although Morgan would term it a village as he reckons nothing of any interest ever happens here. "What am I s'posed to do

18

exactly?" he moaned recently, when I complained about his lack of activity. "I'm *dying* in this place. It's crushing my soul. Why did we ever leave York?" That's where he spent his first seven years until Vince, his father, and I broke up. It made sense then to move to the house my friend Kim had just inherited from her mum and offered to let to me at a ridiculously low rent. Although Morgan welcomed the move — and made friends here immediately — he now views it as unforgivable on my part.

School is an imposing Victorian red-brick building, with part of the playground given over to wooden troughs crammed with pansies and marigolds planted by the children. Although being a dinner lady didn't exactly feature on my plans, I had to find something — a stopgap — to fit around looking after Morgan when we first moved here. I try not to dwell upon the fact that it's been a *very* long time since his school hours have been a factor in my life.

In the kitchen, Amanda, the cook, is stirring an enormous pot of fragrant chicken curry. It's the last day of term, and there's a lightness in the air, a palpable sense of anticipation. "So what are you and Morgan up to this summer?" she asks, briefly looking round from the stove.

"Me and Morgan?" I laugh. "Nothing. God, can you imagine him wanting to come away with me?" I pause, then add, "I think me and Stevie might book a last-minute thing . . ." Why did I even say that? We have never discussed going away for more than a night together, and certainly nowhere other than a motorway hotel.

I pull on my blue school apron and set out plastic cups and water jugs on the tables. My proper job title is an MSA, a Midday Supervisory Assistant. I don't exactly look like your classic dinner lady — the stern auntie type with a perm — but then nor do my colleagues. Whippet-thin Amanda has a diamond nose stud and a bleach-blonde crop, while Delyth is all raucous laughter and glossy red lips, possibly the vampiest woman to ever grace a school canteen. However, she can be rather formidable when crossed; she takes no nonsense from the children. Me, I'm a bit of a pushover where kids are concerned — languid teenagers also, obviously.

"You mean you'd leave your poor boy home alone?" teases Delyth, who finds it endlessly amusing that I fuss over Morgan so much.

"I'm sure he'd survive," I say with a grin.

"Have you taught him to cook yet?"

I shrug. "Well, he can just about fry an egg without setting his hair on fire."

"God, Aud," Amanda remarks with a smirk, "you've treated that boy far too well. He doesn't need to figure out stuff for himself. He's never had to."

Although I shrug this off, something gnaws at me: because that's what Vince says too. He reckons I've pampered our boy, and that it's my fault Morgan seems to think it's fine to undertake nothing more taxing than wobbling about on his unicycle and half-heartedly tossing a couple of beanbags about. Can I add that

20

Vince is the one who started it, by buying our boy a juggling kit last Christmas "for a laugh". He was a bright, sparky kid until the teenage hormones kicked in: excellent at maths, science and history, forever huddled over a book. We'd watch movies and play board games together; it felt as if we were a little gang of two. I can no longer remember the last time he read anything — apart from the Chinese takeaway menu — and these days he seems allergic to my company.

But never mind that because the children are surging in now, the younger years first, jostling into a straggly line at the counter while Delyth and I dish out their meals. It's an Indian banquet today, to celebrate breaking up for summer. The queue has already disintegrated into an unruly gaggle. There are shrieks and giggles and much pushing in. "Calm down, everyone," I exclaim, stopping Joseph from grabbing a handful of mini naans.

"Please, Miss Pepper!"

"No, Joseph, only one naan each."

"Miss, *please*, they're only tiny—"

I glance at Delyth, expecting her to lay down the law. But no, she's smirking while doling out curry and rice from the stainless steel containers. "Go on, let him have two," she hisses.

"It's a special day, Miss Pepper!" giggles Holly, clutching her tray.

I frown, deciding it must be the fierce July heat that's making the children so giddy today. Fleetingly, I wonder whether Morgan has managed to draw his bedroom curtains yet, and picture him staggering back, half-blinded by the sudden exposure to sunlight. Delyth and I finish serving the younger ones, and I deal with a small altercation between a bunch of girls at a table — "I'm saving a place for Shannon!"

"You're not allowed to save places, Lily, you know that . . ."

"*Please*, Miss Pepper . . ." And off they go again, dissolving into splutters of laughter.

Delyth and I serve the older years, who are no less hyped up than the little ones, then it's on to wiping tables as the children begin to congregate at one end of the hall. Normally they'd have surged out to the playground by now. Today though, they're sort of *loitering*. I've never seen this happen before. "Off you go," I prompt them. "Your lunchtime's ticking away. Don't you want to be outside in the sunshine?"

"Not yet, Miss Pepper!" someone blurts out. There's a ripple of sniggered asides. I frown at Delyth, then catch the eye of Moira, the head teacher, who's glided into the canteen, as regal as the figurehead on a ship with her magnificent bosom and glossy black hair piled high.

"Everyone!" she calls out, waving a large white envelope above her head. "Boys and girls, gather round and remember what we said at assembly this morning . . ." Another burst of laughter. ". . . Now, all quieten down while I make a very important announcement . . ."

"What's going on?" I whisper to Delyth.

She shrugs. "No idea."

"Not leaving, is she?"

"Maybe. I haven't heard anything . . ." She clears her throat and studies her fingernails. I glance around the crowded canteen. It feels as if the children, who are clearly having trouble containing their excitement, know exactly what's going on. And it dawns on me, slowly, that *everyone* does — even Delyth, who's clearly trying to suppress a grin — apart from me.

"Shhhh!" Moira hushes everyone as only a head teacher can. As the chatter fades, I realise the entire staff is here — teachers, secretaries and classroom assistants; even Greg, the janitor. Stranger still, everyone is staring at *me*. I sense my cheeks glowing hot and sweep my hands over my ponytailed hair.

Moira raps a table with a plastic teaspoon. The room has fallen silent. "Today," she starts, in her authoritative tone, "is a very special day. Yes, I know it's the last day of term and you're all desperate to get out of here and have fun. But before that, I have in my hand a very special letter . . ."

"We know what it is!" Joseph pipes up.

"Joseph, you *don't* know," Delyth reprimands him, waving a finger.

"We do. We all guessed!"

Moira grins. "You might remember, a few months ago, I secretly asked you all to write a couple of sentences about one of our dinner ladies who's been here for *such* a long time, and has seen so many of our children grow up through the school . . ."

Oh, my lord. Delyth only joined us last year, and Amanda's only been here a couple of terms. She means me.

". . . Ten years, she's been here," Moira goes on. "That's even longer than me, which is saying something . . ." Everyone laughs, and I think: yep, I arrived in the era of jam roly poly and now it's all chopped mango and kiwi. And it hits me: I'm getting some kind of long service award, a carriage clock for the dusty old retainer of the school canteen. Which would be lovely, of course. I do need a properly working clock. But Christ, do I feel *old* . . .

". . . Always been so kind and wonderful," Moira goes on as my cheeks blaze. She turns to me. "I'd like to read out a few of the things the children said about you, Miss Pepper . . ."

I swallow hard as she pulls a sheet of A4 from the envelope. What the heck have they said? "'Miss Pepper is a lovely smiling lady . . .'" It feels like something has caught in my throat. "'She's my favourite dinner lady in the whole world,'" Moira reads on. "'She's always kind and she never gets cross, even when we spill water or drop food on the floor . . .'"

My vision fuzzes as I remember the bad thoughts I had yesterday, beaming hatred at Morgan's boxers and kicking Jenna's thong into the corner of the bathroom to fester with the dusty old bottles of floor cleaner and bleach. When did I become so intolerant? What happened to the fun, perky woman who blithely stepped over the odd dropped item of underwear, and who never seethed over a dressing gown dumped on the stairs, and who was *certainly* never seized by an urge to set it alight? They see only the good side of me here: the woman who runs off to find a plaster for a cut knee,

24

and takes the time to chat to a little girl who's crying because there was no room for her to sit with her friends.

Sure, I'm good with other people's kids. I love their enthusiasm for life. If only they knew what a colossal grump I am at home, fizzling with irritation over scattered trainers and the forever elusive remote control . . . "'Miss Pepper is like a kind friend to me,'" Moira continues, and there's more, so much more: about the time I "helped" Ailsa Cartwright (she means when I spotted a remarkably fat nit crawling in her hair and quietly whisked her to the office and called her mum without anyone else ever finding out). Now Moira is talking about some kind of prize I've been awarded, but I'm not paying full attention. Instead, I'm thinking, what would anyone have done, in that situation? Produced a loud hailer and boomed, "Back off, everyone, Ailsa's crawling with lice?"

"Our incredibly kind, hard-working, long-serving dinner lady," Moira booms across the hall. "So here's to another ten years with the wonderful Miss Pepper, dinner lady of the year!"

"What?" I blurt out as the room fills with applause.

"You're dinner lady of the year!" Delyth exclaims, throwing her arms around me. "What did you think this was about?"

I laugh, shaking my head in amazement. "I had no idea. I mean, I didn't even know there was one . . ."

"Well, there is," she laughs, "and you're *it*."

"Bloody hell . . ."

"Language, Miss Pepper," Joseph giggles.

I smile, tears forming as quickly as I can blink them away. "But what is it? What does it mean?"

"It means," Moira says with exaggerated patience, "there's a national competition to find a dinner lady who does far more than her usual duties . . ."

"Like helping us build that massive snowman," Joseph pipes up.

"And washing the netball team kit," Amanda adds with a grin.

"*And* you let us throw wet sponges at you at the car boot sale!" shrieks someone from the back, somewhat overzealously.

"So we put you forward," Moira adds, "and, well, the judges agreed that you're pretty amazing . . ."

"Really? I don't know what to —"

"Speech!" Delyth calls out, and the children's chatter melts away into a respectful hush.

I give her a quick, alarmed glance and push back a strand of hair that's dangling at my boiling cheek. "I, er, I mean . . . I can't begin to . . ." Oh no. Hot tears are spilling now as I try to scrabble together an intelligible sentence. I have never made a speech in my life; I'm not even keen on being the centre of attention. "I'm delighted," I start, blotting my face with my apron. "This means so much to me. I love my job here, you're all such wonderful people . . ." I tail off, fazed by the sea of expectant faces all turned towards me. ". . . And all I can really say is . . . this is totally unexpected and completely wonderful. Thank you *so* much . . ." There's a cheer as I am handed a huge bouquet — an explosion of red and orange blooms —

26

then a cake appears, carried towards me on a silver board by a grinning Amanda. The outlandish creation is swirled with creamy icing, with *Congratulations Miss Pepper Dinner Lady of the Year!!!* in wobbly pink piping on top. Clearly, one of the kids has had a hand in the decorating. There's more cheering, and paper plates appear, and the cake is cut up and distributed to the children who stuff it into their mouths before rushing outside, icing smeared, to play.

"You really deserve this, Audrey," Moira says, hugging me.

"Thank you, I'm still trying to take it in . . ." I swipe the last remaining piece of cake. It's tiny; no more than a mouthful.

"So which prize are you going to choose?"

"Oh, er . . ." I lick a sticky smear from a finger. "I'm sorry, I didn't actually catch —"

"You weren't listening?" Moira laughs with mock indignation. "You're worse than the kids, Audrey. Mind always elsewhere."

"Well, er, I was quite overwhelmed . . ."

She chuckles. "Okay, there's a prize of a French cookery course — classic cuisine and patisserie in a fancy hotel down south somewhere. Buckinghamshire, I think. I can't quite remember. Come on, I have all the details in my office . . ." We retreat to the tiny, cluttered room where she hands me a glossy brochure depicting the hotel. Wilton Grange is a grand, turreted affair with landscaped gardens and a lake, surrounded by rolling hills and woodland.

"Wow," I murmur. "I've never stayed anywhere like that."

Moira smiles. "I know, it's incredible . . ." She has the decency to flick through a sheaf of paperwork as I pore over the brochure. The oval lake is flat as glass and edged with swathes of yolk-yellow flowers. There are four-poster beds in the traditional rooms, and sunlight streams in through enormous bay windows. Recently, I felt obliged to move out of my own bedroom, which is next to Morgan's, due to being woken up to the toe-curling soundtrack of my son's energetic sex life.

I just couldn't bear it. I tried sleeping on my side and stuffing a pillow corner into the exposed ear, but the terrible noises still forced their way through. Ditto with many types of earplugs: foam, silicone, even wax. "Snoring husband?" asked the woman in the chemist with a snigger, the third time I went in. Apart from the utter *wrongness* of hearing your own child at it — a child whose Action Man still resides in the house, along with his spy's fedora hat and the code-cracker's kit he was obsessed with — it also highlighted how dismal my own love life had become. This was before I'd met Stevie. At that point, I hadn't been to bed with anyone for almost two years. While I vaguely remembered the various anatomical parts, I couldn't actually picture a naked man in any kind of realistic way. If this went on any longer, I feared I'd have to study Action Man just to remind myself. But then, Action Man doesn't have a penis — just an eerie plastic slope — so that wouldn't have been any help. Anyway, I moved into the box room at the far end of the landing. It's tiny. That's fine. I'd rather sleep in a drawer than be subjected to the ecstatic gruntings of a boy who is still barely able to operate a toaster.

Moira is clutching the paperwork to her chest. "So there's that," she remarks, "a five-day residential course with some fancy chef, what's his name . . ." She peers at the brochure. "Brad Miller. Never heard of him . . ."

"Neither have I."

"But it does sound incredible . . ."

"It really does." I nod.

She pauses. ". . . Or there's a cash prize of £5000."

I stare at her. "Really? So I could choose that instead?"

She nods. "I'm so proud of you, Audrey . . ."

"Thank you," I say, folding the brochure and placing it on her desk. Five thousand pounds! Perhaps not an earth-shattering amount to some, but to me? Pretty life-changing. Seriously, I cannot remember a time when I wasn't utterly broke. My Charnock Richard date shoes were from the PDSA charity shop and I'm forever stretching yesterday's food to cobble together another meal today. I don't blame Vince for no longer bankrolling our son, because I shouldn't either; by rights, Morgan should be making his own way in the world. But the reality is that he's not, and some months I struggle to make even our perfectly reasonable rent, although I'd never tell Kim this (she'd probably let me off, which would be mortifying).

"The course is worth twice that," Moira adds.

"Really? I can't believe anyone would pay that kind of money to learn to cook . . ."

"Me neither," she laughs. "Guess some people have more money than sense. So ... have you decided which prize you'll take? Or d'you need time to make up your mind?"

I muster a wide smile and give the brochure one last, lustful glance. "Oh, I'll take the money of course," I say firmly. "I mean, I'd be crazy not to."

CHAPTER
FOUR

Disappointing Soup

I leave school with my outlandish bouquet propped over one shoulder, like a toddler, wondering what to spend my prize money on. Not because there's nothing I need, but because there's so much: a new car, perhaps — one that starts every time? I could upgrade our furniture — most of it is quite pitiful, and our kitchen table has a gouge out of it from when Morgan rammed into it on his unicycle. Or maybe I should stash away the cash to avoid further rent panics?

I call Kim to share my news. "You can't spend it on something sensible," she declares. "For God's sake, it's *prize money*. It's for something treaty and fun, not a bloody kitchen table or curtains or—"

"Yes, but—"

"That's the law," she cuts in, forthright as usual. Kim is a make-up artist: renowned for her ability to beautify not only the bride, but battalions of bridesmaids in record time. "You should have fun with it," she adds. "You're long overdue a shopping spree, Aud. Why don't we have a day out?"

"I'd love to," I fib, remembering our last trip to York together, which culminated in her virtually manhandling me into a spray tan salon. My milky-pale skin turned an alarming shade of terracotta, like a plant pot. "God, Mum," Morgan exclaimed on my return. "I hope that's gonna scrub off."

"Sure you don't want to take the hotel prize?" Kim asks. "Do something for yourself for a change? Or take the cash and blow the lot on a holiday, surprise Stevie . . ."

I laugh, shaking off a twinge of regret that my boyfriend isn't the type who'd allow himself to be whisked away. "He doesn't do surprises, you know that. He operates on a strict schedule."

"Oh, of course," she says dryly. "I forgot."

"I'll think about it, okay? And I'll see you tomorrow . . ."

"Can't wait, birthday girl," she says warmly as we finish the call. I quicken my pace, deciding it's not really about the money, although a spree would be fun; it's the fact I won it at all. Dinner lady of the year! I still can't figure out what I did to deserve it. This sets me thinking, as I stop off to pick up a few groceries for Mrs B's: how much longer am I planning to work in a school canteen? Sounds churlish, I know, after the children wrote such lovely things about me. But something about Moira's speech has lodged in my brain: ". . . *Our incredibly kind, hard-working, long-serving dinner lady . . . here's to another ten years!*" Bloody hell: I'm 44 tomorrow. Do I still want to be dishing out potato wedges at 54?

Laden now with shopping *and* flowers, I trudge along the cobbled driveway which cuts across Mrs B's enormous lawn to her stark, gunmetal grey house. It has the air of an approved school, or a former mansion taken over for governmental purposes. Even the beautiful gardens, the herbaceous borders bursting with colour, fail to raise its spirits. Six of the seven bedrooms are never used — apart from when Mrs B's daughter, Victoria, comes up from London to pay an occasional visit — and the entire upper floor remains chilly and damp, even on a bright summer's day. "The only way I'm leaving here is in a coffin," Mrs B retorted, when I gently asked if she ever planned to downsize.

Spotting me, Paul, the gardener, sets down his wheelbarrow and strides across the lawn. "God, Aud," he exclaims, "they're beautiful. You shouldn't have." I laugh and fill him in on today's events. "That's amazing," he says, sounding genuinely impressed. "You should've taken the rest of today off, done something special to celebrate."

"I couldn't really, not at such short notice . . ."

He smiles, rubbing his five o'clock shadow. When I started working here four years ago — my dinner lady earnings weren't nearly enough, and being a home help and carer seemed preferable to bar work — Julie happened to mention the "sexy gardener" who'd recently transformed Mrs B's grounds. I had to admit that the dark eyes, the chestnut hair and general rugged, outdoorsiness of him all added up to one pretty appealing package. "Doesn't say much, though," she added. It took a few months to learn that Paul's apparent shyness was, in fact, just a desire to get on with his work. "I noticed you swapped with Julie yesterday," he adds. "I had a box of veg set aside for you, don't forget to take them today . . ."

"That's so kind of you," I say, meaning it: I am eternally grateful for the virtually limitless supply of produce he supplies.

"So?" He grins, squinting in the bright sunshine. "Impromptu motorway date, was it?"

"Yep, that's right." I chuckle awkwardly. Hell, what possessed me to tell him about Stevie's preferred venues for meet-ups? I'd only meant to ask him how long it would take me to get to Lancaster Services and then it had all poured out. And now, he won't let it go.

"Lucky lady," he teases. "So where was it this time?"

"Charnock Richard."

Paul barks with laughter. "Oh, Aud. He knows how to treat you special. The romantic drone of six lanes of traffic . . ."

"You could hardly hear it actually," I say, a trace defensively.

". . . The whiff of fuel from the petrol station, the all-you-can-eat breakfast buffet with those coiled-up sausages . . . how much was it this time?"

"A fiver," I say with a snigger.

"Bargain . . ." He smirks. For some reason, he seems to derive enormous pleasure from hearing about my adventures. I'm not sure if he has the odd dalliance himself; there's been no evidence of women around, as far as I've noticed, apart from his ex-wife, who drops off their daughters for weekends at the cottage behind the main house, which comes with the gardener's job. I spot Jasmine and Rose from time to time, helping their father to harvest vegetables, or darting like shy woodland creatures between shrubs. At seven and eight, they clearly love their visits to their dad's.

"It was actually an early birthday treat," I add with a grin.

"Oh, when's the big day?"

"Tomorrow." I smile.

"Not the biggie, is it?"

"You mean 50?" I ask, aghast. "Thanks a bunch, Paul!"

He laughs. "I meant 40 . . ."

"Flatterer. I'll be 44," I say with a smirk.

"Ah, nothing to get too het up about then. C'mon, give me that shopping and I'll help you in with it . . ."

"Thanks," I say, and we make for the house where I give the bell two brief rings — just a courtesy really — before stepping in and inhaling the stale, musty air. "Hello, Mrs B?" I call out, propping my bouquet against the wall in the hallway and taking the shopping from Paul. "It's me, Audrey . . ." As he heads back out to the garden, I drop off the groceries in the kitchen and make my way to the rather faded, chintzy drawing room to greet her.

"How are you feeling today?"

"Just the same," she replies tartly, "sitting here all on my own."

"Oh, hasn't Paul been in to make you a cup of tea?"

She peers up at me through wire-framed glasses. Like a tiny bird with plumage of fluffy white hair, she is perched in her usual spot: squished up at one end of the enormous brown Chesterfield. The rest of the sofa is heaped with unravelling balls of wool and half-finished embroidery projects. "Paul?" she repeats with a frown.

"Yes, Paul. I know he pops in every morning . . ."

"He makes terrible tea," she says crossly. "Far too weak. I keep telling him but he won't listen." On her lap, the newspaper is open at the cryptic crossword. *Here we go . . .*

"Well, maybe Julie could stay longer in the mornings? I'm sure we could work out a rota, or perhaps find a new person to do extra—"

"Never mind that," she cuts in, rapping at the paper with her pencil. "Help me with this. Seven across, eleven letters . . ."

"Oh, you know I'm no good at these, Mrs B." As an avoidance tactic I start gathering up the cups and glasses that litter the numerous spindly side tables.

"'Biblical character jumps ship, perhaps.' Four-five . . ."

"Really, I have no idea . . ."

"Don't be so defeatist."

I pick up a plate bearing the remains of one of those pastries with squashed currants inside. I have to say, Mrs B favours the more dismal end of bakery goods. She is still watching me, waiting for an answer. "*I* know," I blurt out. "I've got it. King somebody . . ."

"Pardon?"

"That king, the one who made the sea go back with his hands . . . King Canute!" I smile, feeling pretty confident that I've got one right, therefore proving I'm not the halfwit she has me down for.

"I don't know how you came up with that," she mutters.

"You know — the sea, jumping ship . . ."

"King Canute is *four-six* . . ."

"Oh yes," I say, feeling chastised as I stack all the crockery onto a sticky wooden tea tray. She gnaws at her pencil and mutters an unintelligible answer before setting the newspaper aside with a sigh. I don't even know why she keeps insisting on pinging incomprehensible clues at me. It's like expecting a plumber to be capable of performing root canal work.

"Didn't anyone ever teach you how to do crosswords?" she asks, as if I lack a vital skill: like tying shoelaces or telling the time.

"No one did them in my house," I explain. "Dad didn't really have time for that kind of thing, and remember I told you Mum left when I was nine? She went off with Brian Bazalgette who delivered our coal. Huge guy, strong as an ox from lugging those enormous sacks from his truck to—"

"Oh yes, your mother married the coal man." Her pale eyes glint with interest.

"Well, she's never married him, but they still live together . . ." *As far as I know*, I add silently. Mum's communications have been pretty sporadic over the years. She doesn't have a mobile, or even a landline at her cottage deep in the Welsh valleys. How can you keep in contact with someone who really doesn't want to be contacted? While I have written to her, sporadically, over the years, Mum is never prompt with a reply, and she doesn't own a computer. I can count on one hand the times she's seen Morgan, her only grandchild.

The first time, a few weeks after he was born, she arrived a little dishevelled at our tiny terraced house in York; the journey from Wales had apparently involved numerous changes of bus. Brian didn't come with her, and all she would say was that "it's not his sort of thing". *What isn't?* I wanted to ask. *Meeting your grandchild, getting to know your daughter or accompanying you on a trip?* I barely knew Brian. With his coal-dusted face and gruff demeanour, I'd always stayed well out of his way when he delivered our coal, and couldn't quite see his appeal.

On her visit, I noticed Mum had swapped the nondescript catalogue clothes she used to wear for a raggle-taggle ensemble of washed-out T-shirt, an unravelling cardi and batik-printed trousers that hung loosely on her skinny frame. She brought with her the potent scent of patchouli and woodsmoke, plus a charity shop sweater for Morgan with a penguin appliquéd on the front. When I asked whether Brian was still in the coal business, she replied vaguely, "Oh, he's just doing this and that." She seemed terrified of holding Morgan, and even Vince, who's pretty generous about most people he meets, jokingly remarked that Mum was "a bit of an oddball . . . I can see where you get it from, Aud."

Subsequent visits have been brief and a little tense. Mum has always been armed with numerous excuses about why I can't visit her in Wales — "We're doing the place up, it's good for me to get away" — and four years have slipped by since I last saw her. I miss her, of course. I especially missed her when Morgan was young, and I wanted to pick up the phone and ask her, "Why is he screaming, d'you think? And how d'you wean a baby? I mean, what do they *eat*? He spits out everything I give him!" Of course, I couldn't do that and, over the years, as I found my feet as a mother and needed her less, I began to accept that this was how things were. At least, how she and I operated. I have never understood why she has never wanted to be a proper grandma to Morgan. When *he* has a child — years from now, obviously — I'll be muscling right in.

Mrs B tuts. "Yes, you did tell me about that. Dreadful situation . . ." She presses her thin, pale lips together and shakes the newspaper at me. "Anyway, *this* is an easy one. Even you'll be able to get this. 'Briefly dying caterpillar mocks snow', nine letters . . ."

"Really, it might as well be in Mandarin . . ."

She emits a withering laugh as I gather up scissors and pin cushions from the sofa. It strikes me that an unhealthy proportion of my life is spent putting things away. It's not that Mrs B — or I — care about everything being neat and tidy. I just don't want her impaling herself on an embroidery needle. "Did you have the rest of that lentil soup for lunch today?" I ask.

"No, I threw it away."

I blink at her. "Really? Was there something wrong with it?"

"It was very bland." She gnaws at the end of her pencil.

"Oh." I clear my throat. "I could make carrot and coriander for tomorrow, if you'd prefer that, or maybe mushroom . . ."

"Hmm, I'm not sure about that . . ."

"Or leek and potato?"

"Ugh, no." She shudders visibly and fills in a clue.

How about tomato and horse testicle? I pause, knowing I'm being played with.

"Just ask whoever's coming to bring me some tinned ones tomorrow," she mutters. "I find they have more taste."

"Fine," I say, fixing on a bright smile. "Look, it's lovely and sunny outside. Would you like to sit in the garden?"

She nods, and her face softens; Mrs B adores her garden. So I help her outside, taking her arm to guide her — she is a little unsteady on her feet — where she sits on the bench in her favourite shady spot. The lupins are looking especially lovely today. Paul has a knack for planting which makes everything seem so casual and effortless, yet the colours merge together beautifully. Before I worked here, I had never realised that gardening is a real art.

While Mrs B browses the newspapers I make her favourite dinner: cod with mashed potatoes (she prefers her food to have no colour at all, maybe *that's* what was wrong with the soup) and carry it out to her on a tray. She is happy to sit out until the evening starts to chill, and I persuade her to come back indoors. As I rattle through my evening tasks — a bit of light housework, helping Mrs B into her seated shower and shampooing her hair — a single thought keeps darting through my brain. *I've won £5000!*

"Make sure you wash out all the shampoo," she remarks, folding her skinny arms over her naked body as I rinse her with the shower attachment.

"Yes, Mrs B." *Apart from a Noddy eggcup in a colouring in competition, it's the first thing I've ever won!*

"And the conditioner."

"I will, Mrs B. I do always rinse you very thoroughly, you know."

Can't wait to tell Morgan! How shall we celebrate? The offy'll be closed by the time I'm finished here . . .

"Well, my head was itchy the other night. I couldn't sleep because of it. Clawed myself half to death . . ."

"Maybe your scalp's a bit flaky?" I suggest.

"In all of my 84 years I've never had a flaky scalp!" she barks, as if I'd mooted the possibility of syphilis. God, she is especially crotchety today. I could murder a drink. Surely there's something at home, a bottle of Jacob's Creek lurking in the cupboard or maybe some brandy left over from the Christmas cake . . .

Having dried off Mrs B, I help her into her peach cotton nightie and sheepskin slippers and lead her slowly from the downstairs shower room to her bedroom on the ground floor. It used to be a dining room; these days, Victoria, her carers and the occasional tradesman are the only people who ever venture upstairs.

Once she's tucked up in bed, I bring her a cup of strong tea and two chocolate digestives, plus her toothbrush and a small bowl of water, for post-biscuit cleansing. I once suggested she snacked a little earlier so her teeth could be attended to in the bathroom, rather than in bed. You'd think I'd suggested she scrub them with the loo brush. "*This* is how I like to do it," she retorted. So I wait patiently as she waggles her toothbrush in the water and try not to reel backwards as she spits violently into the porcelain bowl.

I hand Mrs B a flannel so she can dab at her pursed mouth, then tuck in her sheet and satin-edged blankets — she regards duvets as "a silly modern invention" — and click off her main bedroom light, leaving just the orangey glow of her bedside lamp. This room smells rather stale, despite my obsession with airing it as often as possible. The bowl of pot pourri sitting on the glass-topped dressing table probably stopped emitting scent in about 1972. Yet when I've suggested replacing it she has scowled and said, "It's fine as it is." I pause and glance back at her. She seems even tinier now, like a Victorian doll — the ones that look fragile and a little a bit scary — in her queen-sized bed. Her face is pale, almost translucent, her hair a puffy white cloud on the hand-embroidered pillowcase. As I see her so often, perhaps I don't notice all the changes in her. However, it has struck me recently that she is becoming more frail, and that the arm to steady her in the garden is no longer just a precaution, but entirely necessary. "Anything else you need before I go?" I ask.

"No, thank you." She fixes her gaze on me, as if there *is* something, but she's thought better of asking for it.

"Are you sure? It's no trouble . . ."

"I'm fine," she says brusquely.

Well, that's *me* told . . . "Goodnight then, Mrs B." I turn and make my way out of her room and across the gloomy hallway towards the front door, where I take my jacket from the hook and pull it on.

As I pick up my bouquet, her voice rings shrilly from her room. "Could you come back here a minute?"

Christ, don't say she's fallen out of bed. No thud, though: she probably just needs the loo. Still clutching my flowers I stride back to her room and find her sitting bolt upright, eyes wide. "Are you okay? Has something happened?"

She gasps, then her face breaks into a smile, a *genuine* smile: a rare sighting indeed. Her eyes sparkle with delight. "Oh, flowers! What a *kind* girl you are . . ."

"Oh, erm . . ." My heart sinks as I glance down at the blooms.

"They're beautiful," she adds. "A little brash maybe, but I like that — can't be doing with mimsy little posies. Could you fetch a vase?"

"Yes, of course," I say, scuttling to the chilly kitchen and filling a hefty crystal vase with water, in which I arrange the flowers — my flowers! — before returning them to Mrs B.

"Put them beside my bed," she commands, "so I can smell them as I'm going to sleep."

"Yes, of course . . ." I catch their sweet perfume as I place the vase on her bedside table.

She fixes me with a stare. "I can't remember the last time anyone bought me flowers . . ."

"Victoria did," I remind her, "last time she visited."

"Probably out of guilt," she murmurs.

"I'm sure it wasn't like that." *Guilt about what?* I want to ask. About not coming here more often? Yes, as her only child — and with no family of her own — Victoria could certainly be more attentive. But then, Mrs B and her daughter have never given me the impression of being especially close.

I pause in the doorway. Tonight, I'm sensing a twinge of guilt of my own — at leaving her alone — even though she is always perfectly fine alone overnight, and Julie will be here first thing tomorrow. She glances at the flowers and inhales dreamily. "You called me," I add, "as I was leaving?"

"Did I?" Her gaze remains fixed on the bouquet.

"Yes, was there something?"

"Oh," she says, turning towards me, "I meant to say, next time you're shopping, could you *not* buy plain chocolate digestives?"

"Of course, Mrs B." I jam my back teeth together.

"You know I only like milk," she adds.

"I do remember that now." Mustering a stoical smile I turn to leave, reminding myself that this is my job — a job I need very much — and if it involves having my soup and grocery choices criticised, then I guess it's all part of the service. I'm pretty sure she enjoys our cryptic crossword routine and changing her mind about biscuits. But I can't bring myself to feel annoyed. Maybe when I'm 84, with Morgan still lying there scratching his bottom and leaving stinky tuna cans strewn about, I'll be getting my kicks from spitting in a little bowl. Maybe I should save my prize money for my geriatric care?

Stepping outside, I spot a small cardboard box of broccoli, tomatoes and carrots left beside the stone doorstep. Ah, another gift from Paul. Well, they're more useful than flowers. There's something else, too: a bunch of cornflowers and — I think — freesias, tucked in amongst the veg. A brown parcel label has been tied around them. I squint at the careful, forward-sloping handwriting:

I know these are nothing compared to your prize flowers but it's the thought that counts. Well done you and happy birthday. Not long till the bus pass! P.

Cheeky sod! Very sweet of him, though. I pick up the box, my heart soaring into the clear summer's night sky as I make my way home. I am dinner lady of the year and, actually, a bunch of garden flowers gathered together with garden string is more me than a flashy bouquet. Maybe, I reflect, *this* is the part where my life takes a turn for the better.

CHAPTER
FIVE

Salami Coasters

In fact it does, next day, in the Hare and Hounds' sun-dappled beer garden. I've been festooned with gifts from my three favourite friends and I'm feeling extremely treated. "So what did Morgan give you?" Ellie wants to know.

"Nothing yet," I say, "but he's out shopping in York with Jenna so he's probably choosing me something." I pause. "I mean, I don't expect much. He's not earning at the moment—"

"At the *moment*," Kim adds with an eye roll.

"I know, it's ridiculous really. He needs to find something so he can think about getting his own place, especially now Jenna's virtually living with us . . ."

"Still picking up her pants?" Cheryl asks with a wry smile.

"Well, sort of subtly kicking them to one side."

Kim grins, tucking her sharp auburn bob behind her ears. "You don't actually *want* him to move out, do you? You'll be clutching at his ankles, pleading with him to stay . . ."

"No I won't," I exclaim. "I'll be back in my old room, playing the music he hates, guzzling champagne . . ."

"Nah, you'll never get rid of him," she sniggers. "The years'll scoot by and before you know it, you'll be like an old married couple . . ."

"Jesus." I shudder and gulp my prosecco.

". . . going on day trips to Scarborough," she continues, clearly warming to her theme, "with little greaseproof-wrapped packets of cheese sandwiches and saying 'we' all the time, like, 'We might try Bridlington next summer . . .'"

"Stop it!" I'm aware of a niggle of unease as we all peal with laughter. While Cheryl and Ellie are friends from the school gate years, Kim and I go way back to secondary school. We were united in being shunned by the bright, shiny netball team pickers who excelled at everything. I've seen her slogging away at dead-end jobs until she kick-started her make-up artistry business and bought a natty little mint green Fiat 500 and had *Bridal Make-up by Kim* painted on the side. She now leads a whizzy single, childfree life with a gorgeous flat (*two* roof terraces) and more holidays than I can keep tabs on.

Cheryl sips her drink. "For God's sake, Kim. He's only eighteen. Still a kid really. There's so much pressure these days to have your whole future sorted, some grand career plan all mapped out . . ."

"Like you, Aud," Ellie points out. "I mean, being a dinner lady wasn't what you *planned* to do, but look at you now! You're the best one in Britain . . ."

". . . by some kind of fluke . . ." I cut in.

"So what did Morgan think of you winning?" Cheryl asks.

"Um, he seemed pleased. I mean, he glanced up from his phone for about a second, although that might've just been a tic." I shrug. In fact, I had expected a slightly more enthusiastic response and sloped off, dejected, like a scolded puppy. How pathetic, I mused, to expect rapturous applause — or even a "well done, Mum" — from a teenage boy. "It's no big deal," I add. "All it means is that I'm good at being pleasant to five-year-olds . . ."

"Stop putting yourself down," Kim scolds me. "You always do this, you've got to stop—"

"Oh, imagine the kids writing those lovely things about you," Ellie exclaims. "You were made to work with children, it's obvious . . ."

"Maybe," I say, heading into the pub to buy a round, despite their protests that I mustn't, and that today's their treat. In fact, I did have a plan, as a little girl. At nine years old, just after Mum had left us, I got the chance to borrow a clarinet from school. By some mistake or mix-up — or, I suspect now, an act of kindness on the part of Mrs Sherridan, the music teacher — no one ever asked for it back. I took to it easily and played in my bedroom with the door firmly shut, so I wouldn't be distracted by Dad bashing around in the kitchen.

At first, playing those rudimentary pieces was just an avoidance tactic, in the way that I start busily tidying when Mrs B waggles the crossword at me. Back then, it was maths I was keen to avoid, as Dad — appalled by my shoddy numerical skills — had appointed himself as my unofficial tutor. "We're doing some long division," he'd announce. We'd sit together at the kitchen table, with the numbers making no sense and Dad's irritation rising because *anyone can do this, what's wrong with you, Audrey? What are you going to do with your life if you can't even manage a simple sum?* I'd be trapped there for an hour at least. It felt like months, as if the seasons were changing, the trees shedding their leaves and sprouting new ones as Dad scribbled angry numbers in a raggedy exercise book. While Mum had never been terribly involved with me, her presence had softened the atmosphere somewhat. She'd been kind enough in her own way, when she was still with us, showing a vague interest in my homework assignments and occasionally plaiting my hair. But after she left there was *no* softening. In fact, Dad's moods grew darker, my very presence seeming to irritate him, as if the Brian Bazalgette thing had been all my fault. "I need to do some music practice now," I'd announce, once the whisky bottle had joined the jotter and angrily crumpled A4 paper on the kitchen table. "School concert's coming up and we're doing a full rehearsal tomorrow . . ." As I lost myself in the music I'd stop wondering what Mum was doing, and whether Dad had poured another whisky, and whether I'd ever be a normal girl who could invite friends round after school, as everyone else seemed to do.

I started secondary school and was pinged straight into remedial maths. By now, Dad had given up on me, and himself, or so it seemed: while he'd once worked as a carpenter he rarely left the house these days. Mum's letters had dwindled to one every few months, and in my replies I was careful to stress that everything was fine at home, that I was happy and doing well at school. I'd passed grade 6 with distinction on my clarinet — Mum sent a rather wonkily drawn congratulations card which I treasured for years — and spent every spare moment playing. *See, Dad, I can concentrate. Give me a piece of sheet music that's so crammed with notes it looks like a swarm of ants dancing all over it and I'm fine.*

Better than fine, in fact. While practising really hard pieces I'd stop hearing him stomping about downstairs. I'd be utterly lost in a world of my own, where I didn't need Mum, Dad or anyone. It was only hours later, when I ventured downstairs in the night, that I'd see the smashed cereal bowl (Dad and I consumed a *lot* of cereal), the soggy cornflakes scattered, the milk having already seeped into our matted brown rug. Sometimes I'd wake to hear our rusting old van revving furiously in front of our terraced house. Dad would drive off, fuelled by whisky and despair, and I'd creep down to deal with the mess, because one thing I knew was that milk smells disgusting — like sick — if no one mops it up.

So yes, Ellie was right when she said that being a dinner lady wasn't part of the plan. The dream had been to work my way through the remaining grades and apply for music college, and maybe one day stand on a stage, playing Debussy's Rapsodie, which I loved — it sounded like running water — in a chic little black dress. But by the evening of my fifteenth birthday I no longer had a clarinet, and by seventeenth I no longer had a father either as he died in a car accident whilst under the influence.

I had to leave school then, and Mum rushed up to see me: to "look after you", she said, rather belatedly, even suggesting I move down to Wales with her as I wasn't in a position to pay rent and cook my own dinners and take care of myself. I told her tersely that I'd been cooking my own dinners for years. Convincing her I'd be okay, I packed her off home and managed to nab a job as a live-in cleaner at Sunshine Valley holiday park near Morecambe Bay. And *that's* when my glittering career began . . .

Whoa, daytime boozing! It's sent my thoughts racing as I loiter at the bar while Janice gets our drinks. I need to slow down, drink some water, like everyone says. But then, it *is* my birthday, and I've arranged a day off from Mrs B. So why not? The next few hours pass extremely enjoyably, and by the time I return home at just gone five, I'm so buoyed up that I barely even register the scattering of Hula Hoop packets littering the kitchen.

Morgan and Jenna have returned from their trip and are watching something very shouty on TV. Like Hitler invading Poland, my son seems to have annexed our living room as his private snogging quarters while I beaver away in the kitchen. No mention of my birthday yet, but never mind. I poke my head round the living room door. "I'll do pizzas later," I announce, at which the lovers spring apart.

"Mum! D'you have to just barge in?"

"I didn't *barge*, Morgan. I'm just trying to cater to your needs. Anyway, what am I supposed to do? Wear a little bell around my neck, like a cow, to warn you that I'm approaching?"

"No need to be like that . . ."

"It's just, it is my house too. I actually live here. I'm not just the maid . . ."

Jenna giggles and smooths her rumpled fair hair. Oh God, there's what looks distinctly like a love bite planted on her slender neck. I thought they went out of fashion around 1979, like Clackers. What the heck will her mum say?

The landline trills in the hall beside me and I snatch it from the shelf. It's Vince, my ex. "Happy birthday, Aud," he says jovially.

"Thanks, Vince." It's lovely to hear from him, actually. Once we'd recovered from the break-up, we've functioned pretty well as friends; better, in fact, than as partners. "All the fours, eh?" he adds. "How does that feel?"

"Ancient," I reply with a grimace.

"Doing anything nice tonight?"

"No plans, I've just been out for lunch with the girls, that was lovely—"

"Yeah, you sound inebriated," he teases. Since embarking on self-sufficient bliss in the wilds of Northumberland with his girlfriend Laura — a wispy, jam-making sort — my ex has become rather smug.

"I've only had three glasses of wine," I fib, wandering through to the kitchen to top up Paul's flowers with water.

"Sure you have. Anyway, how's our useless layabout of a son? Any signs of him shifting his arse off that sofa yet?"

"Not so I've noticed . . ."

Vince grunts. "Can I have a word?"

"Of course," I say, striding back to the living room and holding out the phone. Morgan disentangles himself from his lady love and squints at it, as if not entirely sure what it is. To be fair, cold callers and Vince are the only ones who ever ring.

"Happy birthday, Audrey," Jenna says, somewhat belatedly, as Morgan falls into a muttered conversation with his father.

"Thanks, Jenna."

"Yuh," Morgan murmurs, "I'm *lookin'*, Dad. Can't just magic up a job, y'know? It's tough out there . . ."

"So great about your prize," she adds. "Decided what you're going to do with the money yet?"

I hesitate, wishing the focus were more on the accolade and less on the cash. She's a sweet girl, and clearly loves Morgan to bits, but she hasn't shaken him out of his reverie as I'd hoped she might.

Morgan finishes the call — it lasted barely two minutes — and flips open his laptop.

Jenna nudges my son. "Five grand, Morgan! Imagine having all that to spend . . ."

"Uh, yeah . . ." He stares hard at the screen.

"I'd hit Top Shop," she announces. "Oh my God, can you *imagine?* I'd have a St Tropez tan and get HD brows and individual lash extensions . . ." This is how different we are as females. At the prospect of sudden riches, she thinks: beautification. I think: new kitchen table.

"Yup," he grunts while I glance around the room for a beautifully wrapped present with my name on it. Heck, any old thing in a Superdrug carrier bag would do. But all I spot are Morgan's juggling sticks dumped on the rug and the aforementioned pants still strewn around. A packet of salami is lying open on the coffee table; several slices have escaped and are wilting on the glass surface, like coasters made from fatty pork. I glower at them, willing Morgan to shut his laptop and at least acknowledge the occasion. "Oh, man," he blurts out, "that's so cool!"

"What is?" I ask.

"This thing here." He jabs at his laptop. I go behind him and peer over his shoulder at the screen.

"What *is* this?"

"Just a thing, a tutorial thing . . ."

I watch a few seconds of the YouTube clip in which an earnest-looking child is balancing a beach ball on his head while juggling multi-coloured blocks. "But he's just a little kid, Morgan. He looks about eight."

"Yeah." He nods.

"And it doesn't look that difficult," I add.

He rounds on me. "It is! You've no idea . . ."

"Oh, come on," I say, laughing. "It's not as if he's, I don't know, juggling while dancing on burning hot coals or eating fire—"

"You want that poor kid to burn himself?"

"Of course I don't . . ."

He turns to Jenna. "She'll only be happy when he's admitted to hospital for skin grafts."

"Jesus!"

The two of them snigger conspiratorially and, not for the first time, I feel like the intruder here, who's blundered into a world of love bites and YouTube tutorials and meals consisting of salami and crisps, which I have no hope of ever understanding.

"S'good, this," he mutters huffily, having turned his attention back to the screen. "S'giving me ideas . . ."

"Ideas for what specifically?" I ask.

He exhales through his nose as the clip switches to the child balancing a stack of bricks on his chin. "My act," Morgan murmurs.

What act? I want to ask, but can't bring myself to be so cutting, especially in front of Jenna. However, Morgan's childhood yearnings to be an international spy seem entirely achievable, compared to expecting a career to materialise through no effort whatsoever on his part. I miss his youthful drive, his boundless energy, and his fondness for leaving coded notes for me on the toilet cistern: MUM UOY EVOL I. With no interest in college or uni — "I mean, what would I *do?*" — he scraped through his exams, gaining pretty unsensational grades, and in the past year has dabbled with a couple of short-lived part-time jobs. My once-vibrant son has been a packer in the pie factory and a washer-upper at a nearby hotel. Then for the past six months, nothing. I can hardly strap him to his desk chair and force him to write his CV. "Morgan," I say carefully, "if you're not interested in college, you're going to have to find something to occupy yourself."

He nods. "Yeah, I know. I'm gonna do some street theatre."

My heart drops. "As a hobby, yes. I meant something as a real job."

"No, that's what I mean. As my *job* . . ."

I stare at him, lost for words for a moment. "But that's not . . . it's not a career. However long you stood out there, doing your thing, you'd never earn enough to—"

"Nah, nah, I don't mean doing it around here. I'd go to York or maybe, I dunno, even *Leeds* . . ." He says this as if it's Los Angeles. "You need big crowds to make decent money," he adds.

"He's really good," Jenna says loyally. "You should see him." *Sweetheart, enormous chunks of my life have been spent watching Morgan clonking into the vegetable rack on that unicycle* . . . "I know he is," I say quickly, turning back to my son, "but Morgan, you tried that, didn't you? I mean, you set off for the day with your sandwiches and flask and you were back about two hours later . . ."

He shrugs. "It was raining."

"Yes, but this is the north of England. It's cold a lot of the time. It's an occupational hazard, I'd have thought . . ."

"It was freezing! And I only had my thin jacket . . ."

"The thin jacket you chose," I shoot back, "when I'd given you money to specifically buy a proper, insulating winter coat . . ."

He turns to Jenna and chuckles. "Mum wants me to have proper insulation, like a boiler." I clamp my back teeth together as they both giggle away.

56

"I meant a coat that was a *bit* thicker than a doily, Morgan . . ."

"What's a doily?"

I glower at him. "You've got to eighteen years old and don't know what a doily is?"

He makes a little snorty noise, like a horse. "See what I have to put up with, Jen? It never stops!"

I glare down at him, deeply irritated now. I need a proper talk with my son — with capitals, a *Proper Talk* — but how is that possible when Jenna's always here, nuzzling his ear? It's not fair to discuss big, serious issues — like his future, and whether he's been remembering to put ointment on his athlete's foot — with his girlfriend listening in. Anyway, he's hardly likely to give me his full attention while he's absent-mindedly massaging her delicate bare tootsies.

"Ooh, that's nice," she breathes, closing her eyes ecstatically, apparently having forgotten I'm here. Where am I supposed to go while this foot fondling is happening? I can't bear to spend any more time holed up in my bedroom or the kitchen. Maybe I should sit outside in our unlovely back yard, by the wheelie bins? I can't help glancing down at her pretty little feet, the nails painted baby blue, the toes perfectly straight and not curled weirdly towards the big one due to wearing foot-cramming courts in the 80s. What kind of person have I become, to feel bitter that a beautiful eighteen-year-old girl — whom my son loves to distraction — doesn't have any corns or calluses? Christ, it's a small step from wishing a verruca on her.

"Mum?" Morgan's voice cuts into my thoughts.

"Yes, love?"

"Are you . . . okay?"

Hell, I've been staring at his girlfriend's feet. I hurry off like a discreet maid and busy myself with the washing up they've left for me, all the while thinking: *my only child has forgotten my birthday*. The child whose bottom I was once forced to wipe with my original 1960s silk scarf in the park.

I go about my business all evening, dishing up pizza then keeping out of their way, trying not to feel envious when I hear them laughing raucously, and wishing I didn't mind so much that I'm not allowed to join in. When did I become so needy? It's only my birthday, after all, and my friends made it fun. And Vince remembered, as did Mum: *Happy birthday Audrey*, the card said in her quivery scrawl. Stevie didn't bother, but then he doesn't strike me as the card-sending sort.

At 11.20p.m., by which time I have given up on any acknowledgement of the date, I pop my head round the living room door. Jenna is audibly kissing my son's neck: *kiss-kiss-kiss*. I hope she isn't planning to mark him. Can't imagine a freshly sucked neck will do him any favours in the job interviews I plan to set up for him and frogmarch him to, if necessary . . . no, no, I must *stop* this. "Goodnight, then," I say.

Jenna peels herself off him. "Night, Audrey."

"Oh, Mum, hang on a minute . . ." Morgan delves into his jeans pocket. "Here," he says, handing me a bent pink envelope.

"Thank you, darling," I say, unable to erase the trace of surprise from my voice. There's an oily stain on it and MUM has been scribbled lightly in pencil on the front.

He grins and winds an arm around his girlfriend's shoulders. "See what she thinks of me, Jen?" he chuckles. "She actually thought I'd forgot."

CHAPTER
SIX

The Wrong Jelly Beans

My heart swells as I take it from him. It'll be a voucher, probably, which doesn't score terribly highly on the effort front — but at least he's thought about the kind of shops I like. At least, I hope it's for John Lewis and not Asda. I rip it open. It's a birthday card depicting a plump tortoise-shell cat sitting on a windowsill. A bit grannyish, but never mind. No voucher either. But then, he's always broke and I wouldn't feel great about him spending what little he has on me. And it's my money anyway, so it would be like giving cash to myself, and not as if I *need* anything . . .

"Thanks, Morgan," I say, placing the card on the mantelpiece and dropping the envelope into the waste paper bin.

"Don't throw that away!" he yelps.

I blink at him. "It was just the envelope, love."

"No, no, there's something in it . . ."

"Sorry, I didn't realise . . ." I snatch it back out and find a piece of paper inside, folded over and over into a tiny square. "What's this?" I murmur, opening it out.

"Just a list."

"A list?" I squint at his barely-legible scrawl:

STUFF I NEED
iPad
Calvin Klein boxers
Bottle rum for Jake's party
Jelly beans (proper Jelly Belly ones, not the cheap ones, can I have the big jar with 45 flavours??) . . .

I'm aware of both Morgan and Jenna watching me intently from the sofa as I grip the note. Maybe it's a joke. It goes on:

Hair stuff
Ralph Lauren aftershave, orange bottle
Clothes (voucher best, DO NOT CHOOSE ANYTHING YOURSELF!!)
iTunes voucher
Unicycle tyre
Proper (METAL) juggling batons
Money for gig tickets
Black leather wallet (plain)
Guitar . . .

"Guitar?" I blurt out. "Are you having a laugh? What d'you want one of those for?"

"'Cause it'd be cool," he says airily.

"But you don't even play!"

"I could learn, couldn't I? You're always saying I should expand my skill set, whatever that means . . ."

"But it's *July*," I add. "Your birthday's not till next month. Why are you giving me your present list now . . . in my birthday card?"

"Oh, it's not my birthday list," he says with a shrug. "It says at the top. It's just stuff I need."

I stare at him. "Have you gone completely crazy? I don't have the cash for all this—"

"You've got that prize money coming, Mum. It's just a few things, not *that* much . . ."

I'm conscious of breathing slowly, trying not to lose my rag. I keep staring at the note in the hope that I'm just experiencing a mental blip, perhaps triggered by all the prosecco I guzzled earlier, and that the messy scrawl will rearrange itself to read: *Sorry I couldn't afford to get you a present, Mum, just wanted to say how much I love you.* But it doesn't.

"You mean," I say carefully, "I've sometimes bought you the wrong kind of jelly beans?"

He nods. "Occasionally, yeah. Some of the flavours are really weird. The cinnamon ones are horrible."

I glare at him, then back at the note. If I had a lighter to hand, which I don't, having given up smoking twenty years ago — although now might be the time to re-start — I'd show him what I think of it. Is it normal, this urge to burn things? I never used to be like this. I'm becoming increasingly less keen on the person I've become. "So," I venture, "you're seriously expecting me to buy you all this? Not for your birthday but just . . . for no real reason at all?"

He nods. "Yeah, but please don't choose my clothes, Mum. Not after that shirt you got me last Christmas . . ."

"Don't be so ungrateful," Jenna splutters, nudging him.

"That perfectly nice one from River Island?" I remark, arching a brow.

"Er, yeah." At last, he has the decency to look nervous.

"What was wrong with it?" I ask, genuinely bewildered.

"C'mon, Mum," he says, blushing now, "it was kinda like an old man's shirt . . ."

Something shrivels inside me as I stare down at them: two beautiful people with their futures ahead of them — if they can muster the energy to *do* something. And I know how they view me: as a sour, middle-aged woman, who doesn't understand that a guitar would be "cool", and who seems to believe that careers should be planned and worked towards, rather than just expected to land in their laps. Even Jenna seems unwilling to grab opportunities presented to her. As she's studying beauty therapy, I'd assumed she might enjoy assisting Kim on a job. "I've checked with her," I explained, "and she really could do with the help. It'll be great experience for you."

"Yeah, maybe," Jenna winced, as if I'd arranged work experience at the local abattoir, rather than patting powder onto bridesmaids' faces.

In my bedroom now, I perch on the edge of my bed and try to figure out whether I've been perfectly reasonable or overreacted terribly. Maybe Vince was right, and I'm drunker than I realise; after all, Morgan's not that bad as teenagers go. He has never written off my car or — to my knowledge — inflicted pain upon a small animal. No, it's the slow drip-drip of barely significant things that's making me feel as if I am beginning to ever-so-slightly lose the plot: the mocking of a perfectly acceptable shirt. The perpetual canoodling that makes me feel as if I'm trapped in a sex education film and that any moment, a voiceover will warn, "Remember to *always* use a condom." Is it any wonder I find it so hard to relax? Right now, in my tiny, gloomy room, I'd give anything to be in that swanky hotel where the cookery course is happening. Not to cook especially — I mean, I wouldn't dream of foisting my bland soup on anyone — but just to *be*.

To take my mind off the note, I unpack my presents from Kim, Ellie and Cheryl from my voluminous shoulder bag. Gorgeous perfume, a posh palette of lip colours and tiny bottles of bath oil with soothing properties. And here, still in its torn-open envelope, is the letter about my competition win, including a contact number for the organiser: Shirley Michaels, whom I've already spoken to about the cash prize.

I lie back on my bed. My room really is tiny: suitable only for a small child, or possibly just coats. There's space only for a three-quarter bed — no wonder Stevie rarely stays over, he's six-foot-two — plus a small, rickety bedside table and a chrome rail for clothes. God, that lovely hotel. I can't get it out of my mind. Lifting my laptop from my bedside table, I Google Wilton Grange. Judging by the pictures on its website, it's extremely fancy. Without wanting to sound as if I struggle to use cutlery politely, it is far posher than anywhere I've ever stayed. We're talking old-style glamour; all plump sofas, twinkling chandeliers and enormous stone fireplaces decked with the kind of fragile-looking vases you're scared to walk past in case you create a gust and blow them off. There are oil paintings of glowering old men and galloping horses, and in the restaurant the food comes with little blobs and swirls of sauce. Imagine having your food *decorated*.

There's a spa, in which guests are lounging around in white dressing gowns, giving the impression that their lives are totally sorted. While they might stop off at Charnock Richard for petrol or a coffee, it would never occur to them to stay overnight. Their pulses wouldn't quicken at the prospect of a £5 all-you-can-eat breakfast buffet. They have never endured obsessive voucher collecting to buy their child a perfectly acceptable checked shirt which, it turns out, he hates. A son who, rather than buying his mother a small birthday gift — just a token, a pack of sodding Hello Kitty hair clips would have sufficed — presents her with an extensive list of stuff *he* wants.

I should have chosen the cookery course prize, I decide, undressing and pulling on my pyjamas. But it's too late now.

Or is it? That's the thought that spears through my brain when I wake, dry-mouthed from the prosecco, just after nine. I scramble out of bed and grab the letter from my bag and stare at the contact numbers. There's an office number, and a mobile. I shouldn't call on a Sunday but what the hell? I tap out the number on my mobile, my heart rattling away as it rings.

"Hello?"

I clear my throat. "Hello Shirley, it's Audrey Pepper. I'm so sorry to call you at the weekend . . ."

"Audrey Pepper? I'm sorry, I don't think I know—"

"We, um, spoke a few days ago about the Dinner Lady of the Year award . . ."

"Oh, yes, of course. If you're calling about the transfer, I have all your bank details and was planning to put through payment first thing on Monday . . ."

"Um, actually, I just wondered," I cut in, "could I change my mind? I mean, if it's at all possible?"

Small pause. "You mean you'd like to do the cookery course instead?"

"Er . . . yes. Yes, I would." Another pause as she clears her throat.

"Umm . . . I think it's pretty booked up, and I'm not sure if I can get hold of anyone today . . . could you hold for a moment please?"

"Sure," I say, licking my parched lips.

I wait and wait and *wait*. I glance up at the mottled ceiling; it needs a coat of emulsion, the whole place does. I've suggested to Morgan that he might paint it for me, thus acquiring some decorating skills — there's a line of work that's always in demand — but he flatly refused to do it without pay. How would he react, I wonder, if I presented him with an invoice for meals cooked, laundry serviced and cleaning undertaken?

"Audrey? Sorry to keep you waiting."

"That's okay, that's *fine* . . ."

"Now, I'm afraid the week where we had a place reserved for you is all fully booked . . ."

66

"Oh, I see." My heart seems to slump.

". . . But," she goes on, "the course starting tomorrow has one place free. There are no single or twin rooms free, I'm afraid . . ."

It's okay, I'll camp in the ruddy garden . . .

"But there is the honeymoon suite, and seeing as you've won your place they're happy for you to have that."

"Oh!" I gasp. Honeymoon suite? Vince and I didn't have one of those. We stayed in his aunt's guesthouse in Whitby.

"It starts at midday with a welcome reception," she goes on. "I know you're in Yorkshire, and it's an awfully long way to travel down to Buckinghamshire, but do you possibly think . . ."

Yes, I do. I *do* possibly think. "Er, can I check something and get straight back to you?"

"Yes, of course," she says.

I finish the call and phone Julie who, as ever, is delighted to take on my shifts.

"So did Stevie come up with something after all?" she asks.

"Sorry?"

Julie laughs. "For your birthday. I assume he's taking you away?"

"No," I say, with a dry chuckle, "but I *am* going away — by myself. I'll explain when I see you, okay?" Then I call Shirley again, trying to sound level and calm, as if visiting luxury hotels to learn to make tarte au citron is a pretty regular occurrence for me. "I can start the course tomorrow," I say firmly.

"Really? Well, that's great!" She sounds genuinely happy for me. "I know the cash prize was tempting but this is an unforgettable experience, isn't it? Possibly even life-changing."

CHAPTER
SEVEN

Guilt Cakes

Of course I plan to tell Morgan. I'll do it when I've calmed down and feel more kindly disposed towards him. In the meantime, I pull out my wheeled suitcase from beneath my bed, wondering how it'll feel to be there, on my own — with no Morgan or Stevie or Mrs B making any demands upon me whatsoever. Freedom! That's what Wilton Grange represents. I'm not even that fussed about the cookery aspect. What is classic French cookery anyway? Steak and frites? Or things slathered in rich sauces? I have no idea. I have never even been to France. We weren't the going-abroad kind of family but then, hardly anyone was in 1970s Yorkshire.

Plus, I'm not the fancy cooking type. Before having Morgan I pretty much survived on things on toast, and as a mother I've been a distinctly workaday cook, intent on providing the kind of meals my ever-ravenous child would approve of. This has tended to involve an awful lot of crumb-coated things to shove in the oven.

I glance at the hotel's website again. My mild panic about grappling with unfamiliar ingredients is offset by visions of me lying in a huge, claw-footed bath. As for

Morgan, it'll be good for him to fend for himself for a week: a sort of intensive training week in preparation for independent adult life. So in some ways, I'm doing him a favour.

I haven't told Stevie yet either. As I try to play down the dinner lady aspect of my life, he doesn't even know about my award; anyway, we haven't spoken since we said goodbye in the Charnock Richard car park. "Crazy busy the next few days," was his parting shot. Perhaps, I muse, a little break will do us good. Absence, heart fonder and all that.

As per their custom, Morgan and Jenna spend all morning in his room and, when lunchtime rolls around, they amble downstairs and head out without giving any clue as to where they might be going. I'll tell him as soon as they come back. I wonder how best to put it? *I know you had high hopes for that money, darling, but I'm going to learn to do clever things with mussels instead.* Christ, better just get it over with, as soon as he comes home.

I fetch my suitcase and carry it through to my former bedroom, where most of my clothes are stored. So, what to pack for Wilton Grange? Shirley has sent me an email:

> *Casual, comfy clothes are required in the kitchen*
> *(aprons provided)*
> *Flat shoes only*
> *No jewellery please*
> *Long hair must be tied back*

Mine needs a cut urgently but unless I hack at it myself there's no time for that. I dig out trousers and tops, plus a couple of dresses, all found in the PDSA shop: so much more satisfying than shopping in a regular high street chain and just selecting your size off the rail. I mean, where's the challenge in that?

Not bad, I decide, dropping in my utilitarian navy swimsuit for the spa and surveying my neatly folded clothes. I add underwear and pyjamas and gather together my toiletries. Silly, I know, as the hotel will provide them, but just in case . . .

And that's me, all ready and raring to go. It's been eerily simple, and unhurried, compared to the last-minute packing I tend to do when Stevie calls. I plan to leave at 6.30 tomorrow morning at the latest, allowing extra time so I'm not the one rushing late into the welcome reception, whatever *that* is. Now I just want Morgan to come home so I can break the news.

Feeling more kindly disposed now, I drive to our nearest, rather uninspiring supermarket and stock up on enough provisions to nourish my son for an entire month, including Rolos and Fondant Fancies and fruit, which I'm bound to find withered on my return, plus industrial quantities of minced beef. Back home, I make an enormous pot of chilli (Morgan complained that my last batch was "too oniony", perhaps food critic could be another career option?) and another of bolognaise, all to keep him going throughout the week. It feels as if I am preparing for impending war. I know it's ridiculous but it's making me feel marginally better about abandoning my child. In the same vein I also shape four burgers, wrapping them individually in grease-proof paper, writing "1 burger! Enjoy! xx" in felt tip across the top. I realise my catering has involved an awful lot of minced beef but at least he's unlikely to become anaemic.

By teatime — still no reappearance of Morgan — the chilli and bolognaise have cooled sufficiently to be ladled into individual cartons and labelled MON/TUE/WED/THUR/FRI: saves him having to make any tricky decisions over what to eat. We also have chicken nuggets which he's perfectly capable of putting in the oven . . . and then forgetting they're there. Plus there's the Chinese and chippy if he gets really desperate.

Vince would say I've lost my mind. He'd point out that my extensive preparations are a small step from cutting up his fish fingers and tucking in his bib. However, as I plan to make the very most of every moment at Wilton Grange, I don't want to worry for one *second* that Morgan is suffering from malnutrition. And now — perhaps I really *am* losing it — I make a batch of fairy cakes, scooping out their centres when they're done and making them into little wings as if Morgan were seven years old. *Sorry for buggering off like this*, my butterfly cakes say. *Sorry for not getting you the unicycle tyre and for being a mad middle-aged woman who's probably having some kind of hormonal collapse.*

I while away the evening rechecking my suitcase and willing Morgan to show up so I can tell him. I ping him a message: *when u coming home?* No reply, unsurprisingly. We've passed the stage where he felt obliged to keep me informed of his movements.

I text Vince: *I've won a prize! A week at a cook school in Buckinghamshire. Leaving tomorrow. M will be home alone all week.*

Wow amazing! Very proud of you, comes his swift reply.

Thanks, I type, *but M will be ALL ALONE. Am I wrong to be terrified?*

His reply takes longer this time: *He's a fully grown man, remember?*

Easy for him to say, being spared the daily discussions — "naggings", Morgan calls them — about what our son might do next with his life. Rifling through my purse, I dump a bundle of notes on the table, weighted down with the pepper grinder, for emergencies. Guilt money. The one thing I don't do is gather up all the stray pants. In fact, and perhaps I really am losing it now, I drag out the plastic box of Morgan's old toys from the cupboard under the stairs. It's full of ratty old teddies, plus the Action Man I got for a quid on eBay, which he made into a spy — demanding that I made him a tiny Fedora hat, like the dented one here that was pretty much welded to his head during his entire spy phase, and which I found him sleeping in once. There are dog-eared books on codes and cyphers that I've been keeping for . . . what exactly? And here it is, precisely what I'm looking for: the tub of jumbo chalks he'd used to draw mysterious symbols on the pavement outside our house (only other spies would understand their significance).

Selecting the white one, I creep around the living room and carefully draw an outline around each pair of dropped pants. It's just a joke, I tell myself. He'll notice when I'm gone and he and Jenna will have a good laugh about his nutty mum. Only . . . I'm not quite sure it *is* funny. In fact, I fear that I am overly obsessing about pants, and that simply picking them up and depositing them into the wash might be an altogether more sensible solution.

I put the chalks back into the box and shove it back under the stairs, and get on with the task of clearing up the kitchen. That's when I spot it, dumped in the bin: the Christmas present from me, carefully chosen as I thought he liked checked shirts, seeing as he wears one slung over a T-shirt nearly every day of his life. It's red, blue and white, in soft brushed cotton, and is lying there with a couple of wet teabags sitting on it. He has *thrown it away*. I blink down at it, wondering why it didn't occur to him that this might be hurtful to me. I mean, okay, get rid of it — discreetly. Stuff it in a litter bin in the park, hand it to a homeless person or drop it off at the charity shop. But don't dump it on top of the tuna cans and takeaway cartons and — I notice now — the application form for part-time work at the leisure centre that I picked up for him.

The front door flies open, and I hear Morgan and Jenna tottering in. "Hi, Mum," he calls out tipsily from the hallway. "You there?"

"Yes, I'm here," I mutter, fury bubbling inside me.

"Been at the pub. Just gonna go up to bed, okay?"

I glance at my cakes sitting all smugly under their glass dome. "Fine," I growl, scrunching up the empty flour packet and dropping it on top of the shirt.

"Don't know what's up with her," Morgan remarks as, giggling, he and Jenna make their way up to his room.

I don't follow them up, and nor do I inform him of my plans when my alarm goes off with a ping at 5.50 a.m., because a hungover teenager — any teenager in fact — is incapable of conversation at this kind of hour. Anyway, what does he care whether I'm here or not? Instead, I shower quickly and slip into a favourite floral print dress, plus a pair of ballet flats. Then, as quietly as possible, I creep downstairs with my suitcase.

Morgan's wish list is still lying on the kitchen table. The damn cheek of it, and on my birthday as well. On its blank side I write:

Dear Morgan,
Gone away for a bit.
Love, Mum x

CHAPTER
EIGHT

Motorway Muffins

I should feel euphoric as I drive south. After all, I deserve this. I should be zipping along, music blaring and a huge smile on my face, like a woman in a movie about to embark on a life-changing adventure. The fact that I'm not is due to one horrible dark thought, currently flooding my senses: *I didn't leave defrosting/ reheating instructions.* Yes, I'm still angry — but more at myself now for being unable to switch off my maternal concern. Surely Morgan is savvy enough to cope with a Tupperware carton of frozen bolognaise? He's a bright boy, when he chooses to engage his brain. He's hardly going to hack away at it with an ice pick. Even so, I keep picturing his crestfallen face as he reads my note, and another alarming thought engulfs me: *what the hell am I playing at?*

I pull off at a service station — one we *haven't* stayed at, I must alert Stevie to this — and buy an Americano and three muffins, one for now and two for later, in case the hotel restaurant's portions really are as tiddly as they looked on the website. From a small, greasy table by the window I fish out my phone and try Morgan's mobile. It's only 9 a.m., of course he'll still be asleep, I remind myself as it goes to voicemail. "Could you call me?" I say, aware that there's little chance of him even playing the message. "I need to talk to you," I add before ringing off.

Next I try Stevie, who doesn't answer either. "It's me, love," I inform his voicemail. "Look, er, I'm . . ." I tail off. It's not the kind of thing I want to explain via a message, especially with my voice sounding terribly loud in the almost deserted café. "I'm going away for a few days," I explain quickly. "I'll tell you all about it when we speak."

Feeling marginally better, I pick at one of the muffins and call Kim. "I can't believe you're doing this!" she exclaims.

"I know, I really should have told him last night . . ."

"No, not that part." She chuckles. "I mean being spontaneous like this. It's so unlike you!"

"Thanks," I say with a dry laugh, although she's right.

"Well, good for you, Aud. It sounds amazing. It'll be good for Morgan too, force him to stand on his own two feet . . ."

I bite my lip. "Um . . . if you're passing the house, would you mind popping in to check he's okay?"

Small pause. "What on earth for?"

"Oh, you know, just to make sure everything's all right. I mean, it's your place, I don't want it burnt to the ground . . ." I am only half-joking.

She laughs loudly. "Aud, he's not a baby. Just go away and enjoy yourself, for Christ's sake."

"Okay, okay," I say, dabbing at the muffin crumbs on the plate with a wet finger. "I will, promise."

"Good. So repeat after me: 'Nothing's going to happen. Everything is going to be fine.'"

She's right: my boy is old enough to get married, to fight for his country or be sent to a proper adult jail. "*Nothing's* going to happen," I repeat, crossing my fingers firmly under the table, "and everything is going to be fine."

It's terribly picturesque, this part of the world. I see no litter or graffiti as I pass through pretty villages, the kind that still have a proper village store, with a tray of penny sweets, I'd imagine, and a kindly lady serving behind the counter. Then the villages fall behind and it's just winding country lanes for miles until, finally, I round a bend and spot the elegant sign on a high, moss-covered wall:

Wilton Grange Hotel
Luxury accommodation ★ Michelin-starred
restaurant ★ World-renowned cookery school

My heartbeat quickens as I turn in through the gate. The gravelled drive curves between gnarled ancient trees, and a few moments later the hotel comes into view. *Peaceful* is the word that springs to mind. Sunlight quivers on the lake. The hotel is swathed in some kind of dense, climbing shrub and the undulating grounds are dotted with summerhouses and those dinky little shelter things, where a refined lady might enjoy some shade while sipping her gin.

I pull up in the car park, nosing my way in between a Bentley and a Merc. A terribly chic woman in a grey trouser suit gives my car a surprised look before climbing into the Merc and driving away. I wipe my sweaty hands on the front of my crumpled dress. Another car arrives to take the Merc's place: a Saab I think, possibly vintage, although its cream paintwork is so gleamingly perfect it could have purred out of the factory just moments ago. I slide my gaze towards the driver. He is flicking through some papers, making no move to get out.

My phone bleeps in my bag, and I snatch it from the passenger seat. A text from Morgan: *when u back??* I glance at the man again and he smiles briefly. He has a kind face, I decide. He's not looking at me as if thinking, What's she doing here? Maybe he thinks I'm staff. I smile back, hoping to convey the message that, despite the state of my vehicle, I actually come to places like this all the time. *I belong here*, I hope my smile says, *just like you do*. Message transmitted, I reply to Morgan's text: *Saturday*.

His reply pings back instantly: *WHAT??* Oh, so he misses me after all. In fact, this is the longest period we'll have ever spent apart. While Morgan's had numerous long weekends with his dad, in recent times the livestock aspect of Vince's smallholding has put him off ("There's so much *crap* everywhere, Mum! It bloody stinks!") and he always seems pretty relieved to come home. I've never managed to fund school trips

79

to France or Austria, and his main summer holidays were usually camping trips to Cornwall with me, then with a friend and me, because the idea of being trapped alone in a tent with his mother was clearly appalling.

Another text: *Need grey T shirt washing wanna wear tonight!!*

Ahh . . . right. So it's the interruption in laundry services he's concerned about. No, "Where are you, Mum? Is everything okay?" I mean, if I were him — and I frequently do try to see things from his point of view — I'd be thinking, "It's not like her to just bugger off. Maybe I should be concerned about her mental health?" But then, Morgan isn't the type to worry about anything. I could be lying dead on the kitchen floor and he'd step over my corpse to fetch a can of Coke from the fridge.

I stab out my reply — *use washing machine* — and climb out of my car, trying to quell the anxiety that's rising inside me. The man from the Saab gets out too. He is tall, well-groomed and handsome; dapper, you'd call him, with his neatly clipped short dark hair and a light tan. His navy blue linen jacket and casual dark grey trousers look expensive. "Hi," he says with a smile.

"Hi," I reply.

"Lovely day."

"Yes, it is . . ."

He stands for a moment, taking in the surroundings: the sweeping lawns, the well-tended borders filled with pale pink roses, the beautiful building itself. Then he checks his watch and, with a breezy confidence that suggests he is unintimidated by poshness — because to people like him this place isn't posh, it's just normal — he opens the boot of his car and lifts out a brown leather bag.

I start making my way towards the hotel, dragging my wheeled case along the gravel and trying not to churn it up too much. When I glance back, the man is strolling a few metres behind. He flashes another broad smile. I smile back, briefly, and snatch my phone from my shoulder bag as it rings. "Hi, Morgan," I say distractedly.

"What d'you mean, you're back next Saturday? What're you *doing?*"

I clear my throat, aware of the crunch of the man's footsteps behind me. "I explained in my note, I've gone away for a bit."

"A bit? That's not a bit. It's a week! For fuck's sake, Mum!"

"Don't swear at me, Morgan."

"All right, sorry, it's just . . . I thought you'd just gone to the Spar or something . . ."

"I *go* there," I correct him. "I don't go *away* there, Morgan. It's not a holiday destination . . ."

"You've gone on holiday without telling me?" he gasps. "Like, where?"

"Well, it's a sort of holiday. I'm in Buckinghamshire . . ." A peacock struts haughtily across the path, its breast shimmering sapphire blue in the sunshine.

"Where's that?"

"It's in the south of England."

"I mean, what's there? Why're you *there?*"

"I'm doing the cookery course," I explain, keeping my voice low.

Morgan makes a choking noise. "You mean that dinner lady thing?"

"Yes, that's right."

"But I thought you were taking the money! The *cash prize*. That's what you said . . ."

"Well, I changed my mind." I've slowed my pace in the hope that the man will understand that I want him to march ahead so I can conduct this conversation in private.

"You chose a baking course," Morgan laments, "over five thousand quid? What use is *that* gonna be?"

"Probably none," I reply tersely, "and it's not a baking course. It's classic French cookery—"

"You've gone mad," he mutters.

"Yes, I probably have."

He pauses. "So anyway, what about my T-shirt?"

"Sorry, but I can't operate the washing machine from here. It's not remote controlled. Much as I'd love to keep on top of all our domestic concerns from 200 miles away, it's not actually possible to . . ." I break off as the man catches up with me and we fall into step.

"Mum?"

"Just a minute," I hiss.

"But I don't know how . . ."

"For God's sake, Morgan. There's a door at the front. You know the round bit you can see through? Open it and put your T-shirt in. Then open the little drawer at the top and put in some powder . . ."

"Why are you whispering? I can hardly hear—"

"I'm not whispering . . ."

"Speak up!"

"*Put-powder-in-the-little-drawer*," I bark, at which the man raises a brow in amusement.

"Where is it?"

"For goodness' sake! It's the big white appliance, the one that's not the freezer, the one that doesn't have peas in it . . ."

"I mean the *powder* —"

"Cupboard under the sink," I growl. There's some urgent rummaging, then the machine door is slammed shut. Hope he hasn't broken it.

"Now what?" Morgan huffs.

"Select the programme," I instruct him as, mercifully, the man seems to understand that I require privacy and strides ahead. "That's the round dial with numbers on at the top," I add. "30 degrees is probably best. Nothing bad ever happens at that temperature. Okay now?"

I hear clicking noises. "Nothing's happening."

"Have you turned it on?"

"God, Mum, why does it have to be so complicated . . ."

"There's an on button," I snap. "It's not complicated. Just press the damn thing . . ."

"How am I s'posed to know . . ."

"You *should* know," I retort, far too loudly for the tranquil surroundings, "because I gave you that washing machine tutorial, remember? I showed you the dial and the little drawer but you wouldn't pay attention. You wandered off to get ice cream . . ."

"It really wasn't that interesting," Morgan mutters.

"No, I suppose it wasn't, but what if I'd been teaching you mouth-to-mouth resuscitation and you'd wandered off then, more interested in stuffing your face full of Ben & Jerry's than saving a life?"

He splutters. "All right, all right! No need to go off on one. I was only *asking* . . ." Now he sounds genuinely upset. I stop on the path, breathing slowly, and watch a squirrel scampering up a tree.

"I'm sorry, love. I didn't mean to sound so snappy."

"Yeah, well, I was only asking for a bit of help."

Guilt niggles in my stomach. "Yes, I know. Look, I suppose I'm just a bit nervous about this whole hotel thing, okay? And I know I shouldn't have just left like that, without saying goodbye . . ." I trot up the wide stone steps and enter the hotel's revolving doors. In the enormous foyer, the posh car man is waiting to be attended to at reception.

"S'all right," Morgan mumbles.

"I love you, darling."

"Love you too," he says grudgingly.

"Did you enjoy the cakes?"

"Haven't tried them yet, had other stuff on my mind . . ."

I smile. "Like your T-shirt."

"Yeah."

"Have you managed to start the washing machine yet?"

"Nah. Think something's wrong with it . . ."

I inhale deeply and murmur, "Just hand-wash it, darling," and finish the call.

84

An elderly couple drift away from the desk, and the receptionist beams expectantly. "Can I help you?"

"Erm, I think this man was first . . ." I indicate the stranger, noting his soft grey eyes and the dark lashes around them. He has that bone structure thing going on: strong nose, defined jawline and chin. Bet he's the sort who knows about wine and whirls it around and sniffs it instead of tipping it straight down his neck.

"No, no, after you," he says graciously.

"Oh, thank you." I pull my case towards the desk.

"Do you have a reservation?" The receptionist's glossy black hair is tucked behind her dainty ears, and she has the kind of bright, white teeth that make ordinary un-veneered ones — the kind everyone used to have, perfectly serviceable teeth — look like trowels in comparison.

"I'm Audrey Pepper," I say. "I'm here for the cookery course . . ."

She blinks at me. "The residential?"

"Yes, that's right."

There's an almost imperceptible frown as she starts tapping away at her keyboard, still seeming unsure and perhaps suspecting that I'm trying to sneak my way in. "Ah, yes." Her pencilled brows shoot up. "Here you are. Oh, you're in the honeymoon suite! It's beautiful. I do hope you like it . . ."

"I'm sure I will."

"If you could just complete this form . . ."

"Yes, of course . . ." I fill in my details and hand it back to her.

"And if I could just take an imprint of a credit or debit card please . . ." A wave of panic rushes over me as I rummage through my purse.

"It is paid for, the room? The suite, I mean?" *I haven't made some awful mistake and it's not free after all?* Sweat springs from my forehead.

"Oh yes, madam," she says brightly, taking my card and swiping it before handing it back. "Great, all done. I'll ask Jasper to show you to your room . . ." She waves to a uniformed porter across the foyer. I hover, hoping Jasper's too busy to help me because I'd rather find my room myself and avoid some sweat-making tipping scenario (not a problem at a Day's Inn motel).

"I'm on the cookery course too," the posh car man offers.

"Oh, are you?"

His eyes crinkle appealingly. "You sound surprised."

"No, not really — I mean, I have no idea who goes on these kind of things. I won my place in a competition . . ."

"Really?" the receptionist asks. "Which one?"

I sense my cheeks flushing. "Dinner lady of the year."

"Wow!" She bares her perfect teeth. "That's, er, fantastic!"

"Dinner lady of the year?" the man exclaims in one of those rich, rounded voices that carries across a room. "Gosh, you'll be showing the rest of us a thing or two . . ."

"Oh, I don't actually cook at school—"

"Sorry, I just assumed . . ."

"Don't worry, everyone does." I smile.

"So you're not vastly experienced in the world of classic French cuisine?"

"Not remotely," I reply, laughing. "To be honest, I don't exactly know what it is."

He chuckles. "Can't tell you how relieved I am to hear that. We can sit in the dunce corner together . . ."

I laugh, sensing myself relaxing. "Sounds good to me."

He reaches to shake my hand. "I'm Hugo. Hugo Fairchurch . . ."

"I'm Audrey, Audrey Pepper."

"What a lovely, unusual name."

I smile, taken aback by his enthusiasm. "Thank you. I must admit, no one's ever said that before."

"It's charming. Very memorable. See you at the welcome reception then," he says as the ridiculously buff young porter takes my suitcase and escorts me towards the lift. We wait in stilted silence. No one takes you to your room in the kind of places I usually stay at. But then, I have every right to be here, brassy highlights and charity shop dress and all. I can't cook anything fancy but then neither can Hugo, who's bantering away in jovial tones with the glossy receptionist. The lift arrives, and his voice rings out as I step in: "A dinner lady on a classic French cookery course. Isn't that just so *sweet?*"

CHAPTER
NINE

Fungal Popcorn

He didn't mean to be patronising, I tell myself as I gaze around my suite. It's just funny, to someone like him. He probably thinks we still dish up Spam fritters and disgusting mince with a tidemark of orangey grease floating around the edge. Anyway, never mind Hugo; I'm far too excited to feel annoyed about an offhand remark. I managed the tipping scenario by pressing a fiver into the porter's hand (he looked faintly surprised; was it too little? Too much?) and, more importantly, this place is *gorgeous*. Floor-to-ceiling brocade curtains are held back with tasselled golden ropes, and the enormous four-poster bed is strewn with sumptuous furry cushions and throws. It is, I decide, unable to suppress a ridiculous grin, very *Audrey*.

Oh, she probably wouldn't fling herself onto the bed with a whoop of delight — and with her shoes still on — like I do. But who's watching? I stretch out like a giant starfish, relishing the bed's vastness with the baby-soft covers billowing all around me. It feels like a *continent* compared to my bed at home. Thank God Stevie's not here. It's not that I don't appreciate champagne, great sex and a Ginsters pasty. But if he were here he'd be pawing at me already and right now, I just want to *be*.

Scrambling up into a cross-legged position, I scan the room for a laminated card advertising the £5 all-you-can-eat breakfast buffet. Of course there isn't one. No hum of motorway traffic either, or a crappy chipped desk. There's a polished oval table and two plump armchairs upholstered in pink brocade which look as if no human bottom has ever parked itself on them. There's a huge, velvety sofa — how much furniture does one person need? — and from here I can see there's *another* sofa in my other room (*two* rooms, just for me!) perfectly positioned for gazing down at the walled garden below. The bathroom is dazzlingly bright, with white mosaic tiles, a vast oval bath and a shower that's easily roomy enough for four. The elaborate chrome knobs and dials have settings to replicate various weather conditions: fine drizzle, summer rain, downpour. I'll try them all, first chance I get. I'll experience *multiple* climatic conditions.

Feeling peckish now, I bound off the bed and burrow in my bag for the remaining motorway muffins. They're squashed flat in their cellophane wrappers. While I'd normally scoff them anyway, it doesn't feel right in such beautiful surroundings. Instead, I select a plump nectarine from the fruit bowl which has been thoughtfully put out for me, and feel as if I am almost sullying the room by dropping the stone into the waste paper bin.

Further explorations reveal that a gleaming dark wooden cupboard is in fact a fridge filled with booze, plus a multitude of snacks: three types of nuts, including pecans! Packets of thyme and shallot-flavoured crisps! A crinkly bag of truffle popcorn, several biscuit varieties including stem ginger, and a box of red foil-wrapped Kirsch Kisses, whatever they might be! There's even a glass dish with a lid, filled with tiny slices of lemon. At Charnock Richard you don't even get a bourbon biscuit.

I check the time — still half an hour until the welcome reception — and remove all the edibles from the cupboard and set them out carefully on the table. Grabbing my phone, I take pictures of the pleasing arrangement from all angles to show everyone back home. I also take a selfie, my grinning face poking in from the side in front of the swanky snacks. Kim, Cheryl and Ellie won't believe what you get here. Neither will Paul. He eats like a horse; I often spot him marching about Mrs B's garden clutching an enormous doorstep of a sandwich. He never seems to stop to eat lunch. So I stash all three packets of crisps into my case for him — handy to eat while he works — plus the pecans for Morgan as, to my knowledge, he's never tried them. That boy needs to be educated in the world of posh nuts. The Kirsch Kisses will do nicely for Mrs B — nuts get jammed in her dentures — and the ginger cookies will be handy for home. It occurs to me that there's not an awful lot left to last me the rest of the week, but I want to take a few presents home.

To quell my pre-reception nerves — and make use of the lemon slices — I pour myself a gin and tonic, discovering that the fridge has a tiny freezer section at the top, with ice cubes. Can life get any better than this? I prowl around my suite, clinking my glass and taking pictures of the pink chairs, the bed and the sweeping view of the manicured gardens below. In the bathroom I photograph the basket of Molton Brown toiletries and the scented candle in its glass and chrome jar. I try on the fluffy white bathrobe over my dress, then carefully hang it back in the wardrobe. I pop open the bag of truffle popcorn and recoil at the earthy whiff. I'd expected chocolate. It smells like soil and the popcorns are flecked with black bits as if they've been swept up off the pavement. I try a single piece, crunching tentatively; it's sort of *fungal*, bringing to mind Morgan's athlete's foot. I spit it into a wad of super-soft loo roll and drop it into the bathroom bin.

Ping! I snatch my phone from my bag: three missed texts from Morgan. They read *Mum?*, then *MUM?!*, then, *Hand wash T shirt how????* I sip my gin and reply: *Fill sink with warm sudsy water, squish about with your hands and rinse clean.* As I picture my boy, dutifully laundering away at the kitchen sink, my heart swells with love for him. Okay, he's an idiot, but we don't do too badly, I reflect, just the two of us. Well, the three of us now Jenna's virtually a permanent fixture at our place.

Feeling all warm and, admittedly, a little tipsy now, I inhale my room's sweet scent. As there's no obvious source of the smell — no dusty old pot pourri — I can only assume it's being piped in from some secret source. However, while it's lovely here, inhaling vanilla and gin, I'd better get downstairs for the welcome reception. I redo my make-up — or rather, apply another layer on top — and clean my teeth extra thoroughly so no one knows I hurled myself at the booze.

Just before leaving, I check my reflection in the full-length mirror. The vivid orange floral print of my dress seems to have faded to a doleful peach. Never mind, people will probably assume it's properly vintage — and vintage is *meant* to be faded — rather than merely second-hand. Remembering that long hair should be tied back, I rummage in vain through my toilet bag for a hair band or scrunchie. Damn, must've forgotten. I've got to find *something*. I plunder my case and find the sole pair of tights I brought with me. Using my nail scissors I hack off a leg and use it to secure a sort of casual topknot. Then, giving my room one last lustful glance, I glide towards the lift.

Wilton Grange Cookery School is housed in a stable block behind the main hotel. I cross the gravelled courtyard, conscious of a fungally gin taste lurking at the back of my throat. The huge barn-style doors are wide open, and the sound of chatter and laughter drifts out. Sounds like a party's going on. A party where everyone — at least, everyone except Hugo — is capable of creating beautiful French lemon tarts as casually as if they were sticking fish fingers under the grill.

A young woman with flushed pink cheeks and a demure blonde plait spots me from the doorway. "Hi, are you on the course?" she asks brightly.

"Yes, I'm Audrey . . ." I make my way towards her.

"Hello, Audrey. Do come in." She flashes a warm smile. *More* perfect teeth. "I'm Chloe and I'm here to help with any queries you have. Let me get you your apron and badge . . ." The stable block is already milling with what I assume are my fellow guests, or students, or whatever we're called. I fix on what I hope is a confident smile as Chloe hands me my apron: dazzling white and emblazoned with Wilton Grange Cookery school in swirly blue letters on the bib. As Chloe swishes off, I pin on my circular "Audrey" badge and glance around at the gaggle of women — and one man — who are all chatting animatedly. The women exude breezy confidence. They remind me of the popular set at school; the sporty girls, whom the boys would buzz around like wasps. Not one of them appears to be wearing a scrap of make-up. My lipstick feels claggy in the heat, and I discreetly wipe it off onto the back of my hand.

Whilst the women are definitely younger than I am, the sole male student present is *ridiculously* youthful: he has the carefree air of a gap year boy, complete with a mop of long dark hair, messily ponytailed, and an extravagant sleeve tattoo. How on earth am I going to fit in here? I mean, what will we *talk* about? I sense that flurry of apprehension starting up again.

The room is split into several cooking areas, each with its own worktop, oven and sink. The walls are whitewashed brickwork and shelves bear numerous stainless steel containers and bottles of various oils. Clumps of fresh herbs and garlic bulbs dangle from silver hooks, and several women in white overalls are buzzing around efficiently. Heck, I'll just throw myself into the cooking. It's always appealed to me, the idea of being able to rustle up proper, grown-up meals rather than the teen-friendly fare I consume daily. I could start inviting friends round more: maybe even Stevie. Yep, I sense my oven chip days are over . . .

Chloe reappears with a tray of shimmering glasses. "Would you like a drink, Audrey?"

"Oh, thank you."

She smiles briskly. "Wine, sparkling water or elderflower cordial?"

"Cordial please," I say, hoping it'll mask any lingering scent of Tanqueray.

A burst of deep, barking laughter rattles down the room. "That's Brad," Chloe adds with a wry smile, indicating the huge bear of a man who's just strolled in. "He's your teacher. He's an amazingly talented chef, but then, you'll know all about him already . . ."

"Yes, of course," I say quickly, assessing his broad, ruddy face topped off with a mop of cherubic pale blond curls. Several women have gathered around and are gazing at him reverentially while he holds court.

"The plan is to have a bite to eat and get to know each other," Chloe continues cheerfully, "then you'll start cooking . . ."

"Really? We're cooking today?"

She nods. "Didn't you receive your itinerary when you booked?"

"Um . . . no. It was a sort of last-minute thing."

"Well," she says kindly, "don't worry. Just go with the flow and I'm sure you'll have a wonderful time." With that, she scampers away to greet another new arrival.

It's Hugo, thank goodness. He's all jovial smiles as he pulls on his apron, pins on his badge and takes a glass from Chloe's tray. "Do help yourselves to the buffet, everyone," she calls out, and we all drift towards the enormous table which is now entirely covered with platters of beautifully-presented miniature delicacies. There are tiny speckled eggs and prawns blanketed in what looks like fluffy foliage. There are dainty rolls of some kind of ham wrapped around dates, and tiny pancakes with blobs of creamy stuff, topped with little black beads. It's quite dizzying.

"Well, this is quite a spread, isn't it?" Hugo grabs a plate and starts loading it up with enthusiasm.

"It all looks delicious," I agree. "Mmm, I like these pancakes."

"Blinis," he corrects me, adding quickly, "At least, I think that's what they're called. You know, the little Russian things . . ."

"Oh yes," I say as he expertly shells one of the tiny eggs. I want to ask him what kind of bird might have laid it — a pigeon perhaps? — as he seems approachable and I'm warming to him already. At least he's around my age.

"Hang on a sec," he says, putting down his plate and reaching for my badge. "It's the wrong way up," he adds with a grin.

"Oh!" I laugh as he repositions it. "So, um, how are you feeling about the course?"

"A bit apprehensive, I suppose, but who cares if we mess up? I'm just regarding it as a bit of fun."

"Me too. I didn't think we'd be thrown into cooking today, though. I thought, you know, we'd be broken in gently . . ."

"You'll be fine," he insists. "You seem like a very capable person, Audrey."

"Really?" I ask with a smile.

"Yes, um . . . I'm sorry . . ." He flushes endearingly. "Look, I didn't mean to eavesdrop when we were arriving but I couldn't help overhearing . . ."

I sip my cordial, genuinely uncomprehending.

". . . It's just," Hugo goes on, "I gather things don't go too well at home in your absence. And I thought, ah, she's one of those women who runs everything brilliantly, like a well-oiled machine, and whenever she's not on hand it all falls apart . . ."

I peer at him, fascinated by his observation. "Like a well-oiled machine? Whatever makes you think that?"

"Well," he explains, "you're certainly very tolerant, telling your other half how to use the washing machine."

I watch as he pops the egg into his mouth. "You thought I was on the phone to my husband?"

"Well, er, I just assumed . . ."

I laugh loudly. "That wasn't my husband. I don't actually have one. It was my son."

"Oh! Oh, I see . . ." He chuckles awkwardly. "Sorry, Audrey. It's just the way it sounded . . ."

"That's okay," I say, grinning at the thought of my non-existent, appliance-phobic husband. "It's ridiculous anyway. I mean, Morgan's not a baby. He's eighteen and he should be able to cope on his own."

"I'm sure he can," Hugo says firmly.

"You're right. In fact, I suspect he could be perfectly capable. He just botches things up — I mean, if I ask him to hoover I can guarantee he'll choke the tube with a sock . . ."

". . . Smart move," Hugo remarks.

"Exactly. It's his way of getting out of doing stuff . . ."

"Phoney ineptitude," he adds with a smirk.

"Phoney ineptitude?" repeats the slender blonde woman who's arrived at our side.

"It means pretending you can't do something when you're perfectly capable," I explain, checking her name badge: *Lottie*.

"Oh, I don't need to pretend," she exclaims, widening her blue eyes. "I've never done anything like this before . . ."

"Neither have I," I say, flooded with relief. "This hotel . . . it's amazing. There's even a fridge in my room!"

Lottie and Hugo exchange a quick glance. "You mean a minibar?" Hugo asks, raising a brow.

"Yes, with miniature spirits and crisps and stuff . . ." I turn to Lottie. "Does your room have one?"

"I expect so," she says with a tinkly laugh.

"You should check when you go up later." I whip my phone from my bag. There's a text from Morgan — *what you mean sudsy water??* — but instead of replying I show them the photos detailing various aspects of my room. "Look at that lot," I enthuse. "Pecans, cookies, some kind of chocolate liqueurs . . ."

Lottie's lips twitch with amusement. "You took pictures of them all!"

"Well, yes, to show everyone at home . . ."

"There's even a photo of the toiletries," she observes, peering at the screen.

"And you did a selfie with snacks!" Hugo exclaims.

I look around at their bemused faces, unsure whether they're taking the mickey or not. "Yes," I say, more cautiously now, "to prove I was here in case I get home and worry that, you know, it wasn't *real* . . ."

Lottie smiles warmly and beckons a statuesque woman with a bouncy, flame-red ponytail to join us. "Audrey, Hugo — this is Tamara, my best friend. We always wanted to come here so we thought we'd do it together."

There are hellos all around, and Lottie insists that Tamara views all my pics. I have to say I'm especially pleased with the oval table composition, bathed as it is in golden sunlight. It's a marked improvement on our coffee table at home, strewn with sweaty salami.

"You're so sweet," Tamara announces, twitching her freckled nose, "being so excited about a minibar . . ."

I clear my throat. "Well, it's just . . ."

"I don't mean to be patronising," she adds quickly.

"That's okay." I laugh awkwardly. "I wasn't sure about that truffle popcorn, though. It's not what you'd think. You'd expect it to be chocolate, right?"

Hugo shrugs. "Er, I guess so."

"Well, it's not. It actually tastes of *soil*."

Tamara chuckles. "That's because truffles have that kind of taste."

98

I look at her blankly.

"You know when you have truffle oil on a pizza or pasta?"

"Um, I don't think I've ever —"

"That's what they taste like," Lottie explains. "The fungi, I mean. The ones little piggies snuffle out in French forests . . . have you never had them?"

"No. Well, I've had the chocolatey ball-type truffles of course. My son gave me some last Christmas from Marks & Spencer . . ."

Tamara laughs indulgently. "I *do* love your accent, Audrey. Where are you from?"

"I live just outside York . . ."

"So do my parents," offers Hugo. "It's where I was brought up."

"Really?" *You don't have an accent*, I want to point out, but then with people like Hugo it's impossible to tell where they're from. I'm not sure whether their accents are ironed out, or if they never had one in the first place.

"Well, you'll know we don't have many truffle-snuffling pigs up there," I say with a smile.

Hugo grins. "You're right. There's a complete absence of truffle snufflers . . ."

"Oh, I love northerners," Lottie announces. "So down to earth. And, ooh, is that tights in your hair?"

"Erm, yes, I forgot to bring anything to tie it back with," I say, reddening.

I catch Hugo peering at my makeshift scrunchie. "That's very resourceful of you. God, it's refreshing to find someone like you on this course, Audrey. Not knowing blinis, calling them little pancakes . . ."

"And the minibar thing," Tamara adds, "that's just adorable!"

I put down my plate and smile unsteadily as I try to work out whether or not that was meant as a compliment. Maybe it's just as well I didn't ask what sort of bird laid those little eggs.

CHAPTER
TEN

The Right Way to Chop an Onion

The ting of a teaspoon against glass cuts through the hubbub of the room. "Everyone," Chloe calls out, "could you please make your way over to the demonstration area and take your seats? Brad's ready to give his introductory talk."

We all drift towards the row of chairs set out in a horseshoe shape at the far end of the room. Brad sits before us behind a worktop with a built-in hob. He is tall and broad chested, clad in chef's whites, his blond curls illuminated by a shaft of sunlight. "Welcome, everyone," he says in a deep transatlantic tone. "I'm Brad Miller, executive chef here at Wilton Grange and your teacher for the week." He pauses and scans the row of students. There are eight of us — six women, two men — and everyone is gazing at Brad with rapt attention. I also note that everyone apart from me is wearing jeans or casual skirts, plus T-shirts. I feel ridiculously overdressed, which I wouldn't have believed would be possible in a frock that cost £2.49 and with tights in my hair.

"As you know," Brad goes on, "we'll be looking at the basic principles of classic French cookery." He offers a brisk, tight smile. "French cuisine can seem intimidating but in fact, as long as you grasp the basic methods and processes, it's a beautiful way to cook . . ." *Beaudiful* is the way he says it, despite being obviously English. "It's precise," he goes on. "That's the *beaudy* of it. We'll be using quality ingredients and preparing them simply and precisely. That's what it's about — patience, letting flavours *evolve* — and I know that, as competent cooks, you'll all be flying by the end of the course . . ."

I throw Hugo a quick look of alarm. Whilst I'm capable of feeding my son, I worry now that I'm not of the standard that Brad clearly expects. Mrs B certainly wouldn't call me competent ("bland soup!"). Hugo flashes a reassuring smile. "In fact," Brad goes on, "I recognise lots of you from the beginner's course we ran before Christmas . . ."

"Beginner's course?" I hiss. "Did you go on that?"

"Nope," Hugo whispers as Brad runs through some of the dishes we'll create: *moules marinière, boudin noir aux pommes, poulet en cocotte bonne femme* . . . Every time he uses a French word, he says it properly Frenchly with the throaty "r" thing, and obviously I haven't a clue what anything is. I mean, I'd never heard of underground truffles until about ten minutes ago, and I'm still wondering about those little eggs.

I glance along the row of students. With her porcelain skin and fair hair secured now in bunches, Lottie looks like a golden fairy. Tamara, with her ruddy glow and determined chin, has the air of a girl who's just bounded off the hockey pitch. Brad and Hugo aside, I realise now that, without exception, the girls can be no more than late twenties. Their lives are obviously unhampered by festering teenage underwear. They've never had to nag an eighteen-year-old boy to get the Mycil ointment right between his toes.

Brad is fixing me with a quizzical stare. I sit bolt upright. "So," he drawls, "*as I was saying*, I hope you've all got to know each other a little during the welcome reception. Just to help things along, perhaps you could all say a few words about yourselves, and why you decided to do the course?" An expectant silence settles over the room. "Shall we start here?" he says, indicating Lottie.

"Erm ..." She colours slightly. "I'm Lottie and I work in property letting and I'm here because, er ..." She turns to Tamara. "Well, we just thought it'd be a bit of fun, didn't we?" A bit of fun that costs *thousands*. I know plenty of people have tons of money and it's not something I think of normally (I mean, Mrs B is seriously posh. Her house might look shabby but she owns vast swathes of Yorkshire, according to Paul). It's just, I have never met people who are so casual about luxury.

Tamara's clear voice rings out. "... I'm an interior designer and I love having dinner parties but don't feel I've ever learnt the proper classic techniques ..."

Brad's gaze turns approving.

"... And, to be honest," she laughs bashfully, "I've always wanted the chance to study with you."

"Wow, thank you," he says grandly.

She beams at him. "I've followed you since you worked at La Scala in Paris and then when you moved on to Maison Bertrand in St Tropez . . ." Everyone swivels towards her. ". . . and then you were at Howard's in New York, then The Dorrington in Chelsea . . ." Blimey, she's studied him like a project. Should I have read up on his background, or Googled him at the very least? The only chefs I've heard of are the ones on TV.

Brad chuckles — "I'm immensely flattered, Tamara!" — and now it's the turn of the tattooed young man.

"I'm Dylan, I've worked in kitchens since I was fifteen, starting as a porter, then a line cook and a *commis* . . ." So much experience crammed into his tender years. "And now I'm a soo . . ." he adds airily.

Brad catches me looking quizzically at him. "Sous-chef," he explains. "Second in charge in the kitchen army. Great stuff, Dylan. You'll be teaching the rest of us a thing or two." He turns to the next student.

"I'm Kate," she starts in breathy tones, adjusting her quirky spectacles, "and I've only done a couple of patisserie courses . . ." Only! There's no *only* about it . . . "I wanted a broader view of the regional variations of French cuisine," she adds with a hopeful smile.

Brad nods. And so it goes on: everyone, it would appear, is an experienced cook. "I'm Jenny, and I cater for friends' parties. I'm looking to expand and build on my business . . ."

"My name's Ruth. I'm starting a supper club in my flat . . ."

A small hush settles. "Audrey?" Brad prompts me. I lick my dry lips. Can I get away without mentioning the dinner lady thing? It's not that I'm ashamed of it. It's just, I know they'll find it amusing — or *sweet*, as Hugo put it — and I just want to be viewed as me, as someone who's eager to learn culinary skills like everyone else here, and didn't just win it in a competition.

"Well, I'm here because . . ." Ping! Damn, a text. I forgot to switch my phone to silent. I will it to remain quiet in the front pocket of my apron.

"Is someone's phone on?" Brad asks, raising a brow. I pull a baffled look.

Ping! "Sorry, I think it's me," I bluster, swiping it from my pocket. Christ, five texts. Can't check them now, with everyone staring. I switch it to silent and clutch it tightly in my sweaty palm.

"So, Audrey," Brad says pointedly, "you're here because . . ."

"I won my place," I blurt out, thinking, to hell with it, I need to get this part over with so I can nip outside and read my messages. If they're all from Morgan, that's more than he normally sends me in a whole *year*, and suggests that something is seriously wrong on the home front. "I'm here because I won an award," I say boldly. "I, erm . . . I'm dinner lady of the year."

There's a collective gasp. "Really?" Brad gives me an incredulous stare. "You're a dinner lady? Seriously?"

"That's right," I say quickly, eyeing the door.

He blinks at me. "How long have you been one of those, then?"

"Er, ten years."

"Wow." He chuckles in amazement. That's another dinner lady thing: it makes people laugh. No one finds accountants or bus drivers funny. "So what kind of lunches do children have these days?"

"A lot of it's quite traditional," I explain, "although we serve a lot of ethnic food — Indian, Thai, Chinese, as it's a pretty multi-cultural school . . ." *Please* let's get this over so I can check my phone . . .

"So you have a huge repertoire already," he booms, looking genuinely impressed. "In fact, you're probably the most experienced cook in the room . . ."

"Well, no, not really because I don't actually—"

"Come on, don't be bashful. I'm very much looking forward to seeing what you produce during the week, Audrey." I smile unsteadily as he turns to Hugo, who rearranges his long legs. "So — last but not least — what brings you here, er . . ." He peers at Hugo's badge.

"Um, I'm Hugo and it's . . . a little hard to explain." He clears his throat. "I'm here because, well . . . I suppose I had sort of a mad urge to do something new and different and completely out of my comfort zone . . ."

Brad gives him a level stare. "A sort of personal challenge?"

"Yeah, something like that," Hugo says.

"Great, that's very admirable, Hugo. Okay, everyone, it's time to get started." He beams round at all of us. "Don't worry, we're kicking off with a very simple dish: a classic soupe à l'oignon. Just before we begin, I'll give

106

you a quick reminder of the knife skills you'll have learned on the beginner's course . . ."

My back teeth are clenched together as one of the kitchen assistants brings Brad a chopping board and a glass bowl containing three large onions. I wish he'd stop mentioning the beginner's course I didn't even know existed. "As I'm sure you'll all know," he starts, taking an onion from the bowl and fondling it, "everything starts with the knife." My phone vibrates in my pocket. I *have* to check it, but Brad has already launched into his demonstration and clearly doesn't take kindly to mobile-related distractions. I fidget anxiously. "We start," Brad goes on, "by trimming the stem" — he whacks an end off the onion — "but do leave the rude end intact." *Rude end?* "We chop the onion in half lengthwise," he rattles on, "then we peel off the skin and cut parallel to the board, almost but not *quite* to the rude end. We then make vertical cuts, leaving the rude end intact . . ."

"What's the rude end?" I whisper to Hugo.

"The *what* end?"

"The rude end, he keeps saying it . . ."

He chuckles. "He means *root* end, the bit where the—"

"Oh yes, of course," I bluster, as my phone vibrates yet again.

I jump up from my seat.

"Everything okay?" Hugo whispers.

"Yes, but, sorry, I need to pop out for a moment . . ."

"Ah. Need a nerve-calming smoke?" Brad booms, triggering a ripple of laughter. I smile back tensely and scurry across the room, whipping my phone from my pocket as I step outside. There are seven texts — all from Morgan — which read:

Sudsy water??

Mum what dyou mean? Hell, I forgot to respond to his earlier laundry-related query . . .

Like shampoo washing up liquid or WHAT?

Can you phone me Mum?

Nothing to wear for party!

OK T-shirt washed but dripping wet how to dry?

And finally: *OMG Mum am burned!!!!!!*

CHAPTER
ELEVEN

Boiled T-shirt

He doesn't answer his phone. He can't because he's lying in a curtained cubicle at A&E, with a concerned doctor applying ointment and gauze to his wounds while asking, "And where was your *mother* when this terrible thing happened?" I mean: *burns*. What degree are we talking? If I leave now, and really put my foot down, I could be home in three hours. I try again and again, pacing back and forth across the courtyard, and on the fourth attempt he finally says, "Yeah?"

"Morgan? What's happened? I'm worried sick—"

"I'm fine."

"How can you be fine? You just texted me saying you're burned—"

"S'just my hands," he mutters.

"Your hands? My God, darling, don't tell me you burnt yourself on the cooker . . ." A terrible image forms of him trying to defrost a frozen brick of chilli con carne over the gas ring.

"Nah, s'all right. It really hurt at the time, though . . ."

"So it's not a serious burn?"

"Um . . . it's just a bit pink. Well, bright red actually . . ."

"You don't need the doctor or hospital?"

"Stop *fussing*, Mum, I'm not five years old—"

"Fussing? But you texted *me*!"

He blows out air. "Yeah, well, I'm all right now. Jenna's coming over in a minute . . ."

I inhale deeply and lean against the warm stone wall. The sweet scent of onions frying is already drifting out of the stable block. Brad thinks I'm out here having a shifty fag; in fact, occasionally I toy with the idea of taking up smoking again. I know it'd blacken my lungs and probably kill me but, on the plus side, when I smoked — even while working as a cleaner at Sunshine Valley Holiday Park, fishing out grubby knickers from the crevices of sofa beds — I wasn't plagued by constant niggling stress. And now, as a virtuous non-smoker, I'm knotted up with worry pretty much all of the time.

"Please tell me *exactly* what happened," I say quietly.

"Well, I hand-washed my T-shirt like you said . . ."

"Don't tell me you used boiling water out of the kettle . . ."

"'Course I didn't. God, Mum. I just used normal water out of the tap but I had to dry it, didn't I?"

"Er, presumably, yes, if you're planning to wear it tonight . . ."

"Yeah, so it was soaking, right? It was *full* of water. It wasn't spun like when it comes out of the washing machine . . ." A tall, athletic-looking blond boy — he can't be much older than Morgan — strides into the courtyard with a wheelbarrow. On seeing me, he flashes a confident smile and sets about pruning a climbing shrub.

"You didn't try to iron it dry, did you?" I murmur.

"No, I microwaved it."

"You *microwaved* your T-shirt?"

"Yeah?" he says defensively. "I thought that was the best way to dry it quick. But when I took it out it was so hot I burnt my fingers . . ."

"For Christ's sake, love!"

He tuts. "Thanks for the sympathy, Mum."

The gentle snip-snip of the boy's secateurs cuts through the hazy air. "The thing is," I say, trying to keep my voice level, "the microwave basically makes liquids boil, so what you did was *cook* your T-shirt."

Silence.

"Was it all right, just out of interest?"

"Nah, some bits had burn marks and some were still wet. So basically, it's ruined." Another surly pause. "It was from Urban Outfitters as well," he adds.

The gainfully-employed teenager has now moved on from pruning to picking up the little twiggy bits that fell on the gravel. This task is performed with remarkable speed and efficiency, with not one fragment left littering the ground. "Look, Morgan," I add, "I'm sorry about your T-shirt, I really am. But, to be honest, I'm more concerned about how you're managing to cope on your own while I'm away."

"What d'you mean?" he says hotly.

"Well, you're eighteen, love. I hope I can trust you not to do any other crazy stuff—"

"It wasn't crazy!"

"Look, should I come home, or what? Just tell me, Morgan . . ."

"Of course not. Why would you need to do that?"

I inhale the scent of stocks in a nearby rustic tub, and wonder how best to put it. "Okay, I won't, but only if you promise to *think* before you do things . . ."

"I'm not stupid," he mutters.

"No, I know you're not. But you *are* a bona fide adult now and you need to act like one. You can vote, you can get married, you can go off and join the army . . ."

There's an audible gasp. "You want me to join the army?"

"No, of course I don't. I'm just making a point . . ."

"You do. Why not just say it? You want me to get shot! That's charming, that is. Thanks a *lot*." With that, he abruptly finishes the call. I glance at the teenage gardener. He is now hammering a bit of loose trellis back into place. Maybe I could borrow him for a few days, take him home to fix things and pick stuff up from the floor and act as a role model for my son. Bet *he* can use a washing machine. He's obviously been raised properly, by capable, fully-functioning parents — that's the crucial difference. I've done my best but, clearly, have fallen way short of the mark somewhere along the line. Morgan is probably the only eighteen-year-old in Yorkshire who is incapable of safely laundering a T-shirt.

I step back into the stable block, trying to shake off my lingering concerns for his safety. "Thought you'd done a runner," Hugo remarks, shuffling onions around in a saucepan.

"Just had to call home," I say lightly. "God, I'm way behind everyone else. You're all frying already . . ."

"*Sautéing*," Brad corrects me, looming disconcertingly at my side. He watches, sturdy arms folded across his broad chest, as I assess the laminated recipe. Ingredients for the soup have been thoughtfully set out for me, just like chefs have on TV. There are plastic pots containing ready-measured portions of butter, flour, olive oil and grated cheese, and even one of white wine and another of red. After my terse exchange with my son, I'd be terribly tempted to have a shifty swig if Brad wasn't still lurking close by.

Six onions are sitting beside my lime green chopping board. I pause before starting to chop them, hoping that Brad will take this as a signal to move on and watch someone else. It's not that I'm incapable of cutting up veg. It's just that his noisy nasal breathing — which is clearly audible, even above all the hubbub of the room — is putting me off. "Knife skills, Audrey," he murmurs.

"Yes, of course," I say. *Off you pop and see Lottie, I* add silently. *She's looking rather harassed . . .* He remains at my side, waiting, I decide now, for me to mess up so he can crack a dinner lady joke and make everyone laugh. He doesn't seem to be doing much teaching, as far as I can see. Maybe he views himself more as a sort of kitchen personality. Well, I won't give him that opportunity. Taking the knife, I start to chop in precisely the way he showed us. I have learned a new skill, I realise. Okay, I know things are going to become trickier with the fancy tarts and all that, but I can do this! *I can actually chop an onion like a proper chef.*

"Very good," he observes, the wind whooshing out of his nostrils and onto my neck. Hell, does he have to stand so close? Under Brad's intense gaze, it takes what feels like a month to chop the rest of my onions. "Mmmm," he says occasionally. "Good technique, nice firm movements ..." The only thing to do is to mentally block him out, to focus so hard on the task in hand that this world-renowned chef with his shock of blond curls melts away. This is what Morgan does with me, I decide. When I'm getting on his nerves, grumbling about his whiffy bedroom or our unflushed loo, he fades me from his consciousness until I cease to exist.

In the swing of things now, I drop my chopped onions into the pan and start to sauté. *Don't be put off by him,* I remind myself. *You've sautéed billions of onions in your life.* "Hmmm, this is looking lovely," Brad adds.

"Thanks," I murmur, hovering over my pan. The onions slowly turn golden and I carefully sprinkle in the flour, followed by wine.

"Taste," he murmurs into my ear.

I turn to look at him. "Sorry?"

"Taste it, Audrey, every step of the way. *Taste, taste taste.* How can you create a *beaudiful* dish if you don't know what it needs?"

I taste it — mmm, not too bad — and sprinkle in a little salt. I taste again, and add a few grinds of black

114

pepper. God, it's delicious. As I continue to stir, something incredible starts to happen. I am only vaguely aware of Brad ambling away to check on Tamara. And soon, not only our teacher but the other students and bustling kitchen assistants all start to melt away too. It's just me, studiously following the recipe, step by step, and tasting, tasting, tasting. Like sight-reading a new piece of music, all you have to do is relax and give it your full attention. You don't panic and think, "I can't possibly do this, it's all going to go horribly wrong!" You just focus hard and let any distractions fade away. As my soup begins to simmer, other things start to disappear too: the spectre of Jenna's thong on my bathroom floor, and the lingering fear that my son is clearly capable of burning down our house.

I turn my attention to my croutons, slicing a baguette with extreme precision and sprinkling it with grated cheese. I didn't need to come to a swanky hotel to learn how to make cheese on toast but I'm damn glad I did. Yum, this cheese is delicious, I think as I steal a bit. Must try and educate Morgan away from the industrial orange Cheddar he's so partial to.

I remove my croutons from the grill and gaze at them reverentially. I taste my soup, adding another touch of salt, then ladle some into a bowl and float the croutons on top. Brad is back at my side, his nostrils quivering as he peers at it. "That looks sensational, Audrey. Can I try?"

"Yes, of course," I say, not sure if he's having me on: yes, it looks perfectly edible, but it's just *soup*.

He picks up a spoon — my spoon — and slurps noisily. "Oh, that's marvellous. *Beaudifully* seasoned, the onions perfectly caramelised . . ."

I laugh, not knowing what to say. It's clearly an over-enthusiastic response: like when a child splatters pink paint on a sheet of paper and you cry, "That's wonderful, darling!"

"I can see you're a natural," he adds, further mortifying me as he raises his voice and says, "Everyone? As Audrey has demonstrated, the secret to a *beaudiful* French onion soup is to never rush, to let the flavours gradually unfold over time. This" — he turns to me with a beaming smile — "is perfection in a bowl."

"Thank you," I croak, my cheeks blazing as hotly as when I was announced as Dinner Lady of the Year. For years — decades — nothing of note ever happened to me, and now all *this*.

"Teacher's pet," Hugo sniggers as we clear up our work stations.

I pull on rubber gloves and plunge them into the sink. "Beginner's luck," I say with a grin.

With a couple of hours before dinner, I take myself off to my room and am slightly taken aback to discover that it's been *tidied*. Not only that, but my bed has been smoothed over after me throwing myself on it, the covers neatly folded back into a triangle shape. A small red foil-wrapped ball has been placed on one of my pillows. I have only ever stayed in budget hotels and B&Bs, and this kind of thing never happens in those places. On closer inspection the pillow present turns out to be a Kirsch Kiss, like the boxed ones in the minibar. It's too special to eat, I decide, and drop it into my suitcase to take home.

Feeling terribly decadent, I cleanse off the day's make-up and fill the huge, claw-footed bath way higher than I would normally — because places like Wilton Grange *never* run out of hot water — and sink into clouds of lilac-scented bubbles. My pleasure is further heightened by the fact that no one will hammer on the bathroom door announcing that they need to pee. I can carry this off, I decide. I can fit in here and learn all kinds of fancy stuff and run a bath that goes right the way up to my neck. It's going to be okay. Well, of course it is — what was I so afraid of exactly?

I'm feeling immensely cheery as I get dressed for dinner and give Morgan a call. No answer. Still sulking over the fact that I want to send him off to a war zone, probably. Oh well. I consider trying Stevie again, but then, he could call *me*. Too busy, probably. "Always on the road, babe," as he puts it, making out that it's a pain, but obviously thinking it lends him an air of glamour. Instead, I call Kim. "How's it going?" she asks. "I've been desperate to hear . . ."

"I love it," I enthuse. "We've just done our first cooking thing and Brad — he's our teacher — reckoned I made the best soupe à l'oignon . . ."

"Oooh, soupe à l'oignon. You're already sounding a little bit French!"

"I feel it. I really do. Well, I feel *different* anyway. I know it's no big deal — it's not like I've won the Nobel Peace prize — but still . . ."

"It *is* a big deal," she insists, with a hint of impatience. "You won it for being completely brilliant and you need to stop shrugging it off as if you don't deserve it."

"Well," I say, opening my mouth like a fish as I daub on my most lash-lengthening mascara, "it's already making me feel better about cooking generally. I mean, maybe it's not my soup that's faulty. Maybe, when you reach 84 like Mrs B, your tastebuds don't function like they used to . . ."

"Probably," she chuckles. "So what are the others like? The other students, I mean?"

"All way younger but they seem lovely. Actually, no, there is someone around my age — Hugo, quite posh, one of those rich, confident voices . . ."

"Single?"

"No idea," I say, laughing, and knowing where this is leading because she's made it pretty clear that she's not wholly approving of Stevie and his service station ways. "I haven't quizzed him about his love life yet," I add. "We've only had a quick chat at the buffet and, anyway, I'm here to *cook*, you know . . ."

"Gay or straight?"

"Kim, I don't know!"

She sniggers. "You're hopeless. So what does he do? Have you found that out, at least?"

"For a job, you mean?" Kim has this thing of always wanting to know what people *do*. "He hasn't said, actually. But he's funny and—"

"Good looking?"

"Yes, I suppose so," I say, applying lipstick at the dressing table mirror.

"Oh, right, you *suppose* so." She's still chuckling as we finish the call.

As I'm a little apprehensive as I head down to dinner, it's a relief to see that Hugo, Tamara and Lottie have saved a place at their table for me. The first thing that strikes me at dinner is that food here is so tidy, so neatly arranged, as if nudged into position with tweezers. While I didn't expect to see oily discs of salami tossed onto the table, I'm impressed to see that the meaty components of my charcuterie platter — again, so French! — have been carefully folded into dainty cones. I keep wanting to take pictures with my phone. It seems almost criminal to be presented with such beauty and not photograph it to show everyone at home. However, I'm also aware that everyone else is just tucking into their starters as if all of this is normal, so I pretend it's normal too. I'll just have to make do with staring hard at my plate and imprinting a mental image on my brain.

There is wine, of course, and it's free — steady on Audrey! — plus four types of bread which are wafted in front of me in their basket. I am almost frozen with indecision, partly because I'm also wondering whether Morgan has had the forethought to defrost a burger in good time for dinner. Christ, I really should have left defrosting and reheating instructions. I know from my food safety course that e-coli is only properly killed off at 155 degrees, and how is a hapless teenager meant to

119

know that? No, no, I *must* stop this. Anyway, it won't kill him if he resorts to the chippy every night . . .

"That soup you made," Lottie remarks. "I watched you, Audrey. I don't know how you managed to concentrate with Brad hanging over you like that." She wrinkles her tiny nose. "Brad said mine lacked depth. I really did my best to get it right. I've even made it before, at home . . ."

"I just tried to blot him out," I explain. "I was focusing on trying to catch up with you lot . . ."

"Yes," Tamara adds, "there you were, casually wandering back after your ciggie break and getting stuck straight in . . ."

"I didn't go out for a smoke," I say with a smile.

"Oh, I just assumed—"

"Just a bit of drama at home," I add.

"Everything okay, I hope?" Hugo asks with a frown.

I pause, on the verge of regaling everyone with the tale of the boiled T-shirt, but decide not to. Hugo already knows about the washing machine drama and I don't want him thinking my life revolves entirely around laundry. "Everything's fine, thanks," I say lightly.

"Of course it is," he says with a big, warm smile. "You've left an eighteen-year-old boy in a nice comfortable house. He's hardly traversing the Alpine Tundra on a yak."

I laugh. "You're right, of course you are . . ."

"So what do you do, Hugo?" Lottie asks with a smile that can only be described as flirtatious. "You didn't say during the introductions."

120

"Me?" He looks taken aback. "Oh, er, I'm looking to set up something new. It's early stages. I'm sort of looking at opportunities . . ." He pauses. "Sorry if that sounds evasive. I don't mean it to be. Honestly, I'm really not sure what's next."

"So what made you come on the course?" I ask.

"Well, um . . . there's been quite a bit happening over the past year . . ."

"Oh, really?" Lottie asks, wide eyed.

He nods. "Like divorce, actually. A real stinker. Polly and I have been wrangling over the details for months . . ." He looks around at all of us as if unsure whether to go on.

"Sorry," I say quickly, "I shouldn't have asked."

"No, no, it's fine. Ask away." He smiles and sips his wine. "Anyway, when the dust settled I just had an urge, you know, to *do* something. A sort of *oh-sod-it* thing. And I've always loved French food. I know it seems a bit old-fashioned these days but it's what I remember from my holidays, when I was a child — a great gang of us: uncles, aunties, grannies, tons of kids . . . we'd all drive over to someone's crumbly old house in Burgundy . . ."

I listen, transfixed, picturing hordes of people all talking over each other and doing relaxed, Frenchy things like smoking filterless cigs from soft packets and giving the babies wine. Dad and I had just one holiday together after Mum's abrupt departure with Brian Bazalgette: a spectacularly terrible canal trip where it soon became apparent that my father should never have been allowed to take the helm of a narrowboat. A dead rat floated by, inflated by its internal gases like a football, and we collided with a partly-submerged shopping trolley. We chugged along in gloomy silence by day and practised long division at night. Unbeknown to Dad, I was utilising the mental arithmetic part of my brain by calculating how many hours we had left before we could go home. I missed Mum so much during that holiday, it caused an actual ache.

"The sun shone every day," Hugo goes on, "and these amazing lunches were set out by various aunties at the huge garden table and drifted on all afternoon . . ."

Briefly, I recall deciding that Dad and I should eat something, and heating up a tin of beans and chipolata sausages in the dank galley kitchen. I couldn't get the grill to work to make toast so we had them on slices of bread.

". . . Endless plates of food," Hugo continues, "and then desserts, God, the heavenly desserts: clafoutis and tarte tatin and pots du crème . . ." I'm virtually inhaling all these French words. I don't know what these puddings are exactly, but I do know I want to eat them. Plus, Hugo has a lovely voice. Posh, yes, but not gratingly so: the kind of warm, reassuring tones you'd enjoy listening to on the radio — no, the *wireless* — late in the evenings. "Sorry for going on." He laughs, catching himself.

"Oh, I love hearing about this," I say eagerly. "Tell us more . . ."

"Sounds like I'm showing off," he blusters.

"You're not, honestly . . ." A piece of halibut quivers on the end of my fork.

"Well," Lottie says, "I think coming here, in honour of those holidays, is a terrific thing to do."

"Me too," I say firmly.

She sweeps her fine blonde hair back from her face. "I'm sort of here because of a break-up thing too." She breaks off and glances at Tamara. "Well, Ben and I were still together when I booked it, and he went on and on, 'Oh, it's so indulgent, a total waste of money, what's the point, blah-blah . . .'"

". . . That was kind of the trigger, wasn't it?" Tamara cuts in. "For you to leave him, I mean?"

"Yeah." She laughs. "He's only 30 — same as me — but so bloody middle-aged. Obsessed with investments and pensions and the *future*." She shudders and turns to me. "How about you, Audrey? Are you with anyone?"

I bite into a tiny fondant potato. "There's a thing, a sort of on-and-off thing . . ." A pause settles over the table. "It's nothing really," I add, wishing I was still picturing Hugo's jolly posh types and their tarte tatins, and not Stevie with his meat feast slices.

"Just a casual thing?" Tamara asks, spearing a stem of asparagus.

"Guess so," I say quickly, aware that I am ridiculously keen to play down any attachment whatsoever, not that I'm trying to portray myself as single exactly — I mean, what would be the point? It's just that, obviously, I'm a bit of a novelty to them and they'd want to know all about it. Would I tell them about the champagne glasses stashed in his case, and the post-coital Pringles? "I meant to ask," I say quickly, "has someone tidied your room and put a red foil chocolate on your pillow?"

"Er, I think so," Tamara says vaguely, as if she didn't pay proper attention.

I place my fork on my empty plate. "Well, I had one. It's so thoughtful of them to do that."

Lottie gives me a fond look. "Not really. It's just turndown. Lots of hotels offer that service."

"What's turndown?"

"Oh, Audrey," she exclaims, touching my wrist, "haven't you ever had that before? It's when the maid turns back your covers . . ."

"But why?" I ask.

"Well . . ." She shrugs. "To make it more inviting, I guess, so you can just slip straight in."

I picture my bed at home and laugh. "It's the most inviting bed I've ever slept in. It doesn't need to be turned down."

"No," Hugo says, clearly trying to suppress a smile, "but it's a nice touch, don't you think?"

"Yes, I suppose it is."

"It's so sweet that you appreciate these things," Lottie adds warmly, "like the way you were at the buffet today, really enjoying it, tucking into those quails' eggs" — aha! — "instead of taking it all for granted . . ."

"Yes," Tamara adds, "it's lovely to meet someone so . . . *unjaded* by life."

Full of delicious food and a touch too much wine, we all drift out of the restaurant a little while later and

124

settle ourselves into burgundy velvet sofas in a dimly lit corner of the bar. A waiter wearing a bow tie glides over to take our drinks order. As Lottie and Tamara chat away gaily, I sort of settle into the background, enjoying being a part of it, without actually having to take part. The *unjaded* thing could, I decide, be interpreted as patronising. But I decide to take it as a compliment. I know they find me amusing, photographing my pecans and not knowing about truffles or turndown time. But that's okay. They just find me interesting and different, like the way Morgan was fascinated by the giant tortoises at Flamingo Land. Granted, they're not the most attractive creatures at the zoo. But they have their own, gnarly charm, and people seem to enjoy watching to see what they'll do next.

Oh, it *is* lovely here, this hermetically sealed world where the food is carefully organised to give immense pleasure without making you feel like a bloated seal. Where you can lounge in a bar surrounded by attractive, rich-looking people — just like the ones on the hotel website — and your drink is placed before you on a little paper doily.

My reverie is briefly interrupted by the trilling of my phone. I fish it from my bag: Stevie. Taking a sip of my G&T, I leave it to go to voicemail.

CHAPTER
TWELVE

De-bearding Mussels

I assumed the teenage gardener was brought up properly because he knew how to prune a climbing shrub and now I'm thinking, wow, the children here seem incredibly well raised too. Miles of fruit, cereals, hams, cheeses and exquisite-looking pastries have been set out for breakfast; it's like an extravagant harvest festival display. However, the immaculate young guests aren't snatching at muffins and stuffing them into their mouths. Instead, a little boy with chestnut curls selects a boiled egg and a sliver of ham. A strawberry blonde girl has merely chosen a yoghurt and a pear. And it's making me think, perhaps these polite youngsters are the norm — i.e. they're just behaving in a socially acceptable manner, and it's *my* parenting that's fallen short of the mark. Ever the "live wire", as the other mums politely put it, Morgan could barely sit on his bottom for five minutes until he was about nine years old. Ironic, really, seeing as he now spends roughly 90% of his time sitting/lying down.

"Eggs with asparagus and hollandaise, moules marinière, poulet en cocotte bonne femme, tarte au citron and madeleines . . ." Tamara looks up from a typed sheet of paper as I join the table with my own (modest) selection from the buffet.

"What's that?" I ask.

"Today's schedule."

"I haven't seen any schedule," I say, panic rising in my chest.

"Don't worry, no one has. I just saw it lying about in the stable block yesterday and stuffed it in my pocket . . ."

"We wanted to know what we were in for," Lottie says with a smile.

Hugo, who's ploughing into a full English breakfast, looks up. "Good thinking. We can give the dishes some thought and research them if necessary." He turns and beams at me. "Can't have Audrey outdoing us all again," he adds.

Lottie sips her coffee. "Sounds like an awful lot for one day."

"It'll be fine," I hear myself saying. "It's not as if we're going to be thrown to the lions, and Brad's here to help us . . ."

"But he doesn't really help," she points out. "I mean, yesterday all he did was chop an onion and leave us to get on with the recipe."

Tamara nods. "He's not what I expected. I hoped he'd be a bit more, you know, *interactive* . . ."

Hugo sniggers. "I got the impression he'd like to be interactive with Audrey."

"You're joking." I choke on a fragment of Danish pastry, and am almost relieved when my mobile rings:

Stevie again. "Excuse me a sec," I say, jumping up from the table and striding away.

"Hey, babe," Stevie says. "So what's all this, eh? Elusive lady . . ."

He's one to talk. "Hi, darling. Look, I know I should have explained but it all happened in such a hurry. I won this thing, this work thing, and I'm away for a few days—"

"Only teasing," he chuckles. "I know where you are and what you're up to. Couldn't get hold of you last night so I called your landline first thing this morning. Morgan answered. Sounded a bit startled, like he didn't quite know how to take a call."

I sink into a leather armchair at the fireplace in the foyer. Hugo, Lottie and Tamara emerge from the restaurant and head straight for the lift. "I'm amazed he was even awake," I murmur.

"Well, he was definitely conscious. Told me you'd won some prize, some award . . . to do with school, was it?"

"Er, yes." I decide not to elaborate further; Stevie has shown zero interest in my work, not that I'd expect him to be fascinated about the correct way to dish out lasagne.

". . . Said you were in some hotel learning to make cakes or whatever," he goes on. "So where *are* you exactly?"

"Um, the hotel's called Wilton Grange. It's in Buckinghamshire. It's incredibly posh, we're being taught by a Michelin-starred chef . . ."

"Michelin? Aren't they the tyre people?"

128

I laugh. "They do food as well, Stevie. They award stars to the best restaurants . . ."

"Ah, *you're* my star, babe. I miss you. So, how long are you there for?"

"Four more days. The course finishes on Friday but there's a drinks do on Friday night. So I'll be home Saturday afternoon . . ."

He sighs. "Wish I could see you. I'm missing you like crazy, you know."

"I miss you too," I say as other students leave the restaurant — Ruth and Dylan are talking animatedly about wine — "but I'd really better go. Class starts at 9.30 and I need to fetch my apron . . ."

"Your apron!" He chuckles throatily. "Hmmm, I like the sound of that."

"Jesus, Stevie."

"Will you wear it for me next time I see you?"

I snort. "I don't actually know if we're allowed to bring them home."

"Aw, shame. I was hoping you'd model it for me tonight."

"Tonight?" I splutter. "You know I'm away—"

"Yeah, but they're not keeping you prisoner, are they? I mean, they don't chain you to the cooker 24 hours a day?"

"No, of course not . . ."

"Well then, come and meet me tonight. I know you're way down south but you could sneak out later, make it to Knutsford services by, I dunno, about ten . . ."

I laugh loudly. "Are you joking? I'm not driving to Knutsford services tonight, Stevie. I'm staying here. This is quite important to me, you know."

"Yeah, but you're not cooking at night, surely? Unless it's a midnight feast?"

"No, as far as I know we're not doing midnight feasts."

He sniggers suggestively. "We could have a midnight feast, babe. You could serve me some, er, *delicacies*, in your apron . . ."

A waitress glides by with a silver tray laden with profiteroles. "Stevie, I really have to go."

"Ooh, you're being all brisk! I quite like it. Sure you don't fancy Knutsford?"

"Not tonight," I say firmly. "Class starts in ten minutes and I really don't want to be late."

He sounds huffy as we say goodbye, as well he might: it's the first time I have declined the offer of an overnighter. Back in my room, I decide this could definitely benefit what I loosely term our "relationship": me being not quite so readily available. The nerve of it, expecting me to drop everything and drive God knows how many miles — in fact, I don't know where Knutsford even is, maybe my motorway knowledge is patchier than I'd thought — instead of enjoying another evening with my fellow students.

It *was* lovely last night, I reflect, pulling on my apron and tying back my hair (chopped tights again: *resourceful*). I didn't make a fool of myself, I didn't get drunk and start ranting about Morgan and his pants, and no one went on about me being a dinner lady, which suggests they have almost forgotten. While they're not the usual types I come across, Lottie and Tamara are so friendly and lovely and I'm thinking maybe they could teach me some ways of the world (the truffle thing) which would help me to handle myself better in all kinds of company. Like Mrs B, for instance. I mean, she's from posh stock; perhaps, if I dropped in the odd mention of quails' eggs, she might warm to me a little more . . .

Back in the stable block, Brad is giving us pointers on how to make the perfect hollandaise. "We're looking for a silken texture," he drawls, "and we begin by making a reduction, this is *very* important, it's a cornerstone of classic French cuisine . . ." We all watch intently as not Brad but a young assistant bounds towards the hob, and proceeds to add vinegar and twists of salt and pepper to a small pan of simmering water. "Making a reduction," Brad continues — he says it very Frenchly: *re-duuukssion* — "is about creating a concentration of flavours . . ." The assistant transfers the liquid to a glass bowl and places it on a pan of bubbling water. Into the bowl go egg yolks and melted butter, at which point Brad yawns and checks his watch, while the girl whisks and whisks until a perfectly silken sauce is achieved.

"What you want," Brad says, snatching the bowl from her now all the hard work's been done, "is a perfectly light and creamy hollandaise like mine."

"Like *his*," Tamara hisses, and the two of us splutter with stifled laughter.

Now it's our turn. While I follow the recipe to the letter, my hollandaise turns out rather insipid and thin. Instead of concentrating the flavours, I seem to have frightened them away. And although I keep prodding at my asparagus as it simmers, it's a touch overdone, in my opinion. I poach my eggs, lay the asparagus beside them and dribble sauce on top and, thankfully, the whole thing looks better when all the components are put together. It's like when you have a crappy haircut and the stylist manages to make it look presentable by giving it a big, bouffy blow-dry. But you know it's still crappy underneath.

Next we have to de-beard our mussels, which means effectively ripping off their hairy bits. "It's like doing a Brazilian," I whisper to Lottie, who's working directly behind me, when Hugo's out of earshot at the sink.

"Have you, then?" she asks with a quick smile.

"Well, I haven't *done* one, but I have had one done." Hell, what am I saying? I only meant it as a throwaway comment. I glance over at Brad, who's yacking away loudly to the assistants.

"The more often you have it done, the less awkward and painful it is," she says cheerfully. Of course, she's a young person. Having her lady hair ripped off is as normal to her as flossing her teeth.

"I've only actually had it done once," I admit.

"Had what done?" Hugo has reappeared at my side.

"We're talking Brazilians," Lottie explains with a grin as I focus my attention on chopping my shallots — *knife skills, Audrey!* — and throwing them into a pan.

132

"I imagine it's not the most relaxing experience," Hugo remarks.

"No, it's not," I say, laughing off my embarrassment. "It's bloody awful actually."

"So what happens?" he asks, seeming genuinely curious. I look at him as he pours oil into his pan. Whereas Stevie loads virtually anything — an apron, for God's sake — with suggestive undertones, there's a straightforwardness about Hugo that's so refreshing.

"Well," I explain, "first you have to lie on your back with your legs kind of elevated, and then you have to turn over and kneel on a plinth."

"A plinth?" he exclaims. "Like the ones in Trafalgar Square?" I blink at him. "You know, the ones with the lions on, although the fourth one doesn't have a lion, it's sometimes used for art . . ."

"Yes, like the blue rooster," Lottie cuts in. I chuckle above the sizzle of my shallots hitting the hot oil. Probably best not to admit that I have never been to London, let alone heard of any blue rooster on a plinth.

"I mean a little thing to rest your knees on," I explain, "so your bottom's in the air."

"Oh." Hugo gives me a grave look. "Sounds rather degrading, Audrey. Is there really any need for that sort of thing?"

"It was degrading," I say, experiencing a belated tinge of resentment at having subjected myself to such pain — all for Stevie, with him being such a youngster and therefore probably allergic to a woman's natural fuzziness, not that I was prepared to repeat the experience — "but mostly because it's so weird, you know, wearing a jumper with nothing on your bottom half . . ."

"Ugh, I can imagine," Hugo says, looking genuinely concerned.

"I mean," I go on, giving the contents of my pan a cursory prod with a wooden spoon, "we're used to seeing people topless, but *bottomless* is a whole different thing . . ."

Lottie peals with laughter.

"Oh, God," I mutter, glancing into my pan. "I think my shallots are burning."

Hugo peers at them. "They do look rather well browned," he offers.

"I know. I wasn't concentrating."

"Too busy thinking about plinths," he adds with a sympathetic smile.

"Yes. Oh, hell . . ." I scrape at the pan, wondering if the burnt bits might obediently merge in when everything's thrown in the pan, but now Brad is at my side, breathing fiercely against my neck whilst assessing the damage.

"Oh dear. Bit overdone there."

"Yes, I know." I detect booze on his breath, or maybe it's coming from the little pots of wine sitting around on everyone's worktops?

He smirks. "Your mind was on . . . other matters."

"Well, er . . . I lost concentration for a moment and I think I need to start again. Could I have a few more shallots, d'you think?"

"Ooh, I don't know about that," he murmurs. I stop jabbing away at my pan and look at him. I'm pretty sure it's not recently quaffed drink I can smell. More like old booze, lacing his breath.

"Just a couple?" I ask hopefully.

"Sorry, we're all out," he says, teasingly, then gives me a slow, undeniably suggestive wink. "But maybe," he adds, leaning over so as to gust his alcoholic breath directly into my left ear, "I might be able to find you some."

"That would be brilliant," I say levelly. "Thank you."

He beams, exposing large, slightly protruding teeth. "I mean, I might have some kicking around . . ."

I frown. This isn't my kitchen at home, where things — the odd withered lettuce or flaccid cucumber — do, admittedly, "kick around". It's a highly professional organisation. "Tasha!" he calls out, at which the sauce-making assistant beetles over. "Fetch Audrey some shallots please." Said vegetables are duly brought, and Brad wanders away as I set about chopping and sautéing all over again. Mussels go in next, along with garlic and a bouquet garni, then I plonk on the lid and wait a few moments until my molluscs have opened, and the wine and cream are sloshed in.

That's the thing with recipes, I decide: follow the instructions and you won't go far wrong. At least, no disaster will occur. I'm realising belatedly that what I've needed all along is a recipe for the raising of a son.

As we're allowed to eat everything we make here, we all take our moules to the tables behind the stable block for lunch. They have been set with white tablecloths, plus vases of delicate flowers from the gardens; the warm summer's air fills with chatter as we tuck in. Although Brad doesn't join us, we are tended to by bustling assistants who bring us wine and freshly baked bread. "This is lovely," Lottie enthuses, gazing around at the undulating grounds.

"It really is," I murmur. "It's like, I don't know, being at a beautiful outdoor restaurant, only we've done the cooking ourselves." I beam round at everyone, unable to conceal my pride at having produced something so delicious.

"You're right," Hugo says. "Well done us, I say."

"Yes, well done, all of you!" announces Chloe, who greeted us yesterday, and has now swept into the gardens in a chic turquoise shift. "I have to say, you're a remarkably talented bunch." As we all clink glasses, I'm overcome by a surge of happiness: at having made the decision to come here, and somehow fitting in, and cooking — not to mention eating — mussels for the first time in my life. What would Morgan make of them, I wonder? Would he prod at them warily with a fork? Perhaps, if I try hard enough, I can learn to create the kind of lunches Hugo was enthusing about, and even start cooking beautiful (sorry, *beaudiful*) French food back at home. Maybe I could give Morgan wonderful memories of delicious, home-cooked food that he'll reminisce about fondly, the way Hugo did about his idyllic holidays in Burgundy.

Life is so ordinary at home, I decide, dipping bread into my wine-scented sauce. Somehow, as well as the posh crisps and Kirsch Kisses, I need to bring a little Wilton Grange magic back to Yorkshire with me.

136

When we've finished our lunch — our bowls are whisked away by the kitchen assistants — I take myself off to the path that winds around the lake's edge and call Morgan. It's another beautiful day, as if Wilton Grange insists on bright blue skies, and nothing less will do. "Yeah-am-all-right," he mutters once he finally picks up. Clearly not in the mood to hear about yesterday's onion soup triumph.

"So, what are you up to, darling?"

"Nothing much."

"Is Jenna there?"

"Er, yeah?" There's a defensive edge to his voice.

"I was only wondering," I say, focusing on the dazzling pink blooms shrouding the summerhouse. "I'm just making polite conversation, love."

He sniffs. "We're all right, Mum. We're fine."

"Yeah, *you* might be fine," comes Jenna's withering voice in the background, "but I'm not!" And she says something else, something I don't catch as the others have emerged from the stable block, including Hugo and Lottie who are laughing loudly.

"You're so awful!" Lottie giggles in an unmistakably flirtatious tone, distracting me from our phone call. "God, Hugo. That's unbelievable . . ." I glimpse the two of them sniggering together in the corner of the courtyard.

I turn away. "Morgan, is Jenna okay? She sounds . . ."

"She's fine, stop going on."

"Is she drunk?"

He groans. "Of course she's not drunk, it's half one in the afternoon . . ."

I frown. Something's definitely not right; I've never heard them exchange a cross word before. "Um . . . have you and Jenna been . . . *doing* something?"

"'Course we haven't been doing nothing!"

"You haven't been . . . doing drugs, have you?"

"God, Mum. Why are you asking me this?"

"Because . . ." I tail off. Of course I've done the drugs talk, having swotted up on the kinds of stuff kids enjoy stuffing into their bodies these days. I studied legal highs and all manner of chemical substances in the way that Tamara has clearly studied Brad's career. "The trouble with drugs," I said gravely, while Morgan used my car keys to ease out some gunky stuff from between his toes, "is you never know how you'll react to them, and the effects can go on and on for ages." Which, I realised, made them sound like terrific fun.

"Have you and Jenna had a row?" I ask.

He exhales loudly. "No, we haven't."

"Well, has something happened, then? Is the house okay?"

"Yeah, Mum, I'm *telling* you . . ."

"Has there been some kind of disaster, love? Please tell me. I need to know."

"No, there hasn't been any disaster . . ."

"Well, there has, actually!" Jenna shrieks.

Morgan clears his throat. "It's all right, Mum, everything's *fine*. Just get on with your cooking thing, all right? And stop worrying." And with that, he rings off.

★　★　★

As I fry bacon for my chicken dish, I run through as many hypothetical disasters as my mind can dredge up. Something's obviously been trashed in my absence. TV, lamps, windows? The cooker or washing machine? Nothing irreplaceable, I suppose. But still, annoying (and costly) to put right. Maybe, I reflect, scooping out the bacon and dumping my chicken thighs into the hot oil, Morgan should go and live with his dad for a while in the wilds of Northumberland. I *have* mollycoddled him, I decide, cooking his meals, tending to his laundry and replacing his toothbrush the minute I notice it looking a bit splayed. Vince wouldn't have the patience for any of that, and maybe the change of scene would jolt Morgan into action. He'd miss Jenna, of course, but mucking out his dad's pigs might toughen him up a bit. It's not that I'm desperate to palm him off. But I'm out at work a lot and he's often left to his own devices, and I worry that there are only so many YouTube juggling tutorials a person can watch without losing a grip on reality.

Pushing such thoughts from my mind, I focus on what's happening on the hob in front of me. The chicken dish involves boiling potatoes and onions, then placing them in a pot along with the chicken and bacon, basting the whole lot with an insane amount of butter and whacking it in the oven. While that's cooking, I set to with my lemon tart, which involves making pastry — from scratch — which Hugo murmurs is "quite soothing really" (my sole previous experience, for mince pies last Christmas, was less than successful. "Maybe buy them next year," Morgan remarked, "like you usually do"). Anyway, after my conversation with Morgan I am feeling far from soothed. At least he can't have trashed the car, because I have it with me.

"Hmmm, interesting," is Brad's summation of my finished lemon tart which, granted, looks a little lunar in appearance.

"It wouldn't win any beauty contests," I murmur, still detecting booze on his breath.

"No, I can see that. So how's your main course looking?"

Christ, I'd forgotten about my casserole. I whip it out of the oven and remove the lid. "It looks anaemic," I remark.

"I think it looks *great*," Lottie says, loyally, peering over.

I shrug. "I seem to have a knack for taking a classic French recipe and turning it into . . ."

Brad arches a brow. "A school dinner?"

"Yes," I say, forcing a smile.

"Come on, you're being too hard on yourself. I'd say it's a pretty decent poulet en cocotte bonne femme . . ."

"What does that mean, out of interest?"

Brad smiles. "It means made by a good woman, a *beaudiful* woman . . ."

I blink at him. "No, I meant what does the *cocotte* bit mean."

"Oh." He looks taken aback. "It's, er, a casserole. It means cooked in a pot."

I spot Tamara try to quell a snort as he wanders off to get in the way of the sauce girl again, who's busily stacking a dishwasher. "Better watch out, Audrey," Lottie whispers. "He's coming on to you."

"Oh, come on," I exclaim. "Don't be ridiculous . . ."

"No, he definitely is," Hugo observes. "And d'you know, Audrey, that beautiful woman thing — which you are, of course — actually translates as housewife's chicken." We're both sniggering away, and I hope he doesn't resister my reddening cheeks as I turn my attention to my madeleines. Beautiful woman indeed! A jokey remark but still, I have a ridiculous grin on my face as I brush my madeleine tray with melted butter.

"You look like you're enjoying that," Brad drawls across the room.

"I am, thank you," I say, trying not to laugh.

"Remember that baking is a slow, sensuous process," he adds. "It's one of life's simple pleasures, never to be rushed."

"I'll bear that in mind," I say, focusing hard on the recipe. Yet something still goes awry, and my madeleines turn out less pleasing than the ones you'd find in a supermarket.

"A little lumpen," Brad remarks as he glides by.

"Yes, I know."

He turns back and pops one into his mouth. "Um . . . not *too* bad, actually. You've done well, you know, throwing yourself into this thing. You're showing great care and determination and I admire that."

I smile, buoyed up by the unexpected compliment. "Thank you. It's just lovely to be doing something for myself, to be honest."

He watches with interest as I start to clear my worktop. "So, um . . . any plans for tonight?"

"Just having dinner with the others and a couple of drinks in the bar, I'd imagine. But I'll probably have an early night."

I glance over and wave as Lottie, Tamara and Hugo make their way to the door. Only Ruth and Kate are left, washing up their own utensils at the far end of the room. "Would you like to have dinner with me tonight?" Brad asks.

I turn to look at him. "You mean, you'll join us in the restaurant?"

"No, no, I mean with *me*. Me and you, out for dinner." His silvery eyelashes flutter up and down.

My mind whirrs, swiftly throwing up the conclusion that I mustn't read anything into this. Of course it doesn't mean anything; he's just being friendly and God knows, there's probably not much to do in the evenings around here. Maybe it's just a thing he does, asking his students out for a meal? *Course includes dinner with celebrity chef Brad Miller:* it was probably mentioned in the small print.

"Sounds great," I say, mustering a smile.

"Fantastic." He beams at me. "Meet you outside at eight."

CHAPTER
THIRTEEN

Pub Grub

I daren't tell Hugo or Lottie or any of the others who I'm going out with tonight. I mean, we're not going *out* out — it's definitely not a date or anything — and he'll probably ask Lottie tomorrow and Tamara the day after that. Maybe he just likes to get to know everyone better, and find out what we think of the course. However, I still don't want to run the risk of anyone thinking I'm thrilled to be asked. God forbid they'd assume I'm secretly hoping to cop off with him just so I can say I've done it with a Michelin-starred chef. Anyway, I have a *boyfriend*. Stevie definitely falls into that category now, rather than being an on-and-off thing. At least, I have no yearnings to meet anyone else.

For this reason — plus the fact that I am not remotely attracted to Brad — getting ready is entirely stress-free. I pull on another charity shop dress; bluey-green squiggles, prim round neck, utterly devoid of sex appeal. To make doubly sure, I pull on a plain black cardigan and flat pumps and let my hair just dry as it is. Before leaving, I try Morgan's mobile; no answer as usual. "Hope all's okay, love," I tell his voicemail, hoping this doesn't fall into the category of "fussing", and reassure myself that whatever was going on with him and Jenna has probably blown over by now.

Bang on 8p.m. I step out of the lift to find Hugo, Lottie and Tamara loitering in the foyer. Damn, I was hoping to sneak out unnoticed. "Oh, Audrey," Hugo says. "We were wondering if you fancied a quick drink before dinner. It's been a pretty full-on day. We reckon we deserve a spot of liquid refreshment."

"Sorry, I can't tonight," I say.

He gives me a quizzical look, and I realise how much I'd love to sit chatting around the table again, gossiping about Brad and deciding whether boozy breath is just part and parcel of being a chef. "Other plans?" he asks.

"Um, yes, I'm going out tonight."

"Out?" Lottie splutters. "Out where?"

"Going on a nature walk?" Hugo sniggers.

"I'm, er, just meeting a friend for dinner." I check my watch. "Sorry, better dash." I'm aware of the cloud of surprise hovering over their heads as I propel myself towards the revolving doors.

No sign of Brad outside. It occurs to me that, if he whiffed of wine today, being driven by him probably wouldn't be my smartest move. So it's a relief when a taxi appears on the driveway and pulls up in front of the hotel. Brad climbs out from the back seat and, rather grandly, beckons me in. "Audrey! Sorry to keep you waiting. Hop in."

I try to affect a casual air as we both settle into the back seat. "So where are we going?"

144

"Just a little place nearby. You look very nice tonight, by the way."

"Thank you." I give him a quick smile. He's wearing a cream linen shirt and new-looking jeans, plus a brown leather jacket in a sort of blouson style, and his hair looks patted down, perhaps with the aid of some kind of product. It's a little strange, seeing him out of the kitchen environment, and I'm conscious of sweat springing from my palms. *Relax*, I tell myself. *It's probably lonely being famous. He just wants a pleasant night out with an ordinary woman who's unintimidated by his celebrity status.* Yep, that's why he asked me instead of any of the others. He knew the minute I arrived that I didn't have a clue who he was.

"So, d'you live around here?" I venture.

"Yeah, just a couple of miles away." We lapse into silence.

"How long have you been at Wilton Grange?"

"Three years or so," he replies. Christ, he's not giving away much. I wish the driver would put the radio on.

"D'you enjoy teaching?" I rattle on, sensing my underarms prickling disconcertingly.

Brad shrugs. "Yep, it's okay." Oh, for goodness' sake. As conversation falters I study the passing woodland with rapt interest. Maybe, being famous, he's sick of people firing questions at him. I'd hate him to feel I was interviewing him. Should I fill him in on my fascinating life instead? I'm sure he'd be thrilled to learn about Mrs B's crossword fixation and my son's vague notion of being a street performer. Or maybe I could entertain him with hilarious tales from the school canteen?

We meander along country lanes where I study drystone walls and ornamental gates as if gathering information for a project. Finally, we arrive at a quaint, sleepy village, consisting of a cluster of whitewashed cottages huddled around a triangular green, where the driver comes to a halt. "Here we are," Brad says, adding, "Thanks, Martin. I'll text you when we a need a pick up."

"No problem," he says as Brad and I climb out of the taxi.

We have stopped outside a picturesque pub adorned with hanging baskets and window boxes bursting with blooms. "Is this your local?" I ask as we make our way in.

"Sort of," Brad offers. "It's cosy and friendly and has a lot of potential, I think."

I glance at him. What an odd thing to say. He's right, though, about it being friendly; we are greeted by a cheerful young waitress who hands us enormous laminated menus. "This looks great," I enthuse, relieved now that he's chosen somewhere unpreten-tious. The pub is bustling and filled with the aroma of home cooking.

"You think so?" Brad beams at me across the table.

"Yes, it does. So . . . what d'you recommend?"

His mouth twitches in amusement as I leaf through page after page of the menu. It's not that I haven't appreciated the beautifully presented dishes at Wilton Grange. Sometimes, though, nothing beats simple, *un*-decorated pub food. We both order steak and chips, plus a bottle of red wine, and I catch Brad giving me amused glances. I'm feeling oddly observed. "You're obviously enjoying the course," he remarks.

"I am, yes. I'm learning such a lot."

He smiles approvingly. "Well, you're a natural in the kitchen, I'd say. Very instinctive . . ."

"Oh, I don't know about that," I say with a shrug. "I was a bit disappointed in today's dishes, to be honest."

"No, you did very well, for a novice."

"Thank you." Our wine arrives and I take a nerve-steadying sip as he focuses me with an intense stare. "So, tell me about yourself, Audrey."

"Well, er . . ." Another big sip. "I live just outside York with my son, Morgan, who's eighteen . . ."

"Tell me about *you*," he cuts in.

"There's not an awful lot to tell really."

He exhales through his nose. "You have a thing going on, don't you? A sort of self-deprecation thing . . ."

"Do I?" I laugh awkwardly. "It's not intentional. Anyway, you know I'm a dinner lady. I also work as a carer for an elderly lady . . ."

"And before that? What else have you done?"

Now I feel as if *I'm* the one being interviewed. "Um . . . well, my first job was as a cleaner at a holiday park near Morecambe Bay . . ."

Brad frowns. "I'd have thought you were capable of something more, um . . ."

"I just had to find a job," I explain. "You see, Mum left when I was nine so it was just me and Dad after that. And he died when I was seventeen so it was ideal really, being a live-in job . . ."

"Oh, I'm sorry to hear that." He tips his head sympathetically and nods for me to carry on. "So what did that entail? The holiday park, I mean?"

I smirk. "Fishing out rotting tuna sandwiches from under the sofas, mainly. Knickers, socks, the odd pile of vomit to mop up — that kind of thing."

He chuckles. "And worse things than that, I'd imagine."

"Well, yes."

"Like what?" He beams at me. Christ, he wants to know more? Having already tippled a large glass of wine, he refills it to the brim.

"Used condoms in the beds," I say, pulling a face.

"Ugh. Poor you. You must've been a tough little cookie, Audrey."

"I probably was," I say, laughing. "Anyway, I stayed there for a few years and . . ." I pause and look at him. "D'you really want to hear all this?"

"I do. You're a very interesting woman."

I smile, starting to relax a little at last. Can he really find me interesting? Or is he just being kind? "Well," I continue, "I worked there until my early twenties and then I got a better job as a receptionist at a hotel . . ."

"Ah, so you've worked in hospitality?"

"Yes, sort of, but I have to tell you it was nothing like Wilton Grange. It was a hen party hotel called The Last Fling. Cheap as chips, no minibars — I'd never even seen one before I came on this course — and definitely no chocolate on the pillow at bedtime . . . You know the

148

kind of place?" He gives me a baffled look. Of course he doesn't. "But we did offer chocolate fondue parties," I go on, "and the odd oiled-up male stripper put in an appearance . . ."

"Good lord," he says, chuckling. "Sounds dreadful. But you're a very stoical type, Audrey. I'm sure you handled it well."

I pause, wondering what to make of this. Resourceful, Lottie said. And now *stoical*. In fact, compared to Sunshine Valley the hotel was a dream of a job. It's also where I met Vince, who worked there briefly as a security guy; a slightly older, charming man with a shock of red hair, like a fox, and a smile that lifted my heart. "I enjoyed it actually," I say.

"Yes, I'm sure you did, because things have just happened to you and you've made the best of unpromising situations."

I frown, unused to being summed up by a man I barely know. "Like I said, I haven't had much choice." Enormous platefuls of steak and chips arrive, and I tear open a sachet of ketchup, hoping the conversation will shift away from the matter of my rather shabby CV.

"Can I ask you something?" Brad says. I nod and sip my wine. "If you're eating out — with friends, say — what kind of experience are you after?"

"Well, something like this, I suppose. It reminds me of my local, actually, although that's not as pretty outside. But it's friendly, with big helpings . . ."

"Big helpings?" he repeats with a smirk. "That's important to you?"

"Well, er . . ." I falter, suspecting this *is* an interview . . . but for what? And I'm sounding as though my top priority on a night out is a horse trough of chips. "I like the fact that there's a lot of choice," I add, confidence dwindling.

He arches a brow. "You don't find the menu too . . . unwieldy? You know, a bit everything-but-the-kitchen-sink?"

I pause, not sure of the correct answer here. "I suppose they're just hoping to please everyone."

"Ah," he says, leaning towards me across the table, "but don't you think a more *focused* approach might appeal more?"

Hell, now I'm really out of my depth. "Er, maybe," I reply vaguely. He drains his glass and adds, in a lowered tone, "I'm actually in the process of buying this place."

"Really?" I exclaim. "You should! It's a lovely pub."

"Ah, but it won't be like this. We're not talking ten-page laminated menus, Audrey. You see, it won't be a pub at all. At least, not in the old-fashioned boozer sense of the word. I'm talking an experience, a destination, a way of life . . ." I nod, although this is as baffling to me as when Stevie talks about mindful time management. What do these terms actually *mean?* ". . . There'll be great food of course," Brad goes on, "all locally sourced, and accommodation upstairs. There are three acres out back, so there'll be vegetable gardens, a small farm, and I'm looking at producing our own cheeses . . ."

"Sounds amazing," I exclaim, sawing at my steak.

150

"We'll produce honey," Brad continues, clearly on a roll now. "We'll have hives and livestock and grow our own produce: salads, an orchard, our own cider . . ." I glance at the wine bottle, noting that, somehow, we've downed the lot. Or rather, Brad has. Determined not to start prattling drunkenly, I've dawdled over a single glass.

"So when are you thinking of doing all this?" I ask.

"It's not something you can rush," he canters on, summonsing the waitress to bring us another bottle of wine, "but then, there has to be a momentum to it. And the time's right, I just know it. I feel it in here." He prods at his chest. "We're not talking fancy or exclusive, you know. It's just what real people want right now . . ."

"When you say *real*, d'you mean people who'd never be able to afford to eat at Wilton Grange?"

"Correct!" he exclaims, rapping the table and knocking over the little basket so the sauce sachets fall out.

"You mean people who wouldn't dream of spending £100 on dinner?"

He nods eagerly and fixes me with an intense look. "That's it *exactly*," he says. So I was right: in the normal course of things Brad doesn't encounter many ordinary types. This is why I'm here: to be his token "normal person", a sounding board to make sure it doesn't veer away from the kind of place regular, *stoical* types like me would enjoy. "You're a worldly, unpretentious sort of woman," he goes on, "and I'd really value your input . . ."

My stomach flips with excitement. So *that's* why he invited me to dinner: he wants to quiz me about the behaviours and eating habits of ordinary people. "Forget hollandaise sauce," I'll advise him. "I know it tastes good but it's a little bit fussy and, to be honest, a lot of people are iffy about asparagus . . ." Paul gave me a bundle last summer when he'd grown a bumper crop at Mrs B's. Morgan made it clear he wanted nothing to do with it — "makes your pee stink," he remarked — and it slowly decomposed in the fridge.

"I'm looking to build a vibrant, talented team from the very beginning," Brad goes on, pausing to drain yet another glass of wine. "It's not a project one can launch into all by oneself . . ."

"So," I venture hesitantly, "what kind of people will you be looking for?"

"Everyone," he says. "Front of house, kitchen staff, someone to man the cheese farm and hives, not that hives have to be *manned* as such, bees are pretty self-sufficient . . ." A throaty chuckle. "There'll be the hotel to run, and the bar and farm shop and cider farm . . ." He pauses to refill his glass. "I'm looking for passion, commitment . . ."

"Oh, yes," I say eagerly, my heart beating a little faster.

". . . I'm even thinking of taking on youngsters, school leavers — the types who have no direction — and training them up, giving them a chance in life . . ."

"That's such a great thing to do . . ."

"I'm looking to mentor raw talent," he lurches on, lips blackened by wine now. "It's hugely exciting. So, what d'you think?"

152

"Sounds fantastic," I enthuse. "There aren't enough opportunities for young people — at least, if they're not hugely academic and heading straight to university. I mean, my son Morgan, he has notions of being a street performer but —"

"I'm so glad you think so," he barges in, slurring now. "I value your input, Audrey. You have something about you, you know." With that, he excuses himself and totters off to the gents.

I can hardly contain my excitement while he's gone. So he thinks I have something about me! He *must* be planning to ask me to be involved, on some level. Perhaps I could advise from afar, or even take up a live-in position when he gets the thing started? Maybe he wants to mentor *me?* It's all falling into place now: his keen interest in my dinner lady and hotel experience, and the fact that he clearly wanted to talk to me alone.

Another thought hits me: this youngsters-with-no-direction thing. Could Morgan be taken on as a trainee chef? While he certainly lacks basic culinary skills, he does have a keen interest in food. Well, he *eats*, at least. I know he'd miss Jenna but really, would he allow his relationship to get in the way of an amazing opportunity? And it would be far preferable to mucking out pigs at his dad's. It's all I can do not to text him and tell him to prepare for great news.

Having emerged from the loo, Brad catches my eye and waves apologetically; he's now taking a call on his mobile. *Sorry*, he mouths, marching towards the main door and stepping outside. I glance down at the remains of my steak and chips. I'm far too excited to eat now. As I gather up the sauce sachets and stuff them back into their basket, I decide to go all out to impress him, to prove that an ordinary dinner lady from Yorkshire is precisely the kind of person he needs to help him get his project off the ground.

I glance back at the door. Still no sign of him. It's funny, I decide, toying with the vinegar bottle, how people like Brad view people like me. He probably thinks I'd never encountered olive oil before coming on the course — that I cook with lard — and fork spaghetti straight into my mouth from a tin. With a smile, I decide to show him I *do* know stuff, and quickly Google "foodie trends" on my phone (no calls or texts from Morgan, so I can only assume all is well). From a blog called Fashion Plates I learn that kale is terribly last season and that — amazingly — cauliflower is "having a moment" right now. Other veg on the hot list include chard, celeriac and globe artichokes. I decide not to admit that I haven't tried any of them.

Brad reappears, faintly sweaty and full of apologies. "So rude of me to leave you languishing here . . ." He waves the waitress over and pays the bill. "Taxi's outside," he adds.

"Oh." I assume the interview's over, then. "I should probably explain that I don't know much about food," I begin, deciding this is my chance to show how eager I am. "But while you were taking that call I started looking stuff up on my phone . . ."

"What kind of stuff?" He gives me a bemused smile as we climb into the taxi.

154

"Well," I say, "the kind of food that's in fashion right now." I chuckle. "It's amazing that vegetables go in and out of style, like skinny jeans or boyfriend jeans or whatever the thing of the moment is . . ."

"I'm not concerned with fads," he says firmly.

"No, I understand that — your new place is for ordinary people. It's just, I thought it might be useful for me to know that cauliflower's the thing now, did you know that? Well, obviously you do, being in the position you're in . . ."

He casts me a confused glance as we pull away from the pub. "I was vaguely aware, yes . . ."

"But never boiled to oblivion," I go on, thinking: *don't blow this, Audrey. You have about fifteen minutes to impress him enough for him to offer you a job* . . . "It's meant to be roasted," I continue, "like potatoes . . ."

"Really?" Brad smirks.

"Yes, so it keeps its, er, texture . . ." I tail off. "Anyway, I'm going on about cauliflower." I laugh awkwardly.

"You're *very* charming," Brad says, patting my leg and adding, "how about a little nightcap at my place before we whisk you back to the hotel? It's not too far out of the way."

CHAPTER
FOURTEEN

Kirsch Kiss

I say yes because I'm thrilled about this mentoring thing, about being involved with Brad's new venture right from the beginning. To think, being offered this chance at 44 years old! Oh, maybe I'm getting ahead of myself here but, God, it's exciting. Opportunities like this just don't happen to me.

The taxi takes us past the gated entrance to Wilton Grange and along a narrow lane which winds its way through dense, dark woodland. A rogue thought flutters through my mind that Brad might not be planning to talk business but to lure me to a dilapidated shack where he'll proceed to dismember me and package my various parts in sturdy black polythene. At what point, I wonder, would Morgan start to worry? When the cash and the freezer meals ran out, probably. Or when he reaches the end of his rope with hand laundering and decides he really needs to brave the washing machine. I give myself a mental shake and decide I'm being ridiculous as we arrive at a small, red-brick cottage bordered by a clearly neglected garden and a flimsy-looking white fence. It's not quite what I'd expected for a celebrity chef.

Brad thanks the driver and lets us in. The low-ceilinged living room is poky and dark, the well-worn grey corduroy sofa strewn with paperwork and CDs all spilt from their boxes. The shelves are crammed haphazardly with books, and a couple of bobbly old sweaters are strewn over the back of a chair. There is a slight odour of bin. Disconcertingly, it reminds me of Morgan's room. "Sorry about the state of the place," Brad says, switching on a wobbly standard lamp and clicking off the main light, as if that'll improve the atmosphere.

"Oh, it's very cosy," I say quickly. "So, d'you live here by yourself?"

"Yeah, these past couple of years, since the divorce . . ." He grunts. "You probably read all about that."

"No, I didn't actually." I smile tightly. "I don't really bother with celebrity gossip."

"Well, that's refreshing to hear." He pauses. "D'you mind me asking how old you are, Audrey?"

"Not at all. I'm 44 . . ."

"How old d'you think I am?" He grins squiffily.

"Er . . ." Oh God, I hate this game. It's even more stressful than crossword clues. "40?" I ask hopefully.

"Yeah. You're right." He doesn't look entirely pleased by this. "People usually have me down for mid-thirties," he adds, "but then they're used to seeing all those photos in the food mags and such, airbrushed to fuck, most of them . . ."

"I could do with a bit of that myself," I laugh.

"Not a bit of it. Sorry, I'm being rude. I haven't even offered you a drink. Red wine, is it?"

"That would be lovely," I say, turning to inspect a bookshelf — mainly tatty thrillers and ancient-looking cookbooks — while he hurries off to the kitchen. I do hope we'll get around to discussing his job offer soon as I'm keen to get back to the hotel. It's not that Brad is terrible company exactly, but I'm looking forward to hanging out with the others, and I can't wait to call Kim to tell her about the latest developments. While I'm at it, I'll also remind her to drop in on Morgan next time she's passing. It's her house, so I'm not hugely keen on her seeing whatever it is he's broken. But it's probably something of ours, I reassure myself, rather than the actual fabric of the building . . .

Brad returns with two large glasses of red wine. He hands one to me, then gathers up all the paperwork from the sofa and, rather unsteadily, dumps it on a desk in the corner of the room. "Come and sit with me," he says, landing heavily on the sofa and patting the space beside him.

Obediently, I perch beside him. I hope my body language is conveying the message that I'm not really in the mood for lengthy chats, and that I'd appreciate it if he could lay out the terms of his offer as quickly as possible so I can jump into the taxi and get back to the hotel. I'd also love to rub that red wine off his lips with a wet flannel, in the manner of cleaning the mouth of a small child. It's always puzzled me why it goes black on the lips, when the wine itself is dark red. "So," he says, clutching his glass, "tell me about *you*."

158

Not this again. I was hoping this part of the interview would focus more on my skills. I'm already trying to figure out how to make giving Mrs B her nightly shower sound relevant to the nurturing of bees. "Well," I start, "I told you about the holiday park and the hotel . . ."

"I mean *you*," he slurs. A fleck of white spit shoots out of his mouth. "What are *you* all about, Audrey?"

"I don't really know what you mean," I say. Agh, how not to answer an interview question. I picture Brad's other potential candidates — shiny, bright hockey types like Lottie and Tamara — and mentally pull myself together. "I should probably explain that I didn't set out to be a dinner lady," I add.

"So what did you *want* to be?"

I twiddle with my glass. "A musician. Well, a clarinetist specifically."

"So you play?" He widens his rather bloodshot eyes.

"Yes. At least, I did until the age of fifteen."

"Ah," he says, grinning, "and then other distractions got in the way . . ."

"You mean boys?" I say with a small laugh, relaxing a little now. "No, it wasn't quite like that . . ." Brad slugs more wine and nods for me to go on.

"My dad broke my clarinet," I say with a shrug.

He frowns. "Accidentally, you mean?"

I pause, realising how bizarre this is, sitting in a world-famous chef's scruffy cottage whilst talking about my clarinet. I glance around the room. How sad, I decide, to have a Michelin star but live in such dismal surroundings. My place isn't exactly salubrious but at least it doesn't feel soulless like this. "No, it wasn't an accident," I murmur. "He, er . . . wasn't in a terribly good state at that stage of his life. It was my birthday, and I'd assumed he'd be out — he spent most evenings in the pub. So I invited some friends round and we made punch, you know — a little slug from all of the bottles in the cupboard, topped up with lemonade . . ."

Brad sniggers. "You stole his booze, naughty girl."

"Yes, just a bit of this and that so he wouldn't notice."

"And what happened?"

I glance at him. Is this the kind of thing he wants to know? This isn't like my dinner lady interview when all I had to do was chat about my experience and show them the certificates for my food hygiene courses. "He came back early," I continue, "and everyone was, well, not drunk exactly but kind of tipsy and he threw a fit." I pause while he tops up my glass. I don't really want to drink any more, not while I'm trying to convey the impression of being the perfect addition to his passionate team. But nor do I want him to think I'm an uptight sort who won't be fun to have around. "And he threw everyone out," I go on, "and when they'd gone he was kind of mad — you know, drunk, falling about. And my clarinet was sitting on its stand — I'd brought it downstairs to practise — and he grabbed it and smashed it against the wall—"

"Oh, Audrey," he gasps, "that's terrible! Did it break?"

"Yes, of course." I focus hard on a pair of matted grey slippers sitting by the dusty TV. "But . . . y'know. It was just a thing."

160

"Yes, I know, but it was *your* thing. Did he get you another?"

"No." I laugh dryly. "It was a school instrument and we couldn't afford another. In fact, I never asked."

He looks perplexed at this, and glances around the room as if he might have a spare clarinet lying about somewhere. My steak and chips swirl unsettlingly in my stomach. I wish we could get around to talking about his plans for me as it's gone eleven, and I'm now thinking I might skip drinks with the others and just head straight up to my room. That four-poster bed is immensely alluring right now. I wish I hadn't allocated my minibar treats to Morgan, Mrs B and everyone else. Having only been able to manage half of my dinner I could do with something to soak up the wine, like those posh crisps.

"That's a desperately sad story, Audrey," Brad murmurs, his hand brushing against mine.

"Yes, it is, but it was a long time ago." I clear my throat and edge away. "Brad, um, I really should be getting back pretty soon. I wondered if we could get down to business and maybe the taxi driver could—" My words are stopped by his mouth, wet and jamming hard against my lips, and whiffing of steak and onion rings. "What are you doing?" I push him off and leap to my feet.

His stares up, startled. "But I thought you wanted—"

"You thought I wanted to kiss you?" I exclaim. His cheeks are florid, his blond curls fluffed up as whatever product he used has obviously worn off.

"Sorry," he says again, gathering himself up. "I thought, well, you're good fun, you're very attractive and when you said you wanted to get down to business . . ."

"Not that kind of business," I snap. "I mean, I thought we were discussing your new venture . . ."

He shrugs. "We have, and your input's been very helpful."

"I mean," I go on, cheeks burning, "how I could be involved. I thought, you know, I could somehow be a part of the thing — the cider and the cheese farm and bees . . ."

He fixes me with a steady stare. "Bees?"

"Well, not bees *specifically*. I mean, I like them, I know they're important in, er, nature and stuff but I'd be happy to . . ." I tail off.

"I . . . I'm sorry, Audrey . . . did you think I was going to offer you a job?"

I clear my throat, feeling oddly tearful. "Well, you seemed keen to tell me all about your project . . ."

"Well, it's my next big thing," he exclaims, shaking his head, "and it's been great, talking it over with you but, er . . . I think we might be at cross purposes here."

"Oh," I say dully.

He pats my arm and I shrink away. "I thought we were getting along, and I just assumed . . ." He laughs awkwardly. "You know, I did you a favour today, getting you those extra shallots . . ."

I stare at the blob of saliva that's settled in the corner of his mouth. "What do shallots have to do with anything?"

He is chuckling now, raking at his hair with his fingers and still clutching his glass. "Well, we don't normally do that, you know. It just doesn't work if students are constantly saying, 'Oh, I need extra eggs, I've messed up this chicken, can I have another couple of thighs . . .'"

"So," I say carefully, "you thought, just because you gave me those extra shallots — I mean, you only had to ask one of the assistants to fetch them, it's not as if you went out and dug them up from the garden and brushed off the soil . . ."

"Well, no," he blusters.

". . . You assumed I'd be up for it with you just because you gave me a couple of little onions?"

"No!" he exclaims, clamping a hand on my forearm. "God, Audrey, that was a joke. I thought you'd find it funny . . ."

"I mean," I cut in sharply, pulling away, "maybe if it'd been an aubergine or, what are those other things — Jerusalem artichokes . . ."

He stares at me. "You'd go to bed with me for a Jerusalem artichoke?"

"No, *I'm* joking, Brad." I glare at him. "I thought you wanted to, I don't know, mentor me as part of your new business . . ."

He stares at me, his mouth hanging ajar. I glance out of the window where the taxi is waiting. Maybe it's been there the whole time. Or perhaps Brad texted the driver while he was in the kitchen, fetching our drinks, so he'd be able to whisk me back to the hotel as soon as business was concluded. "I'm going now," I add, making for the door.

"Please don't be offended, Audrey," he says, scuttling after me as I step outside. "You're a lovely person and I'm sure you have a lot to offer. But to tell you the truth, the people I'm looking to mentor are, well . . . *young*."

The driver doesn't attempt to chat as we head back to the hotel. Maybe this is a regular thing, ferrying Brad's chosen women from the cottage back to Wilton Grange. I simmer silently in the back seat, studying my hands — unlovely dinner lady hands — wondering what on earth made me think he wanted to involve me in his venture. Things haven't changed since those awful netball selections at school. I'm *never* picked for teams.

Christ, I reflect, I should have taken the money instead of this stupid prize. Never mind a new sofa or kitchen table or any of that practical shit. I could've blown it on a holiday for me and Kim, and even asked Morgan along — he'd have agreed, if Jenna could've come too. *That's* what I should have done, instead of getting carried away and assuming our celebrated teacher planned to appoint me as Head of Cider Pressing when all he wanted was a quick shag. God, how am I going to get through the rest of this week?

I pull out my phone and call Morgan, amazed when he answers. "Hey, Mum, all right?" He sounds a little tipsy for an ordinary Tuesday night, but then, every day's the weekend as far as Morgan's concerned.

164

"Yeah, I'm having a great time," I fib, wondering how my incredible prize has descended into a night of mortification. "So, um . . . is everything okay with you? You sounded a bit out of sorts when we last spoke."

"I'm fine," he says firmly. "*We're* fine. We're just, um . . . hanging out."

I wonder whether to quiz him about whatever he's broken, but decide I can't face a tetchy exchange after the horror of Brad's kiss. "I miss you, love," I murmur.

"I miss you too," he says, and I'm overcome by a rush of love for my son, a fine young man who, for all his faults, at least *respects* women. At least, I'm sure he'd never expect sex in exchange for two shallots.

"Well, darling, I just wanted to say hi."

He sniffs. "That's nice. Glad you're having fun. You deserve it, you know."

"You really think so?" Now I feel quite choked.

"Yeah, you work hard, Mum. Can't remember the last time you had a break."

"Oh, thank you, darling. That's a lovely thing to say." It is, of course, but I also sense that he wants to get off the phone. My heart twists with a longing to see him as we say our goodbyes.

I pull out my purse as the driver parks in front of the hotel. "Don't worry, love," he says, "it's on account."

"Thanks." I smile stiffly and make my way through the hotel's main doors. To hell with it, I decide, heading for the bar instead of the lift. The whole Brad thing is starting to seem pretty funny and, as I spot Hugo, Lottie and Tamara clustered around a corner table, I can't resist sharing it with them.

"You're kidding!" Lottie shrieks as I fill them in on our dinner, the shallots and the forceful kiss.

"They were just normal shallots too," Hugo offers with a smirk. "Not even the more exotic banana kind."

"Oh, if it had been the banana kind she'd definitely have put out," Tamara hoots, and we all dissolve into raucous laughter.

"He was obviously expecting you to stay the night," Hugo observes.

"No, I don't think so. In fact, I suspect the taxi was waiting outside the whole time . . ."

"Oh, God," Lottie giggles. "What on earth made you go back anyway?"

I shrug and sip the gin and tonic that's been deposited in front of me. "Well, it was kind of interesting. We'd been talking about a new business he's planning — a kind of restaurant and farm — and he'd been quizzing me about the sort of experience ordinary people might enjoy . . ." I tail off, deciding to omit the part about me deciding I'd pretty much nailed the position of head keeper of bees.

"You were having a good time," Hugo adds kindly.

"Not really," I laugh. *I'd much rather have been here*, I decide, as the night continues extremely pleasantly and we are joined by Ruth, Dylan and Jenny who have come in search of a nightcap. "Another G&T?" Hugo suggests.

"God, I shouldn't really, not with our early start tomorrow . . ." I turn to Tamara. "What are we making? D'you have that schedule?"

"Lost it," she giggles, "and who cares anyway? Come on, let's have another round."

It's gone 1.30 by the time I finally totter off to the top floor, accompanied by Hugo, whose room is two doors down from mine. "Sure you can manage?" he asks as I fumble with the hefty brass key.

"Yep, I'm sure." I turn and smile. "What a great night."

He laughs. "It's not often you're accosted by a famous chef."

"No, not *that* bit." I pause. "I mean . . . just being here. It's great, you know. I love us all hanging out."

"Me too," he says, as I finally manage to open my door. He seems to hesitate, as if wanting to say something else. In fact, for just a moment, I wish it had been Hugo — my kind, gentlemanly new mate — who'd asked me to dinner, and not a lecherous chef. Which is ridiculous, of course, as Lottie's sparkle seems all the brighter when he's around, and of course I'm not his type, and anyway, I-have-a-boyfriend I-have-a-boyfriend I-have-a-boyfriend . . .

"Well, goodnight then," I say with a smile.

"Goodnight, Audrey." He grins awkwardly, then turns and lollops off down the corridor.

In my room now, I realise the turndown person has been busy again. Everything is neatened, straightened, made just so. It's also apparent that I need something to eat to soak up the booze. I flop onto the bed, visualising the minibar snacks stashed in my suitcase: the fancy crisps and ginger cookies and, hell, even the soily popcorn would go down a treat right now. But I can't guzzle them, not when they're allocated as presents. Another Kirsch Kiss has been placed on one of the pillows. That, too, will be taken home as a gift. It's too special to be used as blotting paper for booze.

Gathering myself up, I wonder if there's anything left in the minibar, maybe a packet of cookies or a soft drink: that'd be sensible. A bottle of water or a Coke. I slip off the bed and throw open the polished wooden door.

My heat soars. A miracle has happened. The minibar has been refilled.

CHAPTER
FIFTEEN

Droopy Soufflé

I don't quite know what happened last night. I remember the pub, of course, and somehow convincing myself that Brad had me earmarked as Queen of Hives, and then that terrible, wet-mouthed kiss . . . then a far happier time in the hotel bar with the others. And gin — I remember that too, if only vaguely. My eyes are still closed and my mouth feels disgusting: dry and not terribly fragrant. On a positive note, I am naked. This means I was at least capable of taking off my dress and shoes and even my underwear which in turn suggests that I wasn't *that* far gone. Which also suggests that, once I rouse myself, my hangover won't be too awful and I'll still be capable of cooking.

On a less positive note, I seem to be lying on gravel which suggests that I am outside.

Holy Christ. I scramble up, awash with relief on seeing the sturdy four-poster and the soft purple covers of my heavenly bed. So it's not gravel I'm lying on. It's a scattering of truffle popcorn which seems to have embedded itself in my skin. I pick it off my bottom and thighs, examining the dimples it's left behind. The effect is of extreme cellulite, coupled with light exfoliation from the salt.

I slip out of bed and check the time. Class starts in ten minutes so no time for a shower. However, as I'm not the kind of woman who'd be happy for the chambermaid to see a popcorn-strewn bed, I rake it together with my hands and dump it in the bin. I'm pulling on jeans and a top when there's a tap on the door.

"Just a minute," I say, raking a brush through my hair.

I open the door to see an eerily un-hungover-looking Hugo. "Was just a bit worried you'd slept in," he explains, "seeing as you didn't show up for breakfast."

"I did oversleep actually," I say with a grimace. "Forgot to set my alarm."

"I thought you might have." He raises a brow in amusement and, from behind his back, produces a blueberry muffin from the buffet.

"Oh, you shouldn't have! But thanks — I could probably do with some carbs. Come in while I get ready . . ." I nibble the muffin feebly and wash it down with a glass of water. "Hope I wasn't awful last night," I add, pulling on my apron and tying up my hair in its now customary manner with tights.

"You weren't awful at all," he says, glancing around. "Oh, your room's lovely. A suite! Mine's a broom cupboard compared to this."

"No, really?"

He grins. "Not quite. But seriously, this is palatial . . ."

We leave my room and, as we travel down in the lift, I try to quell my hangover-fuelled sense of unease. "Don't know if I can face Brad today," I mutter. "I mean, it seemed funny last night but now — I don't know — it's going to be so awkward . . ."

"Nonsense," Hugo exclaims. "He's the one who should be embarrassed, pouncing on you like that. He should offer you a full apology."

"You're right," I say as we step out into the foyer. "He's the one who lured me to his house with the promise of cider and cheese when he just wanted sex . . ."

Hugo gives me a quizzical look. "He offered you cider and cheese?"

"Well, no, not exactly," I say quickly, sensing my paranoia bubbling up again. "I got the wrong end of the stick, really. It's fine, though," I add breezily. "I'm just going to work through today's recipes in a totally professional way. I mean, we only have three more days of cooking. I really want to get the most out of this."

"Good girl," Hugo says with a chuckle. "Cook your socks off and show him you're not remotely fazed." I smile, feeling better already as we make our way across the sun-filled courtyard and into the stable block.

As if remotely controlled, I make my way straight to my workstation without making eye contact with Brad and check today's recipes. Brad doesn't seem to be bothering to do a demonstration, or even welcoming us this morning; he is too busy making idle banter with the assistants. This is good. The less interaction the better, as far as I'm concerned.

Everyone is getting stuck in with the first recipe: boudin noir aux pommes — that's blood sausage with apple, I have now discovered — which seems a little cruel considering my fragile condition. But then, no one strapped me to a chair in the bar last night and poured gin down my throat. I have no one to blame but myself, I decide, trying to breathe my way through a wave of queasiness as I sauté my pungent sausages, then transfer them onto a plate. Calvados — alcohol, ugh — is sloshed into the pan, along with sliced shiny red apples and a glug of cream. By now, I'm aware of a prickly sensation on my bottom and legs, and decide it's another hangover symptom: quite reasonably, my skin is protesting against me getting hammered last night. Scratching — I hope *discreetly* — at my bottom, I catch Brad's amused glance across the room.

I turn away and finish the dish, moving swiftly onwards to duck liver pâté, which involves the sautéing of offal, obviously, plus another slosh of booze — cognac in this case — by which time the entire lower half of my body is prickling unbearably. I nip to the loo to check out my legs and bottom; as I feared, they are worryingly blotchy. Perhaps it's the presence of Brad — and visions of his wet, wine-stained lips looming towards me last night — that's bringing me out in a rash . . .

I'm still itchy at lunchtime, and poke half-heartedly at my pâté at a table in the sun-filled gardens. I simply can't face my boudin noir. "This is delicious," Hugo enthuses, forking in chunks of sausage while I recall Jenna's shortlived vegetarian phase earlier this year.

Really, it didn't impact her dietary habits that much: she just picked the pepperoni off her pizza. Yet now, as everyone discusses the next dish to be cooked, I wonder if I may follow suit.

"Rabbit casserole," Tamara muses. "That sounds okay. Just like chicken, really . . ."

"No, it's not," I cut in. "Morgan's favourite film was *Watership Down*, he watched it over and over for months . . ."

"But these aren't the ones in the movie," Hugo points out. "They're just random, nameless bunnies."

"Yes, I know, but it doesn't seem right, eating something you'd normally see in a hutch."

"Why not?" he asks, looking genuinely perplexed.

I want to explain that it's a small step from sautéing a guinea pig, but don't want to seem pathetically un-French. "Well," I say, shrugging, "they're furry . . ."

"Cows are furry," Lottie points out.

"Well, sort of *fuzzy*," Tamara corrects her.

"They're small, then," I add. "I mean, a rabbit can fit in a handbag . . ."

"And you have a personal rule," Hugo remarks, "to never eat anything you could fit in your handbag . . ." I laugh, realising how ridiculous I'm being. Something about being around Hugo lifts my spirits; even the itching has subsided a little now. By the time we're back at our workstations, jointing our rabbits — "chop them at the elbows and knees," Brad commands — I'm too busy grappling with bones and sinew and God knows what else to even think about my traumatised skin.

In fact, the rabbit casserole is delicious, as long as I can banish thoughts of seven-year-old Morgan, weeping quietly to the strains of *Bright Eyes* in front of his beloved DVD. But by the time we move on to our sweet vanilla soufflés, my confidence has begun to wane.

"Rise, for Christ's sake," I murmur, peering at my creation through the glass oven door. I will it to puff up, to be beautifully cloud-like and prove that I *am* a capable cook — Frenchie style — and that Brad is crazy not to consider me for his team.

"Staring at it won't help," he remarks, having arrived at my side.

"I'm just keeping an eye on it," I say. I glance up at him, expecting him to at least look a little embarrassed, and to whisper, "Sorry about last night. I was rat-arsed and my behaviour was completely disrespectful." But instead he just stands there, hands on hips, gaze fixed upon my soufflé as I lift it from the oven. Rather than rising obediently it has slumped dolefully in the middle.

"It's not too bad," Hugo says, glancing over.

"It's a disaster," I groan. Brad is giving it a pitiful look, as if it's a pet with virtually no chance of survival. In fact, he's clearly delighted with my failure on the soufflé front. *Serves her right*, I bet he's thinking, *for shoving me off her last night.*

"Desserts really aren't your thing, are they?" he asks with a smirk.

"No, clearly not," I say dryly.

"I was watching you," he adds, far louder than is necessary, "and you didn't gently fold in the egg whites. You sort of muddled it all together . . ."

174

I cough. "Yes, um, I realise I went a bit wrong there . . ."

"You seemed distracted," he continues, waggling his pale brows, "as if your mind wasn't really on the job in hand . . . would that be a correct assumption?"

Catching Lottie and Hugo throwing him irritated glances, I turn to look Brad directly in the eye. "I'm actually not feeling too good today."

"Really?" He flashes a teasing grin. "Not been . . . bitten, have you?"

"I'm sorry?" I exclaim, aware now of Dylan and Jenny tuning into our exchange.

"The scratching, Audrey. You seem terribly *itchy* today. Don't tell me there are bedbugs in the honeymoon suite . . ."

"I'm sure there aren't," I bluster. "It's just . . . a bit hot in here. In fact, excuse me, I'm going to step outside for a minute . . ." I dart out to the courtyard where, not caring that anyone might glance through the stable block windows and see me, I claw at my bottom and legs. It's not enough. I need to be naked, sluiced with cool water.

It's an unforgettable experience, isn't it? Shirley, the competition organiser, had enthused. *Possibly even life-changing.* It sure is, I decide, raking at my rear and wondering if I'm having an allergic reaction to all the rich dishes I've been sampling here. Maybe fancy French food isn't for me. Damn Brad, humiliating me just because I wouldn't shag him last night.

Itching slightly subsided, I make my way back into the stable block where I tackle my washing up at lightning speed. "We're going to the spa after this," Tamara remarks. "Fancy coming along?"

I shake my head. "Thanks, but I think I'll just have a lie down in my room. It's been a bit of a trying day."

"Oh, come on," Lottie chides me, "it's just what you need. We've checked it out already and it's amazing. Grab your swimsuit and meet us there."

Up in my room, I strip naked and examine my mottled body, then pull on my undies plus a loose cotton dress: kind to stressed skin. Grabbing my swimsuit and robe, I make my way downstairs and across the grounds to the spa — it's a modern, low-level glass structure, cunningly disguised by trees — where Lottie, Tamara and Hugo are already reclining in robes on loungers by the side of the indoor pool. "Poor you," Lottie says sympathetically as I join them. "Brad didn't need to pick on you like that."

"He's just a pisshead," Tamara mutters. "I mean, what's he taught us all week? How to chop an onion and whip up a hollandaise?"

"The assistant did that," Lottie reminds her.

"Anyway," Hugo adds, looking up from his phone, "you rose above it, Audrey, like the lightest of soufflés. So, well done you."

"Thanks, Hugo." I perch on a lounger and glimpse his screen: it's a shot of a beautiful, raven-haired teenage girl.

He catches me looking. "That's Emily," he says, holding it up so I can get a better look.

"Emily?"

"My daughter," he adds with a grin.

"Really? I didn't know you had any kids. How old is she?"

"Fourteen," he replies.

I take a moment to process this. How strange to not have mentioned her over the past three days. "She's your only one?"

"Yep," he replies, showing me another picture, this time of the two of them, arms around each other in a garden filled with roses.

"She's lovely, Hugo. A real beauty. She looks like you, actually, very much . . ."

"So everyone says," he says with a smile.

"So, um . . . does she live with her mum?" I ask.

"Well, yes, in the holidays. She's at boarding school the rest of the time."

"Oh."

He smiles. "You sound surprised."

"It's just, I don't know anyone whose children go to boarding school. I guess you had your reasons, though—"

"She loves it," he says firmly. "It's a real community, the opportunities they have are amazing. There are incredible trips and career guidance, they all do the Duke of Edinburgh award . . ." Would Morgan still be lying on the sofa, prodding at his laptop, if I'd had the money to offer him that kind of education? I'd have missed him, though. In fact, I realise, scratching my ankle, I'm missing him now.

"I went to boarding school too," Tamara offers.

"Really?" I turn to her. "Did you enjoy it?"

177

"Christ, no, I bloody hated it." She guffaws. "Terrible bullying and a whole load of bulimia thrown in." She glances at Hugo. "Sorry. I'm sure Emily's having a far better experience . . ."

"She's fine," he says, a little defensively now. "She's getting an excellent education."

"I'm sure she is," I offer, my head buzzing with questions: but don't you miss her? Don't you wonder what she's doing, every day? But then, maybe it's me who's overly involved in my son's life: leaving him frozen meals and butterfly cakes, for God's sake.

"Anyone fancy a dip?" Hugo asks, whipping off his robe to reveal an impressively toned body clad in boxer-style trunks. He leaps in with a splash.

"I do," Tamara calls after him, casting off her own robe and striding in a cut-away black swimsuit to the deep end. She dives in a graceful arc, followed by Lottie in a polka dot bikini: gorgeous, the pair of them, their bodies unmottled and devoid of the ravages of time. Hugo is already ploughing energetically along the length of the pool. I catch myself watching him, trying to figure out why he hadn't thought to mention his daughter before.

"Come on in!" he commands with a wave. I grimace, not sure that I'm up to exposing my mottled body in such attractive company.

"Hurry up," Tamara adds. "It's lovely in here . . ." I shrug off my robe and itch at my hip, then absent-mindedly bite at my nail. Salt. My fingertip tastes of salt, from my hip — from the *popcorn*. "I'm all salty!" I announce, springing up from the lounger.

178

"I've been itching all day and I couldn't work out what it was . . ."

"I thought you seemed a bit distracted," Lottie exclaims. "I didn't like to say . . . so, what happened?"

"Oh, *I* know," Tamara remarks. "You managed to fit in a salt scrub before class . . ."

"So *that's* why you didn't show up for breakfast," Lottie adds. "You're supposed to shower it off, you know."

"It wasn't a salt scrub," I say, laughing now as I gather myself up and plunge feet first into the cool, soothing water. Ah: instant relief.

"What was it, then?" Hugo asks, splashing towards me as I come up for air.

"It was the popcorn I lay on all night."

"You slept on popcorn?" He blinks at me, uncomprehending. "What is this, some kind of weird new beauty treatment?"

"No, it wasn't deliberate," I chuckle. "I sort of, er, spilt it in bed. But yeah, I guess I've had a salt scrub."

"Oh, Audrey," Lottie giggles, "you *are* adorable. People pay good money for that."

CHAPTER
SIXTEEN

Champagne in Bed

My son is uncontactable next morning. That's fine, it's only just gone eleven — he's probably still *resting* — and I've only popped out of class to say hi and check all's okay on the home front. However I imagine that, in my absence, he has slipped into an entirely nocturnal schedule, like a mole. I can't understand it. Would any adult human choose to work night shifts and sleep all day, if they could possibly avoid it? Of course they wouldn't. Yet Morgan seems to actively desire this kind of life.

After rustling up a decent wild garlic soup — can't imagine *that* going down a storm with Mrs B — I set about tackling a boeuf bourguignon, with a cow's actual cheeks, plus lashings of red wine and with no direction from Brad whatsoever. In fact he spends the whole time blathering away on his mobile, which is rich, considering how disapproving he is of us prodding at our phones. Still, rather that than him hovering around me. Left in peace to cook, and with my rash now disappeared, I tackle the relatively simple task of knocking together leeks vinaigrette (vegetables, sweet relief!).

Our bourguignons are ready in time for lunch. "I'm not sure about eating an animal's actual face," Lottie remarks, frowning at her dish in the dappled sunshine.

Instantly, I feel better about making such a fuss about sautéing rabbit yesterday. "I suppose it's no different to a thigh really," I remark. Having polished off a bowl of soup, I am now savouring my own bourguignon with a glass of red wine.

"I know it's not in theory," Lottie says. "It's just, all this rich food: it's lovely of course, but who could eat like this all the time?"

"Actually, I think I could," I enthuse. "In fact, I'm going to do a proper French lunch for my friends when I get back . . ."

"What about Morgan?" Hugo asks with a grin, joining us at the table.

"Oh, he'd take exception to the leeks, being plants . . ." I break off as Jasper, the ridiculously buff porter, appears in the garden and strides towards me.

"Ah, here you are, madam. Sorry to interrupt your lunch, but there's someone at reception to see you."

I frown. "Really? I'm not expecting anyone. Are you sure they want me?"

He smiles briskly. "Yes, definitely." Giving the others a baffled look, I trot along beside him into the foyer.

My heart lurches as I spot him. This is wrong, *so* wrong. Dressed down in a crumpled grey T-shirt and faded jeans — *he* doesn't feel obliged to dress up for a place like this — Stevie is leaning on the reception desk with his pert bottom stuck out. He has the tousled air of a rakish young dude paying a visit to his older woman in her swanky hotel suite. Hang on, I realise with a sinking heart, that's *exactly* what he's doing.

"Hey, babe!" Stevie's face breaks into a wide, teeth-showing smile.

"Stevie . . . what are *you* doing here?"

"Charming! I thought you'd be pleased." He feigns a put-out look.

"I am, I really am, but . . . couldn't you have called to warn me?"

"*Warn* you." He laughs dryly. "Well, that's nice, Aud. I'd expected a slightly more enthusiastic reception." He kisses me noisily on the lips and emits another cackly laugh. "Woah, garlic! It's pretty pungent, babe. Still, I s'pose there's a whole heap of that in French cooking . . ."

"Not as much as you'd expect but, yes, we did make garlic soup this morning . . ."

"Hmmm, remind me not to try any, darling." He slides an arm around my waist. Aware of the receptionist observing our exchange, I lead him by the hand to the soft leather armchairs by the fireplace.

"Look," I mutter, "it *is* lovely to see you. I'm just a bit . . . surprised, that's all."

With difficulty, he pulls his chair closer to mine. "That was the whole point. To surprise you, I mean. I was in the area and—"

"Were you really?"

"Yeah, honestly," he insists, "and I thought, well, I'd be crazy to miss this opportunity to see you . . ."

I study his greeny-blue eyes, wishing this didn't feel quite so wrong. "But I'm on a course, Stevie. You know

182

that. I'm just on my lunch break. Class starts again at two . . ."

The beginnings of a sulk settles over his face. "Yeah, okay, I know you're busy. It's just, I felt a bit crap about missing your birthday . . ." He reaches down and unzips his brown leather bag — the one I've seen in many a Travelodge — to extract a tiny parcel wrapped in pale blue tissue. "So I thought I'd surprise you with this."

"Oh! That's very sweet of you. Thank you, darling."

Amazed that he's brought me something — the first gift he's ever given me — I carefully peel away the paper. It's a delicate silver necklace, its interlocked spirals embellished with tiny, glittering pink stones. "It's lovely," I murmur, studying it in the palm of my hand.

He grins. "I thought it'd be nicer to deliver it personally."

I look up at him, ashamed now for greeting him so curtly. "That's so thoughtful of you, honey."

"Go on, try it on." I smile and fix it around my neck. "Looks gorgeous," he says approvingly. "I knew it'd suit you. You have a beautiful neck, babe." I lean over and kiss his cheek. "So how about you show me your room?" he adds.

I laugh. "I can't, not now. I told you, afternoon class starts at—"

"Aw, c'mon, sweetheart, I'll wait for you there until it's finished. I'm sure I'll be able to amuse myself. Won't be long, will you?"

"Well, yes, I'll be three hours or so . . ."

"Three hours?" he repeats, aghast. "What're you planning to do with all that time?"

"Cook," I say, jumping up from my seat. "That's what I'm here for, remember? But I'll take you up and you can hang out there until I'm done."

We kiss in the lift. While it's usually thrilling in a motorway hotel, I sense myself tensing in case it should stop and we're caught locked in an embrace. Maybe, I decide, relieved when we reach the top floor, I'm more of a cheap hotel sort of woman. It never occurs to me to worry what people might think when we're at a Day's Inn or a Travelodge. "Wow, you lucky girl," Stevie exclaims as I let us into my room.

"I know! Isn't it lovely?"

He dumps his bag and grabs me for another kiss, then marches around, checking the lounging area, the bathroom, the sweeping views from the windows. He opens drawers and the wardrobe and fondles the tassel on the thick golden rope that holds back a brocade curtain. He discovers the minibar, flinging it open with a gasp of delight. "Wow, tons of booze. There's even lemon for drinks! They think of everything here. Okay if I have these crisps?" He snatches a packet and rips it open.

"Yes, of course . . ."

"Ugh, they pong a bit, don't they have any salt and vinegar?" He dives back towards the minibar, pulls out a packet of ginger cookies and crams one into his mouth. "Bit too gingery," he announces, wrinkling his nose.

"Stevie, my class starts in fifteen minutes," I say, sensing a twist of annoyance as he whips a Kirsch Kiss from the box.

"Mmm, yum, this is more like it . . ." He grabs another and consumes it in one bite.

"This is important to me," I say, my voice rising a little. "We're doing brûlées, it's the only chance I'll have to learn—"

"Your only chance to make a brûlée," he teases, flinging himself backwards onto the bed with such force that a cushion flies off. "No, it's not. I'll buy you a cookbook, darling. We'll make one together. We'll work through the recipe step by step, you can show me all your special skills with your apron on and nothing underneath . . ."

Despite my irritation, I laugh. "Behave yourself. You'll dirty my bed with your shoes on."

"Oh, c'mere, give me another kiss. Just a quick one, promise." I smile and lie beside him, and we kiss again — he tastes of chocolate and kirsch — and it happens, even though I know it shouldn't: my top and jeans fall away and I'm down to my non-matchy underwear, the lace on my bra gone bobbly from too many washes, the knickers a tad baggy around the bottom. Now he's kissing the swell of my stomach, sending little sparks shooting through me and breaking off only to murmur, "Hang on a sec. I've got another surprise for you, babe."

"What is it? Another present?"

"Yeah, yeah. Just lie there and close your eyes . . ."

I shift position on the bed. "Stevie, I really don't have the time. Brûlée's pretty technical and I don't want to miss—"

"It'll only take a minute," he cuts in. With a trace of exasperation I close my eyes, torn between curiosity and a burning desire to get off to class and prove to Brad that desserts *are* my thing, actually.

"Hurry up," I murmur.

"I will if you absolutely promise not to open your eyes."

"Okay, okay . . ." There's the soft pad of his footsteps, then he slithers next to me on the bed. "Keep your eyes shut," he whispers into my ear, recommencing the kissing, around my neck and décolletage now which, under normal circumstances — i.e., somewhere on the M6, with a juggernaut revving outside the un-open-able UPVC window — I'd find extremely pleasing. "You're so gorgeous," he murmurs, trailing his fingers along my inner thigh.

"What time is it?"

"Shhh, stop worrying, there's plenty of time."

"Seriously, Stevie, I need to—" My eyes ping open to the sight of Stevie in his pants, grabbing at my wrists and lashing something firmly around them. "What are you doing?" I shriek.

"Oh, c'mon, Aud, it's just a bit of fun . . ."

"You're *not* tying me up. Let me go!"

He laughs, and for a moment I'm too stunned to react as, having firmly tied my wrists together, he lashes the ends of the rope to opposite posters of the bed. "See, I knew you'd like this."

186

"You're mad. Christ, how did you do that so fast?"

"I was in the Scouts," he sniggers. "Got my knotwork badge, babe."

I am laughing now, at his sheer nerve and, I have to admit, his ingenuity as I peer at the rope and spot a dangling tassel. "It's the rope off my curtains!"

"Yeah," Stevie chuckles. "Like I said, they think of everything here."

"Very funny. How *resourceful* of you. Now stop all this and let me go . . ."

He pulls a mock forlorn face. "Aw, c'mon, darling, when do we ever end up together in a bed like this?"

"Never," I reply. "Never ever . . ."

"So let's use it then . . . hey, I've got an idea!" He bounds off the bed and lurches for the minibar.

"You're not having more chocolates. I want to take them all home for—"

"Nah, babe, this . . ." He pulls out a mini bottle of champagne and pops it open.

"I can't drink that, I already had a glass of red at lunch-time. I need to be fully compos for brûlée . . ."

"No, but *I* can," he chuckles, crawling back onto the bed and sloshing some onto my stomach.

"Christ, that's freezing!" I glare down, seeing it pooling in my bellybutton and dribbling over my sides onto my velvety covers.

"Lie still," he commands, positioning his head at my stomach and lapping at the champagne like a dog.

"Stevie, stop it," I snap. "Okay, you can have the champagne — have anything you want — but please drink it out of a glass . . ."

"This is much more fun," he murmurs.

"Untie me *right now!*"

He rears up his head, in that way that a tortoise might do, and wipes a dribble of champagne from his chin. "Woah, I didn't mean to upset you, babe, you're not normally this uptight . . ."

"No, because I'm not in a posh hotel in the daytime with a custard to make. Just *do* it, Stevie. I mean it. Untie me now."

He tuts loudly and shuffles towards one of the posters where he starts to fiddle ineffectually at the knot. "Jesus, it's bloody tight. It's 'cause you've been tugging on it . . ."

"Untie me!"

"I'm trying, I'm trying, Christ's sake . . ." He rakes back his hair. "What a waste of a room, that's all I can say . . ."

I glare at him, fury bubbling inside me. "A room isn't wasted just because I don't want to have sex in it, Stevie."

"You don't usually need much persuading," he huffs, still picking feebly at the knot.

"Oh, that's charming that is. That makes me feel really good about myself, that I'm usually desperate . . ."

"Well," he says, with an infuriating snort, "you are!"

I glare at him, about to retort *how-bloody-dare-you*, but of course he's absolutely right. Who else but a desperate woman would dash off down the motorway to have sex in miserable hotel rooms and finish off with a meat feast slice? "Just get this thing off me," I yell, at which the door flies open and Hugo stands there, gawping as if caught in headlights, then backs away into the corridor and disappears.

CHAPTER
SEVENTEEN

Curdled Custard

"Who the fuck was that?" Stevie exclaims. I close my eyes momentarily. I am actually *dying* here, from acute mortification. The staff will have to smuggle out my body without the other guests seeing. They'll probably shove me out of some back entrance where deliveries come in.

"No one," I murmur. "It doesn't matter. Just get these ropes off me right now . . ." Grumbling under his breath, Stevie frees one wrist, then the other. Turns out they were easy to untie after all. What a star scout he must have been. I must ask him to demonstrate other skills sometime, like lighting a fire by rubbing two sticks together or constructing a shelter from branches and ferns.

I clamber off the bed and pull on my top and jeans. "C'mon," Stevie mutters, tugging on his T-shirt, "he probably didn't see much."

I glare up from putting on my shoes. "No, of course not. Only me in my underwear, tied up. *And* you soaked my bed, just look at it, the turndown lady'll wonder what the hell's been going on . . ." I point at the mottled patches on the throw where the champagne's sunk in.

"Turndown lady?"

"Yes, the woman who brings chocolate . . . oh, never mind."

Stevie sniffs. "Who *was* that guy anyway? And don't say no one. He obviously knows you well enough to march straight into your room . . ."

"That was Hugo," I reply, in the bathroom now, pulling out my improvised scrunchie and brushing out my dishevelled hair.

"And this *Hugo*" — he affects a ridiculously posh voice — "thinks it's okay to barge into your room like that?"

I emerge from the bathroom and glare at him. "He probably heard me shouting. He was only trying to help . . ."

"*Help*," Stevie repeats with a sneer. "Is that what you call it?"

I stare at him. "What are you inferring?"

He shrugs. "Oh, nothing. Nothing at all. So you're, um, what . . . friends? Lovers?"

"Don't be ridiculous!"

"Well, what am I supposed to think? Is that what's been going on here? Oh, I can imagine. Getting pissed in the evenings, everyone hopping from room to room . . ."

"For God's sake, of course we haven't. There's been no *hopping* . . ."

"Look, I know what these posh types are like," he goes on in a sneering tone I've never heard before. "Shagging each other at gymkhanas, groping each other's arses in jodhpurs . . ." I gawp at him, watching his now decidedly unappealing mouth as he rants on.

"I think you're confusing a French cookery course with *Riders* by Jilly Cooper, Stevie."

"Yeah, whatever . . ."

I inhale deeply, my gaze settling upon his leather bag. Presumably his little champagne seduction kit is stashed in there as usual. He needn't have bothered when there's plenty of posh booze in my minibar. As he's discovered, they think of everything here.

"Well," I say firmly, "you can think what you like, but Hugo's just a man on the course, just a friend . . ."

"So you've made a new friend," he says bitterly.

"Yes, is that a problem?"

He blinks at me, and his face softens. He steps towards me and slides his arms round my waist. "Sorry, babe. I'm just a bit . . . hurt, that's all. You don't seem too happy to see me . . ."

"It's just not a good time," I mutter.

He kisses the top of my head. "Don't rush off. Let's chill out, have a drink . . ."

"I don't want a drink," I snap. "You can stay here, do whatever you like. I'm going out."

"Off to brûlée class?" he calls after me as I make for the door.

"Just *out*, if that's okay with you?"

"It's just custard with a burnt crust on top," he shouts after me. "How difficult can it be?"

I'll never know, I decide as I travel down in the lift, because, clearly, I can't face Hugo today, or ever again for that matter. I'll have to feign illness until the end of

192

the course, surviving on room service meals and self-medicating with minibar booze — but then, what would be the point of that? I'd be lonely and bored up here all by myself, and the turndown lady would tell the other turndown ladies about the pitiful drunk woman lying on a damp bed in the honeymoon suite. No, I'm better sneaking back to my room and sending Stevie packing, then grabbing my stuff and leaving too.

I step out through the revolving doors. It's a cool, breezy day with a bright blue cloudless sky. I inhale deeply, in the hope that the fresh country air will somehow lend me an air of purity after being lashed to the bed and splattered with drink. I stop and watch a pair of ducks gliding serenely across the shimmering water. Another option would be to throw myself into the lake, but how would Morgan feel, being informed that his mother had come to a watery end having left him only a few measly tubs of chilli and bolognaise and forty quid? He won't get far on *that*.

I slip a hand up my T-shirt and touch my stomach experimentally. It's sticky from the champagne, further adding to my sense of tawdriness as I replay recent events: being wetly snogged by a celebrity chef (unwanted) and tied up with a curtain rope (*doubly* unwanted). Life was a whole lot happier when I was just going about my business, tending to the kids at school and Mrs B — and Morgan, of course. Maybe I'm really not cut out for this kind of life.

A figure emerges from the hotel and looks around the grounds, as if searching for someone. I glance back at the lake and focus hard on the ducks. "Audrey?" the man calls out.

Christ, it's Hugo. My heart quickens as he strides towards me. *Please go away. I can't discuss the curtain rope thing now.* I will myself to split into billions of particles and disappear. "Hey," he says, crossing the perfect lawn and sitting on the bench beside me.

"Shouldn't you be in class?" I ask weakly.

"Yeah, in a minute." He touches my arm. "You okay?"

"No, not really," I mutter.

He clears his throat. "Look, I'm so sorry for barging in on you like that. I shouldn't have—"

"No, *I'm* sorry . . ." I dig the toe of my shoe into the gravel.

"It's just, I heard you yelling. I was worried. You screamed, 'Get it off me!' and I thought — I don't know — that you were being stung or something . . ."

"Stung?" I repeat, turning to him.

"Well, yeah." We lapse into silence. "And your door wasn't shut properly," he adds. "Class was just about to start and I knew you wouldn't want to miss—"

"I can't go to class today," I cut in. "I just can't face it. Could you tell Brad I've, um . . . had a bit of a turn?"

He blinks at me. "A bit of a turn, like an old lady?"

I fiddle with my birthday necklace. "Well, I *feel* like an old lady."

"Oh, come on. It's not that bad. No one knows, only me . . ."

"Hugo, *please* don't tell anyone."

"Come on," he exclaims, "how old d'you think I am, nine? Of course I won't tell anyone! Anyway, I take it that was your on-and-off thing?"

"Yep, he's the one," I say flatly.

He smiles, and his eyes crinkle kindly. "I assume he's on at the moment?"

I shrug. "Yes, I suppose so. He just showed up without any warning. He's still in my room, annoyed about being left alone, probably . . ."

Hugo smiles warmly. "He's a grown man. I'm sure he can take care of himself."

"Yeah." I turn to look at him. "I'm just not sure what I'm doing here, Hugo."

"What d'you mean?"

"Well," I say, focusing on a blaze of bright yellow roses, "I don't know what the point is. I mean, you're here because you had that what-the-hell thing, you wanted to do something spontaneous . . ."

"Isn't that why you're here too?"

I consider this. "No, I'm here because I was mad that Morgan threw away the shirt I'd bought him for Christmas."

Hugo frowns. "That was rather ungrateful of him. Was it covered in galloping reindeer?"

"No, it was a perfectly nice check."

"Sounds pretty inoffensive." He pauses. "I'm glad, though. Not about the wasted shirt," he adds quickly, "but that you're here."

I smile ruefully. "Well, at least I've provided you with some entertainment . . ."

He touches my arm again, and now I wish we could just sit here, the two of us, and that Stevie and Brad and the whole cooking malarky would just melt away. "How about coming to class now?"

"I'm really not sure, Hugo . . ."

"But it's brûlée! It's the classic French dessert. Come on, it's why you're here, isn't it? To learn, to stretch yourself, to do fancy stuff with a few eggs and whatever the heck else goes into it?"

I smile, because he's right: and aren't I always on at Morgan, urging him to get out there and make the most out of life? "I would like to be able to make a brûlée," I say firmly.

"Come on, then. Let's do it." He beams at me, squinting in the sunshine, as we stride together back to the hotel.

Everyone's already beavering away at their workstations. "Sorry I'm late," I murmur, silently challenging Brad to make a sarky remark.

"Another ciggie break?" He throws me a resigned look.

"Not exactly, Brad. I actually gave up twenty years ago." I smile briefly and take my place next to Hugo who begins to crack eggs into a glass bowl. I pick up the laminated recipe and study it hard: *Heat the cream and vanilla in a saucepan.* Sounds simple enough. I pour my cream into the pan, aware of Brad making his way over and watching, arms folded, a smirk on his face. "You missed the demonstration," he adds. Whoah,

196

so he's actually bothered to do some teaching today. Or maybe the hollandaise girl did it for him?

"Yes, I'm sorry, I lost track of time."

"She was a bit tied up," Hugo murmurs, at which I splutter while focusing hard on the laminated sheet of A4.

"The thing is to heat the cream slowly," Brad adds, "in the pan."

Well, I didn't plan to heat it in an egg cup, smartass. I smile sweetly as he wanders away to lavish praise on Tamara's perfectly smooth custard — maybe she's his next target for a dinner date — and try to concentrate on the matter in hand instead of picturing Stevie, growing restless in my room. He's probably glugging his way through the minibar and making a cack-handed attempt at fixing the curtain rope back in its proper place.

I wrestle my thoughts back to my brûlée and scan the worktop for vanilla. "Pretty necklace," Brad remarks, arriving back at my side.

Instinctively, I touch the silver chain. "Er, thank you."

"Although you shouldn't be wearing jewellery in class." I catch Hugo shooting him a look of annoyance, and quickly take it off and place it on the corner of the worktop.

"Sorry, I forgot."

"That's okay," he says with a grin. "You haven't tied your hair back either."

"God, no. I'll go and do it now . . ."

"No, no, just get on with the recipe, Audrey. You seem to have a real sense of . . . *determination* about you today."

I inhale deeply, still looking for my missing vanilla. There are only egg yolks, two kinds of sugar and a gnarly old leaf on my bench. Looks like the assistant forgot to set some out for me. I'm reluctant to ask Brad in case he assumes that fetching me some means he's entitled to a sexual favour. If he reckoned he was due a quickie for a couple of shallots, what would he expect for a glug of vanilla essence?

Brad has now levered himself up and is sitting on the corner of my workbench. "Looking for something?" he asks.

"Just vanilla," I say distractedly.

He picks up the withered brown thing and holds it in front of me. "Know what this is?"

I shake my head.

"It's a vanilla *pod*," he says slowly, as if addressing a child. "We don't use essence here."

"Right, of course . . ." I force a smile and take it from him. So what to do now: chop it, boil it or just bung the whole thing in? I glance over at Hugo, who's charged ahead: his brûlée has already been poured into four ramekins.

"If you'd been here for my demo," Hugo adds, "you'd have seen that we prepare it by making a slit along its length, peeling it open and scraping out the sticky paste."

"Of course," I say, unruffled by his patronising tone as I tackle the pod as directed.

198

"Very good. Now bring the cream to boiling point but *don't* let it boil."

"Okay . . ." *I'm not illiterate, I can read a recipe . . .*

"Now beat the egg yolks and caster sugar . . ."

"Right-ho," I chirp, a phrase I've never used in my life.

"Now pour your flavoured cream into the bowl with your sugar and eggs . . ." Oh, *I* get it. He's still trying to pay me back for rebuffing his advances. Making fun of my bottom scratching didn't work, so now he's opting for the over-attentive approach. What he doesn't know is that, having been seen tied up with a curtain rope, nothing can ruffle me now.

I stand over my pan, slowly stirring, trying to block out the sound of Brad breathing boozily at the back of my neck. As lumps begin to form, I quicken my stirring in the hope that it'll smooth everything out . . . but no.

I turn off the heat and gaze down at the scrambled mess.

"*Ahhh*," Brad observes, unable to erase the note of triumph from his voice. "Looks like you've got one hell of a curdled custard there, Audrey."

My heart's not in the macarons that follow. While Hugo's are pretty shades of lemon and pink, mine bring to mind those "a hint of a tint" paints that were once so popular as an alternative to white. "Macarons are tricky," Lottie says generously, although hers, too, are picture perfect.

It's almost a relief to finish cooking for the day and head up to my room where Stevie is lying diagonally on the bed, leafing idly through the hotel's glossy magazine. "Hey," he says, brightening, "here at last. So how did it go?"

"Fine," I say flatly, pulling off my shoes and curling up on my side next to him. Not that I've forgiven him exactly; I just need a little lie down.

"Good. Well, babe, I have to say, I can totally see why you chose this trip instead of the cash prize. What a place! They're working you too hard, though. You look knackered." Hmmm, a comment guaranteed to boost a woman's morale. "A girl came in to tidy up," he adds, stretching out to his full length. "I told her not to bother. She left one of those red foil chocolates, though . . ."

"Oh, where is it?"

"I ate it. Bloody delicious they are." He smiles lazily. "Come here, darling, give me a cuddle . . ." He tries to gather me up in his arms, but I edge away.

"Not now, Stevie." I reach for my phone.

"What're you doing?"

"Just texting Morgan . . ."

"You're always prodding at your phone. Always something else on your mind, darling. First your custard, now your son . . ." Choosing to ignore this, I tap out my message: *Everything ok?*

Yeah, comes the illuminating reply. Well, at least he's replied. I don't expect an extensive account of everything he's been up to during my absence. Stevie tuts. "C'mon, Aud, put your phone away and give me a shoulder rub. I'm all knotted and stiff from the

200

drive . . ." He whips off his T-shirt and positions himself face down, ready for servicing.

I cast a cursory glance over his back. A very attractive back, granted, lightly tanned and just muscly enough, but not one I wish to start working on now. "I'm not really in the mood."

"Aw, babe. Not still annoyed about that *thing*, are you?"

"It's not that," I mutter, sitting up and drawing up my knees to my chin.

He props himself up on an elbow and frowns. "So what's wrong?"

"Oh, it's just . . ." I sigh loudly. "The brûlée. It was supposed to be cooked on a gentle heat, and I *thought* it was, but it still curdled, looked like bloody rice pudding by the time I'd finished . . ."

Stevie blinks slowly at me. "You're kidding me, Aud."

I turn to face him. "No, that's what happens. If you heat it too quickly you're basically scrambling the eggs."

He shrinks back slightly. "D'you realise what you're doing here? I've driven all this way to be with you—"

"You said you were in the area!"

". . . and you're *still* talking about custard."

"Well, it's important," I exclaim. "I tried to rectify it, I poured it into ramekins and blowtorched the hell out of their surfaces . . ."

"They have blowtorches here? What were you doing, stripping paint?"

"They're for caramelising . . ."

"Whoo, *caramelising*," he parrots, infuriatingly. I glare at him. "C'mon, forget the brûlée, babe. Put it out of your pretty little mind . . ."

"Could you be a little more patronising, Stevie?"

"Aw, don't be like that. Let's go downstairs and get something to eat . . ."

"We're too early for dinner. If you're hungry you can have the rest of those crisps and cookies from the minibar . . ."

He looks crestfallen. "It's a five-star hotel, Aud. We can have whatever we want, whenever we want it. That's what they're here for, to *serve* us . . ."

I sense a slight chill as I look at him. "The thing is, I can't really take you down to dinner. We all sit together, there are set menus for the students on the course . . ."

"Let's order a takeaway then, get cosy in here . . ."

I laugh involuntarily. "What were you planning, phoning for a Domino's pizza?"

"Ooh, gone all haute cuisine have you now, Aud? Isn't a pizza good enough for you?"

"Of course it is. For God's sake, Stevie. What I mean is, we're in the middle of nowhere. There aren't any takeaways around here."

He flips off the bed and grabs the leather-bound directory from the mahogany desk. "Room service, then? Is this included in the prize? I mean, can we have anything we want?"

"You can choose something if you like, it's not a problem . . ."

"Great, I'm starving. Looking forward to breakfast tomorrow. Bet there's tons to choose from . . ."

"Breakfast?" I stare at him "You mean . . . you're planning to stay the night?"

"Yeah, 'course, unless you're expecting me to camp in the grounds." He reaches for my hand but I back away. "What's wrong with you, Aud? You seem so tense."

"No, it's just . . . you're not meant to be staying here. I mean, you're not officially booked in as a guest."

He shrugs. "No one would know . . ."

"But what if everyone smuggled in their boyfriends and girlfriends?"

"Well, they haven't, have they? And who cares if they did? Anyway, we're consenting adults in the honeymoon suite. What d'you think normally goes on in here?"

"That's different, they'd be booked in as a couple . . ."

He snorts. "If it bothers you that much, I'll hide in the bathroom when the room service guy comes up . . ."

"That's not the point!"

He laughs hollowly. "I know what it is. You're embarrassed by me in front of your new posh friends. In front of *Hugo* . . ."

"Don't be ridiculous."

He studies my face, then his gaze slides a little lower. "Where's your necklace, babe? Don't say you've lost it already."

Instinctively, my hand goes to my neck. "I had to take it off. Jewellery's not allowed at cook school . . ."

"So where d'you put it?"

"It's okay," I say quickly, "I left it on my worktop. I'll pop down now and see if the stable block's still open."

"Oh, just leave it," he says tetchily.

"No, I don't want to lose it," I say, striding to the door. While it's true that I'd like to retrieve my present, I am also keen for a breather from Stevie's demands. Room service, a massage, lashing me to the bed with a rope: it's all a little too much. Having a boyfriend really is more trouble than it's worth.

My heart is thumping hard as I travel down in the lift and hurry out towards the courtyard. Stevie, showing up like this: what will the others think if he insists on coming down for breakfast and loading his plate with sausages? I can hardly stop him, if that's what he wants. I can hardly barricade him in the wardrobe. Maybe I can persuade him to stay in my room and smuggle him up a croissant? It's not that I'm ashamed to be seen with him. It's just that *he isn't supposed to be here.*

And neither am I, I figure, trying the handle of the stable block door and discovering that it's unlocked. I creep in and peer around the immaculate workstations where the assistants have put everything away. Everything, that is, apart from my necklace, which is sitting in a small glass bowl on my worktop. I fix it on and perch on a stool for a minute, relishing the sense of calm. This is what I came here for: to get away from it all, and to change my life somehow. But it hasn't turned out that way. I picture everyone gathering in the hotel bar before dinner, congratulating Tamara on her perfect brûlée. I imagine my new friends creating beautiful dishes tomorrow — our last day of cooking — while Brad makes barbed remarks about mine.

I step out of the stable block and close the door quietly behind me. By the time I return to my room, Stevie's brown leather bag — and Stevie himself — have gone.

CHAPTER
EIGHTEEN

A Dazzling Array of Canapes

The atmosphere at cook school is different today.
There's a noticeable absence of chatter as everyone
gears up for the day's tasks. Our mission is to create a
myriad of small dishes — canapés really — utilising the
skills we've picked up during the course: pastry making,
sautéing, creating the perfect *redukssion*. I study my
laminated recipes:

> *Tapenade and Aubergine Caviar with tiny toasts*
> *Salmon mousse choux pastries*
> *Scallops with parsley butter*
> *Gruyere tartlets*
> *Tuna rillettes*
> *Baked Camembert with caramelised onions*
> *Cherry clafoutis*

Blimey. Just as well I'm hangover-free — having
skipped the bar last night — and raring to go. *I'll show
him*, I decide. Brad can hover over me, gusting nose-
breath on the back of my neck, and I will not mess up.

I am also fuelled by simmering anger at Stevie for
upping and leaving last night. How dare he, just

because sex wasn't on the cards? I might have been persuaded, if he hadn't been quite so demanding. And he had the nerve to call *me* desperate! I haven't phoned him for an explanation, and nor has he been in touch to apologise; I sense a no-calling stand-off happening. Well, *fine*.

"All ready?" Brad booms out. There's a collective murmur of readiness. "Remember," he goes on, "today's challenge is to work through the recipes in a methodical way. You'll be working on several dishes at once, switching from one to another and juggling *many* tasks, so it's vital to keep a clear head and focus fully . . ."

Lottie throws me an alarmed look.

"Don't panic," Brad goes on. "Panic is the enemy of, er . . . well, everything really. So keep your nerve, and when you're all done we'll enjoy a buffet lunch so you can all try each other's dishes. You'll have the afternoon free, and we'll gather together at seven for this evening's farewell drinks before dinner . . ." He has an air of relief about him, as if he'll be glad to see the back of us.

I start by making my pastry for my gruyere tartlets. While they're baking blind in their fluted tins, I knock together the savoury filling and make yet more pastry, this time choux. Pastry overload, as far as I'm concerned — but this time, everything seems to be going right. I blend tuna, mayonnaise, lemon juice and dill for my tuna rillettes which, I discover, are just little pancakes, or blinis, or whatever you want to call them. These, too, must be made from scratch.

The tapenade and aubergine caviar are easy — dips, basically, although Brad would probably shudder at the term — and, by some miracle, when I check my tartlets in the oven they have just reached peak goldenness. "Ooh, they look great," Tamara enthuses.

"Thanks," I say quickly, turning my attention to caramelising my onions — slowly, to coax out their sweetness — and popping my camembert in the oven, then whipping up my salmon mousse to wrap up in choux. In fact, preparing so many dishes at once is somehow less stressful than focusing on just one thing. With so much going on, I've clicked into sight-reading mode: allowing distractions to fade away as the various components come together like notes on a stave. I whip together the batter for my cherry clafoutis, which I remember Hugo reminiscing about from his idyllic French lunches, and discover it's basically a fat pancake filled with fruit.

"Those scallops are almost done," Brad remarks, casting a quick glance as I shuffle them around in the pan.

"Oh yes, I think so too." I smile sweetly and add a generous dollop of butter and a scattering of chopped parsley.

"I'm way behind," laments Lottie from the workstation opposite. "Look at you, Audrey. Your tarts are finished already!"

"How did you manage that?" Hugo remarks, sounding impressed.

"I'm just taking it step by step," I say, looking around at everyone beavering away and realising, finally, that I *do* belong here. Stevie has gone, nothing terrible appears to have happened at home (Morgan is still living and breathing at least) and — if I say so myself — my clafoutis looks pretty damn perfect.

"Excellent effort," Hugo declares as I transport my finished dishes to the huge oval table.

"Think so?" I say.

He grins. "Oh, yes. Maybe you *are* a dessert person after all."

"She's more than that," remarks Dylan. "Blimey, Audrey, you've done yourself proud today . . ."

"And don't you dare say it's beginner's luck," Hugo laughs, startling me with an unexpected hug.

"Wow. Thank you." Blushing, I pull away and stand back as Lottie brings her finished dishes to the table, followed by Tamara. The room is filled with a palpable air of relief as we all congratulate each other.

The ding of a spoon on a glass causes the hubbub to die down. "Everyone!" calls out Chloe, who greeted us all on our first day. "Welcome to our final buffet, a little early in the day to call it a last supper but . . ." She chuckles. "I think — and I know Brad agrees — that you've all done fantastically this week. And I know you're all dying to try these wonderful dishes . . ."

"I certainly am," says Brad, not entirely sincerely.

"So thank you, everyone," Chloe adds, "for being such great sports and making the most of the opportunity to learn from our brilliant chef . . ." Hugo catches my eye and smirks. "I hope you've all enjoyed . . ." She breaks off as Jasper, the male model porter strides in and murmurs something to her.

"Audrey?" She turns to me. "Jasper says there's been a call for you at reception."

"Oh." I frown. "Who was it?"

He hands me a small piece of paper torn off a notepad with a single word — Marvin — written on it. "Marvin?" I say, frowning. "I don't know any Marvins. Are you sure it was for me?"

"He definitely asked for you," the young man says. "I'm sorry, Genevieve on reception said he wasn't speaking very clearly. She asked him to repeat it but he rang off without leaving a number. She said he sounded a bit, uh, *agitated* . . ."

Something tightens in my chest. "Could it have been Morgan?"

He shrugs. "No idea. Sorry I can't be more helpful . . ." My blood seems to turn cold. "If there's anything I can do to help," he adds, scuttling along beside me as I rush out to the courtyard and fish out my phone from my pocket. *Six* missed calls, all from Morgan. I've been so engrossed in all that fiddly cooking, I haven't even thought to check.

"My God," I mutter, trying his number. Jasper hovers uncertainly. "I'm fine, thank you," I say, grateful when he heads back to the hotel.

Morgan's phone is off. Where's the logic in making a panicky call, and then being unavailable? I try our landline as I march in through the main doors to reception. No answer. I picture him burned in some terrible microwave catastrophe and feel sick. "Excuse me," I say, causing the receptionist to look up from her

210

screen. "Er, I'm Audrey Pepper, someone called for me?"

"Oh, yes. Marvin, I think it was . . ."

"Morgan actually, but never mind. Did he say anything else? Did he say why he needed me?"

She purses her lips and frowns. "Um, no, I don't think so . . ."

"It's just, I think it must've been pretty urgent."

"He just said, um . . . could you call him please as something's happened . . ."

I stare at her. "*What's* happened?"

She widens her hazel eyes and smiles apologetically at an elderly man who is clearly waiting to check in. "Sorry," she says, signalling that our exchange is over, "he didn't say."

I step back outside and pace the grounds, trying his number over and over whilst leaving increasingly agitated texts for him to ring me back. *JUST SAY YOU'RE OK*, I type frantically. *JUST ONE WORD WILL DO. OK!* The capable teenage gardener is out here, hoeing a flowerbed ablaze with blush-pink geraniums. Seeing me, he raises a hand in greeting. I nod distractedly back.

It'll be nothing serious, I try to reassure myself. *He'll have hand-washed his boxers using my coconut bubble bath and is now upset because they whiff of Bounty bar. Christ, there are far worse things pants can smell of . . .* But no, in my heart of hearts I know it's not that. Calling the hotel means he'd have had to remember its name — or find it out somehow — and Google it for the phone number, which would have amounted to a colossal amount of effort and ingenuity on his part . . .

I turn and virtually run back to the hotel where, instead of wasting precious time waiting for the lift, I charge upstairs two at a time and fumble in my pocket for my key. The maid has been in, neatening and straightening, making everything smooth and orderly. I perch on the edge of the bed and try Morgan's mobile again. Still turned off. I try Jenna's — she doesn't answer either — and of course I don't have her mum's mobile, or their landline. I have never had any reason to call her.

I swallow hard, my mouth bone dry, and try to think of other options. "Kim?" I bark into the phone.

"Hey you, how's it going?"

"It's been, it's been . . . fine but look, Morgan called the hotel in some kind of panic—"

"He's probably run out of milk," she says, chuckling.

"No, it wasn't that. I'm sure it wasn't. I mean, he tried my mobile six times and when he couldn't get through he managed to find the hotel number . . ."

"It can't have been hard, Aud."

"No, don't you see? He wouldn't have bothered unless it was urgent . . ."

"Oh, love," she cuts in. "Please don't panic . . ."

"I'm not," I fib, "but if you're around my way today could you just pop by?"

"I would but I'm on my way to Manchester, I'm nearly there now . . ."

"Ah, okay, don't worry. I'll come home."

"Home?" she exclaims. "But I thought you weren't due back till tomorrow."

"Yes, that was the plan but it doesn't matter . . ."

"It *does* matter," she barks. "Christ, Aud, it's your last night! What on earth could have happened? He's a perfectly capable young man. Why are you doing this?"

"Because he *needs* me," I say, rather hotly, as we finish the call.

I fetch my case from the wardrobe and set it on the bed. I'll never sleep in a bed like this again, I muse, snatching clothes from drawers and hangers. Well, that doesn't matter. I don't need four-posters — no one's going to be tying me up anytime soon — or a mattress the size of a car park. I just need to know that Morgan's okay.

I throw my clothes into my case on top of the mound of minibar snacks. It's a squash to jam everything in: I've been packing away all the edibles to take home, apart from the ones Stevie scoffed. With a knot of panic in my stomach I grab my bits and pieces — including the book I brought to read in the evenings in case there was no one to hang out with — plus the posh toiletries and the scented candle from the bathroom. The whole operation has taken less than five minutes. I zip up my case and wipe a slick of sweat from my brow.

Picking up my key, I take a last glance through the enormous window onto the sweeping grounds, the vegetable garden and lake, the elegant summerhouses and swathes of yellow blooms. Then I dash out of my room, nearly barging into a chambermaid wheeling a trolley of toiletries along the corridor and take the lift to the ground floor.

Focusing determinedly ahead, to minimise the chance of making eye contact with anyone and having to explain, I drop my brass key on the currently unmanned front desk and stride out to my car. The gravy smell seems more pungent than ever, probably due to the fact that I've spent the past five days in a heavenly place where there are no horrible smells at all — just *aromas*.

I make another attempt to contact Morgan: phone still off. I consider calling Vince, but he's a three-hour drive away and would think I'm panicking over nothing. One thing about being a mother is that it always comes down to *you*; you're the one who mops up the mess when things go wrong. It's all very well Vince declaring that Morgan should be standing on his own two feet by now, but look what happens when I leave him.

I dump my case on the back seat and climb into my car, picturing Brad assessing our dainty dishes and perhaps — I allow myself this small, pleasing thought — conceding that my clafoutis is beautifully textured. I didn't even get to taste today's efforts, not that that matters now. I mean, I've survived perfectly well to the ripe old age of 44 without ever trying a bloody clafoutis. I do not need a cake in my life that I can't even pronounce. Nor do I care that everyone will be gathering together tonight in the cosy bar, laughing and gossiping and cementing the friendships we've built up over the week. Well, I decide, swiping away a bitter tear from my cheek, I don't mind *much*. Morgan needs me, and that's that.

Wiping my face on my sleeve, I pull out onto the drive. I switch on the radio, and try to conjure up sweet vanillaish scents in order to blot out the lingering whiff of gravy in my car. But I can't.

CHAPTER
NINETEEN

Minibar Snacks

Our car can't be that crappy as it somehow manages to propel me northwards without me having very much to do with it. I am on autopilot, notching up miles as the sky fades from Wilton Grange blue to a watery grey.

As fine rain spits at my windscreen, I try to banish a terrible image of Morgan, screaming in pain from an ironing injury. No, that definitely hasn't happened. He's never ironed anything in his life.

I drive on, deciding now that something was bound to happen, and that perhaps I'm just not cut out for a luxurious life. It didn't feel right, having someone place a proper cloth napkin on my lap when I sat down to dinner, and calling me madam as if it were 1875. No, actually, I'm lying. I loved having my drink brought over on a tray with a little doily! I loved the chocolates on my pillow, and the fact that I only had to take a few sips from my wine glass for a charming waiter to scurry over and top it up. I'll admit it: I loved the whole damn thing. Not even Brad's slobbery kiss — or being lashed to the bed with a curtain rope — spoiled it, because nothing could. Nothing except this . . .

216

I drive for over two hours before light-headedness sets in. Better eat something, I decide, turning off at a service station. More importantly, I need to try and call Morgan again.

It's now raining heavily, and my flat shoes slap against the puddled tarmac as I race for the building. Shivering now, I hover by the pinball game as I try Morgan's mobile, followed by our landline which rings and rings, like some relic from a bygone era.

What the hell has happened to him?

I buy an Americano and a clammy chicken sandwich which embeds itself in my molars. I manage about a quarter of it, and check my phone for missed calls, even though it's been wedged in my hand the whole time. There must be someone else I can call. I run through terrifying scenarios of Morgan being knocked down in the road, or in a fight — he's not a fighter, but has someone attacked him? And now I can't shift the image of terrible injuries from my mind. Yes, he was still capable of finding the hotel number and making a call — but all that tells me is that he could operate his laptop and speak on the phone, in a not entirely intelligible manner . . .

A wave of dread washes over me as I try to figure out which hospital he'd most likely be in. If there's been an accident at home — and I'm now assuming there has, as he rarely strays from his natural habitat of sofa/bed — he'd be at Park Vale, which doesn't have a proper A&E department but then, Morgan wouldn't know that. And surely, if he managed to propel himself there, they'd at least make some attempt to treat him? I

Google the number and call. "Hello," I start, "I wondered if a Morgan Pepper's been admitted today?"

"Morgan *Pepper?*"

"Yes, that's right. He's eighteen, he's my son, I think he might have had an accident . . ."

"Oh, we don't have A&E here, love. You need Watley General . . ."

"Right, of course. I just thought . . ." I bat away a tear from my cheek. "Thank you." I try Watley General where the receptionist puts me through to A&E, and where the line remains unanswered as, clearly, everyone is too busy patching up my darling son to answer it.

Finally someone picks up. "A&E?"

I rattle off my concerns.

"Hang on a minute, please." As the minute stretches on and on — more like twenty, it feels like — I become aware of a smart-looking woman at the next table glancing at me with a mixture of sympathy and disdain. Few sights can be more pitiful than a middle-aged woman mopping up her snot in public with a paper napkin.

"No one of that name, I'm afraid," a bored-sounding woman says finally.

Okay, so he's not at hospital. This fails to reassure me. I fire off a text: *Morgan phone me NOW!!*, then wait some more, wondering if time has distorted because my coffee, which was lip-burningly hot a few moments ago, is now tepid.

And then my phone rings. "Morgan," I bark, "are you okay?"

"Yeah," he mumbles, "s'pose so."

"You suppose so? What happened? Did you call the hotel?"

He coughs awkwardly. "Er, yeah, sorry 'bout that. Just wanted to, y'know . . . talk to someone."

"What about? I've been worried sick, darling. What's going on?"

"Aww . . . it's been pretty bad, Mum . . ."

"Are you hurt or what?"

"Yeah, I was pretty hurt, still am, it's just . . ." His voice wobbles, and the words dissolve. My heart seems to break. I can't remember the last time he cried.

"Please, darling, just tell me what happened . . ."

He sniffs loudly. "It's nothing, Mum. Is *nothing*, all right? It's just, Jenna's dumped me."

I shouldn't mind, I tell myself as I drive through torrential rain towards home, that it's only his heart that's broken. I mean, there's no *only* about it, not at eighteen years old — not at any age in fact. For months it felt as if my own heart was shredded, *desiccated*, after Vince and I broke up, and I'd been the one to leave. Anyway, all I've missed are the goodbye drinks and dinner and a final night in the most enveloping bed I've ever had the pleasure to sleep in. I mean, it's only *that*, plus the exchanging of contact details which would have been nice — but would we really have kept in touch once we'd all scattered back to our everyday lives?

I left in a panic because Jenna finished with him, is the single thought that loops through my brain as I drive north. *And by the time I arrive home they'll probably be back together again.*

It's still raining when I pull up and let myself into our rather stale-smelling house. "Morgan?" I call out from the hall. "Morgan, I'm home, are you in?" Silence. I dump my suitcase in the hall and dart into the living room. The pants are still there, in precisely the same positions as I left them, as carefully marked by their chalked outlines. Never mind that. In fact, I'm a little embarrassed about that now. In the light of Morgan's heartbreak, it seems like a terribly petty gesture.

On the coffee table lies a note from my son: *Hi Mum gone for a walk.* A walk? I don't like the sound of that. He must be in a pretty poor emotional state to be propelling himself forward, under his own steam, for no particular reason at all.

I investigate the kitchen. There's a lingering greasy whiff, with a top note of angst, bringing to mind a burger being fried by a crying boy. Well, at least he's been eating. The sink piled high with dirty plates and glasses offers further evidence that he's been nourishing himself. Not on my butterfly cakes, though. They are still sitting there, now hard as grenades, apart from one which appears to have been ground into crumbs and liberally sprinkled across the worktop. Investigation of the freezer reveals that he hasn't consumed any of my home-cooked offerings either. I peer into the bin where numerous oily Chinese takeaway cartons are jammed on top of the offensive checked shirt. So, he made use of the guilt money I left him, at least.

220

Up in Morgan's bedroom the curtains are drawn, and the bed is a tumble of crumpled duvet and sheets. His rather grubby, fat pillows — he insists on six, like a sultan — are lying all over the floor as if flung about in despair. In the bathroom his trainers are lying by the unflushed, pee-splattered loo. They are bright white and vast, like motor yachts moored on our sparkly blue lino. Jenna's lemon thong is still scrunched up in the corner, near the bottles of Domestos and Cif. At least nothing appears to be broken. Maybe he managed to fix, or replace, whatever it was.

My mobile trills weakly from inside my bag, and I race downstairs to the hall to answer it. "Hello, may I speak to Audrey Pepper please?" It's a polished female voice.

"Yes, speaking?"

"Ah, great, it's Genevieve from Wilton Grange here. I think you left without checking out?"

"Yes, sorry. There was, er, something urgent I had to attend to at home."

"That's fine," she says, adopting a brisker tone. "So if we could just settle your extras . . ."

"Extras? What d'you mean?"

She coughs politely. "Your minibar bill, madam."

"Oh! Yes, of course, I forgot about that." Damn, I assumed that stuff was free. Still, it was only a few packets of crisps and biscuits . . .

"No problem. We have your debit card details so we can just charge it to that, if that's okay . . ."

"Yes, fine," I mutter.

"Okay, so that comes to, ah . . . £462.37."

"What?"

"£462.37," she repeats primly.

I lower myself shakily onto the bottom stair. "It can't be that much. Are you sure you don't have someone else's room?"

"No, it's definitely the honeymoon suite . . ."

"But . . ." I glare at my suitcase. Sure, it's jammed with minibar presents, and I realise pecans aren't cheap, and that each individual piece of that truffle popcorn was probably rutted out by a snuffling pig. But still . . .

"I can run through it for you," she chirps, a trace of impatience creeping into her voice.

"Er, if you wouldn't mind . . ."

"Right. So we have four boxes of stem ginger cookies, four packets of truffle popcorn, twelve packets of crisps . . ." I tune out while she rattles away, realising that the last time I was presented with a list I didn't want — jelly beans, unicycle tyre — I stomped off and booked the damn course instead of opting for the cash prize. Morgan was right. *You chose a baking course over five thousand quid? What use is that gonna be?*

"Four jars of pecans," Genevieve goes on, "two Cokes, three sparkling waters, one bottle of champagne . . ."

"Could you stop there please? I didn't drink any champagne."

"I'm sorry, it's definitely on your bill . . ." *Christ, she's right. I didn't drink it, it was sloshed into my belly button. What a criminal waste of good booze . . .* "One gin, one tonic," she continues, "one scented candle . . ."

"I thought it was okay to take the candle?"

"Yes, of course, guests are welcome to purchase them, they're £45 . . ." Holy Christ, for a candle that burns away! "Four boxes of Kirsch Kisses . . ."

"Thank you, that's *fine*," I cut in, imagining a newly arrived guest — a dapper elderly man with a clipped silvery moustache — smirking to his wife whilst waiting to be attended to. *Gosh, Daphne, what an absolute glutton! Probably never had access to a minibar before. Some people just don't know when to stop . . .*

". . . You didn't have any newspapers," she adds helpfully.

Small mercies and all that. "No, I didn't."

"Great," she says brightly. "I'll just pop the transaction through now . . ." My mind whirrs as I try to figure out how the bill could possibly amount to that much. But without knowing how much everything was — there was probably a price list in that leather-bound directory, I never bothered to check — it's impossible.

"I'm sorry," Genevieve says, "there seems to be a slight problem." Ah, so it *is* someone else's bill! Or the "extras", as she calls them, were in fact included in my dinner lady prize and I'm being let off and she's going to apologise. *Terribly sorry to have bothered you, madam . . .*

"I'm afraid your card's been declined, Miss Pepper."

"Oh. Um . . ."

"Do you have another I could try?"

I picture her, frowning, with more guests arriving, all waiting to be checked in. "I'm afraid I don't," I murmur.

"Not a credit card?"

"No." Hell, I must have reached my paltry overdraft limit. "Could I send a cheque?" I ask feebly.

"A cheque?" she repeats as if I'd suggested paying with plastic beads. "Um . . . yes, I *suppose* so."

"I'll put it in the post tomorrow," I say, figuring that my pay from Mrs B should be in my account by the time she receives it, if I send it second class.

"Great," she concludes. "I'll pop a copy of the bill in the post to you."

"Thank you very much," I say tersely.

That'll look fantastic framed on the bathroom wall, I decide. But what does a stupid bill matter when my son's out there, crying, roaming the streets? I wheel my case to the kitchen and pace around, wondering whether to go out and look for him or whether he just wants to be left alone for a while. Yes, that's probably the purpose of this "walk" thing. Instead, I unzip my case and dump my clothes on the table, discovering that the loose Kirsch Kisses have oozed out of their red foil wrappers onto my orange print dress.

I unpack the ruinous snacks, set them out on the table and glare at them, as if they snuck out of the minibar and stowed away in my suitcase without me having anything to do with it. And I don't even like soily popcorn! That imaginary man with the silvery moustache was right: I'm a foolish glutton who, even in rarefied surroundings like Wilton Grange, cannot manage to conduct herself in a proper manner. Those children politely selecting their yoghurt and pear at breakfast showed more restraint than I'll ever have.

224

I make myself a coffee and, just to taunt myself further, fetch my laptop and Google Wilton Grange, just to gawp at the unadulterated luxury I've left behind. A lump catches in my throat as I survey the spa, the gardens, the sumptuous rooms. I slam my laptop shut and embark on a frantic tidying up session. How stupid, I decide, stomping through to the living room, to refuse to pick up pants. I mean, what's the point of going on strike when no one notices or cares? All it results in is a faintly depressing home. So I gather them up and study the chalked shapes left behind: like the outlines of bodies left at a crime scene. I fetch a damp cloth and rub my frankly unhinged markings off the sofa, the carpet and rug, then throw the offending underwear into our hideously complicated washing machine with its baffling two knobs.

As it whirrs into action, I realise how seamlessly I've switched back from being Audrey lounging in her four-poster bed to ordinary, everyday me. My heart feels heavy as I realise that all I have to show for my Wilton Grange stay is a pile of minibar snacks I no longer want, and a colossal bill.

Still, things could be worse. At least they didn't charge me for those lemon slices.

CHAPTER
TWENTY

Lacklustre Mousse

Morgan has returned to the nest with a bottle of Coke and a saveloy sausage from the chip shop. "Sorry, Mum," he mutters as I attempt to hug him.

"It's all right, darling. I was just so worried when you called."

Despite his cry for help just a few hours ago, he now shrugs me off as if I am an irritating aunt. "You needn't have been."

"Of course I was worried! I had six missed calls and you didn't leave any messages—"

"You know I hate leaving messages. I never know what to say. What would I have told you? 'My girlfriend's finished with me?'"

"Well, that might've been a good starting point, seeing as that's what had happened . . ." He fixes me with a steady gaze. His hair, which is usually washed daily with the Toni & Guy shampoo he insists on — no pound shop products for *his* lustrous tresses — flops greasily around his hollow cheeks. Dark shadows lurk beneath his eyes, and there's a tiny cold sore on his bottom lip, like a fragment of crisp. "Look, I'm really sorry, darling. I know how much you love her. But you phoned the actual hotel, you went to the trouble of finding the number. I thought you'd been in an accident or beaten up or—"

He shrugs. "It wasn't that hard, Mum. I just did a search, y'know: hotel, French cookery course, Buckinghamshire . . ."

"Really? I'm amazed you remembered."

"I do have a brain, Mum," he snaps.

I meet his hostile gaze, deciding that now isn't the time to inform him that I'm missing tonight's farewell drinks on his account, and that I'm not happy about him chomping at his sausage from its polystyrene carton whilst sprawled on the sofa either.

I perch beside him. "Look, hon, maybe it's just a blip. Relationships go through all kinds of ups and downs." He darts me a look which suggests that, at my stage of decrepitude, I can't possibly know the first thing about love. "I'm just saying," I add, "maybe she just needs a bit of space, and the two of you can work things out . . ." He shuts the carton abruptly, sausage only a third eaten, his eyes wet with tears. "Oh, darling . . ." I go to throw my arms around him but he lurches away.

"I'm okay, Mum!"

"Honey, you're *not* . . ."

Tears are falling now: big, splashy boy tears that I haven't witnessed since he fell over a hurdle at school and I was summonsed to collect him, sobbing with a profusely bleeding knee, from the sick room. My own vision blurs, and my heart actually hurts, as if it's me who's been dumped, and driven to roaming around town with a carton of fried food. "Come through to the kitchen with me," I murmur, briefly squeezing his hand. "I'll make you a hot chocolate."

"All right," he croaks, gathering himself up and following me like a dog. While I heat the milk, he prowls around the table, as if unsure where to put himself. In the hope of perking him up, I throw open the cupboard.

"Look at all these snacks I brought back, darling. You can have anything you want."

He narrows his eyes. "Crisps and biscuits."

"Yes, but not any old crisps and biscuits," I say, considering whether to tell him about the stratospheric extras bill, thinking it might amuse him. No, better not: he's depressed enough without learning that several unicycle tyres could have been bought for the price of a load of fancy popcorn that no one's going to eat.

Instead, I hand him his hot chocolate in his favourite mug and open the posh cookies, placing a few on a plate — they *deserve* a plate.

"No thanks, Mum."

"Come on, hon, they're stem ginger . . ." He shrinks away as if they might have been spat on.

As we sit across the table from each other, I try to figure out how I can help him. It's so much easier when they're seven and fall off the swing and you cuddle them and dust them down and everything's okay. "So," I start gently, "you and Jenna . . . d'you want to tell me what happened?"

He sips his hot chocolate. "It's just kinda . . . *happened*."

228

"Really? You had no idea she wanted to break up?"

Shake of the head. I reach across the table and place my hand over his, wanting to say, *You're only eighteen, you're handsome and smart and a lovely person, you'll meet someone soon* . . . He places his mug on the table and gets up from his chair. "I'm going out," he announces.

"What, for another walk?"

"Nah, I'm going over to Dan's . . ."

"Are you sure?" I ask.

"Yeah. Haven't seen him for ages. Might get a few beers in, crash out there for the night . . ."

"Oh," I say, a little put out seeing as I've just made a 200-mile mercy dash to be with him. But he's off — the front door slams — and of course it's natural to want to spend time with a friend, whom he's neglected, frankly, since he got together with Jenna, and who won't patronise him with biscuits.

My phone trills. "Hi, Stevie," I say flatly.

"Babe, hope I'm not interrupting your posh dinner . . ."

"No, I'm home actually. I, er . . . decided to come back early."

"Really? Well, guess they weren't really your type . . ." What the heck does that mean? "Listen, Aud," he goes on, "sorry for leaving like that. I was just a bit hurt, y'know . . ."

"And I was a bit mortified," I cut in.

"Huh?"

"You know: bedroom, curtain rope, that kind of thing . . ."

He clears his throat. "Oh yeah. Well, I was phoning to apologise but it sounds like you're still in a mood . . ."

"I'm not in a mood," I say tersely. "I've just had a long drive, that's all."

"Aw, honey, you feeling blue? Get that son of yours to cook you a nice meal . . ."

"He's just gone out actually."

A small pause. "You're home alone? Can I come over?"

I consider this. I could spend the evening alone, perhaps scouring our unsavoury toilet whilst thinking of Hugo and Lottie and Tamara all chatting and laughing in the hotel bar, or I could have some company. Twenty minutes later, Stevie appears, all beaming smiles on my doorstep, planting a passionate kiss on my lips.

"We've got the place to ourselves, babe!" he exclaims, tossing his jacket onto an armchair and gathering me for another kiss.

I pull back and study his handsome face: the glinting greeny-blue eyes and the mischievous mouth that somehow always looks so suggestive. "You are allowed to come over when Morgan's here," I remark.

"Yeah, I know, but it's not the same . . ." It irks me, this unwillingness to at least engage with my son, and try to get to know him a little; plus the implication that, as enthusiastic sex is out of the question when Morgan's at home, Stevie would rather not bother coming over. "Fancy going up to bed?" he breathes into my ear.

230

"Not right now, Stevie."

He frowns. "Why not?"

"Because . . ." I pause. *Because I'd like to do other things. You know, coupley things, like . . .* Christ, I actually don't know. Have a conversation, maybe? "It's, like, only ten past eight," I mutter.

He laughs. "It's, like, only ten past eight? Why're you talking like a teenager, Aud?"

"I'm not. It's just . . . you know what? I'd actually like us to go out."

"Out?" He looks startled by the concept. "Out where?"

I shrug. "I don't know, just a pub or something. I'm pretty hungry actually . . ." *Do something normal*, is what I mean. *To make up for you being such a petulant twerp and buggering off without saying goodbye . . .*

"Not keen on the pubs around here," he says sulkily.

"Well, how about we drive somewhere, to that old watermill place maybe, the one that's just been done up? It looks lovely . . ."

He pulls a comic frown. "Yeah, if you really want to."

"Well, if you're not in the mood . . ."

"Aw, c'mon," he says, grabbing my hand, "don't be like that. Sure, we can go out. I just want to spend some time with you."

He doesn't mean it, though, I can tell.

His jaw remains firmly set as he drives. He fails to show any interest in my success with clafoutis, or the fact that I'm considering expanding my culinary repertoire beyond my usual vats of mince-based meals. He doesn't even seem impressed that I know what to do with a gnarly old vanilla pod. "I might take Morgan on one of those French camping holidays," I muse. "Take his mind off Jenna. Maybe his mate Dan would like to come too. I'd give them plenty of space to do whatever they wanted — I mean, I wouldn't tag along, forcing them to go to museums or making them come swimming with me. God, seeing a 44-year-old woman in a swimsuit, in a swimsuit with a *slenderising* panel, that could cause a teenage boy serious psychological damage . . ." I glance sideways at Stevie. "They've split up," I add.

"Hmm?"

"Morgan and his girlfriend. She's broken up with him."

"Well, that happens, doesn't it? He's only nineteen . . ."

"Eighteen actually," I growl.

As we lapse into silence, it becomes apparent that Stevie is not really in the mood for chit-chat. Well, no wonder: we simply don't know how to talk to each other. As far as I can recall, we've only had three normal dates; all the rest have been motorway stop-overs. It's becoming apparent that we haven't the faintest idea how to enjoy the normal things proper couples do. "Are you going away this summer?" I ask, in the manner of a hairdresser making polite conversation with a client.

"Nah, don't think so, babe. Got an awful lot on."

More silence. With a start, I realise I don't know what else to say, and that I am mentally gearing myself up for our dinner. Is this right, to feel that a date must be "geared up" for? My phone pings: a text from Paul.

Hope you're enjoying your last night. Mrs B seems to be really missing you. It's not like Paul to text me. I hope it's not his gentle way of letting me know she isn't doing too well.

Came home early, I reply, *will explain when I see you, hope all ok?*

All ok, comes his brusque reply. In fact, it's Mrs B who fills my mind as Stevie and I arrive at the watermill and settle on a window-side table. Apart from an elderly couple in rain macs, the place is empty. As I gamely work my way through tepid battered cod — and peas which have the appearance of being recently liberated from a tin — I realise I'm looking forward to getting back to work and seeing Paul again. Maybe he'll have put together a veg box for me, and I can try to tempt Morgan with garlic soup?

"So, the course was fun, then?" Stevie asks, toying with a chip.

"Yes, it was, um . . . an experience."

He nods and chews and sips his Coke. Maybe that's why he's put out — because he's driving and therefore not quaffing wine — or, and this is more likely, he's been denied sex since our session at Charnock Richard. We finish our mains, and I dip my spoon into a lacklustre chocolate mousse. It's gluey, not terribly chocolatey and possibly from a packet; Angel Delight comes to mind. Brad would not be impressed.

"It wasn't really about the cooking," I explain. "It was about, well, meeting new people . . ."

Stevie smirks. "You sound like a Miss World contestant. 'I enjoy meeting new people' . . ."

For some reason, this enrages me more than it should. "I just mean it was good for me to have a break from normal life . . ." I pause to watch him shovelling in a hillock of apple crumble. ". . . and not feeling as if I'm just a mother and a dinner lady and a carer, you know . . ." His mouth makes a slapping noise as he chomps down his pud. "And I felt, you know, that I could be *anyone* there. Does that make sense? No one knew me, you see. No one had any preconceived ideas about me. Oh, sure, they were amused by the dinner lady thing. But that soon wore off, and I felt accepted, and it made me realise how small my world had become — just working and cooking and cleaning, basically — and that, maybe, I should start thinking about, I don't know, doing something *different* with my life . . ." I tail off, suspecting he's not listening. "Stevie?" I prompt him. "D'you understand what I'm saying at all?"

He looks up and wipes his mouth on a napkin. "Huh?"

Christ, who's the teenager now?

"I'm trying to explain what it was all about for me . . ."

"Oh, yeah, I get that," he says quickly, "and I'm not surprised you came back early. Sounds like they were a load of knobs."

I stare at him across the table. "Why d'you say that? That's not why I came home. I came back because of Morgan—"

"Yeah, they weren't exactly your type though, were they?"

234

"What makes you say that? They were actually really nice people. You didn't even meet them . . ."

He splutters. "Apart from that jerk who burst into your room."

"I wouldn't call that a proper meeting, and he *wasn't* a jerk. What's wrong with you tonight?"

"Nothing," he exclaims, too loudly. "We're out, aren't we? Having a nice time?"

I watch as he noisily scrapes up the last of his crumble. "*You* don't seem to be having a nice time. You're being quite prickly, to be honest."

He sighs heavily. "Aw, sorry, Aud, I'm just a bit tired tonight."

Funny, he showed no signs of fatigue when he was keen to hotfoot it to my bedroom. "Shall we just get the bill then?" I suggest.

"Yeah, my treat."

"No, no, I'll get it, I was the one who wanted to come out tonight . . ." I pull out my purse, relieved that I have enough notes stashed in there to cover it, considering that my card might well be declined.

Stevie smiles. "Thanks, that was lovely."

"It wasn't really," I say with a grimace.

"Well, *I* thought it was," he remarks as we get up to leave. "You've been spoilt, that's your problem, living it up in a five-star hotel."

It was just a joke, I tell myself as he drives us home. And he's right: my stay at Wilton Grange *has* altered the way I view things. Not that I'm going to start insisting that Morgan turns down my covers for me. It's more the way I'm viewing Stevie, and how he's written off the people I met just because they could afford to treat themselves to a swanky course. Why the hell shouldn't they? Lottie, Tamara and Hugo wanted to do something for themselves, just as I did. We're not that different after all.

"I won't stay over at yours tonight," he says, indicating to pull into a petrol station.

The cheek. As if he's invited. "That's okay," I remark.

"Early start tomorrow," he adds. "Gotta head over to Liverpool first thing . . ."

"Fine," I say flatly.

"Next time," he adds, patting my knee before climbing out of the car. While he fills up, and although I don't particularly *want* him pawing at me tonight, I mull over the fact that he's passing up the possibility of sex. It's most unusual. Perhaps he's just not keen on sleeping with me in a normal house, where we don't have to check out by eleven. Or maybe it's the lack of Cumberland sausage? He struts towards the shop and joins the small queue waiting to pay. A bald man in scruffy blue overalls seems to be having some kind of altercation with the young woman behind the counter. The queue shuffles impatiently. I glance around Stevie's car, which still smells factory-fresh, even though he's had it since I've known him.

For something to do I open the glove compartment. There's just the car manual and a slim red, faux leather-covered notebook. I glance towards the shop, where the argument is still going on; another staff member has been called over to sort things out. The queue is growing agitated and Stevie and the man in front of him are shrugging in exasperation. I flick my gaze back to the notebook. Probably something to do with work, the training "products" he implements, which baffles me slightly; the word product makes me think Marmite or Persil, something you can hold in your hand. As if dragged by a powerful magnetic force, my hand moves towards it.

I pick it up and flick through the pages. There are lines of letters and numbers in Stevie's tiny, meticulous handwriting: 27/3, J16, M6, D. 28/3, J9, A. 31/3, J18, M6, C . . . It goes on and on over page after page, and makes no sense whatsoever. Yep, it's probably a work thing. When I've tried to fathom out what "mindfulness in the workplace" — his company's slogan — actually means, Stevie has just flung mysterious terms at me: creative empathy, emotionally intelligent appraisals, and I've been none the wiser because we never had any of that at Sunshine Valley Holiday Park. "What kind of training were you doing today?" I asked him recently.

"Data assimilation," he said vaguely. That's probably what this is: data, waiting to be assimilated. But it's weird that he jots it all down in a little book. As far as I can make out, Stevie's entire life — certainly his professional life — is all contained within his top-of-the-range laptop.

He has reached the front of the queue now and, before I can even figure out why I'm doing it — in the way that I didn't exactly consider my actions before I chalked outlines around Morgan's pants — I've snatched my phone from my bag and photographed one of the completed pages.

By the time Stevie hops back into the driver's seat, my phone and the notebook are back in their rightful positions, and I manage to pull a sympathetic face as he mutters, "Bloody hell, Aud, some tosser in there was convinced the poor girl had short-changed him by 10p."

CHAPTER
TWENTY-ONE

Soothing Broth

Morgan and I spend the next morning trying not to get in each other's way. He is making it clear that he doesn't want me asking questions, or even lending a sympathetic ear. I'm starting to wonder why he called the hotel in the first place. It's as if he *thought* he needed me, like when he was little, but I only irritated him with my hugs and urge to force hot chocolate on him. He probably wished I'd bugger off back to Buckinghamshire. It occurs to me that — apart from the provision of food and cash — he no longer has any need for a mother at all.

So I am officially redundant, and not even working today as I'm supposed to be on my way home from Wilton Grange. So when Kim calls on the off chance I'm free for lunch — "Come on over, I need to hear all about it!" — I jump in my car.

Kim's apartment is in a modern development on the outskirts of York. There's a gym in the basement, and a coffee bar, but never mind that: if I lived in a flat like hers I doubt if I'd ever leave it. It's all glass frontage and white brick walls, with a dazzling tangerine sofa and jaunty stripy rugs dotted about the polished floors.

There's no clutter at all; the few decorative items have been carefully chosen and positioned, rather than merely dumped on any available space. There are no crisp packets or tuna cans strewn around — but then, she doesn't have an eighteen-year-old son.

With the radio playing quietly in the background, she throws together an impressive salade niçoise which we take out to the balcony in the glorious afternoon sun, and soon I'm telling her all about Brad swooping in for a snog, and Stevie with the curtain rope. "Aud," she declares, "you can't see that man any more. I absolutely forbid it."

I laugh loudly. "We'll see how things go. It's just a bit of fun, you know."

"That doesn't sound like fun. What a nerve. You were off doing something for yourself for the first time in God knows how long, and he thought he could just show up without warning . . ."

"He wanted to bring my birthday present," I cut in.

"Yeah, sure. And when you couldn't spare the time for a quickie he tied you to the bloody bed!"

"It wasn't quite like that . . ."

"Yes, it was. That's exactly what it was. He didn't like you being unavailable."

I nibble on a tomato. "To be fair, I've never told him I have a problem with these impromptu dates. And it *is* fun, you know. I mean, it's different for you. You have no shortage of attention . . ."

"I don't know about that," she laughs.

"Well, the Stevie thing . . ." I pause. "It makes me feel, I don't know . . . *young.*"

240

"You're only 44," she reminds me. "There are plenty of decent men out there who aren't so, I don't know . . . *weird*. Wasn't there anyone on the course?"

"I was there to cook," I remind her with a smile. "But yes, there was Hugo."

Her eyes widen. "Oh yes, you mentioned him. So go on, tell all . . ."

"He was lovely, actually." I smile. "Very sweet, kind, well-mannered . . ."

"That makes a change," she says dryly.

". . . And if I hadn't rushed away I think, I *hope*, we might have stayed in touch as friends, but . . ." I shrug. "It was probably one of those things when you're thrown together for a few days and when you meet up again it's awful and you realise you have nothing in common."

"Let's Google him," she says, and before I can stop her she's leapt up from her chair and marched into the open-plan living area where she starts tapping away at her laptop. "I'll do an image search," she murmurs, and up pops his jovial, smiling face.

"That's him!" I yelp. "That's definitely him . . ."

"Ooh, very handsome . . ." She grins at me. In fact, there are lots of pictures of Hugo. He obviously has quite an online presence. I focus on one particular image. It's definitely the Hugo I know — with his bright, wide smile and warmth shining from those soft grey eyes — but there's something odd about the picture. He is wearing a white jacket, with two rows of buttons down the front, just like Brad's.

"He's wearing chef's whites," I remark. "But he's not a chef . . ."

"What does he do?" Kim asks.

I shrug. "I'm not really sure. He said he's kind of in-between things at the moment . . ."

"Oh, one of *those*." She chuckles and rolls her eyes.

"No, I mean he's looking to set up some kind of business, waiting for the right opportunity . . ." I pause. "Maybe he's done a cookery course before . . ."

"Or could it be fancy dress?" she suggests.

"Let me see," I say, leaning over and clicking on the link. It's a local newspaper article.

The village of Hambleton Willows is delighted by the arrival of chef Hugo Fairchurch at the Cap and Feather, a much-loved pub that's been serving delicious lunches to its loyal customers for well over 75 years . . .

"He *is* a chef!" I exclaim. "Why didn't he say?"

Hugo's arrival will mark a new chapter in the Cap and Feather's history: fine bistro food with a contemporary twist. "I'm delighted to join the team here," Hugo explains, deftly filleting a sole as we chat to him in the bustling kitchen . . .

"Deftly filleting a sole?" I splutter. "Christ, Kim, he reckoned he could barely operate a whisk. He said we could sit in the dunce corner together! What the hell was he playing at?"

"God knows," she murmurs as we examine the photo forensically. I read on: "*My background has mostly been in big London restaurants, but I'm keen now to bring that experience to a small, intimate local establishment which already has a reputation for great home cooking . . .*"

"Perhaps he just wanted to be a regular student," Kim ventures, "like everyone else?"

I nod. "But there was another chef on the course. More like he thought I'd be intimidated if he admitted he could actually cook . . ."

"Maybe," she says, and a phrase pings into my mind: *phoney ineptitude*, just like Morgan's hapless attempts at housework. There are plenty of things I can't do well: delight Mrs B with my soup, or help her with crosswords, or inspire my son to get out into the world and make something of himself. I don't feel the need to *pretend* to be rubbish at anything.

"Hang on," I say, "when is this from? I mean, is it recent?"

Kim checks the date. "Yes, June . . . so are you going to contact him?"

I shake my head. "What's the point?" I shut her laptop, deciding that's the end of things there; for whatever reason, Hugo couldn't be honest with me. "I bet the others all knew and were laughing behind my back," I mutter.

"Oh, Aud, don't think the worst of everyone . . ."

"Honestly," I retort, "the way he made a big deal of praising my cooking, as if he was genuinely impressed!"

"Well, maybe he *was*."

"How could he be when he's worked in all those big London restaurants?" I sigh heavily. "What a liar. I'm glad we didn't exchange contact details. They'd have all been having a good old snigger about it after I'd left . . ."

"Stop doing this," Kim exclaims. "Stop imagining everyone's laughing at you when they're not. Why would they be? Okay, you won your prize, but that's because you're a lovely, amazing person. You work hard and the kids love you. You deserved to be on that course, just like everyone else."

I nod, taking this in, and swerve the conversation towards Kim's recent date with a builder she met at a wedding. However, Hugo's deceit is still niggling at me as I hug her goodbye and set off for home.

Morgan is still holed up in his room. I knock politely on his door and interpret his grunt as permission to go in. He is lying on his unmade bed, hair a greasy tangle, phone clutched to his chest. He blinks at me as if I am an unexpected room service person. "Are you all right, darling?"

He nods grimly.

"Heard anything from Jenna?"

"No?" he replies, as if that would be as unlikely as a call from the Pope.

"Have you eaten today?"

"Yeah."

What have you had? I want to ask, *because you're looking pale and gaunt and there's no sign of any recent food preparation having taken place in the kitchen . . .*

244

"I, er, made a sandwich," he fibs, his small, terse smile signifying that I may leave now.

"Would you like a hot chocolate?"

"No," he barks, at which I slope out of his room. At a loss how to comfort him, I try to settle on watching TV but find myself channel hopping, coming across far too many food programmes featuring celebrity chefs — is there nothing else on telly these days? — and make Morgan a bowl of chilli which he pokes at morosely. As I'm clearing up my mobile rings. "Paul?" It's unlike him to phone me.

"Er, hi," he says, sounding distracted. "Hope it's not a bad time—"

"No, of course it's not . . ."

"You said you came home early . . . no drama, I hope?"

"Just a small one at home. Well, not so small, but . . ." I tail off. "Is Mrs B okay, Paul?"

"It's . . . it's kind of hard to say. Look, I know you're probably busy this evening and you're not on the rota till Monday, but she's pretty agitated, won't settle. Julie said she hardly touched her dinner tonight . . ."

I frown. "Oh, that doesn't sound good."

"And she keeps asking — no, *demanding* — for you to come over . . ."

"Really? She asked for me specifically?"

"Well, sort of," he starts, and a child's voice pipes up: "*Daddy, get off the phone . . .*"

"Just a minute, Jasmine . . . Sorry, kids over today . . . girls, could you just pipe down for a minute? I've asked you to put your pyjamas on . . ." Their squeals fade away. "She actually said the one who gave me that

245

showy bouquet," Paul continues with a chuckle. "Julie said we shouldn't bother you, it's not fair when you're supposed to be off, but I wondered, if you wouldn't mind . . ."

"Of course I don't mind," I say. "I'll come over right now."

"Thanks, Aud. I think she'll really appreciate that."

I set off, realising why Paul's call has made my spirits rise. While my son doesn't particularly want me around, a certain 84-year-old lady does, even if she can't remember my name.

Mrs B's garden is bathed in evening sunlight. It looks as if everything has been tinged with gold. I spot Paul in the distance, and although he waves, his attention is caught up with his two little girls who are darting between bushes in their pyjamas. "I'm seeker, Daddy," declares Rose, the younger of the two. Ah, hide and seek. This is one game my own mother would occasionally be cajoled into playing with me. I'd go off and hide — squeezed into a wardrobe, or huddled behind the heavy velvet living room curtains — until it became apparent that no seeking was going on. I'd creep out, and eventually find her curled up on her bed, having a nap. I swallow hard, spotting Paul crouching behind a rhododendron with Jasmine fidgeting excitedly at his side, then make my way to the house.

"She didn't want to sit in the garden today," Julie explains as I let myself in, "and she took herself straight off to bed after dinner. I don't know what's wrong with her. Dr Carpenter's been, but he said she's not running a temperature and she kept insisting she was okay, virtually shooed him out of the house . . ."

"Don't talk about me as if I'm not here," Mrs B barks from her room.

Julie and I look at each other. "I've got a migraine coming on," she mutters.

"Why don't you head off early then? I can sit with her for a while."

"Oh, are you sure? I'd really appreciate that." She grabs her coat from the hook as I step into Mrs B's bedroom.

"Oh, it's you," she says vaguely, looking tinier than ever in the enormous bed. Her fluffy hair seems to have thinned lately, and lies in soft wisps across her scalp.

"Yes, Mrs B," I say, perching on the spindly wooden chair beside her bed. "Paul said you'd been asking for me . . . Is everything okay?"

She twists a corner of the newspaper that's lying on her lap. "I'm just very disappointed, that's all I can say."

"I'm sorry?" Although she's often cranky, the tone of her voice still takes me aback.

"You went away," she says gruffly.

I stare, amazed that she even noticed. "Yes, I was on a French cookery course . . ."

"You didn't tell me."

"Well, I didn't think . . ." *I didn't think you'd be interested*, is what I mean.

"It sort of happened very suddenly," I say.

A trace of interest flickers in her pale eyes. "So you've learnt to cook?" The words *at last* hover in the air, and I smile.

"Yes, Mrs B. I'll cook you a real French feast one day."

At that, her face seems to soften, and she lies back and closes her eyes. "That would be lovely. But now, I think I need to sleep."

Leaving her doesn't feel right, so I potter about in her living room, tidying and straightening and trying to freshen the place up by changing the water in the vase of hollyhocks which Paul must have cut for her. When I check on her just after ten, she is sound asleep. Although she never has a carer overnight, I'm still concerned about leaving her alone. So I unpack the baby listening device which her daughter Victoria bought for when she needs round-the-clock care, and plug it in in the hallway. I step quietly outside and take the other part to Paul's cottage.

"Hey, you're still here," he says with a look of surprise. "Everything okay?"

"I'm just a bit concerned about Mrs B." I hold out the baby listener. "I hope you don't mind, but I thought, just in case . . ."

"Of course, not a problem. I'll plug it in in my bedroom. Come in . . ."

"Oh, it's late, I know your girls are here . . ."

"It's fine, they're in bed. Well, they're meant to be. Took a bit of persuading tonight, all revved up after hide and seek." He grins. "Their mother'll kill me."

I smile and step into the small, cosy living room. It's far neater than I'd imagined; wrongly, I'd assumed a lone man — a gardener — would live more chaotically. Abstract landscapes in bright, splashy colours adorn the bumpy white walls, and framed photographs of Jasmine and Rose are clustered on the mantelpiece.

"Can I get you a drink?" Paul asks.

"No, I'm fine, really."

"Or some soup? It's broth actually, made from garden veg. I took some over for Mrs B's lunch and she seemed to enjoy it . . ."

"Better than mine?" I ask, grinning.

Paul laughs. "Well, let's just say it looked as if she'd finished it, but who knows? She might've poured it down the sink. So, can I get you some?"

"That would be lovely," I say, realising now how hungry I am. It's delicious, and perhaps the aromas filter through to the girls' bedroom as first Rose, then Jasmine appear shyly in crumpled PJs and snuggle close to their dad on the sofa.

"Hi," I say, hoping they're not shocked by my presence.

They watch me with dark, solemn eyes. "This is my friend Audrey," Paul explains. "Say hello, girls."

Jasmine turns and whispers into her father's ear. "Don't whisper, sweetheart," he says.

She focuses on me, her face sleepy. "You're the dinner lady," she murmurs.

I smile. "Yes, that's right, how d'you know?"

She turns to her father. "Daddy told us."

"He said you have two jobs," Rose adds, resting her head on Paul's chest. "That's a lot."

"Well, being a dinner lady doesn't take up too much time," I explain, surprised by how pleased I am that Paul has talked about me to his girls. Yet the three of them look so cosy, all huddled up together, I sense I shouldn't really be here.

"I'd better get back," I say. "Thanks for the broth, and for listening in to Mrs B . . ."

"Any time," Paul says, getting up and giving me a brief hug goodbye, which startles me. He has never seemed like the hugging kind.

"Goodnight, girls," I say, feeling curiously restored as I stride out to my car. The soothing properties of broth, perhaps. Yes, that must be it.

The effect is short-lived. Jarring music is blaring from Morgan's room, some terrible rap thing with repeated mentions of "bitch" and "ho" that I try to view with an open mind. But it baffles me, how Morgan can enjoy such violent and misogynistic tripe when his favoured activity — at least until recently — was cuddling Jenna and gently stroking her hair.

I call out hello, which he probably doesn't hear over the din, and busy myself by setting out my Wilton Grange toiletries on the bathroom shelf. In such ordinary surroundings, they don't look quite as impressive; I wonder what possessed me to get so excited over a few miniature bottles of shower gel and shampoo. I light the scented candle which I mistakenly "bought" from the hotel, in the hope that the scent of honey blossom and lime might somehow cancel out the abrasiveness of the lyrics still blasting from Morgan's room. However, all I can think is this is costing me about a quid a minute to burn, and besides, our bathroom will never share the serenity of the

250

honeymoon suite, not with Jenna's thong still scrunched up in the corner.

I start running the bath and stare at the thong. I can't just leave it here. While Morgan isn't especially observant, he's bound to spot it eventually and it'll upset him horribly: who wants to be confronted by the knickers of the girl who's broken his heart? I pick it up bare-handed, and flip up the lid of the bathroom bin. It's full to the brim of boxes and bottles, scrunched-up wads of loo roll and discarded razors — obviously Morgan didn't bother to empty it in my absence — and, although I don't mean to pry or even look, because God knows what else is lurking in its depths, I can't help seeing it sitting there: the white plastic stick, a pregnancy test, with a clearly visible thin blue line.

CHAPTER
TWENTY-TWO

A Bun in the Oven

I decide to leave it to the morning to talk to Morgan because I want to broach this carefully. I didn't fancy barging into his room and making him turn off his music; we'd get off on a very bad footing. While I'm aware that it will hardly be the easiest conversation we've had, tossing and turning all night in bed has given me time to mull over possible, less terrifying explanations than the obvious: i.e., perhaps I imagined it (even though I've been up twice in the night and re-checked the bin, before quietly lowering the lid and creeping miserably back to bed). Or — not that I'd wish to foist an unwanted pregnancy on anyone — maybe there's the *tiniest* chance that Morgan invited a horde of people over during my absence and it's one of those random teenagers who did the test. *Don't jump to conclusions*, I tell myself, staring at my bedroom ceiling as dawn begins to creep into my room. *Wait until he's up, then have a mature and reasonable discussion . . .*

At 6.47 a.m. I'm rapping on his door. "Morgan? Are you awake?"

"Uhh?"

252

"I need to talk to you," I announce, sweeping into his room.

"What are you doing?" His eyes ping open in the half-light. "It's still night!"

"No, it's not," I say briskly. "This is the time normal people get up and go to work . . ."

"Like who? Bin men?" He glowers at me. "And it's *Sunday*," he adds, as if every day in his life doesn't offer limitless potential for leisure.

"Look, Morgan . . ." I clear my throat. "I found something in the bathroom bin, and I wanted to—"

"You've been raking through the bathroom bin?" He looks aghast.

"No, not *raking*. I just happened to be dropping, er, something in, and I saw it, I couldn't help it . . ."

"What was it?"

I'm aware of my heart rattling away as I lower myself onto the edge of his bed. "A pregnancy test, love. A positive one . . ."

The defiance melts from his face. "Oh. Uh, yeah . . ."

"So . . . is there something you need to tell me?" He peers at me from his duvet nest, looking hopeless and lost. "Morgan?"

"Yeah, Mum," he mutters. "Jenna's pregnant."

I stare at him for a moment, lost for words, and reach for his rather clammy hand — amazingly, he allows me to hold it — as this information swills around us, finally settling like dust. "Oh, darling," is all I can think of to say.

"Yeah, I know, Mum." He pulls his hand away from mine and tugs the duvet up to his chin.

"Did you find out while I was away?"

He nods again. God, what was I *thinking*, curdling custard while they went through this trauma alone? "Is that why you called the hotel?" I ask gently.

"What d'you mean?"

"Well, to tell me . . ."

"No," he snaps. "No, Mum. I was just upset, y'know? She'd finished with me, I didn't really know what I was doing . . ." As if he's ashamed at having tried to reach out to his mum.

"Okay," I say quietly, glancing around his room. Sitting on the top of his wobbly white bookcase is a matted teddy, Bobby, whose original eyes I had to replace with buttons from an old jacket. Although Morgan has probably kept him in an ironic, "Look, I still have my teddy!" kind of way, I suspect he is still pretty fond of him. "So," I venture, "what's she planning to do? I mean, what d'you both want to do? Have you decided?"

"No, she just said it was my fault . . ."

"Oh, come on, it's not one person's fault. I mean, if a condom split . . ." The words shimmer awkwardly in the air. "I mean," I struggle on, "if you'd known there'd been an accident, she could have got the morning after pill . . ."

"Yeah." He flips over so I can only see the back of his head. "Too late for that now, though."

"Well, yes, obviously . . ."

"She didn't get it," he adds, "'cause the woman who's always there in the chemist — the fat one with moles and a nose ring—"

254

"She was afraid of the woman with a nose ring?"

"Yeah, well . . . not exactly. But she's a friend of her mum's."

I stare at his messy dark hair. Ridiculously, even though he is part-responsible for having conceived a child, I am overcome by an urge to brush it. "Couldn't you have gone in for her? Or gone to the doctor with her or . . ." I tail off, because he's right, it's too late for that. A beautiful girl, who weighs little more than a packet of marshmallows, is pregnant at eighteen years old. My darling son is possibly going to become a father when he sincerely believed it was okay to microwave a T-shirt. *That's* what matters, not any steps they might have taken to stop things reaching this stage.

"So," I murmur, "you have no idea what she's planning to do?"

Slowly, he turns back to face me. "No, Mum. She won't talk to me."

"Have you tried, though? She's probably just upset . . ."

"Yeah, of course she is," he exclaims. "She did the test at home, brought it round to show me. Practically shoved it in my face. I didn't even know what it was. Said I'd ruined her life, her future, we had a bit of a fight . . ."

"Not a physical fight?" I gasp.

"No, just shouting, it's when you phoned . . ." Oh, of course. And to think I'd been worried about a broken lamp or TV. ". . . I've texted and called her loads," he goes on, his dark eyes filling with tears, "but she never answers."

"What about going round to see her?" I suggest.

A look of terror flashes across his face. "I can't do that! What if her mum and dad were there?"

"But darling, you'll have to face—"

"They'll *kill* me, Mum." He starts to cry properly, his shoulders heaving with each gulp.

"Oh, darling," I murmur as he blunders out of his duvet and flings his gangly arms around me. We're hugging, our hot faces gummed together with tears. Despite the less-than-ideal circumstances, it's lovely to hold him close.

"Oh, for fuck's sake," Vince exclaims. "What a raving bloody fool."

"Well, it's happened," I say.

"Holy shit," he mutters. "And they're sure, right?"

"Well, the test was positive and they're hardly ever wrong . . ."

"So what're they planning to do?"

I sigh. "It doesn't sound like they're planning anything — at least, not together. Jenna's finished with him, won't reply to his phone calls or texts . . ."

"Jesus Christ."

"I even said he should write her a letter — you know, a proper letter, with a pen and paper. You'd have thought I'd suggested he send her a telegram."

Vince sighs. "So, how does he seem?"

"A mess, frankly. Pretends he's okay, then breaks down in tears . . ."

256

"Oh, God, I can't remember the last time I saw him cry . . . Want me to drive over?"

"No, there's no need at the moment . . . maybe you should talk to him, though?"

"Yes, of course." I call Morgan from his room. Despite it being almost lunchtime, he has yet to emerge from his lair. He slopes out in saggy pyjama bottoms, blinking as if emerging from hibernation, and snatches my mobile before disappearing back into the fuggy cave of his room. I potter about in my bedroom, aware of his muttered tones. The muted conversation lasts for over ten minutes, which must be a record, in terms of Morgan's communications with his father.

He ambles out of his room and hands the phone back to me. "How did that go?" I ask Vince as I head downstairs.

"To be honest, I have no idea."

"He's devastated," I add, "but I'm not sure if it's the pregnancy part, or the being finished with part or—"

"Look, are you sure you don't want me to come over?"

"No, really, we'll be okay," I say. "I don't want it to seem like a big drama . . ."

"It *is* though," Vince says, "as dramas go. I mean, I can't imagine many situations being much bigger than this."

"Yes, I know. I'll keep in touch, okay? And thanks, Vince."

"Uhh," he groans, "I just wish I was nearer." So do I, I decide as we finish the call, if only because sometimes, I run out of ideas of what to do.

Morgan appears, perhaps drawn from his room by hunger as he's now peering into the cupboard at the minibar snacks.

"Didn't they have any *normal* stuff at the hotel?"

"Like what?" At least he's showing an interest in food. As far as I'm aware, all he's had since I came home are roughly two inches of saveloy sausage and a meagre bowl of chilli.

"Dunno, like normal crisps?" He grabs a packet and glares at it. "Shallots," he says, grimacing. "What are they?"

"They're just like onions, love." I pause. "I'll make you a cooked breakfast," I add, "but first I'm going to have to call Natalie."

"Who?"

"Natalie, Jenna's mum."

"What?" he barks, shutting the cupboard with a bang. "But you don't even know her!"

"I've met her a few times, actually. Anyway, that doesn't matter. We need to talk . . ."

"What, like, have a *summit meeting?*" His eyes fill with horror.

"No, nothing like that. But I'm your mum, and I'm concerned, and I'm sure Natalie and, er, what's Jenna's dad called again?"

"Mark or Mike or something else beginning with M. *I* dunno. He doesn't really talk. So, you hardly know them but you're just gonna call with, like, no warning?"

I give him a level look. "I'm not sure how to warn someone I'm planning to call them, love."

"Well, you just can't phone out of the blue!"

"I'm sure she's expecting me to get in touch. I mean, I'm not just going to pretend it's not happening, am I? There needs to be some communication . . ."

"Yeah," he mumbles, "but not the kind that's like all the mums getting together . . ."

I go to touch his arm but he swerves away. "It's not *all* the mums. It's just two. So, can I have her home number please?"

"Her what?"

"Jenna's home number. Her landline, I mean."

"You want to call her house phone?"

"Yes, darling."

He opens the fridge door and shuts it again. "Don't have it."

"Come on," I say firmly, "you must." He peers at me through his fringe. "Please, Morgan, just tell me . . ."

"What're you gonna do," he says, backing away, "shine a bright light in my eyes and force it out of me like the Gestapo?"

"Morgan, don't be ridiculous. You've been seeing Jenna for over a year, you must—"

"I don't know it!" he shrieks. "I don't have it, all right?"

I stare at him and slowly step away. Something tells me that perhaps my son isn't quite ready to be a father. I try to find Natalie Barnett's number through old-fashioned directory enquiries, which seems in keeping with using the antiquated landline, but of course she's ex-directory, everyone is nowadays. So, as I head towards Mrs B's — I'm on the early shift today —

I scroll through my mobile contacts to find someone who might know someone who knows her.

I sense a stab of nostalgia at the sight of the names of the mothers of Morgan's primary school friends, friends he peeled away from once secondary school started and we parents no longer congregated at the school gates. I try Sophie Trainer, an organised sort who always seemed to know who was having work done on their house or had put out their recycling bin on the wrong day. "Audrey," she exclaims, "it's been a while!"

"Yes, well, you know how things are . . ."

"So how's Morgan doing? Where did he decide to go, in the end?"

I cannot bring myself to say: *the sofa*. "Er, he's still kind of deciding on courses."

"Ah, right. Well, er, some take a bit longer to find their way, don't they?"

"Yes," I laugh hollowly. "So, how's Freddie doing?"

"Oh, loved his first year at Durham. Works far too hard, though. Grafts all through the night. I wish he'd let his hair down and party more!"

"Yes, I know what you mean . . ."

My stomach feels leaden as we wind up the call. She didn't have Natalie Barnett's number, and it occurs to me that I *should* have it, and should have remained in regular contact with her when Jenna started staying over. First time it had happened — when it had become apparent that Jenna wasn't going home — I'd hung around, pottering about until there was no more pottering to be done. I'd offered them tea and toast; I'd even polished the lamp flex, for goodness' sake. At

1 a.m. the two of them were still clumped all over each other in the living room.

"D'you need a lift home, Jenna?" I ventured.

"No, it's fine thanks," she replied.

"Are you sure? It's awfully late . . ."

"Jen's staying over, Mum," Morgan explained.

"Really?" I blinked at them. "Are you sure, Jenna? I mean, does your mum know?"

"Yeah, of course!" she said brightly. "She's fine with it." It must be okay, I decided; they're both adults now. By their age, I had already spent a year fishing out pubey clumps from the shower drains in the Sunshine Valley chalets. A few days later, I spotted Natalie in Tesco and scampered down the poultry aisle after her. I vaguely knew her from when Morgan and Jenna were at primary school together. She was always the smartest mother at the school gates; in a crisp white shirt, black pencil skirt and a sharp pair of heels, she always looked as if she were about to swish off to some meeting. She was no different that day, and I was aware of her gaze flicking over my hastily ponytailed hair as we exchanged greetings.

"Haven't seen you for ages," I blustered.

"No, it's been a while," she remarked.

"Last time must've been when I was going around bothering everyone, trying to drum up prizes for the community centre bottle stall . . ."

Her mouth tightened. "That was a long time ago."

I sensed my heartbeat quickening. "Erm, isn't it lovely about Morgan and Jenna?"

"Yes, it's very sweet," she said, looking as if she were experiencing mild pain.

"And it's okay, um, for her to stay over at our place? I mean, you're okay with that, are you? Because if you're not—"

"She's a very sensible girl," she said, before making her excuses and striding away with her basket. I mean, what should I have done? Charged after her, and alerted her to the fact that two young people, who loved each other deeply, might just possibly be having sex? I just couldn't do it.

I've worked myself up into quite a sweat when I make the next call: Heather Watson, a jovial woman whose daughter Jessica was terribly keen on Morgan when they were about twelve years old. "How *is* lovely Morgan?" she asks warmly.

"Oh, he's fine, he's looking into, er . . ."

"Bet he's doing something terribly clever with science or maths. Oh, I remember his spy thing. Obsessed, he was. What a fantastically quirky boy . . ."

"Yes, haha, he really was . . ."

". . . Inventing all those codes," she goes on. "The coloured dots, the symbols, the time he wrote Jessica a letter in invisible ink . . . my God, she talked about nothing else for weeks!"

"Really?"

"Yes! She was besotted with him, kept the letter for years. Never told me what it said, of course. She had to heat it under the grill to read it, nearly set the kitchen on fire . . ." She chuckles. "So inventive. The brains of that boy!"

262

I laugh awkwardly. "So, erm, what's Jessica doing?"

"She's starting law in Manchester, doesn't want to be a high street solicitor, though, nothing boring like that. She's aiming for international law, human rights, that kind of thing. You know, to make a real *difference* in the world . . ."

"That's great," I manage, hoping she forgets to follow up on the science/maths line of questioning.

"So, what about Morgan?"

"Oh, he's, er, changed direction quite dramatically."

"Everyone's allowed to do that . . ."

"Yes, he's, er, into performing now."

"Performing arts? Acting?"

"Sort of, yes."

She enthuses some more, and of course we must get together over coffee and, yes, she happens to have Natalie's number. "I'll see you at Ellie's birthday lunch on Friday," she adds. "It'll be so good to catch up."

At Mrs B's gates now, I glimpse Jasmine and Rose huddled over a picnic set out in the woodland at the bottom of the garden. Paul is nearby, balanced on a small stepladder, pruning a tree. Seeing me, he raises a hand in greeting and climbs down. "Thanks for having the listener last night," I say as he strides towards me.

"No problem at all. She was quiet as a mouse and I looked in on her first thing. Everything seemed fine."

"Great." I glance over at his daughters. "Lovely day for a picnic . . ."

"Want to join them? They'd be delighted."

"Better not," I say, forcing a tense smile. "I really should see to Mrs B." He nods, and as he heads back to his stepladder I realise I can't start my shift until I've made this call. My heart is hammering as I tap out the number.

"Hello?" It's Natalie who answers.

"Er, hello, Natalie, it's Audrey here."

"Oh," she says ominously.

Small silence. "Look, I, erm . . . I've only just found out, and I thought perhaps we should get together to talk . . ."

"Yes, because you were away, weren't you?"

"Sorry?"

"You went away and left them alone for a week."

I frown, wondering what she's implying. "It was five days actually. Well, it was meant to be five but I came back early. Morgan phoned in a bit of a state, they'd broken up . . ."

"Yes and no wonder," she hisses.

"Natalie," I start, "could Morgan and I come over to talk to you? I really think we should all meet up. Would tomorrow morning be okay?"

"I suppose so," she says resignedly.

I pause, wondering how to proceed. "I can understand why you're upset. I am too, I mean, I know it's far from ideal . . ."

"Upset? Of course I am, Audrey!"

I bite my lip. "But . . . you did know that Jenna was staying over with Morgan . . ."

"Yes," she mutters, "but I thought they'd be supervised."

This knocks the wind out of me. "How on earth d'you think I'd have supervised them?"

264

"Well, I would've," she declares. "I'd have found a way. I'd have made them keep the bedroom door open or . . ."

"You're not serious," I exclaim.

"I would have done *something*." Yes, but what? Sit all night on a chair on the landing, like a watchman? But of course she's upset, she's allowed a rant and hopefully — I cling onto this thought — she'll be okay when she's had time to come to terms with it all.

"Natalie," I say, as calmly as I can manage, "I'm very upset too, but these things happen . . ." God, no, that sounds so trite, as if someone has broken a vase. "We'll see you tomorrow," I add. "I'm sure we can work everything out."

"Really?" she snaps with a mirthless laugh. "God, you must be feeling pretty optimistic because this is one hell of a mess."

CHAPTER
TWENTY-THREE

A Touch of Salt

The stale air hits me as I step into Mrs B's house. "Hello?" her reedy voice rings out from the living room.

"It's me, Audrey." I find her wide-eyed and looking a little anxious, perched on the edge of the sofa.

"You didn't knock," she remarks.

"No, I'm sorry, I didn't think . . ." I start to fold up a pile of unfinished embroidery projects on the sofa in order to make space to sit beside her.

"Why are you moving things?" she enquires.

"Just to make space to sit with you."

She turns to me and scowls. "Someone's always hiding things."

"Have you lost something? Can I help to look for it?"

"*You* wouldn't know," she says tersely, "but things are going on around here, things I don't like . . ."

I study her face, wondering whether her fears are justified, or a sign that she's becoming muddled and confused. Instead of sitting and chatting with her — she's clearly not in the mood — I gather together a scattering of craft magazines from the coffee table (which will probably be interpreted as moving/hiding things) and switch on Radio 4, her preferred station. "If you're worried about something," I add, "you can always talk to me, or one of the others . . ."

"It's nothing you can help with," she says briskly, picking up today's newspaper and emitting powerful leave-me-alone-now vibes. Considering that she'd been asking for me while I was away, my presence doesn't half seem to annoy her.

In the kitchen now, I chop carrots for disappointing soup and, while those are sautéing, I knock together the topping for an apple and berry crumble. I am beavering away, "keeping busy" as people do when they don't want to think about the thing they really should be thinking about. Spotting some ageing bananas in a wooden bowl, I dig out an old recipe book — grease-splattered, with spine peeling — and make a banana loaf. The process isn't as soothing as it should be; baking isn't the slow, sensuous experience Brad enthused about. But then, he hadn't been reeling from the shock of possibly becoming a grandparent.

Without warning, tears start to drip down my face. I don't mean to cry, but then no one thinks, "Right now, at my place of work, is an ideal moment for red, puffy eyes and a blotchy face." Natalie was right: somehow, I should have prevented this from happening. Maybe I just haven't been around enough, keeping an eye on what they were up to. I've been too wrapped up in providing, in getting things done — plus nipping off to meet my boyfriend on the motorway — to take notice of the bigger picture. And now, as tears plop into the cake mixture — I quickly beat them in — I'm wondering if my contraception talk wasn't up to the mark. Maybe I'm just not very good at conveying information. The fact that Morgan wandered off to stuff Caramel Chew Chew ice cream into his face during my washing machine tutorial would suggest that this is the case.

I pour the banana loaf batter into a tin and place it in the oven. As it bakes, I take Mrs B a slice of quiche and salad for her dinner, and wonder whether I should have at least run a compulsory refresher course. That's it: I should have forced him to watch me cramming a condom onto a courgette. Or would that have seriously messed up his mind regarding sex, and vegetables? It's difficult enough trying to persuade him to eat anything green . . . Anyway, too late now. Like harping on about the morning after pill, it's a little late in the day for sex education.

It's just not the way I'd envisaged things would turn out, I muse as I lift my loaf from the oven and turn it out onto a wire rack. My son is heading for fatherhood before his life has even properly started. Then to top it all — and right now, this disappoints me more than any Wilton Grange failure — my loaf is burnt at the ends and saggy in the middle. It appears to be over- *and* under-baked.

I help Mrs B to shower and, once she's in bed — before the bowl-spitting regime — I saw a slice off the loaf and take it through to her with a cup of tea. I stand back, awaiting her critique.

She nibbles it tentatively. "Oooh, this is good. Not too sweet. In fact it's almost . . ." She slaps her lips together. "Almost salty. What did you put in it?"

"Just the usual ingredients," I say lightly. *And a bucketload of tears.*

"See," she adds, "you could do it, if you applied yourself."

I stop and look at her. "You mean bake?"

"Well, yes," she jabs at the newspaper beside her, "*and* this."

"The crossword," I say, my heart sinking.

"Yes, you're a capable woman. You're a mother, a worker, an excellent cook . . ."

"But my soup," I remind her. "You said—"

"Oh, take no notice of me. Everything tastes bland to me these days." She grabs a gnawed pencil from her lap and pats the edge of the bed. "Now sit here with me and use your brain for once. I'll show you how it's done . . ."

My chest tightens as, obediently, because Mrs B has that way about her, I perch on the bed. She could be teasing, or perhaps it's just an offhand remark. My gaze drops to the crossword. "If you'd just focus," she goes on, "you'd do fine, but you just give up without trying. So look, here's how to break down this kind of clue . . ." She starts filling in clues, explaining how she's figured them out. But I'm not listening. In fact, I'm not here at all, in Mrs B's gloomy bedroom with its heavy maroon curtains, but back in the pine-and-Formica kitchen of my childhood home, after Mum had gone, and Dad had made it his mission to make a maths genius out of me. *It's only long division! Just concentrate. What on earth's wrong with you, Audrey?* The thump of a fist on the table, the numbers in my dog-eared jotter blurring before my eyes. *Crying isn't going to help. You need to try, don't you understand? You're going to amount to nothing with an attitude like this!*

I get up and take her crumb-strewn plate. "Audrey?" The word jolts my ears. Mrs B has never called me by name before.

"Yes, Mrs B?"

She peers at my face. "I haven't . . . upset you, have I?"

"No, no, of course not."

She frowns. "Your eyes look a bit pink."

"No, honestly," I say briskly. "There was something, uh . . . something earlier today . . ."

"What was it?"

"Trapped my fingers in the car door," I say quickly.

"Ooh. That sounds nasty."

I force a smile at this frail old lady who I'm paid to look after, and can't even bring myself to be annoyed with. "I'm fine now," I add, flitting off to fetch her toothbrush, toothpaste and the porcelain bowl. "Would you like anything else before I go?" I ask, when we've been through the spitting routine.

A thin smile spreads across her face. "No thank you, dear," she says. *Dear?* Now, there's a first.

As I'm leaving, I spot a box of vegetables placed on the step for me. It's a whopper this time, too heavy for me to carry home. So I pick it up and carry it across the garden to Paul's cottage. "Thanks for this," I say as he opens the door. "Can I take it home next time I'm here? I'll bring my car . . ."

"Oh, I'll drive you home," he says. "Jackie's just been to pick up the girls."

"Really? If you're sure it's no trouble."

"I know you like to walk to work," he says, "and of course it's no trouble. C'mon." I smile at his bluffness and hand the vegetable box to him, which he loads into the back of his truck. "So how did she seem today?" he asks as I clamber into the passenger seat.

"Kind of . . . tetchy, a little irrational . . . but then quite sweet. Called me 'dear'."

"Dear?" He grins.

"Yeah, I know. It's pretty worrying." I pause. "Actually, I'm not sure how much longer I can keep working here, Paul."

He throws me a startled look as we pull away from the cottage. "But why?"

"Oh, I know she was asking for me while I was away but . . ." I shrug. "I just seem to irritate her really."

"But you're so good with her," he insists.

I smile. "I'm glad you think so. I'm not sure Mrs B does, though. I mean, it's not as if I expect to be showered with gratitude. It's just, there's been quite a lot going on lately and I'm always on at Morgan to get out there, to make something of himself. And maybe I should do the same, you know? And find a job where I can really make a difference."

"But you do! You make a huge difference to Mrs B." He stops at red lights and glances at me.

"I just think I could set a better example to Morgan," I mutter.

We pull away from the lights and fall into silence for a moment. "Aud," Paul says hesitantly, "has something happened? I don't want to pry, but—"

I nod. "Morgan's girlfriend is pregnant."

"Oh. God . . ."

I look at him, taking in the soft brown eyes, amazed that I've told him at all. After all, not even my friends know yet. No one does, except Jenna's parents, Vince and me. I inhale deeply, deciding Paul won't judge. He won't imply that, somehow, I could have prevented it from happening.

"How old are they?" he asks gently.

"Both eighteen."

Another small silence settles around us. "Pretty young," he offers. "But not the end of the world, maybe."

"Yes, maybe not."

"I'm sorry, Aud. It's not what you'd have wanted, but don't do anything rash just because you're upset. You're good at your job. You're needed there, not that you should feel trapped, but—"

"It's not that, Paul."

"And you'd miss your vegetable boxes," he adds, smiling now. "There are globe artichokes in there."

"Oh, they're *very* on trend."

"Are they? I had no idea." He chuckles.

I smile, sensing my tension subsiding. "My road's next on the right. You can drop me at the corner if you like."

"No, let me take you to your door."

"Thanks," I say. "It's last on the left." He pulls up and insists on carrying the vegetable box into the kitchen for me. I glance around, regarding the place through his eyes, terribly conscious of the unwashed dishes dumped on the worktops. "Teenagers," I say, turning on the taps at the sink and pulling on Marigold gloves.

He sets the box on the table. "Please don't start clearing up because of me."

"Oh, it's disgusting. I'm sorry." A thumping bass starts up from Morgan's room as I wipe up a scattering of granulated sugar from the worktop. Something about bitches, hos and ass. "Christ," I say, picturing Paul's wholesome daughters enjoying their picnic.

"Aud, it's fine."

"I'm sorry, this is what boys are like. At least, *mine* is . . ."

"Hey, stop apologising . . ." My mobile starts trilling on the table: Stevie. I leave it go to voicemail, and immediately he calls again. "Excuse me a sec," I say as I answer it.

"Hey, babe," Stevie says, "you working tomorrow night?" No, *how's things?* I sense myself bristling with irritation.

"Yes, I'm on a late shift . . . why?"

"Want to ask someone to swap shifts with you?" I give Paul, who's hovering in the kitchen doorway, an apologetic glance.

"I can't, not at such short notice."

"Aw, just for one night?"

273

"I can't do it, Stevie. Julie covered the days I was down at Wilton Grange. I can't keep doing this, expecting the others to jump in and help me out . . ."

Stevie sighs. "Maybe next week, then? If I give you a bit more *notice?*" His voice is tinged with bitterness.

"Maybe," I say. "Look, I've got to go. Speak to you soon."

Paul smirks. "So how *are* things with Motorway Man?"

"Oh, you know." I shrug. "I'm not sure where we're going, really."

"Down the M6, probably," Paul chuckles.

"Yes, I know, I must be mad." I turn and open the cupboard, reeling back as a crinkly packet tumbles out. I snatch it from the floor. "Snacks from the hotel minibar," I go on, feeling faintly ridiculous as what seemed so exotic and thrilling at Wilton Grange now just look like . . . well, *crisps.* "I brought some back for you," I add as Morgan's music thumps on.

"Thanks," Paul says, looking genuinely pleased as I gather up the packets and hand them to him. "That was so thoughtful of you . . ."

"There are chocolate liqueurs for Mrs B," I add. "I must take them next time —" I stop abruptly as Morgan saunters in, stopping abruptly at the sight of the stranger. "Morgan, this is Paul," I say quickly. "He's the gardener at Mrs B's. Paul, this is Morgan, my son . . ."

"Hi, Morgan," Paul says easily. "So, what're you up to?"

"Just this and that," Morgan says with a shrug.

274

"Working at the moment?"

"Nah," Morgan says levelly. "I'm kinda looking, though." Really? That's news to me . . .

"Ever done any gardening?"

Morgan shakes his head.

"You've done a bit," I prompt him, "at Dad's . . ."

"Oh, yeah. He's got, like, a small farm with pigs and chickens and stuff. He makes me help out and he pays me a bit . . ."

"Well," Paul says, gathering up his crisps, "I might be looking to take on some extra jobs."

"On top of working at Mrs B's?" I ask.

He shrugs. "You know what it's like. There are school trips to pay for, all the stuff they need at birthdays, Christmas . . ." He gives Morgan a big, blokey smile. "Maybe I could give you a call sometime, if you're still looking for work?"

"Yeah," Morgan says airily. "I'll see what I'm up to, okay?"

"But Morgan," I retort, "you're not up to anything."

"Look," Paul cuts in, "I'll leave you to think it over, okay?"

"Yeah," Morgan grunts, throwing me a curt look.

Paul turns back to me. "Well, thanks for the crisps."

"And thanks for the lift and the veg," I add. "Um, I'll see you out, Paul." We step out into the cool evening. "I don't know why he said that," I add. "It's not as if he has a crammed schedule."

He laughs and clambers into his van. "Well, the offer's there. It's up to him if he wants to take it."

275

"Yes, I know, and I really appreciate it. Thank you." I wave him off and head back into the kitchen, where Morgan seems to have emerged from his gloom.

"God, Mum," he splutters, "what were you giving him *crisps* for?"

"As a present," I say defensively.

"Is that a thing, then? Giving people crisps?"

"No, it's not a *thing*. They were in my minibar at the hotel and I thought he'd like them." I sense my cheeks simmering.

"You're bright red, Mum. You look like your face is gonna catch fire."

"I'm just hot," I bluster, plunging my hands into the bowl of washing up and aware of him smirking behind me.

"Why's that, then?"

"Probably my hormones," I say lightly. "My oestrogen's dwindling, darling. I can feel it draining away, day by day . . ." That'll make him drop this line of questioning.

"Ugh, God." He clears his throat. "So, does this mean you've got rid of Stevie?"

I turn around to face him. "No, why d'you say that?"

"'Cause you just brought *him* round . . ."

I laugh stiffly. "I told you, love, he's the gardener where I work. And I didn't *bring him round*, he just gave me a lift with that heavy box of veg . . ."

Morgan snorts. "Is this, like, an old people's ritual then? He brings you cabbage and you give him crisps?"

"It's not cabbage, it's globe artichoke . . ."

"Whatever it is, don't expect me to eat it."

"Don't worry, I won't force it on you, darling." He pokes through the box, seemingly disappointed to discover yet more vegetables: broccoli, runner beans and carrots. "That job offer, though," I add. "I really think you should consider it."

"Mum," he snaps, "I've just got a lot on mind right now, okay? I've *said* I'll think about it . . ." He rubs at his face.

"Okay, love." I blink at him. "Look, are you okay about this thing at Jenna's tomorrow?"

He shrugs. "'Course I'm not! I don't see why we have to do it."

I start unloading the box. "It just feels important. I'd just like Jenna and her parents to know I — I mean *we* — are fully supportive, you know? I want them to know we're all together in this, as a family." He nods glumly. "Would you like Dad to be there?" I ask hesitantly.

"Er . . ." He glances at me, as if trying to gauge my reaction. "Yeah, I would actually."

"You think it'd help?"

Another nod. "Yeah. It's just, you can be a bit . . ." He gnaws at his lip. "Y'know."

A bit what? I want to ask. *Concerned, in precisely the way a mother should be?*

"You tend to blow things up," he mutters. I'm about to say, *what does that mean exactly?* But instead I text Vince, willing him to say yes.

No prob, comes the swift reply, *I'll be with you by ten*.

"Dad's coming tomorrow morning," I tell Morgan, with a sense of relief.

He nods. "Aw, okay. That's good."

I study my son, wishing he'd open up to me more, and tell me how he really feels about this baby. But clearly, he doesn't feel he can. "You really think I blow things up?" I ask gently.

"Yeah."

"Like what, love?"

"Well, like, er . . ." Ah, he can't think of a single example. "Like the pants thing," he announces, triumph in his voice. "Drawing round them, I mean, with chalk."

"Ah, you did notice then. I wondered if you had."

"Yeah, 'course I did. Very mature, Mum. All you had to do was ask me to pick them up."

CHAPTER
TWENTY-FOUR

Breakfast at Natalie's

Vince arrives dead on time in his grotty old pick-up truck. He has clearly made quite an effort, as he looks spruce in a navy needlecord shirt plus smart black trousers (grubby jeans and raggedy T-shirts are his usual attire). He looks, I decide, interview-ready. "We can't turn up at Jenna's in that," Morgan declares, peering at his father's vehicle through the living room window.

"Why not?" Vince looks genuinely hurt.

"'Cause it smells, Dad. It smells of animal and we'll take it into their house with us."

I chuckle. "You mean it'll stick to us?"

"Yeah!" Morgan says, looking appalled.

"I think that's the least of our worries," Vince says, clearly teasing, which Morgan fails to notice.

"Yeah," he says hotly, "it's gonna be bad enough without us walking in being the Stink Family."

I catch Vince's eye and we smile. "The Stink Family," Vince muses. "I quite like that."

"And my car still smells of gravy," I add. "We don't want to take that in with us either. We don't want to be the Bisto Family. Maybe we should walk? That way, we won't pick up any terrible smells at all."

"Nah, let's not walk," Morgan says, looking quite rattled at the thought.

I glance at him. "You don't want to be spotted walking through town with your parents?" Again, it occurs to me that he may not be up to the task of winding a colicky baby in a few months' time.

"It's not that," he insists. "It'd be okay normally. It's just, y'know, we're gonna have those looks on our faces like we're going to, I dunno, *court* or something."

"You think you're going to be put on trial?" Vince asks, raising a brow.

"No, but . . ."

"C'mon, love," I say, touching his arm, "we're both here for you and I'm sure Natalie's parents are going to be perfectly reasonable."

"You reckon?" Morgan exclaims. "How was she on the phone?"

"Er . . . reasonable," I fib.

"Yeah, bet she was."

"What's she like?" Vince asks. "I mean, have you any idea what we're in for here?"

I pause, wondering how to put this. "Well, *okay*, she's hardly going to be cracking open the champagne. She's stressed and worried, of course she is. But I'm sure she's a perfectly decent person and we'll manage to sort everything out." I turn to Morgan. "What's she like, love? I mean, you know her better than I do . . ."

"Not really," he says with a shrug. "I mean, we're hardly ever there, Mum. We prefer it at ours." Hmmm, no wonder. Natalie doesn't strike me as the sort who'd

280

tolerate mugs and Coke cans and salami being scattered about.

"Come on, I'm sure she likes you, darling. You were invited to their party at Christmas and she always seems friendly . . ."

"Does she? Like, when?"

"Erm . . ." I try to dredge up an example. "Remember when I was asked to gather all the prizes for the bottle stall?"

"What's that got to do with anything?" Morgan asks.

"Well, some people handed in rubbishy bubble bath but she donated a bottle of sangria shaped like a bull."

Vince barks with laughter. "Oh, right. So obviously, everything's going to be okay."

We drive in my car (gravy rather than farm) because Morgan seemed to be genuinely freaking out about us being spotted with "court faces", and I didn't want to add to his stress. I, too, am a little agitated as I ring the bell of the immaculate detached house at the end of Jenna's quiet, affluent cul-de-sac. There's a small front garden, with pansies planted equidistant apart, and the glossy red panelled front door has a stone surround, with a pointed bit on top, possibly to make it look Georgian. *Do not be intimidated by a door*, I tell myself as it opens.

Natalie appears, wearing a resigned expression, as if we have come to check her home for rot. "Hello Natalie," I say, forcing a smile.

"Come in," she says flatly.

"This is Vince, Morgan's dad," I add as she leads us through the living room, in which an L-shaped beige leather sofa runs along two entire walls.

"Hello, Vince," she says without turning round.

We glance at each other. "Good to meet you, Natalie," he says, his easy charm faltering as we arrive at a formal dining room with a polished table and the kind of high-backed chairs that force you to sit bolt upright.

I glance at Morgan, who is peering down at the porridge-coloured carpet as if he has never encountered such a floor covering before. Natalie has yet to acknowledge his presence. "Please sit down," she says, pushing back her short, dark crop and adjusting her tortoiseshell glasses. She is wearing a crisp cream blouse and smart black trousers. The room smells strongly of Mr Sheen. The three of us sit in a row, with Morgan between us, as if we are protecting him from attack. "Tea, coffee?" Natalie asks primly.

"Coffee would be lovely, thanks," I say.

"That'd be great," adds Vince.

She looks at our son. "D'you drink coffee, Morgan? Or would you prefer, er, a fizzy drink?"

"Yes please," he mutters, blushing wildly.

She blinks at him, and I have to stop myself from saying, *He means he'd like a coffee*. He's old enough to make a baby, for crying out loud. He doesn't need me to speak for him. He doesn't want me to squeeze his hand under the table either, which I desperately want to do. "So . . . which would you like?" She fixes him with a cool stare.

282

"Coffee please," he croaks. I'm conscious of my heart rattling away as Natalie disappears to the kitchen.

"You okay?" I whisper to Morgan.

"God, Mum," he mutters. "I didn't think it'd be like this . . ."

"Feels like a job interview," Vince adds, although Morgan is unfamiliar with the concept. We fall into a gloomy silence punctuated only by the distant tinkle of crockery in the faraway kitchen.

"D'you think Jenna's going to join us?" I ask.

"Dunno," Morgan growls, "*you* set this up."

I inhale deeply, trying to quell the jitters inside. "Hi, Morgan." We all turn to the source of the small, breathy voice in the doorway.

"Hi, Jenna." Morgan smiles unsteadily.

She looks tiny in her vest top and frayed denim shorts. It hardly seems possible that she's pregnant. She takes a seat at the far end of the opposite side of the table, so as not to be facing any of us directly. "Jenna," I start, "this is Vince, Morgan's dad . . ."

"Hi," she says sweetly, getting up as he reaches to shake her hand across the table.

"Are you okay?" I ask, wanting to go round and hug her, but not sure how her mother would view that. Her wide blue eyes water as she nods. "I just thought it'd be good for us to all get together," I add, trying to sound reassuring as Natalie reappears with a tray of coffee, plus, disconcertingly, a plate of terribly sticky-looking iced Danish pastries. Not that any of us are likely to eat anything. "This looks lovely, thank you," I manage as Mark, or Mike, or something else beginning with M, appears in a striped blue shirt, a shiny purple tie and office trousers. He looks around nervously, as if wondering what it is he is expected to do.

"Pour the coffees, please," Natalie commands. He duly obliges as she takes the seat next to their daughter before lurching straight in. "So, we've made our decision and we'd just like to run through it with you, if that sounds okay?"

The three of us gawp at her. "Your decision?" I ask weakly.

"Well, yes."

My breath seems to have caught in my throat. I had it all planned out, what I'd say: that I'd like Jenna and Morgan to feel fully supported in whatever they decide to do. Now my voice won't work properly. Neither Vince, nor Mark/Mike/another M-name — it's too late to ask now — has spoken either.

". . . Jenna very much wants to continue with the pregnancy," Natalie explains, her voice devoid of emotion, "and we'll support her, of course, although it's *not* what either of us would have wanted for her . . ." She turns sharply to her husband. "Is it?"

"No," he says hurriedly, bobbing down onto the seat next to her and taking a noisy slurp from his cup.

Natalie twiddles her daisy-shaped earring. ". . . So, what we're proposing is . . ."

"Sorry to butt in," I say quickly, turning to Jenna, "but that's what you've definitely decided, is it?"

Jenna presses her lips together and nods.

"Well," I say gently, "that's fine."

284

Natalie widens her eyes at me. "I think you'll find it's far from fine!"

"No, what I mean is—"

"What Audrey means is . . ." Vince cuts in.

"Vince, just a minute please." I'm surprised by the forcefulness of my own voice. "Natalie," I start, "I don't think it's fine, of course I don't. I mean, they're only eighteen, it *is* very young, but it's happened and I think we need to accept it and help both of them as much as we can, even if they're not together . . ." I glance at Jenna. Tears are now spilling into her cheeks. I'm not sure if her mother has noticed, or is too preoccupied to comfort her. I glance at Morgan, who throws me a pleading look, as if silently requesting instructions on what to do.

"Well, that's part of it," Natalie says. "We have decided, as a family, that Jenna won't see Morgan any more, or have anything to do with him. We'll take care of—"

"But what d'you think of this, Jenna?" I cut in.

She looks at me, too choked to speak. I feel a surge of sympathy for a daughter who's not even mine.

"That's the thing," Natalie charges on. "It's not really about their *relationship* or whatever it was . . ."

"Of course it's a relationship!" I blurt out, at which Morgan kicks me under the table.

"Yes," Natalie continues, "but that's not the issue now. We're keen for Jenna to continue her education, and we'll do all we can to enable that to happen — on the condition that Morgan is out of the picture."

For a moment, I am too stunned to speak.

"But . . ." Vince starts, "what about these two? Shouldn't we see how they feel about it? And about each other?"

Natalie emits a sort of gasp. "Maybe, if *you* had a daughter, you wouldn't be quite so laissez-faire about it all."

Something ignites in me then, as I run my gaze over the mute husband, the distraught daughter and, in the middle, Natalie, in full flow again: "I will *not* have it, do you understand? I want my daughter to have a happy, fulfilled and successful life with someone who deserves her."

I stare at her, realising how idiotic I'd been to assume this would be okay, just because she donated that manky old sangria to the bottle stall and which, *actually*, was returned unopened to the next community centre fundraiser. I imagine the disgusting stuff is still in circulation now. "That's a very disparaging thing to say," I say firmly, glancing at Morgan who seems to have shrunk to his eight-year-old self. "And," I go on, "I think it's extremely unfair. We're not even giving Jenna or Morgan a chance to speak, to say how they feel . . ."

Natalie sniffs. "We should have stopped this, nipped it the bud . . ."

"But they're eighteen," Vince reminds her. "How were we supposed to nip it exactly?"

She glares at him. "Well, there's not much *you* could have done. I gather you're not really around . . ."

"Can we stop this please?" I blurt out in a voice which, although it's apparently coming from me, doesn't seem to be mine. "It isn't helping at all. Look how upset Jenna is — and I can't even imagine how Morgan's feeling right now. And you know what? It's not about us making rules and deciding whether they can or can't be together. It's not fair. It's not the way the world works. They love each other — anyone can see that — and what's happening here, this laying down the law, feels so wrong and I won't be a part of it."

I stand up and noisily push back my chair. Natalie's eyes are wide, her mouth hanging open. "Vince," I bark, "I think we should leave Morgan and Jenna to talk things over — by themselves." I turn back to Natalie, then glance at her husband, having forgotten he was there for a moment. "So, Vince and I will leave you now." I touch Morgan's shoulder. "Maybe you and Jenna could go for a walk, get some time on your own?"

He looks up at me and nods.

"You're okay if Dad and I go home?"

"Er . . . yuh." He looks as fearful as when I left him in the classroom on his first day of school. I almost want to check that he's remembered his lunchbox.

"Well, thank you, Natalie," I say tightly, glancing briefly at the untouched Danish pastries, "and thank you, er . . ."

"No, thank *you*," says the husband, darting up from his seat before Natalie escorts us out. Her jaw is set, her face waxily pale. She doesn't even say goodbye.

Vince and I step outside, and the door shuts firmly behind us. I try to ignore the nausea swilling through me as we climb into my car and where, unexpectedly, he gives me a brief, firm hug. "God, Aud," he exclaims, "you were fantastic in there. I never knew you had it in you."

In years gone by, when Vince had visited, he and Morgan might have headed into York to do something boyish together: see a Bond movie, eat a pizza, or run about in some dark, mysterious warehouse armed with laser guns. Now, of course, Morgan isn't here, and even if he was, he wouldn't want to do anything with his dad. His absence is palpable as I knock together lunch from odds and ends in the fridge.

"Think they'll work things out?" Vince asks.

"I hope so. It's hard for Jenna, though, when her mum's laid down the law."

"Surely she can't stop her from seeing him. What's she planning to do, barricade the poor girl in?"

"No, but she can make life difficult." I pause. "God, Vince, we're going to be *grandparents*. I'm only 44!"

He laughs weakly. "Jesus, Aud. Still haven't got my head around it, to be honest."

"Me neither."

"Think he'll cut it as a dad?"

I shrug. "He'll have to, I guess, if he's allowed to play a part in it."

Vince nods. "He might rise to the challenge."

"You really think so? I don't know, Vince. How on earth is he going to contribute? I've gone on about courses, apprenticeships, finding any old job to tide him over . . . the gardener at Mrs B's even asked him if he'd be interested in some casual work."

"Will he go for that, d'you think?"

I pick at my slightly wilted ham salad. "He wasn't exactly raring to go, put it that way."

"And he still thinks this street theatre thing's a goer?"

I smile. "He hasn't mentioned it for a while so hopefully he's started to see sense." I look at Vince across the table: a caring, well-meaning father, with no more clue about how to shake Morgan out of his ennui than I have. "I know you think I've mollycoddled him," I add. "Of course I want him to get out there and do something. But I can't go on at him all the time. Life would be hell. I don't want him to hate me, Vince."

"Hey," he says gently, patting my arm across the table. "You've done a brilliant job."

"You really think so?"

"Yeah, I really do. He's just in a . . . slump, that's all. It happens. He'll have to shape up when he has a child to support and then he'll be off your hands, and we'll wonder what the hell we were worrying about . . ." He breaks off and grins. "Anyway, how about you? Seen much of your man lately?"

"Oh, he turned up at the hotel without any warning, can you believe it? Wanted to stay the night in my suite . . ."

"Bet he did! Sounds like it was a step up from a Travelodge. So, did you let him?"

I chuckle, grateful for the easiness between us; not that I'll be sharing any details about being tied up and dowsed in champagne. "No, I did not. I was there to cook, Vince."

"Yeah, of course," he says, raising a brow.

"I've seen him once since then, and that was weird too . . ." I fish out my phone. "I found a book — a notebook — in his car . . ." I scroll through my pictures to find the shot of the page. "Look. What d'you make of this?"

Vince takes it from me and frowns at the screen. "No idea. I don't even know what I'm looking at, Aud . . ."

"It's a page from his notebook. I took a picture while he was paying for petrol . . ."

He turns to me and grins. "Can I ask why?"

I laugh in embarrassment. "I don't know. It just seemed odd. It *is* odd, the whole thing, and I just had a feeling . . ."

"Could it be something to do with his work? What it is he does again?"

"Oh, it's that mindfulness stuff, focusing on the moment. I don't fully understand it."

"Why doesn't anyone have a proper job any more?"

I shrug. "I don't get it — the little notebook, I mean . . ."

The front door opens, and Morgan shambles in. "Hi darling, how did it go?" I ask.

"Dunno really," Morgan says, joining us at the table. "I think she's just scared of what her mum'll think if she sees me . . ."

"Aw, don't worry," Vince says, wrapping an arm around him, "she'll come round, once the dust's settled. Jenna's a lovely girl, son. God knows what she sees in you."

"Thanks, Dad." He grimaces.

"I'm joking. Anyway, wasn't your mum brilliant today?"

Morgan shrugs. "She was all right."

"C'mon, she was more than all right!"

"She was, uh, *direct*," Morgan offers with a weak smile.

"Hey," Vince adds, "here's something to take your mind off Natalie and whatever the bloke's name was. Your mum was showing me something, maybe you can help . . ."

"He's welcome to have a look," I say, turning to Morgan. "Go on, love, see what you make of it. You used to be great at all this stuff."

"What stuff?" He frowns.

"Figuring out codes, secret messages and all that," Vince says. "Don't s'pose you fancy resurrecting those spying skills, do you? Maybe that's a career path worth investigating . . ."

"Dad, that was when I was, like, *ten*."

"Ah, you were pretty good at it, though," Vince teases, "writing mysterious notes full of symbols . . ."

"I spoke to Jessica Watson's mum yesterday," I cut in. "She thinks Jessica still has that letter you wrote, Morgan." He looks blank. "Remember the invisible ink one?"

"Oh, God, yeah."

"The love letter," I add slyly. "Well, her mum reckons she kept it for years . . ."

He grins, his cheeks glowing. "She can't have read it, Mum."

"She did, her mum said . . ."

He laughs bashfully. "Remember that spy book I had? There was a thing about how to make invisible ink from onion juice but it stank so bad, I just used water. So," he adds with a snigger, "there was nothing to read."

"Well," I add, "her mum said it was definitely a love note, that she was besotted with you, darling . . ."

"*Stop* it, Mum."

"Maybe," Vince says sagely, "she interpreted it the way she wanted to."

Morgan shakes his head. At, least he's perked up. "Anyway," Vince adds, thrusting my phone at him, "what d'you make of this, spy kid? It's a page from a notebook your mum found in lover boy's car."

With a small shudder, Morgan takes it from him and peers at the screen. "Well, it's dates, isn't it?" He turns to me. "Where d'you usually meet him, Mum?"

"What d'you mean?"

"Stevie, when you stay overnight."

I clear my throat. "Er, *you* know. At motorway services . . ."

"Well, yeah, er . . ." He tails off.

"What is it?" I exclaim.

"Dunno, Mum. I think it's pretty obvious, though, don't you?"

I take my phone from him and squint at it. "You mean you don't know, or it's obvious? Which is it, Morgan?"

"Mum . . ." He throws me a pleading look. "I think it's kinda, um . . . a diary-sorta-thing."

"Really? A diary of what?"

"Well . . . of his motorway, erm, *things*."

"What things?"

He looks a little queasy. "His, um . . . the stuff he does." He stands at my side and jabs at the screen "See the J bit? That's the junction, and the M bit's the motorway, obviously . . ."

"And the other letters?" I prompt him. "The D, C and A?"

"Well, I'm only guessing," he mumbles, "but I'd say, there's the date and the motorway and junction numbers, and the letters are, er . . ." He breaks off and looks at me. "Well, the A is you."

I stare at him. "Oh. So . . . what are the C and D?"

He reddens as his dark eyes meet mine. "I don't think it's *what*, Mum. It's *who*."

CHAPTER
TWENTY-FIVE

Dinner for One

Stevie doesn't favour motorway hotels because of the fuzzy ball toothbrushes. Nor is it their proximity to Pringles or a tepid Meat Feast Slice. It's their convenience, the fact that they're right there at the roadside. They are anonymous stop-offs for salesmen and shaggers.

Yep, shaggers. If I am the A, then the D is — who, Donna? Denise? And the C . . . could she be Caroline or Cathy? I have no idea. I do know, though, that the little red notebook is a logbook of motorway-related activities and suggests that Stevie is a very busy man. So he has excellent time management skills after all. Bastard. No wonder he's made a career out of it. I wonder if C or D lets him tie her up and slurp booze from her bellybutton? Maybe they both do. He certainly seemed well practised with knot work, and I don't believe for a moment that he was in the Scouts.

Vince has headed off home now, having persuaded Morgan to go back to his place for a couple of days. "Just for a change of scene," he suggested, "to let you think over this whole scenario and decide what you want to do." To my amazement, Morgan agreed. "It'll be good for him," Vince added, as Morgan disappeared to pack a bag. "Give him, and you, a bit of space."

I'd desperately wanted space when I'd headed off to Wilton Grange. Now, in our eerily silent house, I am not so certain.

"Are you sure that's what it is?" Kim asks when I call her. "I mean, is there anything else it could be?"

"Definitely not," I reply. "I've checked my diary and all the A dates match up to the nights I met him."

"Jesus," she breathes. "So he's kept a record of it all . . ."

". . . Yep, probably so he can remember who he's taken to which one," I add. "God forbid he ever remarked that he'd been there before, forgetting that it'd been with someone else."

"It's so weird," she murmurs.

"Kind of creepy," I agree.

"Oh, Aud. I'm so sorry."

I consider this. "You know, I thought there was something odd going on. I just told myself it was the easiest way for us to get together, with him travelling so much . . ."

"Well, it sort of made sense," she murmurs.

"No, it didn't. Not really, when you think about it. The whole thing felt wrong. Just tell me, am I the stupidest person you've ever met?"

"Of course not," Kim retorts. "You're smart, Audrey. You just . . . wanted to believe it was okay."

"I'm gullible then."

"No, you trust people. There's nothing wrong with that. Look, I'm doing a make-up rehearsal today for a wedding next weekend. But I could pop over later?"

"No, I'm fine, honestly." I pause, wanting to tell her about Morgan and Jenna and the baby, but can't bring myself to load that on her now, on top of the Stevie debacle. Plus, it's really too soon to share the news; I should never have blurted it out to Paul.

"So what are you going to do?" Kim asks.

"I'm not sure. I need to think about it . . ." In fact, as soon as we finish the call, a plan lays itself out before me. I am free today; Victoria, Mrs B's daughter, has arrived to "take over the reins" for a few days, as she put it, asking Julie to alert me and Claire that we wouldn't be needed during her stay. Not exactly convenient for the others — but after today's confrontation with Natalie (that's what it felt like: a *confrontation*) I could do with a break. I spend the afternoon de-stinking Morgan's room — he'll hate me for it but I can't help myself — and make a dinner for one; a defrosted portion of bolognaise which I realise now was meant for two (Morgan and Jenna) and which I can barely stomach anyway.

I don't call to say I'm coming over. I just set off at 7.30p.m. in the gravymobile, knowing it's likely that Stevie won't be home. Fury simmers inside me as the undulating countryside fades into the affluent suburbs. I try to calm myself by thinking of soothing things, like slowly browning onions for soup, which no one will want because Morgan will only tolerate Heinz tomato. So that fails to calm me. Instead, I switch my thoughts to the lovely evenings spent with Lottie, Tamara and Hugo — but then, what was all that about, making out he'd be consigned to the dunce corner when he's a bloody professional chef? Does *no one* tell the truth any more?

I'm finished with men, I decide. At least, apart from my son. Kim was right: he'll be living with me when he's 47 and we'll be having greaseproof-wrapped sandwiches on Bridlington beach.

I pull into Stevie's narrow street and park on the corner, to allow myself a few moments to calm myself rather than being someone who "blows things up". His office sits in between a solicitor's and a dentist's in a bland modern block. There are several bare, reddish patches where the pebbledash has crumbled off. *Stephen Dudley Mindfulness Training*, reads the tarnished gold lettering above the window. There's a lamp on in the window of the flat above; not that that means he's home. The entrance to his flat is next to the office. There's an intercom, and I should buzz really — but then, there are lots of other things I should have done, like practised my pelvic floor exercises and taught my son to hand wash a T-shirt without microwaving it to buggery, and made a point of having relationships only with decent, honest men. So, bypassing the intercom, I push the door — it's unlocked — and walk straight in.

The bleak, narrow hallway is bare apart from a small shelf bearing a scattering of mail. The wallpaper is of the woodchip type, and peeling in places. I tread lightly up the bare wooden stairs to the landing. The door to

Stevie's flat is of the cheap, flimsy type, badly painted with white gloss. The one time Stevie invited me here, I was faintly thrilled by how basic it was, the way he existed unhampered by clutter with the tiniest size of milk carton in the fridge (skimmed). He gave me cheese on toast — value Cheddar — and a large glass of cheap Argentinian red. I felt a wave of youthfulness, imagining that this was what being a student at music college might have been like. However, I could understand why he wasn't keen for me to come over again. He was embarrassed by its sparseness, I decided. "It's pretty tragic," he kept saying, "for a guy of my age."

Low music is filtering through the door. I hover for a moment, awaiting instructions from my brain as to what to do next. My options appear to be: creep back downstairs and drive away. Or, knock on the door and, when he answers, explain that I was just passing and that, last time I saw him, I found this little book, and was compelled to take a picture of it and . . . oh, *God*. Maybe Morgan was wrong, and it was nothing to do with motorways after all. I mean, it's been a good eight years since he abandoned his career as a spy.

That's it, I decide: I've jumped to conclusions. Stevie is just a busy man, and motorway hotels fit into his schedule—

I jump back as the door flies opens. "Oh!" A woman — no, a *girl* — is staring at me.

"Hello," I say, in a ridiculously chirpy tone.

"Er . . . hello, can I help you?" She's so young, is all I can think. She's a tiny doll of a person, with reddish brown poker-straight hair that falls all the way to her bottom, which is pretty much where her tight black dress ends too. She was probably born in the 90s, for crying out loud.

"Erm, I'm here to see Stevie," I say, in an eerily level voice.

The girl frowns. She's clutching a packet of Silk Cut and a cheap plastic lighter, and a silvery bracelet glints at her wrist. "He's just popped out. I was just going out for a cigarette . . ." I catch her looking me up and down and quickly figuring that I can't possibly be anything other than a vague acquaintance, or perhaps a neighbour. "He hates cigarette smoke," she adds, her expression softening. "Won't even let me lean out of the window, says it wafts back in . . ." She laughs self-consciously.

"I'll come down with you," I say, as she shuts the door behind her.

"D'you want to leave him a message? Is it anything I can help with?"

"Er, no, I don't think so," I say, sensing myself ageing rapidly as we trot downstairs together. While I'm still wearing the sensible pale blue shirt and black corduroy skirt I chose for the summit meeting at Jenna's, this girl looks like she's about to go clubbing. I could be her mother, for goodness' sake.

She lights up as we step out into the cool evening. I am horribly tempted to ask her for one. "Is it something important?" she asks, looking uneasy now and repeatedly glancing down the street.

"It is quite," I reply.

She gusts out smoke and picks at a nail. They are long and sugary pink, possibly false, and each one has a sparkly jewel stuck in the middle. "How d'you know Stevie, if you don't mind me asking?"

"Oh, just from round and about," I reply vaguely.

She shivers in her thin dress. So this is the kind of girl he sees when he's not with me. A *girl*, not a woman. I knew, of course. I just didn't allow myself to dwell on it because it felt so good, making love with a man I'd have imagined to be way out of my league. I glance at her as she puffs away, tapping her foot on the pavement. She has a tiny lizard tattoo above her ankle and her shoes — extravagantly strapped, with huge, chunky heels — appear to be squishing her toes together. She needs a cardigan, I decide, and I hope she's not planning to wear those shoes all night.

I check my watch. I could make my excuses and leave, and she'll just say, "Some woman was looking for you", when he returns from the shops. Maybe he's bringing her Pringles. Poor thing, I reflect, assuming she has a good thing going with a successful, handsome older man who happens to be bloody brilliant in the sack. Of course he is. He's had plenty of practice. It's like Mrs Sherridan, my music teacher, kept reminding me: work hard at the basics — breathing, tonguing, running up and down those pesky arpeggios and scales — and the more technical stuff will come easily.

She continues to smoke in silence. "I'm Audrey, by the way," I venture.

"I'm Danielle." She flashes a brief smile, and I decide there and then to just leave it because he'll arrive with his shopping and it'll be terrible and, anyway, now I know. Danielle is the D, and someone else is the C, but it's not my job to tell her. Maybe she'll never find out.

"Look, I think I'll just go," I murmur.

She looks faintly relieved. "Okay. So, shall I just say Audrey was here?"

"Yes, if you wouldn't mind."

"And he'll know what it's about?"

"I'd imagine so, yes." Now I just want to get away, to spare this shivering girl a terrible scene when all she wanted was a quick smoke. Her expression turns quizzical as she drops her gaze to my neck. "*That's weird . . .*"

"What is?" I frown.

"That. Your necklace. Look, it's just like my bracelet . . ." She raises her arm. My heart turns over as I study the silver coils dotted with tiny pink stones.

"There must be a lot of them around," I say, with an awkward laugh.

"No, there can't be. He had it made specially for my birthday. He asked what stones I'd like and I said pink diamonds" — she laughs tightly — "and he said, Bloody hell, they're only the most expensive gemstones in the world, so he got something cheaper, but as close as he could to the real thing, y'know? 'Cause it was my 21st . . ." Her *21st*! For Christ's sake, she is three years older than Morgan.

She examines my necklace and reaches out to touch it. I flinch as her nails brush against my neck. Shit, here comes Stevie, ambling down the street with a carrier bag. He spots us, and his expression freezes. For a moment, he looks as if he might be sick.

"Stevie!" Danielle calls out sharply. "This lady — Annie, was it? — wants to see you . . ."

He walks towards us and stops. "Audrey. Er . . . hi."

"Hi," I say dryly.

Danielle looks at him, then me, and crushes her cigarette end with her shoe. "What . . . what are you *doing* here?" he croaks.

"Like Danielle said, I just came to see you." I feel eerily calm as I fix my gaze on his. Those eyes, which always looked so teasing and suggestive, are now filled with fear.

"Shit, Aud," he mutters.

"Yes, it is a bit shit, isn't it? That's exactly how I'd have described it."

He swallows hard, his Adam's apple bobbing. I'd never noticed how prominent it is before.

"What the fuck's going on?" Danielle snaps.

"Nothing!" he exclaims.

"It doesn't seem like nothing," she shoots back, waggling her wrist in his face. "See this bracelet? The one you had specially made, 'cause you know how much I love pink?"

"Yeah, yeah." He tightens his grip on his Londis carrier bag.

"Well," she adds, "her necklace . . . it's just the same, isn't it?"

He frowns, pretending to study it carefully, as if not entirely sure.

"Did you give it to her?" Danielle ventures.

302

"Er, well, she's a friend, I should've said . . ."

Her eyes widen, and she steps backwards, her pert, young person's breasts barely contained in the low-cut scoop of the dress. "Don't tell me you're *seeing* her?" She glances at me, as if barely able to believe it might be possible.

"Well, I, er, um . . ."

"*I* know what it was," she yells, rounding on him. "It was one of those jewellery sets — the necklace, bracelet and earrings all in the same design. I've seen them. You bought one and split it up, you tight bastard!"

"Whoah!" he cries. "No need for that . . ."

"Where did you get it?" I cut in.

He purses his lips. "Just some store."

"Where exactly?" Danielle demands.

His cheeks colour, and a middle-aged man passing by with a terrier on a lead pauses to smirk at us. "I think it was BHS," Stevie mutters.

"*BHS?*" Danielle crows. "Well, that's lovely, that is. That's real class, Stevie . . ."

"So . . . who got the earrings?" I enquire.

"Nobody! Listen, I never said . . ."

"You said you designed and commissioned it," she shrieks, "just for me—" He starts to protest, but she storms past him and into the entrance to his flat. "I'm getting my stuff," she yells back. He stands, still clutching his carrier bag, looking at me in a *what-did-I-do?* kind of way.

"Well, that was nice," I say coldly. "You're just a lying shit and you keep a note of us all in a little book."

"*What?*" There's a crack of breaking glass as he dumps his bag on the pavement. Liquid — wine, probably, or maybe even champagne — starts to leak from the bag and pool around his feet.

"I saw it in your car."

"Oh, for fuck's sake," he snaps. "I didn't ask for any of this . . ."

I observe him in a detached way, as if he might be the sort of ranting stranger I'd normally cross the street to avoid. "You sort of did, actually."

"Aud, for God's sake, you can't just turn up at my place without any warning. I have a *life*, you know. You should've called—"

I climb into my car and lower the window. "I was just in the area, Stevie. Bye."

CHAPTER
TWENTY-SIX

Emergency Booze

Maybe it's me, and I just don't know the rules of modern dating. Maybe the way things go is that, unless someone says, "At the present time I am only intending to sleep with you", then they are probably shagging so many other people they need to keep track of it all in a logbook of lays. I should start one, I decide as I drive home. Should be easy to keep: i.e., pages of blankness, stretching to infinity. I wouldn't even need to bother looking for a pen.

I let myself into the house. It feels oddly quiet without Morgan in it, and I prowl from room to room, putting things away, crunching morosely on stem ginger cookies and deciding I need a drink. It's gone midnight when Stevie texts me: *Sorry babe but I never said we were exclusive.*

I *absolutely* need a drink. There must be something. I rake through our cupboards and fridge.

Inventory of booze found:
1 bottle Tia Maria (raffle prize, unopened)
Dregs of Baileys (contains cream, and not kept in fridge: possibly ill advised?)

1 can cider

2 cans lager

Bottle of brandy, about a quarter full and untouched for several years

Four boxes Kirsch Kisses (melted loose ones dispensed of)

Dregs of a bottle of red cooking wine, containing sediment

Rum and raisin ice cream (joke)

Deciding to opt for the brandy, I tipple some into a glass, noticing how pale it is, almost watery-pale. I try a sip. It *is* water, albeit with a faintly alcoholic tinge. You could feed it to a baby with no discernible ill effects. Surely my darling son hasn't been nicking my booze and topping up the bottle with water? What a cheek, after all the beer and cider I've bought him. I finish the glass anyway — despite it being disgusting — and pour a Tia Maria, which is okay-ish, although not my usual tipple of choice. But this is an emergency. I down it and pour another glass, alternating between sips and bites of Kirsch Kisses and promptly feel quite sick — of Stevie, of myself, sitting here in the kitchen drinking all on my own, and of life itself.

Being a sensible, *stoical* sort, I carry on in this manner, having fetched my laptop now with the purpose of Googling Stephen Dudley Mindfulness Training and glowering at the picture that pops up on the website: my cheekily grinning ex burbling on about a "flexible approach to facilitate clear, effective communication".

"Arsehole," I mutter, not terribly mindfully, then — fuelled by more Tia Maria and a perverse desire to make myself feel even more wretched — I mull over another time I was lied to, deceived, whatever you want to call it, by a man. "We can sit in the dunce corner together," Hugo said, when he knocks out top-quality dinners for God knows how many, every night of the week. I Google him, and his jolly beaming face appears. Although I try to beam fury at it, I just can't. The kind grey eyes, the warm, wide smile: it's just not a glaring-at sort of face. Anyway, compared to cheating on women and splitting up sets of BHS jewellery, playing down your culinary abilities no longer seems like a terrible crime.

I'll let him off I decide, sipping from my smeary glass. I'll tell him I know his secret, and that it's okay, and what does it matter anyway? I hiccup loudly, wiping my chocolatey mouth on my shirt sleeve and Google his pub, The Cap and Feather in Hambleton Willows. *I'm* the one who needs to say sorry: for subjecting him to the terrible sight of me in my industrial bra and pants, lashed to the bed with a curtain rope. If he can recover from that, maybe we could stay friends? I pull off my shoes, toss them across the kitchen floor and take another big swig of Tia Maria for Dutch courage. Realising I'm having to focus quote hard on the keypad, I tap out the number of the pub.

"Hello, Cap and Feather?"

"Hello," I start in my best sober voice, "could I speak to Hugo if he's there, please?"

"He might be busy just now," says the efficient-sounding woman, "but I can ask someone to check . . . who can I say is calling?"

I gulp yet more drink. "Just a friend."

"Could I take a name please?"

"I, er, sort of want it to be a surprise."

"Oh." She pauses. "Okay then. Hang on please . . ." While she's gone, I refuel with more booze and chocolate, wondering if this is how normal people, like Lottie and Tamara, while away an ordinary Monday night.

"Hello?" comes the quizzical male voice.

"Hugo!" I blurt out too loudly. "Is that you?"

"Er . . . yes, it is. Who *is* this?"

"It's Audrey from cook school, remember?"

"Oh! Yes, yes of course I do. So, er . . . you've tracked me down . . ." He coughs awkwardly.

"Yes, it was easy, and it's fine, okay? It really is! And I'm sorry I dashed off without saying goodbye . . ."

"Was everything okay? We were all a bit worried . . ."

"Yes. Well, no. My son's pregnant. I mean, my son's *girlfriend's* pregnant . . ."

"Gosh, Audrey. That sounds more serious than the washing machine . . ."

"It is," I declare. "God, yes, it is!" A pause hangs in the air, filled with the background hubbub in the Cap and Feather and lasting just long enough for my booze-fuelled confidence to subside. "I'm sorry, you're at work, this is probably a terrible time . . ."

"Well, er, I'm okay for a couple of minutes . . ."

Oh, I know what this means: *please get off the phone*. "I shouldn't have called," I mutter, picking nail polish off my big toe. "It's just, well, I've had a bit of a crap evening, to be honest."

"Sorry to hear that," he says. "I can imagine things are pretty tense at home . . ."

"No, no, it wasn't that. Remember Stevie, my, er . . . friend? The one who—"

"Yes, I remember," Hugo says quickly.

"Well," I charge on, "I knew something was going on so I went round tonight and there was a woman there, well, a *girl*, she's only 21 — that's definitely girl rather than woman, wouldn't you say?"

"Um, probably," Hugo agrees.

"So he's seeing her and, God, I feel stupid . . ." Without warning, my voice wavers and a tear rolls down my cheek.

"I'm so sorry to hear that," he says gently.

"It's okay," I snivel, wondering what's possessing me to tell him this stuff, and why I've mistaken a man I barely know for a shoulder to cry on.

"Audrey, listen . . ."

"No, it's all right," I whimper, tippling more Tia Maria into my glass. Another tear drips down my face. "Anyway," I go on, "I don't know why I called you. I was just feeling, I don't know, a bit lost, I suppose. Morgan's away at his dad's until tomorrow. Not that he'd be interested. Got enough of his own stuff to figure out . . ."

"Yes, of course he has," Hugo murmurs. "Are you going to be all right tonight?"

"Yeah," I say firmly, "I'm fine. I shouldn't be bothering you. Look, I know you're a chef, okay? Of course I do. You *know* I know. I just phoned you at the pub and I shouldn't have. I'm sorry . . ."

"Please, Audrey," he interrupts, "could you listen for a minute?"

"You *are* a chef, aren't you? A proper one in a white jacket, like Brad?"

I hear him inhale. "Er, well, yes, I must admit I do have some experience in the catering trade."

I laugh bitterly. "You're making it sound like you've dished out soup in a church hall. D'you have proper chef's knives?"

"Um, I do have knives, yes. They're kind of pretty essential . . ."

"And a blow torch for burning the tops of things? D'you have one of those too?"

"*Please*, Audrey, listen . . ."

I try to sip from my glass, but it's empty. "Remember I told you about Morgan jamming the hoover by sucking up socks? Phoney ineptitude, you called it. Pretending you can't do something when really you can . . ."

"Yes, I think I might have said that," he says with a trace of exasperation, "but look, I just wanted to say—"

"You don't need to explain," I trill, knocking the bottle with my elbow. As I try to catch it, my phone flies out of my hand. The bottle shatters on the floor, and shards of glass skid in all directions across the kitchen. I stare down at my mobile, which is sitting in a puddle of Tia Maria. "Oh, God," I groan, scrambling up from my chair and retrieving it. Its screen is cracked, and it appears to be dead. At least, Hugo isn't there any more. Maybe he heard the bang and thought I'd shot myself. Bet he's just relieved I'm not still babbling on at him. He's probably sauntered back to the kitchen to deftly fillet some sodding sole. I dry my phone with a tea towel and lower myself back onto a kitchen chair.

That was sensible, I decide: calling him while pissed. If anyone's ever needed to make a complete arse of themselves, I'm your woman. Maybe that's a career path I should consider: that of a middle-aged joke, cheated on by a man I was never properly in love with. Sex, that's all it was. Tons of hotel sex, followed by oily sausages and coffee from a machine in the morning. A fleeting image of Stevie and Danielle pops into my mind. So she's allowed to visit his flat, *and* she gets the whole hotel routine too. Christ, I'm amazed she can even drive. Bet she still lives with her mum and dad and has piles of teddies on her bed . . .

My thoughts turn to Morgan who at least is far away from this pitiful scene, at Vince's. That's what I need to focus on: not men who don't matter, but on setting a good example to my son.

I stare down at the mess on the floor then, still clutching my sticky phone, step barefoot through the shards of glass to the living room as if that will make everything go away. I curl up on the sofa, aware of a spiking sensation on the sole of my left foot. Prodding at it makes it worse, and my fingers come away sticky and dark red. Further investigation reveals that a fragment of glass has embedded itself in my foot, and blood is oozing from the wound. I try, ineffectually, to squeeze it out like a splinter and, when that doesn't work, I close my eyes in the hope that, like when you can't be bothered to take off your make-up, it will miraculously disappear during the night.

CHAPTER
TWENTY-SEVEN

Fish Bone

I wake up on the sofa at 4.27 a.m., with memories of Danielle in her tight dress and heels filtering as if through dirty gauze into my dehydrated brain. As I peer around the living room — at least the curtains are drawn, sparing anyone passing the sight of me sprawled in my shirt and knickers — more recollections nudge their way in: a broken phone and — oh, God, calling Hugo ... My eyes, which had been momentarily opened, clamp shut again. So this is what my life has come to: getting drunk on a spirit I don't even like, without mixers. But then, I *am* over eighteen, and we didn't have any Coke, and I'd just discovered that my boyfriend's been sprinkling cheap jewellery all over Yorkshire. So I was allowed, surely?

I scramble up and examine my hands. This is becoming a habit, I realise: waking up thinking I was lying on gravel, and now wondering why my fingers are all bloody. Either my memory is deteriorating or I am simply drinking too much. Did Stevie and I have an actual fight? Surely not. I've never hit anyone, apart from Marianne Cheadle at primary school when she said I was a swotty little bastard for playing the clarinet ...

My foot throbs, and I hoik it up to examine it. Of course, the broken bottle. I peer at my sole and try to ease out the glass with my fingernails. It won't budge. Grabbing my phone and crumpled skirt from the floor, I dress quickly and hobble upstairs to the bathroom, briefly wondering how Natalie would view me now. We shall be sharing grandmotherly roles: her with her posh grown-up blouses and pencil skirts, me with my cheap highlights and booze injuries. I'm sure she'll be delighted. Having washed my hands and foot, I finally manage to extract the glass with the help of my eyebrow tweezers. My sole's still sore to walk on, which feels sort of *right*: punishment for my foolish actions last night. I slope up to bed and, without bothering to undress or even slither under the duvet, I sink into a heavy sleep.

Within what feels like minutes my phone trills by my ear. That's good, at least: it's come back to life. "Hello?" I croak.

"Audrey? It's Victoria, Elizabeth's daughter." My fuddled brain takes a moment to process that Elizabeth is, in fact, Mrs B. "D'you have a minute?" she chirps.

"Yes, yes of course." I sit bolt upright in bed and glance at the clock; it's just gone 9 a.m. "Is everything okay?"

"No, not really. In fact, it's far from okay. That's why I'm calling a staff meeting . . ."

"Victoria," I cut in, "is your mum all right?"

"She is *now*," she says tersely. "Everyone else can make it today at one . . . would you be able to pop over?"

"Yes, of course . . ." I lick my parched lips. "I hope it's nothing serious?"

"I'll explain everything when I see you," she says primly.

Having showered and dressed, I spend the morning glugging pint glasses of water and attempting to erase all traces of my appalling behaviour. The Tia Maria seems to have coated the entire kitchen floor, and it takes several attempts to obliterate the stickiness and lingering alcoholic whiff. As I scrub specks of blood off the sofa, it occurs to me that I have no right to feel cross about Morgan leaving a few crisp packets strewn about.

I arrive at Mrs B's to find everyone — Julie and Claire, the other carers, Rosa the cleaner, and even Paul — assembled awkwardly in the living room. There's no sign of Mrs B, and clearly, we haven't been summonsed here for good news. "Ah, *here* you are," Victoria says, as if I delayed proceedings. Paul gives me a quick, ominous glance. Victoria is pacing around, curiously ageless — although in her late fifties, at a guess — with her pale hair scooped up into a haphazard bun. Reminding me of a particularly unapproachable teacher, she is decked out in pastels: peach top, fawn trousers. Although I have only met her a handful of times, I gather that she favours a washed-out wardrobe. "Please sit down," she says. Paul moves up on the sofa to make space for me. "I'll get tea and coffee," she adds.

As she flits off I glance around at the others. "What's going on?" I murmur.

315

"No idea," Julie replies, "apart from that something happened when they went out for dinner last night . . ."

"They went out for dinner?" I gasp. "Why didn't they just eat here?"

"Victoria doesn't cook," Claire whispers with a roll of her eyes.

Paul turns to me. "There was some kind of incident in the restaurant." He pauses. "You okay, Audrey? You look a bit peaky."

"I'm fine," I bluster, "just didn't sleep too well last night. So where's Mrs B?"

"Mum's having a nap," Victoria announces, gliding back in with a tray laden with clinking china. I leap up and take it from her and busy myself by pouring coffees and teas and handing around delicate, rose-patterned cups. "The whole thing's been exhausting," she adds, clutching at her brow.

"You mean looking after your mum?" I venture.

"Well, yes. Honestly, I thought it would be a treat for her, for us to have some time together and go out for a lovely meal . . ." She briefly closes her eyes. "So, we arrived, and she was terribly fussy about the menu and said something about fish . . ." She blinks at me. "Do you often cook her fish?"

"I do, yes. It's her favourite."

"Hmm. Well, they did it for her specially — it had to be *completely* plain — and then she got a bone caught in her throat. She insisted she could still feel it, even after I'd given her dry bread to eat and water to drink, and she wouldn't let it drop . . ." She sighs, pushing back a loop of stray hair and looks around at us all.

Apart from being on committees for various charitable institutions, I have no idea what she does. "So I had to take her to A&E for an X-ray," she adds as if this, too, had been a terrible chore.

"So what happened?" I ask.

"Well," Victoria exclaims, "of course there was nothing there."

"Maybe it had shifted?" Rosa suggests.

"And left a scratch," I offer. "That can happen with fish bones. It scratches the throat so it still feels like it's there, like a sort of *phantom* bone . . ."

"Well, whatever it was, it ruined our evening. Three hours, we had to wait at A&E. And by the time we got home the bone — or the *phantom* bone or whatever it was — had gone."

"Well, that's good, isn't it?" Julie remarks.

Victoria flares her nostrils. "I suppose so, but the whole situation made it clear to me that this can't go on." We all stare at her. "She needs constant care," she continues. "Someone at hand in case this kind of thing happens again . . ."

"A fish bone sort of thing?" Paul asks, raising a brow.

"Yes, well, no — anything really. She's far too vulnerable to live in this huge house all by herself and, as you know, I can't be here permanently."

I swallow hard and glance at Julie. We all need our jobs, especially Paul; he lives in the grounds, for goodness' sake. But more than that: this is Mrs B's home, *and the only way I'm leaving here is in a coffin.* "Victoria," I begin hesitantly, "I know it's a big house and a lot to look after, but your mum isn't alone for much of the day."

"And I'm pretty much always here," Paul cuts in.

"Yes, in the garden," Victoria says.

He clears his throat. "Well, not always. Not these days. I always come in when the morning carer leaves, make her a cuppa, have a chat . . ."

She peers at him. "She needs more than a cuppa, Paul."

"Yes, I realise that but we all pull together, we're a pretty good team." He glances at me, a tinge of frustration in his dark eyes. "Audrey popped over the other day," he adds, "when it wasn't even her shift . . ."

"It's still not enough," Victoria cuts in.

"Could you increase her home care then," I suggest, "just to put your mind at rest? We could help you find another carer to cover the nights . . ."

She shakes her head. "It's not that. It's just . . ." She looks around at us all. "I need to look ahead and plan for the future."

I glance at Paul.

". . . So we need to get the house ready, which means a huge effort from everyone . . ."

"What d'you mean, get the house ready?" I blurt out.

"I mean," she says firmly, "we need to start tackling this place, freshening it up, making it more appealing . . ." My heart seems to sink. "Rosa," she continues, "perhaps you could increase your hours, start decluttering, set aside things you know Mum doesn't use? We can go through them together, donate to charity, whatever . . ."

318

Rosa has paled. "Er, okay, but why are we—"

"Just do as many hours as you can and let me know. Cost isn't an issue."

Rosa nods and looks at the floor.

"And Paul," she goes on, "the main thing is to get the garden knocked into shape as quickly as possible."

He looks confused by this. "It *is* in pretty good shape. Mrs B was saying the other day that it's looking the best it has in years . . ."

"Yes, I know the borders are the way Mum likes them — crammed with flowers, untended and cottagey . . ."

"Untended?" he repeats hotly.

She frowns at him. "I'm just saying they're not to everyone's taste. Plus, there's that overgrown woodland area which would put anyone off. And if I'm going to sell the place—"

"You're selling the house?" I exclaim.

"Well, yes, that seems to be the best option. So, Paul, we need everything neater, trimmed back, tamed . . ."

"Victoria," I venture, beyond caring about offending her now, "is your mum okay about all of this? You know how much she loves her home and garden, and she's often said she absolutely refuses to move."

Her pale eyes beam into mine. A Latin teacher, I decide, that's what she could be — not that I ever did Latin. "Thank you, Audrey, but this is a family matter, and until I find suitable alternative . . ."

"You mean a care home?" Claire looks around at all of us in horror.

"Well, some sort of supported accommodation." She pauses. "So, everyone, if you could carry on as you are, taking on extra duties if you can spare the time — the clearing, the sorting and what-not . . . I'd like us to *move* on this, please. I'm hoping to have the place entirely spruced up by the end of next month, ready for it to be surveyed and valued . . ."

"That quickly?" I gasp. "But surely it's going to take more time—"

"Not if we all pull together." She glances around the room. "I'm sure Mum will agree that this is the best plan for everyone."

If she were here, I'm sure she would *not*. Okay, she may have become a little *hazy* lately, but when it comes to things that matter — her home, her preferred biscuits — she is razor sharp.

We are dismissed and wander outside, rather dazed. As we can't be seen hanging around and gossiping — we are all rather scared of Victoria — we make our way to the gate.

"Selling the place?" Claire mutters. "You know she'll never agree to that."

"Can Victoria go ahead anyway?" Julie asks.

"I doubt it," I say. "I mean, it's Mrs B's house."

"She seems determined, though," Paul mutters. "All that talk of planning ahead . . ."

". . . As if her mum's already dead," Claire says bitterly.

I turn to Paul. "What about you? What'll you do?"

He shrugs. "Move on, I guess. Victoria's made it clear what she needs us to do, so we'd better just get on with it."

His bluffness stings me. "Not yet, though," I say quickly. "It could take months — *years* — to sell a house like this. Not many people have that sort of money . . ."

"No," he says firmly, "I'm going to get the job done, get the garden *tamed* . . ." He grimaces at the word. "And in the meantime I'll definitely have to start looking for more work."

"Another live-in job, you mean?"

He shakes his head. "That happened at the right time, when Jackie and I split up. I left her the house and needed somewhere to live and . . ." He pauses. "I can get my own place now and there's plenty of work around here. Maybe Morgan could help me out, just until I get the job done?"

"I'll mention it," I say, which should raise my spirits. But as I walk home I can't help thinking that a part of my life — a part that's far more important than a cheating boyfriend — has come to an end.

Back home, I can't stop thinking about Mrs B. It's not that I have anything against care homes, or supported accommodation or whatever Victoria has in mind for her mother, if that's what the elderly person wants. My own Granny — Mum's mum — lived in a delightful place, Cedar Villas, that served afternoon teas and had quizzes and games and all sorts going on. Someone was often tinkling away on the piano, Granny was surrounded by friends and, as a little girl I always regarded visiting her as a treat. Maybe it's because it was something Mum and I did together. When I try to remember being with her, before Brian Bazalgette happened, there aren't too many memories to choose from.

My birthday cards are still sitting on the mantelpiece: from Morgan, Vince, my friends, and Mum. To be fair, she never forgets my birthday, or Morgan's, for that matter. There are never any presents, but I don't expect any. I used to send her drawings Morgan had done — more like diagrams really — of the thrilling gadgets spies might use. *It looks like the man is wearing a flower on his jacket*, Morgan would write, *but really it's a weapon and tiny knives shoot out of it!!* As Mum rarely responded, Morgan, understandably, gave up.

I won't, though. She needs to know that, at the relatively tender age of 65, she is going to be a great-grandmother.

I find the pale blue Basildon Bond notepaper I haven't used for years. Although it's only A5 the page looks vast, and I have no idea how I'll fill it. Chewing the end of my pen, and wondering if the lingering Tia Maria scent is just in my imagination, I curl up on the sofa and start:

Dear Mum,

I'm writing to tell you some ~~exciting amazing~~ pretty startling news. Morgan and his ~~girlfriend~~ ~~ex-girlfriend~~ sort-of-girlfriend are expecting a baby . . .

Christ, no wonder people hardly ever write letters any more. And to think I suggested Morgan wrote one to Jenna! It's excruciating and, as I hardly ever use a pen these days — does anyone? I'm amazed Morgan didn't write that wish list on his phone — my handwriting is appalling.

I rip off the page and start again:

Dear Mum,
   I wanted to let you know that Morgan is going to be a dad.
   Love,
   Audrey

   PS Our landline number, in case you've mislaid it, is 01632 767294

CHAPTER
TWENTY-EIGHT

A Hail of Falafel

I pick up Morgan next day at York railway station. As he hasn't eaten "for, like, *hours*" — negotiating the buffet car must have been beyond him — I take him to his favoured 50s-style diner in the hope that the humungous portions will make him more open to a glittering career in gardening. "I'm not sure, Mum," he says, liberally dowsing his chips in vinegar.

"What aren't you sure about exactly?" He looks less peaky, less light-starved having spent a couple of days with his father. I was hoping a blast of outdoor grafting might have ignited an enthusiasm for fresh air.

"I'm just not sure it's my thing."

"But it's money, isn't it? And it's close to home, you could even walk there . . ."

"Walk?" he repeats suspiciously.

"Well, yes, I mean I walk to Mrs B's, don't I? But if that's the issue I'm sure I could arrange for you to be transported there by sedan chair . . ." He shakes his head, as if *I'm* the exasperating teenager. "And Paul really needs some help," I continue. "So which part aren't you sure about?"

He bites into a chip. "The gardening part."

"You mean good, honest, physical work?"

He laughs dryly. "You sound like Dad. Know what he had me doing yesterday? Building a wall!"

"Well, that's good. You'll get fit, doing that kind of thing. It's a useful skill to have."

"How is it useful, Mum?"

I peer at him. "Well, virtually everything's made from walls, isn't it? Houses, shops, churches, factories—"

"Yeah, but look at my hands," he exclaims, thrusting them, palms up, towards me. They are entirely unblemished and baby-soft, as if they've spent eighteen years shrouded in soft cotton gloves.

"They look fine to me. In fact they're perfect, love. They could be used to advertise hand cream. Now that's a career you could think about — being a hand model. D'you know they really exist? People are paid vast amounts of money just to hold things in adverts, now *that* doesn't sound strenuous—"

"Mum," he cuts in, "will you stop thinking up possible careers for me? So far we've had builder, gardener and model and I've only been off the train about fifteen minutes. Got any more ideas?"

My stomach clenches. Once upon a time, we'd have giggled about the hand model thing and come up with a list of the World's Easiest Jobs. "That was a joke, actually," I mutter. "Being a hand model, I mean."

"Hmm," he grunts, turning his attention to his burger.

"Anyway," I continue as he chomps and slurps, "sorry to go on, Morgan, but you say gardening's not your thing. The problem is, *nothing* seems to be your thing. It's been over a year now, and apart from those few weeks at the factory and hotel, you've done absolutely nothing at all."

"Please, Mum, give it a break."

"But you can't live this way!" I exclaim. "I can't afford to support both of us and have you lying about the house and not bothering to help out there either. It's just not fair."

"Yeah, but I don't wanna be a gardener, all right?"

I peer at him, conscious of my heart galloping away. He's right, I shouldn't be getting on at him now, when he's only just come back from his dad's. But then, there's never a good time to address it. "Okay," I say, trying to normalise my voice, "how about thinking about what you *do* want to do, rather than what you won't even consider?"

He slurps his shake. Its pungent laboratory banana whiff is detectable across the table. "Actually, I was thinking about this on the train."

"You were *thinking*, on the train?"

"Yeah." He shrugs. Christ, maybe I should shovel him off to his dad's more often. "And what I was thinking," he continues, tearing off a wodge of burger bun and stuffing it into his mouth, "is that I *definitely* don't want a job where I'd need a briefcase." He gnaws away and takes another noisy slurp of shake.

"A briefcase? What's wrong with a briefcase?"

"You know what I mean. They're just . . . ugh . . ." He shudders dramatically.

"D'you mean an accountant or a tax inspector or something like that?"

"Yeah, the kind of jobs where everyone hates you."

I laugh dryly and bite into my own burger. It's bouncy, like the foam used for sofa cushions, and tastes entirely of grease. Wilton Grange feels a terribly long way away. "Okay, so what else did you decide?"

"That I don't want to work in an office."

I frown at him. "That rules out an awful lot of opportunities, Morgan. I mean, I know you think, office, boring, but it's just a building with desks and telephones. It's just a *place* . . ."

"Yeah, but I don't wanna work in that kinda place."

I blink at him. "I think you're being too fussy. I mean, when I started out—"

He groans loudly. "Please, Mum, don't give me all that stuff about going out to earn a living when you were seventeen and having to wear brown paper for shoes . . ."

My mouth falls open. "I've never said I wore brown paper for shoes!"

He laughs, oblivious to a little boy at the table behind us who's twisting round, clearly enjoying the show. I sip my Coke, aware that I must not overreact — or *blow things up* — or remind him that I only took a live-in job because my dad had just died, having slammed our car headlong into a parked tractor after downing an entire bottle of Grouse.

"Mummy," the little boy pipes up, "why does that lady have brown paper for shoes?"

"Shush, William."

"But why—"

"It's what happened in the olden days," she hisses, "to poor children."

I look down at my plate and inhale slowly before meeting Morgan's gaze. "So, I take it it's a no with the gardening, then?"

He bites his lip. "Well, what I decided on the train was, if I'm gonna be there for Jenna and, like, support the baby and stuff . . . 'cause she wants us to be together, it was just her mum saying I wasn't good enough, all that . . ."

I nod encouragingly. "I'm glad the two of you are trying to make it work, love."

"Yeah, and I was thinking I really should follow my heart and give it everything I've got."

I stare at him. "What d'you mean?" As far as I can see, there is no *it*.

"Street theatre, of course."

"What?" I exclaim. "You mean as your actual job?"

"Yeah?" he counters. "'Course I do . . ."

For a moment, I'm lost for words. I thought we'd moved on from all this. "That's not a *job*," I exclaim. "It doesn't fall into that category, Morgan." A vein has started to pulsate in my neck.

"What is it then?"

"I don't know — a hobby. A thing you do to fill your copious spare time. It's not a way of earning anything like enough to support a young family. What does Dad think? Did you actually tell him this is what you're planning to do?"

"Nah. I will, though, once I get going . . ."

"See, you know it's not viable. You're living in a fantasy world . . ."

He glares at me and starts to tear up a paper napkin into tiny flakes. "You know what, Mum? It was actually really nice being at Dad's."

"I'm glad," I mutter. "You should see him more often."

"Yeah, I might," he snaps, "because he's not always on at me like this. He believes in me. He says *positive* stuff . . ."

"I say positive stuff!"

"When, Mum? When d'you ever say, 'Well done'?"

I stare at him, scrabbling for words and aware of the little boy watching us intently: the young, shouty man and his mum who's on the verge of crying in sheer frustration. "I've said it millions of times,". I mutter.

"I can't remember the last time. *When* was the last time?"

I glare at my cold chips. Actually, I can't remember. Maybe I haven't for years. God, isn't that awful? But what are all these well dones meant to be for? Flushing the loo occasionally? Managing to emerge from his bedroom at some point before noon? We descend into a stony silence. "I'm sorry you feel like this," I mumble.

"Yeah, I am too."

I look up at him, my handsome boy with whom I have managed to fall out when it was supposed to be a fun lunch. "Do your street theatre, then," I say firmly. "It's your decision."

"Yeah, it is. Thanks for that, Mum. Thanks for acknowledging that I do have some choices in life." And now he's up on his feet, throwing his bag over his shoulder with such force, he almost clonks a young girl clearing tables.

"What are you doing?" I cry.

"I'm gonna go and do some street theatre *right now*. Maybe then you'll stop putting me down . . ."

"But it's raining! And you don't even have a proper waterproof coat . . ."

"Why are you obsessed with coats?"

"I'm not. You don't have your stuff either. Don't be crazy, Morgan. Sit down and finish your shake . . ."

"I've got my batons in my bag," he retorts, already making for the door. "I practised loads at Dad's, *he* said I was really good."

"You are good, I know you are . . ." I, too, am up on my feet, aware of the little boy and his mother gawping at me.

"Don't worry, I'll get a bus home . . ."

"Morgan, wait! Please—"

But he's already gone, catching the eye of two willowy girls sitting at the window table, who nudge each other and giggle as he swishes by.

I look down at our messy plates and pay the bill. And as I leave the diner I catch the little boy staring pointedly at my feet, as if checking whether my shoes really are made of paper. He looks quite disappointed that they're not.

He's just agitated, I tell myself as I wander around the shops. Not that there's anything I want to buy. I'm still smarting from our lunch, but try to convince myself that once he's calmed down he'll start to see reason and possibly even take up Paul's offer of paid work.

I meander into a chemists' with the purpose of buying something small, like a nail polish, to cheer myself up. But there are far too many colours and sparkly decorations to stick on them, which remind me now of Danielle's embellished nails, so I leave the shop, wondering whether I should have *my* nails profession-ally done, and all my body hair ripped off while I'm at it, or just remain unadorned and fuzzy. I'm not sure that looking like an oversized eight-year-old girl down there exactly goes with a middle-aged face.

As for the hair on my head, having glimpsed my reflection in a mirrored shop sign, I realise it desperately needs a trim if I'm likely to be attending job interviews soon. It could do with de-yellowing too. It seems to be turning brassier by the day. I peer into a tiny salon with no customers inside, and a sign that reads "Appointments Not Always Necessary", and venture in.

"Yes, I can do something now," says a young girl with a brow piercing that, to my untrained eye, looks rather angry and is therefore possibly recently done.

"Just a trim, please," I say, figuring that the half hour this'll take will give Morgan the chance to reflect on his frankly ridiculous tantrum, and decide that I *do* encourage and believe in him. I'll phone him when I'm done and we can drive home together and put our tetchy lunch behind us.

The hairdresser lifts a clump of my hair and frowns, as if it might be radioactive. "You definitely don't want colour? I'm doing a special deal today, half-price tints. It'd really freshen you up . . ." Like I'm a shabby porch in need of a lick of emulsion.

"I'm not sure," I reply. "It's been lightened a lot, and I'm wondering whether I should give it a break."

She tweaks it again and purses her lips. "Yeah, I see what you mean."

"You mean I've wrecked it?"

The girl winces. "I wouldn't say *wrecked*, but . . ." She disappears to fetch a swatch of hair samples. "Look, instead of your, er, quite *harsh* blonde, how about toning it down? These are conditioning colours for hair that's looking a bit frazzled. What d'you think?"

Frazzled! Maybe she'd be better just hacking it off? "They're awfully dark," I say.

"Well, I just think, for the more *mature* woman . . ." Oh, here we go. ". . . More flattering to your skin tones," she goes on, "and I promise, it'll take years off you."

I nod resignedly, doubting very much if it will. "Okay, let's go for it."

"Warm brunette? It's a lovely milky chocolate shade."

"Yes, why not?" Hell, I don't really have the funds for this either — with a jolt, I realise I still haven't posted the cheque for the minibar bill — but at least it's half price.

Without bothering to make small talk she pastes on the colour as if daubing a door frame, then sits me under a heat lamp with a ragged copy of *Take a Break*. My phone rings: it's Kim, and in muttered tones I fill her in on my impromptu visit to Stevie's. "God, Aud. She's 21? What a creep!"

"*And* he split up a BHS jewellery set and gave her the bracelet and the necklace to me . . ."

"What?" she exclaims, then peals with laughter, which sets *me* off. "Where are you now?" she wants to know.

"In town, just round the corner from that 50s diner, having my hair done. I'll be finished in about an hour."

"Great, I'm in town too. Meet me for coffee, Millie's at two?"

"Sure," I say, aware of the hairdresser tuning in — now seeming fascinated that a "mature" woman might have these kind of love dramas going on. And from then on, her demeanour changes to one of rapt attentiveness. My scalp is thoroughly massaged as she shampoos off the tint, and I slip into a sort of reverie in which Morgan and I are friends again, and he's not storming out of a diner but gamely digging horse manure into the borders with Paul.

"This colour looks amazing," the girl enthuses, now combing out my hair. It looks dark, I think: dark and wet. "Can we try something different with your style?"

"Sure," I say, still blissed out from the head massage. She beams at me in the mirror and starts to cut. I watch, fascinated, as clumps tumble until my hair hangs at my jaw, sort of choppy and layered and now being blasted vigorously with the dryer. She squirts on some kind of goo and rubs it in, before giving me another quick blast and a ruffle with her hands. She stops and gazes at me expectantly.

"Well?" she asks with a hopeful smile.

"I . . ." I meet my own gaze. It's not ordinary Audrey, who ladles out macaroni and peas and has been shat on from a great height by her boyfriend. It's a new person, with a younger, brighter face. Even my eyes look more alive. The warmth of the milky brown tint seems to somehow lighten me from the inside, and I realise I am grinning inanely. "I love it," I exclaim, touching my hair. It no longer feels as if it has been baked.

"You look amazing," the girl says kindly, "and, uh, I'm only going to charge you for the cut, okay?"

"No, really?"

"Yeah." She beams at me. "You deserve it and, to be honest, it was me who persuaded you to go for it. I'd never used those colours before, you see. I'm just the junior here — the owner's out on her lunch break. I just wanted a go."

"So I was your guinea pig?" I say with a smile, fishing out my purse.

"Yeah, I guess so." She blushes. I thank her again, and virtually skip out into the street, feeling light and renewed and no longer frustrated by my son.

When I catch sight of myself again in the mirrored sign, I'm so cheered by what I see that I decide to pick up a few gifts for Morgan's birthday in a few weeks' time. What was on that wish list again? Jelly beans (I take care to buy the right kind) and hair stuff (*is* it the right kind? With the vast array of putties and pastes on offer it's impossible to tell), plus — veering off-list here — a giant Toblerone which I know he loves. That can

334

be a peace offering. While Ralph Lauren aftershave is pushing it, I find a big bottle of fragrance on a market stall that smells vaguely similar to the one he likes.

It's lovely, I decide, giving presents — which reminds me, I still haven't taken in the chocolates for Mrs B. Wonder what Paul will make of my new, choppy, dark hair?

I find Kim already installed in Millie's where she enthuses loudly over my brand new do. "Wow, I love it, Aud. I hardly recognised you when you walked in. You're so brave!"

"Glad you like it," I say, glowing with pleasure.

"So how d'you feel?"

"Brave," I say, laughing, and we quickly down our coffees as she's keen to embark on her favoured activity (shopping). We do the high-end chains — Hobbs, Whistles, which do nothing for me, even if I could afford the clothes — then a couple of charity shops which yield all kinds of treasures, and which Kim tolerates, although I know she objects to the faint, worn-before whiff. In Boots, she brandishes a lipstick for me to try. "It's too bright," I tell her, my hand hovering over a subdued pinky-brown.

"No, it's perfect for you," she insists, "with your new hair."

"It won't suit me, Kim."

"But it's cherry red," remarks the sales assistant, "and that suits everyone . . ."

"She's right," Kim says, pulling out her purse and handing over the cash.

"You don't need to buy it for me!"

She takes it from the assistant. "I already have."

Back out in the fine rain, we make our way along bustling cobbled streets. "Did you ever get in touch with that chef guy?" she asks.

I grimace. "I'm afraid so . . . when I was pissed. Called him at his pub. Oh God, Kim. It was mortifying. I started ranting on about Stevie and that girl — as if *he* cared — and then I dropped my phone and . . ." I break off. "I shouldn't be allowed to make calls after 9 p.m."

"Idiot," she says with a grin. "At least he *knows* you know."

"Yeah, I'm sure he's hugely concerned about that."

"Oh, Aud. He still sounds like a decent guy. I'm sure he had his reasons . . ."

"Reasons I'll never find out," I say briskly, dropping a pound coin into an accordion player's hat, and figuring that maybe I'll buy those coveted Calvin Klein boxers from the wish list too, a better class of pant to strew about the living room . . .

Kim tugs at my sleeve. "Look! Is that Morgan?"

I follow her gaze to the paved area in front of the church. She's right. My gangly boy is tossing batons with aplomb; it's actually quite an impressive sight.

"He's not bad," Kim exclaims. "From what you've said, I thought he'd be awful . . ."

Was he right, *am* I always putting him down? "He said he was practising at his dad's," I murmur.

"Let's give him money," Kim announces.

"No, he'll hate that."

"He hates *money?*"

"No, he'd hate us giving it to him. He'd think we were humouring him. He'd find it patronising . . ."

She laughs and shakes her head. "Teenagers are *so* weird."

"In fact," I add, "he'd hate us watching. Come on . . ." I grab at her arm and we shrink back into a disused shop doorway in order to watch more discreetly. Silver batons fly in graceful arcs, each expertly caught. It's not just his performance that's startling. It's also seeing him from a distance like this — standing upright, unaided — rather than lying prone on the sofa. I hadn't realised how tall he's grown. He towers over most passers-by. No one is stopping to watch, though, let alone toss coins into the woollen beanie hat at his feet. They're just hurrying past in the light rain. *Hey*, I want to shout, *stop and watch this guy for a minute. He's my son!* "He'll get soaked," I add.

"He'll be okay, he's wearing a jacket . . ." Yes, the pathetically thin one he chose, no better than a fly sheet, despite costing £125. A bread wrapper would be more effective at keeping out the rain. I don't tell Kim this. Nor do I point out that he's wearing those pitiful canvas shoes that merely draw the moisture in. That can't be good for his athlete's foot . . .

Although he glances in our direction, he appears not to see us, thank God. I shouldn't be here, not really. It's like when I agreed to let him play in the park with his mate Dan and then lurked in the bushes, spying, in case a stranger appeared with a bag of sweets and tried to bundle them into a van. Of course, nothing bad happened. I was just being a neurotic mother, as I am now. My poor boy, soon to become a father of a tiny, utterly dependent baby, gamely tossing batons to make some money to buy baby things. My heart aches for him.

A rabbly group of young men — also unsuitably attired for the weather, in tight jeans and lurid fluorescent yellow T-shirts — are making their way noisily along the cobbled street. Looks like a stag party. They are jostling and laughing and taking up most of the street. A tall, stocky man with overly gelled hair buffets into an elderly lady with a wheeled shopping trolley, and she throws him a look of disgust.

He mutters something at her, then peels away from the others and meanders unsteadily towards Morgan. "Lads," he calls back, "come and watch this tosser!"

I glance at Kim in alarm. "For God's sake," I mutter. "There's no need for that!"

The others all amble towards him. While Morgan is all rangy limbs — there's not a spare ounce on him — these are broader, altogether more solid types. The batons soar higher as Morgan gamely juggles on. The men are sniggering and — I think — teasing him, trying to provoke a reaction. His gaze remains upon the batons as they shoot up into the air. "Wanker!" shouts one of the men.

Something inside me clenches. How bloody *dare* they? How would they feel, trying to earn enough for a moses basket and a sterilising unit in the bleak Yorkshire rain?

"You're shit," yells another of the pack.

338

"Bastards," I whisper to Kim, having to forcibly stop myself from marching over because I know Morgan would hate that, he'd be *mortified* to see his mother rushing to his aid. Then something else happens, something that pushes away all thoughts of what Morgan would think because one of the men — the tubbiest one, arse spilling over the back of his jeans — appears to be doing something that's caused my beloved, *talented* boy to stop juggling. His batons clatter onto the ground and he backs away. "They're throwing stones at him!" I yell, and before I know it I'm rushing over, forgetting about Kim or my shopping or the fact that my son will probably disown, me for this.

I round on the culprit who's smirking infuriatingly. "What d'you think you're doing? How *dare* you?"

"Fuck's sake, missus," he blusters, teetering away and guffawing at his mates.

I indicate Morgan, who's still backed into the decorative arch of the church. "Is that reasonable, to throw stones at a boy who's just trying to make a few quid?"

"Stones?" he repeats gormlessly. "They weren't stones."

I catch Morgan giving me a pleading look. "They looked like stones, from where I was standing. You could have had his eye out—"

"Who are you anyway?"

"His mum," I snap.

"Oooh, his mummy's rushed over to rescue him!" he cackles, thrusting a foil carton in my face. "It weren't stones. It were these."

I peer into the carton to see a small heap of rather doleful-looking falafel, plus a scattering of shredded iceberg lettuce. "You were throwing *falafel* at him?"

"Yeah, we were only having a laugh," he says, pulling a hurt expression befitting the wrongly accused, before they all make their way in an ungainly clump down the street.

I turn to Morgan, who's glaring at me. "Falafel," I exclaim. "I wouldn't have thought that'd be their kind of thing."

Morgan steps towards me. "Mum, d'you have *any* idea what you've just done?"

"Yes." I nod and take my bag of shopping from a rather shell-shocked-looking Kim. "I made assumptions about what those men would eat, based on their appearance and behaviour."

"For God's sake," he mutters, retrieving a baton from the ground. I scurry to retrieve one that's rolled into the gutter, and he snatches it from my grasp.

"Did they hurt you?" I ask, reaching for his arm.

"Mum, stop trying to touch me! Leave me *alone*, okay? No, it didn't hurt, it was just a bit mortifying, that's all . . ."

"I know, darling, they were outrageous . . ."

"I don't mean them," Morgan says, picking up the last baton. "They were fine. I mean, at least they were showing some interest . . ."

"You want that kind of interest?"

"Yeah. No. I mean you, Mum, storming over and scaring people off . . ." He throws me another furious look. "Are you completely insane?"

"No, I'm not. What am I supposed to do, just stand back and allow that to happen?"

"I am *not* seven years old!"

I clamp my back teeth together and glance at Kim, who musters a stoical smile. "Morgan," she says, "I think your mum's new hair made her a bit *too* brave."

CHAPTER
TWENTY-NINE

Tea and Sympathy

Conversation is strained as I drive us home. To break the chilly silence I try quizzing Morgan on the precise type of wall he helped his dad to build: "Drystone or cemented?"

"Cemented," comes the curt response.

"So you learnt how to use mortar, with a trowel? Like a proper builder? Maybe you could get an apprenticeship—"

"Mum, please stop patronising me."

"It was only a *suggestion*," I remark, my stomach twisting uncomfortably. Never mind the behaviour of errant boyfriends. Nothing spears the heart of a middle-aged woman like a cruel remark from her son. "So, that stag party group," I struggle on. "I'd have expected them to be more your chips or kebabs type-people, not wandering around with vegetarian chickpea-based snacks . . ."

"Can we leave the falafel now please?"

I glance at him, yet again stung by his sharpness, and rack my brain for something else to talk about. Jenna and the baby are probably too sensitive a topic when he's still smarting from the street theatre incident. "I bought you a giant Toblerone," I murmur, as I pull up outside our house, wondering if this, too, might be viewed as patronising. *I'm eighteen years old, for God's sake! I don't need a massive chocolate bar!* But he musters muted thanks as I rummage through my bag on the back seat and hand it to him.

"Kim thought your act was really good," I add.

He looks at me from the passenger seat. "How about you? What did you think?"

"I thought you were great, darling. Very confident and professional."

"Yeah, right."

"No, I really did . . ."

He pauses, as if wondering whether to believe me. "Um . . . Jenna's coming over in a bit, okay?"

"Really? So, are you two back together?"

"I'm just letting you know so you can give us a bit of space," he remarks, climbing out of the car.

"Yes, of course I will." I scuttle after him and let us into the house, deciding to give him his presents now, instead of holding them back for his birthday; hopefully, they'll cancel out any bad feelings caused by the falafel incident.

"Thanks, Mum, this is, er, *great*," he says, wincing at the fake Ralph Lauren scent. "Um, Jenna's on her way now, okay?"

"Yes, love. I'll give you some space." Exiled to my bedroom, I figure I'm far enough from the living room/kitchen or indeed any other parts of the house where they might wish to hang out, without resorting to sitting in the back yard in the rain. The front door opens, and there's a tetchy exchange as Morgan lets her in.

"So how much money did you make?" Jenna's voice, sounding shriller than usual, carries upstairs from the hallway.

"It wasn't about the money," he replies.

"What *was* it about then?"

"It was about developing my act . . ."

"You're always developing your act. When are you going to stop *developing* and just get on and do it?"

"Hey, I thought you were on my side! You're sounding just like Mum . . ." Something twists inside me.

"It's different now," she shoots back. "We're having a *baby*. We're going to need more than the few coins people throw in your hat . . ." I know I shouldn't be listening. But as they're talking loudly, at the bottom of the stairs, it's impossible not to hear.

There's more muttering, then, "It's, it's just a *mess*, Morgan, and you seem to think it's all gonna be okay . . ." I am frozen, perched on the edge of my bed, wanting to help, but feeling helpless.

"Mum!" Morgan yells upstairs.

I lurch out to the landing. He is standing — alone now — in the hallway. "What is it, darling?"

He pushes his hair out of his eyes. "Got a minute? Jenna wants to talk to you." I pause. "I mean you can come down now," he adds.

"Oh. Is everything all right?"

He declines to answer as I scamper downstairs and find Jenna hunched on the sofa.

344

She throws my son a significant look. "Morgan?"

"Yeah, yeah, okay." He slopes out of the room; looks like he's the one being exiled now.

"Jenna . . ." I sit gingerly beside her. "Are you okay?"

She picks at her nails. "Not really."

"Well, I'm not surprised, love. I'm sorry it was so . . . awkward at your place the other day. I hope it didn't make things worse."

She shakes her head. "No, that's just Mum."

"She's bound to be upset. But what about you? You and Morgan, I mean? I know your mum doesn't want you to have anything to do with him . . ."

"Yeah, but I told her, after what you said at our place. I said, it's up to us whether we're together or not. Not her . . ." She musters a weak smile. "Thanks for standing up to her. No one ever does. Not even Dad. Well, especially not Dad . . ."

"I couldn't just sit there," I say firmly, realising that, despite her regular visits over the past year, this is the first real conversation we've had. Although I've tried, it's been hard to get to know her in any real way when she's been forever glued to Morgan's side. "Are the two of you back together?" I ask hesitantly.

"Dunno." She sniffs loudly. "He's driving me a bit mad, to be honest." Hmm, I can relate to that . . . "Could you . . ." she starts. "I mean, I know it's not easy 'cause he doesn't want it . . ."

"Morgan doesn't want the baby?" I gasp.

"No, not that. He does. We *both* do. I mean that job, that gardening thing . . . can you make him do it?"

So *this* is why she wanted to talk to me. I squeeze her hand, flattered that she believes I can influence him. "Well, I'll try. Short of frog marching him down to Mrs B's garden, I'll do whatever I can."

She musters a smile. "Thanks for being so kind to me, Audrey."

My heart seems to swell. "Oh, it's nothing, sweetheart. You know you can can talk to me anytime—"

"I don't mean right now," she says quickly. "I mean letting me come over all the time and hang out . . ."

"Jenna, it's nothing. You're always welcome here."

Her eyes well up as she holds my hand tightly. "It's so much nicer here than at ours. You're such . . . such a cosy, comforting person . . ." She's making me sound like a onesie, but it's still lovely to hear. "I wish *you* were my mum," she adds.

"I'd be different," I say gently, "if I were your mum."

She manages another smile. "So, what's it like?"

"You mean being pregnant," I ask, "or giving birth? Or actually being a mum to a baby?"

She laughs dryly. "All of it."

What can I tell her? That her slender body will change beyond all recognition, and that it won't be teensie knickers she'll be wearing but massive mummy pants and a nursing bra? Or that having this baby will change her life forever? That's the thing: you can never switch off. You might be able to nip away to a motorway hotel, or even take yourself off to de-beard mussels and cock up a custard; but you're still responsible, still to blame for the reckless microwaving of a favourite

346

T-shirt and the aiding and abetting of the conception of a child.

I put an arm around her shoulders. "I don't think anyone can truly tell you what it's like. But if there's anything I can do, anything at all . . ."

She turns to looks at me. "There *is* something."

"Really? What is it?" My heart soars at the prospect of being able to offer sage advice.

"Er, my favourite thong. It's pale yellow, lacy . . . I think I must've left it here. Don't s'pose you've seen it lying about?"

I frown, feigning bafflement. "No, but I'll keep an eye out for it," I say.

To give Morgan and Jenna the chance to talk things over, I head over to Mrs B's. Although it's not my shift, I plan to drop off her chocolates and catch up with Paul if he has time for a chat. Seeing me arriving at the gates, he clambers off the ride-on lawnmower and strides over. "Great hair," he enthuses. "Really suits you. But why the big change?"

"The hairdresser reckoned it's more befitting my age," I say with a grin.

"Oh, I liked you blonde, but I like this more, I think." His cheeks colour a little, and I sense mine flushing too.

"Thanks." He looks especially handsome today with his dark hair dishevelled and a smattering of stubble, his tan enhancing his chocolatey eyes. "Look, I'm sorry about Morgan," I add quickly. "He seemed so ungrateful when you offered him some work . . ."

"That's just boys," Paul says with a shrug.

"Yep, anything I suggest, he rejects out of hand. I've sent off for course prospectuses and found job ads online and he just says no — it's his default reaction. So how about you contact him direct?"

"I'm happy to try," Paul says. "Could you text me his number?"

"Sure," I say, then make my way through the sun-filled garden towards the house. Pink lupins soar between swathes of white stocks and the rare blue poppies Paul is so proud of. Victoria was right: the woodland area, where his daughters love to play, could be tidier. But it wouldn't be *this* garden — all Paul's work — which I've witnessed slowly blossoming into an eye-popping display.

As I knock and let myself in, I spot Victoria's drab grey mac hanging in the hall. So she's still here. Of course she is; despite her brusque manner she's bound to be concerned. I wonder if Morgan will fret about me when I'm 84, and he finds me slumped on the floor in a puddle of Tia Maria.

"Hello?" I call out from the hallway.

"In here," comes Victoria's prim voice from the kitchen. I find her sitting at the table with a fat folder of paperwork in front of her.

"Hi, Victoria. Hope you don't mind me dropping by. Just thought I'd pop in and see how your mum's doing."

She purses her lips, looking less than delighted. "That's very kind of you, Audrey, but she's napping at the moment."

348

"Well, if I could just—"

"Go and see her, then," she says briskly. "But please don't wake her if she's asleep . . ."

"Of course I won't," I say, trying to maintain a pleasant demeanour as I leave the kitchen. I find her mother sitting up in bed, her mouth set in a frown, the room heavy with the scent of stocks in a vase at her bedside. "Hello, Mrs B," I say, perching on the chair beside her bed. "I brought you these. I hope you like them." I take the box of Kirsch Kisses from my bag and place them on her bedside table. With a start, I remember I still haven't settled that minibar bill. Christ, I hope I'm not accruing interest . . .

"That's very kind of you," she says, sounding rather surprised. "Could you put them in my drawer? I don't want anyone else having them."

"Of course," I say, wondering if she realises her beloved garden is being tamed, her house being prepared for sale. "I heard you had trouble with a fish bone," I add.

"Yes," she says, her eyes glinting with mischief. "Victoria thought I was imagining it, making a fuss . . ."

"I'm sure it was there, if you could feel it."

"Of course I could! No one listens to me . . ."

"We *all* listen," I say gently, taking her hand. She fixes her gaze on me. Her face, once soft, has become more angular over the past few months, and hollows have appeared beneath her cheekbones. Her wrists are skinny and her wedding ring, which once fit snugly, now shifts easily along her bony finger as she twiddles with it.

"Audrey?" Victoria appears in the doorway. "I think Mum should have a rest now."

"I'm fine," Mrs B huffs. "I keep telling you, there's absolutely nothing wrong with me . . ."

"Er, I'd best be off then." Reluctantly, I get up to leave, and instinctively bob down to give her a quick hug.

"Oh!" Mrs B emits a tinkly laugh.

"Bye, Mrs B. See you soon."

Instead of saying goodbye in the hallway, Victoria accompanies me outside. I feel stung, as if I am being escorted off the premises in case I steal something. "Victoria . . ." I pause on the front steps, wondering how to put this. "I've been thinking, you know, how much your mum loves this place. Is there any way she could possibly stay here?"

"I'm sorry," she says firmly, "but I've made my decision."

"But does she even know what you're planning?"

Her jaw tightens, and she touches her string of cut-glass beads. "You're making it sound as if I'm doing this behind her back."

"Well, *aren't* you?" I'm shocked as the words fly out of my mouth. Maybe it's my new hair, or seeing Mrs B, shuffled off for a nap in the daytime when she'd far prefer to be sitting out in the garden with her newspaper. "She doesn't seem to have any idea," I go on. "At least, she hasn't mentioned the house being sold. Of course, none of us will say anything. But I do feel she needs to know. I mean, it's her place—"

"In this case, it's not," Victoria says firmly. "It's actually my house and my decision to sell."

I blink at her. "Your house? But I thought . . ."

"We looked at the whole situation a few years ago and decided it would be better, *simpler*, to sign it over to me."

I feel as if I've been punched. "Oh, I see."

"And someone's interested in buying," she adds.

"Right." I am lost for words.

"Bye, then," she says, turning back to the house and shutting the door firmly behind her.

I stride towards the gate, pausing only to wave to Paul in the distance. So that's that, then. A care home for Mrs B, despite the fact that she's arranged her life in precisely the way she wants it — which, despite her trickiness, I have to admire: that fierce determination to do things her way. Until Victoria waded in, and now it appears that she doesn't have any choice in the matter at all.

CHAPTER
THIRTY

Packed Lunch

I am woken by an unfamiliar sound. The insistent droning seems to be coming from downstairs: on and on, sounding like — no, it actually *is* the hoover, apparently being operated without me having anything to do with it. Maybe there's been a freak electrical fault and it's somehow turned itself on. I slip out of bed and pad downstairs in pyjamas to be greeted by the startling spectacle of Morgan dragging the appliance around the living room.

He grunts in greeting as I watch, transfixed. I'd be no more surprised to find him operating on a newborn's pancreas. There's a tinny rattle as he sucks up a pen lid and possibly a scattering of loose change. He moves the nozzle towards the surface of the coffee table where a few stray crisps, plus my eye liner — worn down to a stub, but *still* — fly up the hose. "Well, this is good to see," I manage.

"Aw, I couldn't sleep," he says, now vigorously raking at the rug.

I smile, deciding not to point out that 8.17a.m. is officially classed as morning. I'm still awestruck by the fact that he managed to find the hoover and turn it on. "Feeling okay, love?"

"Yeah, I s'pose."

"Any plans for today?"

"Yeah, I'm working, Mum."

"*Working?* What d'you mean?"

He smirks. "Aw, y'know, going out and doing a job for money . . ."

"Yes, I understand the concept but—"

"That man, that *friend* of yours called yesterday and I said, yeah, I'll give it a go . . ." Ah, so it worked! ". . . seeing as I've got a bit of time on my hands," he adds.

"You're helping Paul with the garden? That's brilliant, darling."

Morgan sniffs. "Just till something better comes along."

"Yes, yes, of course. So what time d'you start?"

"Nine, I'd better get ready . . ." Leaving the hoover dumped in the middle of the living room, he plods upstairs.

Well, this is *fantastic* news. Never mind that he has never so much as watered a pot plant before. My son is entering the world of paid employment! I dart to the kitchen, thrilled at the thought of him learning new skills, perhaps falling in love with horticulture and being able to prune and fix things like that capable teenager at Wilton Grange.

I set to work, making a cheese and pickle sandwich and selecting the best-looking apple from the bowl, giving it an extra polish with a tea towel. I pause, trying to remember the other components that should go in a lunchbox. It's been years since I've packed one for

Morgan — he reckoned taking one to secondary school would have resulted in "having my head kicked in" — and we no longer have mini cartons of Ribena knocking about the place. I'd force shallot crisps upon him if I hadn't given them to Paul . . . *I know*: a jar of pecans, for protein. His lanky frame will need building up if he'll be hacking at branches and strimming undergrowth. Christ, a strimmer. I trust Paul will be issuing him with protective clothing?

Morgan reappears, having "got himself ready"; i.e., pulled on wrecked-looking trainers with the laces left undone. "I was wondering what to put your packed lunch in," I remark.

He glances at the nourishing items set out on the kitchen table. "My what?"

"Your packed lunch, love. You'll need something to carry it in . . ."

Air gusts from his nostrils. "Guess you could use my Action Man lunchbox."

I grab a yoghurt from the fridge and a spoon from the drawer. "That'd be perfect. Any idea where it is?"

Morgan guffaws. "Mum, I'm kidding. I'm going to work, not primary school. I'm not taking a lunchbox and I'm not taking . . ." He breaks off and picks up the jar of pecans. "What the hell are these?"

"They're pecans . . ."

"What am I, a squirrel?" He grabs the cling film-wrapped sandwich and rams it into the back pocket of his jeans. "This'll do."

"But what about a drink? It's going to be a hot day, you'll be parched, you might get dehydrated . . ."

"I'll drink water," he says, already making for the door.

"But we don't have any bottled—"

"Nah, it's okay, Mum. It just comes out of the tap."

I arrive at Mrs B's an hour later, with the rest of his packed lunch in my bag and vowing to myself not to keep an eye on him. I want to, of course, in case he gets a thorn in his finger or prongs himself with a rake. He could run over his own foot with the wheelbarrow. Garden hazards are many and varied and I fear for my son's safety even more keenly than when he was being pelted with falafel in York.

To occupy myself, I tackle Mrs B's laundry and make more banana bread, as it's one of the few offerings she seems to have enjoyed recently. She and Victoria are out in the garden, on a swing chair. "Mum needs more fresh air," she declared. "She shouldn't be cooped up indoors."

I don't point out that she's usually eager to usher off her mother for daytime naps, or that Mrs B enjoys plenty of fresh air — but in the shady spot rather than in blazing sun. At least she is wearing a hat.

I take them out tea and banana bread, which Victoria pronounces "quite *cakey*", which I do not take as a compliment. In the distance, Paul and Morgan are working together, clipping an enormous climber that shrouds an entire wall. While Paul nods in my direction, Morgan stares blankly as if he has never seen me before in his life.

It's clear that I must not acknowledge that we have any connection whatsoever. Obviously, I cannot rush over with the pecans and yoghurt and apple. He doesn't need me, I decide, and with Victoria here I feel *doubly* redundant. So I dust the bookshelves and sweep the floors, even though Rosa did the rounds yesterday, and when there's nothing else to do I make a coffee and sit nibbling at the nuts. The thought of that minibar bill, and the fact that no one else on the course would have been so thrilled as to stash all those goodies in their case, makes them stick in my throat. Three days have passed since my drunken call to Hugo. Bet he swapped numbers with Lottie and Tamara and they've all had a good laugh about it. I pull out my phone and scroll through my calls to find the number of his pub. Should I call or not? As he doesn't have my number he can't phone me. Probably doesn't want to, after my inebriated ramblings. But what if he does? The least I should do is apologise for phoning under the influence.

My heart quickens as I make the call. "Sorry," a girl says, "he's not available right now. Would you like to leave a number?"

"Sure," I say, rattling off my number and asking her to repeat it, to make sure she has it right. I make another pot of tea and carry it out on a tray to Mrs B and Victoria in the garden. Victoria is engrossed in a historical novel and grunts her thanks as I set down the tray. Her mother is asleep, her chest rising and falling softly, cheeks already a little pink from the sun.

My phone rings as I step back into the kitchen. "Audrey? It's Hugo . . ."

356

"Oh!" I bluster. "I didn't expect you to call back so soon . . ." If at all, if truth be known. "Erm, I hope you don't mind me phoning again. I sort of wanted to apologise."

"Apologise? Whatever for?" He sounds perky and bright and not remotely appalled to hear from me.

"For . . . for phoning you drunkenly the other night. I'm so embarrassed. It's just, when I found out you were a chef I felt sort of . . . stupid, you know? As if you'd been humouring me and—"

"Well, I'd like to explain . . ."

"No, no, it's fine. It's none of my business whatever it is you do . . ."

"Audrey, can I just say—"

"No, can *I* just say, I'm not usually like that, and I'm sorry—"

"Audrey, stop apologising! Honestly, you have nothing to be sorry about."

Small silence. "Oh. Well, that's all I wanted to say, really. I guess you'd better get back to work . . ."

"I should," he says, sounding endearingly flustered now, "but I wondered, erm . . . look, I know this is a long shot. You're probably busy this weekend . . ."

"What is it?" I ask, intrigued.

"There's, um, a festival on. Not a huge thing — I mean, it's hardly Glastonbury — but should be fun . . ."

"You're inviting me to a festival?" I exclaim.

"Yes. Well, if you think you'd enjoy it, of course. It's not too far from you. About an hour and a half's drive at a guess. I thought of you straightaway but of course, I had no way of contacting you . . ."

"That's, um, really lovely of you," I say, wondering how I'll break it to him that, while I have no idea how much festival tickets cost, I do know I can't afford one.

"I have free weekend passes," he goes on. "The pub I work for, we're rolling out food stalls at festivals this summer, it's our first year . . ."

"So you'll be working?"

"No, no, not at all. I'm just going for the music, the experience. It kicks off tomorrow night . . ."

I am astounded by this: the fact that he seems to want to spend the weekend with me. But as what? Are we talking separate tents, or . . . "Oh, I'm meeting friends for a birthday lunch tomorrow," I say quickly.

"Could you come Saturday, then? I'm hiring a tent . . ." Yep, he's envisaging a one-tent scenario, which could, I must admit, be fun: hanging out with Hugo, having a laugh and a dance, a few drinks . . . and seeing what happens. Only, after the Stevie debacle, I'm not so sure . . . ". . . Everything's provided," Hugo continues cheerfully. "Camp beds, sleeping bags, even lanterns. I guess you'd call it glamping . . ." He laughs. "I don't mean, er — what I should say is, it's a big tent with separate pods for, you know, sleeping . . ."

"Right," I say, thinking, *okaaaay* . . . so he's inviting me as a friend. Still, there's the whole festival thing to deal with, and I've never been to one before. Oh, I know all ages go; I've seen them in magazines, cool middle-aged women in wafty prints and wellies,

358

perhaps with a dash of pink hair colour and lots of jangly jewellery. But how would I fit in with that?

". . . It's very laid-back and friendly, so I've heard," Hugo adds. "A real mix of ages, fantastic food—"

Hell, why not? "Okay, yes — I'd love to come."

"Fantastic," he says, sounding genuinely delighted. "I'll text you directions. Reckon you could make it by lunchtime?"

"Sounds great," I say, finishing the call, and hoping Morgan doesn't think I'm desperate, upping and offing as soon as I'm asked to go anywhere. This is different, though. It's about music and it's not on the motorway. And it's definitely just a friendly thing, which is fine — I'm starting to think that being single is good for a person. Kim goes for weeks — months sometimes — between dates and she manages to achieve more than anyone else I know. She is asked to do make-up for so many weddings and functions these days, she's taking on an assistant. As for Morgan — well, although he's seen Jenna she hasn't stayed over since I've been back from Wilton Grange, and look at him now, quite the horticulturalist. Well, he's operated some secateurs . . .

And of course I'll be fine at a festival. After all, I've been to a cookery school on my own. I visualise myself drifting around barefoot, nibbling on falafel — no, not falafel, I've sort of gone off it. Hand-made burgers, then. Little pots of noodly things and probably some earthy, honey-scented cakes. My stomach swirls in anticipation.

I'm preparing lunch when Victoria appears, face pink from the sun. "Have you seen Mum?" she asks briskly.

"No, I thought she was out in the garden with you?"

"Well, yes, she was, and I must have dozed off — this whole thing, it's been so *exhausting* . . ." Her beads tinkle as she shakes her head. "And when I woke up she was gone."

I frown. "Surely she can't have gone very far."

"No, well, I wouldn't have thought so."

"Let's check the house and gardens . . ." While Victoria darts upstairs — not that Mrs B ever ventures to the upper floor — I hurry out to the garden where I find Paul tending rows of lettuces.

"Have you seen Mrs B?" I ask. "She was sitting with Victoria on the terrace and she seems to have wandered off . . ."

"Really? That's not like her." He frowns and dusts his soily hands on the front of his jeans. "I'll check the front garden, the sheds, the garage . . ."

"I'll try the back." I stride off, scanning the woodland area and dense borders, expecting — or hoping — to see her merely having taken a stroll to smell the flowers. If this were my garden, I'd want to enjoy it *my* way — in peace — before it was snatched away from me.

I find Morgan, beavering away with a hoe — it's even the right way up — in a far corner of the garden behind the house. "Mum, I'm *fine*," he says brusquely.

"I'm not here to check on you. Mrs B's gone missing. Don't suppose you've seen her?"

He shakes his head. "Never even met her."

"You've seen her, though . . ."

"Yeah, from a distance."

360

"Well, there's no mistaking her," I say, trying to keep a trace of exasperation from my voice. "She's the only old lady around here, love."

He shrugs. "Been kinda busy, Mum." He jabs the hoe into the ground. "Is she, y'know, a bit . . . mad?"

"No, darling. She's frail but not at all mad."

He grins with relief. "So I'm not gonna see her, like, wandering naked across the lawn?"

"No, you don't have to worry about that . . ."

"Thank God for that," he exclaims with a shudder.

I find Paul at Mrs B's front door, having been directed by Victoria to check the nearby streets. "She's called the police," he says, "and they're sending someone over. So I'll start looking—"

"I'll help you," I say, although I have no idea where she might have gone. Morgan appears, clearly having recovered from picturing an elderly lady wandering about naked.

"I'll come too," he says, startling me with his eagerness. He glances at Paul, as if looking for approval.

"Good lad," Paul says. "The more the better."

We set off, the three of us splitting up and heading for different streets. My spirits rise every time I glimpse an elderly lady with a puff of soft white hair, then plummet when it's not her. I don't understand this sudden urge to wander; while we take her on outings, Mrs B generally seems perfectly content to remain at home, or in her garden. Her care works perfectly well when it's left to us — but then, Victoria *is* her daughter, and whatever happens next is down to her.

I check the grocer's, in case Mrs B has nipped in to buy herself the right kind of biscuits, plus the newsagent's and bakery in the small parade of shops. No one has seen an elderly lady wandering around alone. Well, not *our* elderly lady. My mobile beeps with a text, and I snatch it from my pocket. *Festival's in grounds of Rosetta Hall, Little Inchingham, fairly close to Derby. Easy to find once you're in the area. Any probs call me. Looking forward to seeing you, Hugo.* I slip my phone back into my pocket, wishing I could feel more excited but unable to think about anything else than finding Mrs B. Should I start calling hospitals again, like I did when Morgan went AWOL? Surely Victoria's doing that. I scan a few side streets of neat, red-brick terraced houses. The only people in sight are a bunch of young mums pushing prams, and a couple of elderly men chatting over a garden wall.

My phone rings. "Morgan? Have you found her?"

"Well . . ." He stops. "There's an old woman sitting on her own in that café . . ."

"Which café?" I bark.

"The one no one ever goes to."

I inhale deeply. "Can you narrow it down for me a bit, love? What's it called?"

"Uh, it's the Italian place . . . hang on a minute . . . Angelo's."

"You think Mrs B's in there?"

"Well, like I said, I've never seen her close up but—"

"What does she look like?"

"Like an old lady. *I* dunno. They all look the same to me . . ." Now is not the time to inform him that people over the age of 30 are in fact human beings too, each with their own quirks and individualities.

"Please, just go in and ask her her name."

"I can't do that," he bleats. "For God's sake, Mum!"

"Why not?"

"You know what old people are like. She'll probably think I'm gonna snatch her purse."

"Of course she won't. You don't look remotely like the purse-snatching sort. Just go in now and ask her if she's Mrs B." I wait, phone pressed to my ear, marvelling at how he can get it together to juggle in public yet is frightened to politely approach an elderly lady in a public place. But then, he doesn't encounter many old people. He hasn't seen my mother for years; her birthday and Christmas cards are greeted with cool indifference, and Vince's parents — although generous at birthdays — have a gaggle of grandchildren and tend to focus on the little ones who are thrilled to see them, who don't play rap music or talk out of the corners of their mouths. It seems a little unfair that Morgan's appeal as a grandson appears to have dimmed over the years.

"It's her, Mum," Morgan blurts out.

"Really? You're sure?"

"Well, yeah, she says so. I didn't ask for any ID." I laugh, and call Paul as I make my way towards the café, and by the time I arrive he has joined Morgan and Mrs B, who are all sitting companionably at a window table.

"We've been looking for you, Mrs B," I exclaim. "Everyone's been so worried."

"I've called Victoria," Paul says quickly. "She knows we're here."

"Never mind that," Mrs B says, raising her cup of tea. "I've been having a chat with this nice young man." She beams across the table at Morgan, who grins awkwardly.

"She was telling me about moving," he offers, fiddling with the newspaper that's lying open at the crossword on the table.

"You mean *not* moving," she says sharply. "Victoria seems to think I'm going to some sheltered place where everyone eats together in a canteen." She shudders.

"Er . . . so you do know about this?" I venture.

She fixes me with a stare. "Yes, of course I do. I've heard her on the phone. She seems to think I'm deaf. I hear everything," she adds, tapping at her right ear.

"Yes, we know you do," Paul says with a smile.

"Well, I don't need to go anywhere," she says firmly. "Why would I? I like my house, thank you very much, and I'm staying right where I am."

"I think Victoria's just concerned," I start, "because the house and garden are such a lot to manage."

"I have plenty of help."

"Yes, I know that, and no one's going to force you to move if you don't want to." Paul gives me an ominous look. How can I say that, when that's precisely what's going to happen?

She takes a fierce bite out of a slice of dark, gooey-looking loaf. "This isn't as good as yours, Audrey. The salty banana kind, I mean."

364

I smile. "Thank you, Mrs B. But maybe, when you've finished your tea and cake, we should think about going back . . ."

"Never mind that," she says with an impatient shake of her head. "Now, come on, Morgan, *concentrate*. Order us another pot of tea and help me with seven across." She glances at me. "He's far better at these than you are."

After Paul has fetched his van and whisked Mrs B back to her house, Morgan and I wander home together. "I'm going to a festival on Saturday," I say, feeling far shyer about my weekend plans than any time I've nipped off to a motorway hotel.

"A festival? What kind of festival?"

"Just a *festival*, love. You know — where there's music outside and people camping . . ."

He splutters. "You mean one for, like, middle-aged people?"

"No, for *all* people," I retort. "For all of mankind to gather together and have fun." He throws me a queasy look. "I don't think there's an age restriction, hon."

"So what're you planning to do there, then?"

I grin. "What d'you think? Just — you know — enjoy the music, hang out, dance . . ."

"Dance? When d'you ever dance?"

"I love dancing actually. I really do. I just don't get the opportunity very often."

He blinks at me and starts to smile. Then he laughs, far too long and loudly in my opinion, so much so that a woman and her small daughter, both clutching ice creams, stare from across the street. "God, Mum," Morgan splutters. "That cookery thing you went to and now you're going to *dance*, in front of people, like a lunatic. What's happening to you?"

Although I can't put it into words, because he'll think I'm "being weird" and won't get it at all, I know exactly what's happened. I might have won dinner lady of the year but — far more important than that — I also seem to have stepped out into the real world again. I am no longer just chief picker-upper of pants. "I'm just going to a festival, love," I say with a smile. "It's really no big deal at all."

CHAPTER
THIRTY-ONE

Sparkling Sundaes

We are gathered together — Ellie, a couple of friends she made through their kids' swimming team, plus me — for her 50th birthday lunch. "We should do this more often," she announces, already several glasses of prosecco down. "Not just for birthdays, I mean. We should have a boozy lunch every weekend!"

"We definitely deserve it," declares Heather, mum to Jessica, long-ago recipient of the invisible ink love note. "You're looking amazing, Audrey," she adds. "I love your new dark hair. Suits you so much better than the blonde . . ." She catches herself. "I mean, you looked great before, but this is so much more . . ." She struggles for the right words. "Anyway, did you manage to get hold of Natalie the other day?"

"Yes, thanks for the number . . ."

"What was that about?"

"Oh, um, Morgan and Jenna are sort of, well, seeing each other."

"Aw, how lovely," says Bernie, whom I know only vaguely, and whose son Jack went to a nearby private school. "Bet it's a big love thing."

"Yes, I guess it is." *Plus, a big pregnant thing.* How would they react if I announced, I'm going to be a grandmother?

"Sometimes I wish I'd had my kids younger," muses Heather, turning to me. "Like you, Aud. Popping one out at . . . how old were you again?"

"Twenty-six. It's not that young."

"Well, these days it is. You're so lucky, you know? He's all grown up and he'll be off and away soon and—"

"What *is* he planning to do?" asks Bernie.

I sip my fizzy water. I'm hoping to do some shopping later; Morgan's birthday is fast approaching. I intend to treat him to the other (affordable) items on his list and would rather avoid making any tipsy purchases. "He's just started a new job actually."

"Oh, really?" Heather beams. "The performing arts thing?"

"Not exactly. He's doing a bit of gardening work." A small silence settles over the table.

"Oh, what happened to the street theatre?"

"That's kind of on hold right now."

"Well, I think it's great," Ellie exclaims. "Fresh air, exercise, being close to nature . . ."

I suspect Bernie is trying to look suitably impressed. "Sounds great!" She turns to Heather. "I heard Jessica's been accepted to do law at Manchester. My God, you must be *thrilled* . . ."

"Yes, we couldn't believe she got in . . . how about Jack? Where's he going?"

Bernie tips her head to one side. "Music school, Liverpool Institute for Performing Arts. He's doing tuned percussion . . ."

Heather swings round to face me. "Morgan should go somewhere like that . . ."

"Yes, he should," I say, glad of the distraction when more prosecco is poured. I remind myself that it *is* brilliant, this stage of life, and the fact that Morgan is toiling away at Mrs B's borders does not make him a lesser person. In fact, I am hugely relieved that he will now have to leave the house, on a regular basis; that, to me, is an achievement in itself. And what he's doing is incredibly useful. He'll discover how to make edible things grow, and we all need vegetables, right? He'll be the provider of vitamins for a future generation of lawyers and percussionists. How can they do their amazingly clever things if they're malnourished?

When we've all parted company I nip into John Lewis to buy Morgan his preferred brand of underwear, then find myself in the baby department where I'm overwhelmed by the sheer quantity of stuff there is these days to keep a baby warm, dry and safe. There's a nightlight that doubles as a thermometer to alert you if the baby's bedroom is too hot or cold. There's a video monitor so you can watch your child as he sleeps. Vince and I didn't even have a normal baby monitor. We just had Morgan, hollering his lungs out if he needed attention and it worked fine for us, without any need for a surveillance device.

I'm browsing the toys now, the forest of mobiles all gently bouncing. There's one just like Morgan's, and I

369

sense a stab of nostalgia at the sight of Eeyore and Tigger dangling there, just like the one Vince and I chose for our baby before he was even born. We were madly in love, and hadn't the faintest notion of what it would entail to care for him. Vince worked long hours in a variety of jobs — kitchen porter, taxi driver — and, without either of us intending it to happen, or even noticing, we slipped from being lovers and friends to sleep-deprived housemates. Consumed by looking after our screamy, colicky baby, I barely noticed us drifting apart. Then our demanding baby wasn't a baby any more; he was a delightful, hilarious five-year-old boy, and I looked at Vince one day and said, "Should we be together?"

"I don't know," he admitted. There was a lot of hugging and gallons of tears, and we both agreed he'd move out and get a place just around the corner. I loved him still, but I wasn't *in* love; I was still idealistic enough to believe in crazy bonkers adoration.

But what if crazy bonkers adoration doesn't exist?

They look in love: the couple with arms entwined at the far end of the baby department. They are admiring a display of nursery clocks on the wall. He wanders off to examine the buggies, while she browses cots. She is honey blonde, petite and incredibly pretty — mid-thirties at a guess — with a suggestion of a bump beneath her pale pink linen dress. He is tall, with light brown hair curling down the back of his neck. "How about this one, Carrie?" he calls over.

She turns, as I do, at the sound of his voice.

Stevie. And Carrie . . . C, from his little red book.

Occasionally, I've wondered who sits on the chairs you sometimes see in department stores, not as part of a furniture display but for customers to sit on. Maybe they're for people who are having a turn, like the one I'm experiencing now. A *bit of a turn*, as Paul put it, *like an old lady*. Overcome by dizziness, I lower myself onto the chair that's been conveniently placed by the brightly-painted toy chests.

Carrie is perusing the baby bedding now: adorable quilts appliqued with rabbits and sailing boats. Something grips my stomach as he strides over to join her. Does he lie to her constantly too? *I'm actually thinking of selling the company. Sick of all this travelling, babe.* Does he spin her the same lines, whilst pouring himself a glass of champagne and handing her a soft drink from the 24-hour shop? Is she treated to a meat feast slice, or does she favour a Cheddar and onion pastie? *I need to get myself a proper place — a home — somewhere that's not just a crash pad . . .*

Stevie winds a protective arm around her waist while she enthuses over gingham cot bumpers until, interest clearly waning, he checks his watch. Carrie turns towards me. As she wanders closer I can see she's a little tired — there are faint grey smudges beneath her eyes — and that her earrings, silver spirals with a hint of sparkly stone, look familiar. I can't be certain, though, and I'm not about to stop her and ask to examine her jewellery.

In fact, what am I doing here at all? Natalie will probably buy most of the essential equipment; she is clearly a highly organised sort. Although I'll festoon the baby with tiny outfits and toys and a Winnie the Pooh mobile, I do not need to be prowling about in John Lewis's baby department when my unborn grandchild is the size of a poppy seed. Nor do I care what Stevie gets up to. I am a single woman, going to a festival tomorrow, like Kate Moss — well, no, not exactly like Kate Moss, but I'm *going* at least. I'll dance in a field and feel happy and free.

Stevie rakes back his hair and yawns without covering his mouth. That's when he spots me, and he sort of freezes, mid-yawn, then shuts his mouth like a trap. "D'you think we'll need a playpen, darling?" Carrie asks.

He blinks at me, as if I might be a store detective who's spotted him cramming a silver christening spoon into his pocket. "Stevie?" she prompts him. "What d'you think? We could put it in the nursery maybe, for when she starts to crawl . . ."

The nursery. So he has a proper home — he must have — with a room that's probably already decorated for the baby girl they know they're going to have. My heart aches, not for me, but for her: she's not Danielle, his young thing, or me, grasping at opportunities for fun. She is having his child.

Stevie's cheeks have reddened, and he has acquired the demeanour of a man who would dearly love to leg it out of the store. Catching my eye, he mouths something to me: *sorry,* I think he's saying. I look right through him, then turn quickly and walk away.

CHAPTER
THIRTY-TWO

Contraband Chocolate

So what *does* a person wear to a festival? I've Googled Glastonbury types — models, singers, the willowy offspring of 70s pop stars — and gawped at a sea of fringed waistcoats, tiny shorts and jingly jewellery. I own no such items. Even my wellies, which haven't been worn for years, have a split in them so water leaks in. I'd been thinking a couple of floral summery dresses but now, on this bright and breezy Saturday morning, I'm not sure I'm capable of making any decision at all.

I barely slept last night. I tossed and turned, thoughts of Winnie the Pooh mobiles spinning around until the pale sky filtered in through my curtains. No matter how many times I reminded myself how lucky I am to have found out — and to be rid of Stevie with his creepy Travelodge ways — I still feel like a colossal fool. And now I'm wondering: why has Hugo asked me along? This tent-with-pods thing: okay, he made it clear he isn't a Brad type, anticipating a shag in return for a couple of shallots or even a free festival pass. But still, there'll only be a sheet of the finest nylon between us — as thin as Morgan's preferred coat — which seems somehow conducive to . . . *stuff happening.*

By late morning I have opted for jeans and an embellished, floaty top, changed my mind and pulled on my orangey dress, and dithered excessively over the nightwear conundrum. Sleeping naked is out of the question, obviously: I don't fancy scrabbling for clothes in the dark if I need to venture out to pee. My fleecy Dalmatian-spot PJs don't seem terribly Kate Moss dangling off a rock star's arm, and nor are they remotely sexy, should such a situation present itself. On the plus side, they're cosy and entirely body covering. I stuff them into my case.

I head downstairs to find Morgan clipping his toenails at the kitchen table.

"Morgan, they're the kitchen scissors!"

"Yeah, couldn't find any nail ones."

"You can't use those, it's so unhygienic . . ."

"You're going to a festival," he reminds me, continuing to snip. "How're you gonna handle that, being a hygiene freak?"

A shard of nail shoots across the room and pings against the fridge. "I'm just saying, the scissors I use for chopping the rind off bacon probably shouldn't be used on the toes of someone who has athlete's foot. I wouldn't say that makes me a hygiene freak . . ."

"Yeah, thanks for that, Mum." He peers up at me through his thick dark hair. "So, is Stevie picking you up?"

I hand him the floor brush to sweep up the clippings. He frowns at it in confusion. "I'm not going with Stevie, love. That's finished."

"Aw, really? I just assumed . . . so what happened?"

374

I busy myself with making toast which I have no interest in eating. "Well, the notebook thing, the code thing . . . turned out I wasn't the only one he was seeing."

"Oh, *Mum*."

"Yes, I know."

"That's so shit . . ." He props the brush against the fridge and drapes an arm around my shoulders.

"It is a bit," I say, taken aback by his impromptu display of affection.

"So who're you going with? Paul?"

"No. Erm, you don't know him, love. His name's Hugo, I met him on the cookery course . . ."

"Hugo," he sniggers. "Sounds posh. So, is he loaded, then?"

"I have no idea, it's not important—"

"Be handy, though . . ."

I smile and kiss his cheek, which causes him to spring away, then indicate the brush. "C'mon, sweep up your clippings. There's plenty of food in the freezer for tonight — you'll be spoilt for choice. Just remember to lock the front door when you go to bed and call me any time, anything you're worried about . . ."

"Stop fussing, Mum." He drops the scissors into the sink, snatches a slice of toast and slathers it with butter.

"What'll you do while I'm away?"

"Uh . . . I dunno. Smoke crystal meth, trash the house . . ." I smirk. "Nothing much," he adds. "Probably just have a few mates round."

"How many's a few? Are we talking two or three or—"

"Mum, just *go*," he exclaims. "Just get out of here and have a great time. I'm perfectly capable of looking after myself."

Of course he is, I reassure myself as I climb into my car. I mean, last time was fine; apart from the microwaved T-shirt and the trauma of a positive pregnancy test, nothing untoward happened at all. And Jenna would still have been pregnant, even if I hadn't waltzed off to Buckinghamshire. It's not as if I could have reversed the fertilisation process merely by being in the same house.

My mobile rings as I put my key in the ignition. "Aud? It's Paul. Sorry, I know you're not due in today . . ."

"It's okay," I say quickly. "Is everything all right?"

"Not really. It's kind of hard to tell. Victoria was adamant I shouldn't phone you but, well, she and her mum have had some kind of row, I've no idea what about, and now Mrs B keeps saying she wants to see you to — I don't know — thank you for something . . ."

I frown. "What on earth for?"

"Honestly, I have no idea."

"Well, I could pop in. I'm actually on my way to a festival, would you believe? It's a sort of . . . well, not a date exactly . . ."

"Oh, you should've said," Paul says briskly. "Just forget I called."

"No, it's fine, there's plenty of time and I'm only five minutes away."

376

It's Paul who lets me in. "Thanks for coming over," he says. "I have to warn you, she's acting really oddly. You'll see for yourself." We stop in the gloomy hallway.

"I'm glad you called," I say, meaning it.

"Well, I'd better leave you to it. Don't want Victoria thinking I'm slacking with the garden . . ."

I look at him, wondering whether I'll ever see him again when he has to leave the cottage. "None of this feels right, does it?"

He shakes his head. "You can say that again . . . will you give me a shout if you need anything?"

"Yes, of course I will." He forces a stoical smile before letting himself out.

I step into Mrs B's bedroom. Victoria, who's sitting bolt upright in the chair beside her mother's bed, gives me a terse smile.

"Oh, you've come," Mrs B says, smiling.

"Yes, it was no trouble . . ." She is sitting up, with embroidered pillows at her back, her bony fingers laced together on her lap. "How are you feeling?" I ask gently.

"I'm fine," she says firmly. "I don't know what all this fuss is about."

Victoria turns to me. "Mum's been very . . . animated all morning. Chattering away, not making too much sense at times, to be frank. She's exhausted herself, that's why I insisted she needs a rest . . ."

"Victoria," Mrs B cuts in sharply, "could you please stop talking about me as if I'm not here?" She turns to me, eyes shining, cheeks flushed pink. "I just wanted to thank you," she adds.

377

In the absence of a chair to sit on, I hover at her bedside. "What for, Mrs B?"

She indicates the empty chocolate box on her bedside table. "These."

"Oh, did you enjoy them? I hoped you would."

"They were delicious," she exclaims. "Quality dark chocolate — the kind I like, not like those cheap biscuits you're always buying me . . ."

"They are lovely," I say. "In the hotel I stayed at, for the cookery course, someone put one on my pillow every evening . . ."

"How very thoughtful," Mrs B says.

I glance past her, to Victoria, who has fixed me with a cool stare. "What d'you mean, Audrey?"

"You know — turndown time. When they fold back your covers to make your bed look more—"

"Yes, I *know* what turndown time is. I mean these chocolates." She picks up the box and frowns at the curly gold script on the lid. "Kirsch Kisses. What are they exactly?"

"Erm, just a present I brought back for your mum . . ."

Victoria fixes her pale grey eyes upon mine. Just for a moment, I feel sorry for her. My own mum wasn't around; she'd hotfooted it to Wales with nothing more than her books, a box of photos and a small holdall of clothes. We had neither a tricky nor a warm, loving relationship, because there wasn't any at all. Somehow, the brittleness between Victoria and her mother seems sadder than having a mother who simply decided she needed to be somewhere else.

"But these are *alcoholic* chocolates," Victoria remarks.

"Yes, but there's only a tiny bit of booze in them. It's mostly cherry and chocolate . . ."

A furrow has appeared between her sparse eyebrows. "Mum shouldn't have any alcohol at all. We don't know how it mixes with her medication." She turns to her mother. "So this is why you've been so difficult today."

"It's *fine* with my pills," Mrs B snaps, eyes flashing angrily. "I asked Dr Barlow last time he was here and he said it was allowed, I told you . . ."

Victoria looks aghast. "Mum, I'm only concerned. I just thought it was best to avoid drinking . . ."

". . . Haven't been allowed a drink for over a year!" Mrs B exclaims, turning to me. "Can you imagine what that's like, Audrey?"

"Er, no," I manage truthfully, "I can't."

Victoria gets up, smoothing down the front of her leaf-patterned dress.

"I'm sorry," I murmur. "I just thought your mum would enjoy them."

"Well, yes, clearly she did. She's polished off the whole box."

"There were only nine," I murmur.

She looks at me levelly. "Could I have a quick word in private, Audrey, if you're not dashing off anywhere?"

"Yes, of course." In fact, I *would* like to be heading off now; the thought of wandering around a field, filled with happy people, feels far preferable to being reprimanded like a naughty child. Victoria leads us to the kitchen, where she indicates for me to take the seat opposite her at the huge oak table.

"So," she starts, "those liqueurs. You are aware that kirsch is something like 70% proof, it's basically *brandy*—"

"Look, Victoria, I'm really sorry if your mum's a bit off colour today, but I'm pretty sure it's nothing to do with the chocolates."

She presses her lips together. "Thank you for your diagnosis, Audrey, but it's always been made very clear to the staff that Mum should not be allowed alcohol."

I nod. "Okay, I am sorry. It won't happen again."

"And *I'm* sorry," she adds, a little tic appearing beneath her left eye, "but I'm going to have to let you go."

I stare at her, unable to form words for a moment. "You mean you're sacking me?"

"Yes. Well, no, not exactly . . ."

". . . But I've helped to look after your mum for four years! She's used to me, she *likes* me . . ." Of course she does, I realise now, despite — or maybe because of — my crapness at crosswords.

"You're just a carer, Audrey," she remarks. "It's a purely professional arrangement."

Something twists in my gut. "Yes, I know, but we've got to know each other pretty well. I mean, she asks for me when I'm not here. And you're firing me because of a box of—"

"It's not just the chocolates," she cuts in. "It's, well, as you're aware, I'm here more these days. I'm looking after things now . . ." *Right: parking her in the garden*

380

in full sun, and not even noticing when she takes herself off for a wander, alone . . . "So we won't need your help any more," she adds. "I'll pay you for the whole of August, of course."

Don't bother, is how I want to reply, but I can't because I need the money. "So that's that, then," is all I can manage as I get up and, with tears prickling my eyes, scurry for the door.

I glimpse Paul grafting away with his strimmer in the woodland area as I stride along the path. "Audrey!" He waves across the garden. "Everything all right?"

"Everything's fine," I call back, quickening my pace towards the gate and clambering into my car, all the while telling myself it *is* fine, and I'll be okay, just like I've always been okay. But why the hell didn't I just give her the ginger cookies?

CHAPTER
THIRTY-THREE

Sunshine Crêpes

When crap happens there's a choice to be made. I could decide I can't face a night in a tent, pod or no pod, not after being sacked. Morgan was right — the hygiene aspect is concerning — and there must be a reason why people never talk about festivals without mentioning blocked/ flooded loos. But then, do I want to be the kind of woman who misses out on new experiences due to concern about toilet facilities? I mean, how very middle-aged. Roughing it never used to faze me. As teenagers, Kim and I set off on a camping trip to Whitby, and when our tent flooded we spent the night in a bus shelter and it was *fine*. So I drive south, radio on low, congratulating myself on getting fired on a day when I wasn't even supposed to be there.

It's a job that's exasperated me sometimes ("In all of my 84 years I've never had a flaky scalp!") but which I've become oddly fond of. No, not oddly fond: just *fond*. I've felt useful there, wanted and needed, and now I'm figuring out how to break the news to Morgan that we'll now have to survive on my dinner lady's salary until I find another job. Plus his gardening earnings, of course. I can't help smiling at the irony:

that *he's* now the one gainfully employed. Maybe he'll start suggesting ways in which I could increase my skill set?

I find Little Inchingham easily. Picture-perfect stone cottages border a village green, and a sign proudly announces the winning of the Derbyshire Villages in Bloom award three years running. There's a tea room, a red phone box which I'll bet no one has ever peed in, and numerous signs pointing towards Rosetta Fest: Britain's Friendliest Festival. My spirits rise as the site comes into view: a gorgeous scoop of a valley, surrounded by woodland and almost entirely speckled with tents. A stately home sits proudly in the far distance.

I pull into the car park and call Hugo. "Great, you found it!" he enthuses. "Can you make your way to Willow Field? I'll meet you at the entrance."

"Sure," I say, telling myself it's okay to be wheeling along a small suitcase, as if I'm off to a Travelodge, rather than having a jaunty rucksack slung about me like the smattering of other latecomers who are drifting towards the camping fields.

Bunting is strung between trees, and jazzy music floats above the hubbub of chatter and laughter from the sun-dappled fields. I pause for a moment, realising the music is coming from a small group of musicians who've set up outside the main festival area. Three teenage girls, all with shiny fair hair and make-up-free faces, are playing a double bass, percussion and a clarinet in the shade of a huge oak. Girls whose music lessons are just normal to them, who were taught proper techniques instead of having to figure things out for themselves. I stand watching, transfixed, until a voice cuts through the air: "Audrey! *There* you are."

"Hugo, hi!" Before I can even process how different he looks — he's wearing a checked shirt over a faded blue T-shirt, plus khaki board shorts — he's pulled me in for the kind of hug you'd only give to someone you're genuinely happy to see. "So great you've come," he adds, grabbing my case and wheeling it towards the camping field entrance.

"Well, thanks for asking me," I say, seduced immediately by the delicious smells wafting from food stalls and the sense that everyone is here to have fun. Teenagers are strolling in languid groups, and families are picnicking beside their tents. There are jugglers and dogs and numerous, mostly barefoot children scampering about. "This is wonderful," I add.

"It's lovely, isn't it?" Hugo says. "Last night was great but the line-up's better tonight." In fact, I've already checked the bands on the festival's website and hadn't heard of any of them. But no matter. Like my five days at cook school I'll regard it as an educational experience.

We arrive at Hugo's tent, where I'm introduced to his friends — Joey and Mick, jovial beardy types who are manning the food stall — and immediately handed a beer. "You can leave your stuff here," Hugo says, showing me into the enormous, clearly brand new tent, which does indeed have the promised separate pods. Mine has already been set up with an inflatable bed, plus a pristine sleeping bag and a proper pillow. "Look comfy enough for you?" Hugo asks with a grin.

"It's perfect," I say, parking my case and emerging from the tent to glimpse a group of teenagers spreading out a blanket a few feet away. The three girls and three boys — all around Morgan's age — flop down on it and proceed to tuck into slices of pizza. Someone strums a guitar, and another takes pictures with her phone. "Look at those kids," I murmur to Hugo. "I assumed they'd all be off their faces by now but they're having such a cool time."

"Yeah, I don't think they'll bother us," he says. "I was a bit worried when I saw they were in the next tent."

"I don't mind being near teenagers," I say, laughing. "I'm kind of used to it, you know?"

"Yeah, of course you are." In fact, I almost wish Morgan were here, to witness these kind of young people: the girls chatting animatedly and one of the boys now — amazingly — sewing some kind of appliqued patch onto the front of a T-shirt. That's another life lesson I should have taught Morgan: how to sew. I should have given him a tutorial on my ancient sewing machine — the one Mum didn't bother taking with her when she left. He could be running up his own clothes now instead of getting his girlfriend pregnant. The sewing boy catches my eye and smiles. "All right?" he asks.

"Yes, I'm good, thanks."

"Perfect day, isn't it?" He beams up at the searing blue sky.

"It really is," I reply, deciding it *is* possible for teenagers not to be allergic to adults, and regard us as spoilers of fun.

Hugo and I set off to explore, meandering through bustling fields and past the acoustic stage, where a girl with her hair secured in dozens of tiny plaits is singing a beautiful lilting song. I whip out my phone and take pictures of a woman in a Flamenco outfit — who poses obligingly — and a man on stilts, hula-hooping with aplomb. Let's hope Morgan doesn't see *this* on YouTube. "Documenting everything again," Hugo remarks.

"Can't help it," I laugh. "I don't understand why I've never done this before. Been to a festival, I mean. It's such a lovely atmosphere."

Hugo smiles. "It's actually my first time too."

"Really? I got the impression you did this every summer, that you were an old hand . . ."

"Nope, it's one of those things I've never got around to doing, you know? The opportunity came up and I thought, why not?"

"Like the cookery course?" I ask, giving him a quick look as we wander past stalls selling rainbow-emblazoned T-shirts.

"Yes, sort of." We have arrived at a clearing in the field where families have gathered, all chilling out in the sunshine. We buy beers, and Hugo shrugs off his checked shirt and spreads it on the grass. "Here, you can sit on this."

"On your shirt? I don't need to, really."

386

"Please, you don't want grass stains on your lovely dress." Such manners. After being lurched at by Brad — not to mention *three*-timed by Stevie — it's extremely pleasing. "Remember there was something I wanted to explain?" he ventures, plucking at the grass.

I glance at his handsome profile and nod. "About you being a proper trained chef?"

"Yeah." He pushes back his hair distractedly. "I'm sorry about that. I should've said."

"It doesn't really matter," I say lightly. "It's none of my business . . ."

"Yes, it is," he says firmly.

I shrug. "Well, it did seem a bit weird, you know. Being so evasive, I mean."

"Yeah, I know. I wish I'd just been straight with you from the start. But, you see . . ." He exhales. "When I first saw you, and you were having that washing machine conversation, I was, I don't know . . . intrigued by you. You weren't the kind of person I'd have expected . . ." He breaks off. "Whatever I say is going to sound awful. What I mean is, I thought it would all be Lottie and Tamara types, like the girls I went to school with, and there you were, a dinner lady . . ."

Ah, here we go . . . "Did you think I'd be intimidated by you?"

"No, not exactly. But I thought, she looks interesting, I'd like to get to know her. And I reckoned, if you thought we were in the same boat — you know, beginners together — then I'd have a better chance . . ."

"A better chance of what?" I'm smiling now, while Hugo fidgets awkwardly.

"Of getting to know you," he says quietly.

I am dumbfounded by this. "You didn't have to pretend," I say.

"No, I know that now. That's why I asked you here, to make it up to you so we can just, y'know, hang out, have fun . . ."

"Hugo, it's fine, really. I'm so glad I came." I sip my already tepid beer. "So, why did you go to Wilton Grange anyway?"

"To learn classic techniques from one of the best . . . well, *reportedly* one of the best . . . just like you, really." He grins. "Honestly, it still feels as if I have a lot to learn. So . . . d'you forgive me?"

"Of course I do," I exclaim.

He reaches out and squeezes my hand, and little sparks shoot up my arm. "C'mon," he says, pulling me up, "we should grab something to eat."

We find Mick manning Hugo's pub's stall, where a sizeable queue has gathered. "On the house," Mick says, handing me a flatbread crammed with pulled pork and slathered in spicy sauce; it's utterly delicious. We eat, and we drink, and amble about with no particular destination in mind, the afternoon stretching on in a lovely warm, beery haze. We watch a boisterous Cajun band, and discover three girls with beehives singing impeccable harmonies in a marquee. I glance around at the crowd that's gathered: all ages, from older ladies wearing their long greying hair loose, to children in fancy dress outfits and dreamy-looking young women carrying their babies in papooses. Bet they're not the kind of mothers who "blow things up".

388

Hugo and I leave the marquee and amble past a steam-powered merry-go-round, its golden horses gleaming in the early evening sun. Somehow, without me realising how it happened — or which of us made the move — Hugo and I are now holding hands. So it's *not* just a friends thing, I decide. It's a date, of sorts. An overnight date, not in a faceless hotel but a tent, with pods, and who knows what'll happen? "Can I get you anything?" he asks, as we arrive at more food stalls, the air heady with sugary scents from the crêpe stall.

"Ooh, I'd love one of those," I say. "I'll get them, you've been buying everything—"

"No, no, allow me." I smile as he darts off, returning with perfectly golden crepes on paper plates, plus a bottle of water I hadn't asked for but which now, after a steady trickle of beer all afternoon, I'm grateful for.

"You're very kind, Hugo," I say. "Chivalrous, I mean. I know that sounds terribly old-fashioned."

He chuckles. "Well, I try, you know. It seems important. I've always been that way."

I study his soft grey eyes. "You mean holding doors open, walking on the road side of the pavement, that kind of thing?"

"Yeah." He grins. "You're okay with that?"

"I . . . well, I'm sure I would be. I've just never known anyone like that before."

"You wouldn't find it patronising?"

I laugh. "No, of course not. Everyone wants to be treated nicely, don't they? I don't see anything wrong with that."

"I'm glad you feel that way. With my ex, Polly, I'd always squeeze out her toothpaste onto her toothbrush ready for her before she went to bed."

"Wow, that's so thoughtful." Mrs B's bowl-spitting routine flits into my mind. "So . . . what happened with you two, if it's okay to ask?"

"Yes, of course it is. She blamed the hours I was working, and she was probably right — I'd be at the restaurant from ten in the morning till 2a.m. some days. It wasn't exactly conducive, you know?"

I nod. "So she was at home, doing the parenting thing . . ."

"Well, no, not exactly." A trace of defensiveness has crept into his voice.

"I just meant, you know, being on your own with a child can be tough. It couldn't be helped, you were working, supporting your family . . ."

"No," he says quickly, "Emily's at boarding school, remember?"

"Yes, but I meant when she was younger . . ."

"Well, she went when she was seven."

"Seven?" I gasp.

He looks at me and pulls a strip off his crêpe. "I can tell you're shocked. You see, in our families — mine and Polly's, I mean — it's just what we do . . ."

"Hugo," I cut in, "I'm not judging you. I'd be the last person to do that. Anyway, I guess she always comes home for the holidays . . ."

"Sometimes, yes, but then there have been summer schools, activity camps, music courses, that kind of thing . . ."

I nod as we finish our crêpes. A huge, sprawling family wanders past: mum and dad, plus five children, ranging from a wild-haired toddler to a stunning teenage girl in frayed denim shorts and a bikini top. They are joking with each other in the way close families do, the way Morgan and I would, on our trips to Scarborough when he viewed a whole day with me as a fantastic treat. However far from ideal my own set-up might seem — just Morgan and me, mucking along together — I really wouldn't have planned things so very differently. Maybe, if he'd had a posh education, he'd have headed straight to university instead of getting his girlfriend pregnant. But it's happened and, I decide, we'll all muddle through; I *know* we will.

Hugo grabs my hand. "Hey, there's a band I'd like to see at eight. Let's go down to the front."

As we stroll down the gently sloping hill, I tell myself: *be open-minded about the boarding school thing*. It's just the way things are done, in Hugo's milieu. We merge with the crowd before the main stage, and wend our way towards the front. He wraps an arm around my shoulders and I catch a hint of his scent: deliciously cirtrussy and fresh.

My heart soars as he squeezes my hand, and the band starts up: a band I should have heard of but haven't, because it feels as if my head has been filled with mundane practicalities for as long as I can remember. I'm transfixed by the bluesy music that seems so right for this glorious August evening. The four young men are throwing themselves into their music, giving it their all just as I did as a girl, standing

391

alone on the dusty school stage. I felt brave then, fearless, actually — even though there was no parent watching proudly in the audience — just as I do now, at the prospect of being a grandmother and finding a new job. It'll be okay, I decide. I've made a proper French lemon tart and fought off an amorous celebrity chef. Really, what is there to be afraid of?

Hugo and I join in with the cheers for an encore as the band leaves the stage. They reappear and play on as the sky turns from lilac to inky blue, and I turn just as Hugo does. We look at each other, and he smiles, and then we are kissing and kissing with music floating all around and the stars twinkling above. The sewing boy was right. If a day can be perfect, this has definitely been it.

CHAPTER
THIRTY-FOUR

Mr Whippy Ice Cream

Just go with it, I tell myself as we make our way back through the crowds. *See what happens.* Just because we've kissed — which was completely lovely — doesn't mean there'll be any hopping from pod to pod tonight. And if we do, which doesn't seem entirely out of the question as we are walking with arms entwined, then that's fine. It'd be a new thing for me, doing it in a tent. Vince and I went camping a few times — it was the only kind of holiday we could afford — but with Morgan sleeping between us there was no chance of any kind of shenanigans happening. So, if it does happen it'll be a first for me, doing it with just a layer of the thinnest nylon to separate us from the outside world. Heck, we'll have to be quiet.

I catch myself, thoughts racing ahead, jumping the gun as usual, wondering if our entwined bodies will somehow be silhouetted against the nylon for all to see. I didn't bring any condoms either. Terribly remiss, I know, but it didn't actually cross my mind. Stevie always brought supplies and I'm long out of the habit of carrying any about my person "just in case". Until that night in York, when I met my philandering bastard of a boyfriend, *just in case* never seemed to happen.

And now, I realise with a racing heart, it really could. It's 1.20 a.m., and the festival is in full swing. Still holding hands, we stop to watch a man in a pom-pom-covered hat playing some kind of home-made stringed instrument made from a biscuit tin, then wend our way back to the camping field. "Oh, Christ," Hugo murmurs as his tent comes into view.

"What's wrong?"

"Those kids. The teenagers. They're still up."

I laugh. "Of course they are. I wouldn't have imagined they'd be tucked up in their sleeping bags by ten o'clock."

He smiles tensely. "No, but look — they seem to have multiplied." I follow his gaze, and he's right: the sewing boy and his friends have been joined by a dozen or so more, and they have congregated in the space between our tents.

"They're not causing any trouble, though," I add.

"Yeah," he mutters, "guess so." There are smiles and nodded greetings from the kids, and one couple are kissing fervently.

"Sorry," slurs a boy with a fuzz of ginger hair, as Hugo and I tread carefully between them. "Are we in your way, mate?"

"Not at all," Hugo says gallantly, stepping over a girl who is clearly inebriated, her head resting on the sewing boy's lap. Hugo disappears into the tent and emerges with two bottles of beer, one of which he hands to me. We find a small patch of vacant grass and sip from our bottles.

"It's been such a lovely day," I venture.

"Yes, it really has." He glances over as the teenagers burst into rowdy laughter. "I hope they're going to calm down, though," he adds.

"I'm sure they will."

"D'you think so? They look like they're up for the night to me."

I stifle a yawn. "Does it matter?"

"I s'pose not," he says. "You're tired, though, I can tell. Shall we turn in for the night?"

I smile. *Turn in*, how very quaint: it's what you should do after turndown time. "Maybe we should," I say. We head into the tent, the teenagers' chatter still audible. "Well, goodnight then," I add, wondering if my Dalmatian pyjamas are going to put in an appearance tonight.

"Goodnight, Audrey." Hugo's gaze meets mine. "Look, I'm sorry if I seem a bit out of sorts tonight. You see, I deliberately chose what I thought would be the quietest field, I really didn't expect—"

"It's fine," I cut in, laughing. "Honestly, I don't mind a few rowdy kids . . ." I pause, and just as I'm thinking, he has a lovely mouth and I'd very much like to kiss him again, he kisses *me*. It's such a gentle, tender kiss, it takes my breath away. Even the noise of the boisterous teenagers seems to melt away as he pulls me close. We are kissing harder now, and I shiver with desire.

"You're so lovely," Hugo murmurs into my ear. "I thought that the first time I saw you . . ."

"You're fucking mad!" A girl's voice cuts through the air.

We spring apart.

"No I'm not," someone snaps. "If you'd just listen to what I'm saying instead of being so bloody *right* all the time . . ." Sounds like sewing boy.

"So you're saying he was a good guy?" the girl shrieks.

"Who?" yelps someone else. "Who're you on about now?"

"Hitler," sewing boy barks.

"Oh, for Christ's sake," mutters Hugo.

"You're saying Hitler was a hero?" someone slurs. "You're mental, Tom . . ."

"Nah, nah, what I'm saying is, you could look at it like he's a genius, right? I mean, if you forget all the bad stuff he did . . ."

"Like killing millions of people," someone cuts in.

"Yeah, yeah, if you forget about that, look at what he did . . ."

"Like what?"

"Well, he designed the VW Beetle . . ."

Someone honks with laughter. "He wasn't a fucking car designer, Tom."

"Nah, nah, what was it he invented then . . . Mr Whippy ice cream?"

"Jesus Christ," Hugo exclaims as I suppress a laugh.

"That was Margaret Thatcher," adds one of the other boys.

"Is that true?"

"Yeah!"

"Nah, it was Hitler, he had this thing about making ice cream . . ."

"Mr Whippy wasn't around then in, like, the forties."

"How d'you know?"

"I just *know*."

"Chrissakes, I can't stand this," Hugo mutters, making for the door of the tent.

"What are you doing?" I hiss.

"I'm going to tell them to shut the fuck up."

I grab at his arm. "Please don't. It'll seem so, I don't know—"

"So what?" he counters, nostrils flaring.

"Middle-aged," I exclaim. "Just leave them to it. They'll quieten down soon . . ."

He turns. "D'you want to spend all night listening to a load of pissed kids ranting a load of nonsense?"

"No, not especially, but I don't really feel like some big confrontation—"

"What would you do if Morgan was behaving like this?"

I stop short, dumbfounded by his question. "You mean, if he was going on about Hitler and Mr Whippy?"

"Yes!" Hugo exclaims.

"Well . . . I'd probably find it funny."

"Really?"

I look at him, wondering how I might explain. "That's teenagers, Hugo. They think they know everything, and that we know nothing. In fact, it's a miracle we've managed to feed and clothe ourselves for forty-odd years . . ."

"Yes," he counters, "but they're all off their faces."

"But don't you see?" I shoot back. "Even when they're not, they're just as opinionated. Isn't Emily like this?"

He looks horrified. "Christ, no, not like this." He shakes his head distractedly. "Sorry, Audrey. It's just, I didn't imagine we'd have to listen to crap like this all night . . ."

"Yes, I know, but *please* don't go out and confront them. They won't take any notice anyway."

He frowns, looking exhausted now. "You think so?"

"I know so," I say, meeting the gaze of this kind, handsome man who's bestowed me with a free festival pass and behaved more chivalrously than anyone I've encountered since Vince and I got together. I know it's possible — we could fall into a pod together and do all manner of lovely things — but the moment has passed. "Shall we just go to bed?" I ask. "Separately, I mean."

"Of course," he says quickly. "I didn't expect . . ."

"Look, Hugo, I just . . ." I shrug. "I'm not sure it'd feel right, you know?"

"No, no, it's fine," he says. Then he kisses me, very chastely, like a cousin might, on the cheek. "Goodnight, then," he adds, clambering into his own pod and zipping up the entrance very swiftly, right to the top.

The teenagers continue to party throughout the night. While I'm not sure if Hugo is hearing all of this, I am aware of several noisy and dramatic puking incidents, which don't seem all that shocking really: Sunshine Valley Holiday Park was littered with vomiting teens and the staff were used to mopping up the damage. Maybe it's me, I reflect, snug in my sleeping bag, my Dalmatian pyjamas buttoned up to the neck. Maybe this kind of behaviour *is* out of order, and I should be outraged, as Hugo clearly was. Perhaps I've just been too lenient.

Hugo's soft snores drift from his pod. He's a good man, I decide; successful, considerate and certainly a catch. Not for me, though. Maybe he's thinking the same or, more likely, he's still simmering in annoyance over those teenagers. They have calmed down now, as I said they would; although they're still chatting, they seem to have forgotten about Hitler and Mr Whippy.

I sit up, wide awake now, and unsure whether I have slept at all. Somewhere in the far distance, someone is playing an acoustic guitar. I pull on a sweater over my pyjama top and creep out, with the intention of making my way to the loos. There's just the sewing boy, and a girl with a cute pixie haircut, huddled close together on their blanket. "Hiya," he says lazily.

"Hi," I say.

He grins awkwardly. "Sorry if we've kept you awake."

"That's okay. I'm not sure I'd have slept anyway."

"You want some of this?" He holds out a half-empty wine bottle.

"No, I'm okay, thanks."

"Look," the girl says sleepily, "at all the stars."

I glance up: the sky is sparkling, as if sprinkled with glitter. "It's beautiful," I murmur.

"Tom knows about stars," she adds.

"Really?"

He smiles. "Yeah. I'm studying astronomy."

"Wow, that must be amazing."

"Yeah, it is, and it's a perfect sky tonight. C'mon, lie down and look." He indicates a vacant expanse of blanket.

I pause, frowning, reluctant to intrude. "Go on," the girl says. "Tom'll tell you the names of all the constellations."

"Okay," I say, stretching out on my back beside them.

"So that's Orion," he starts, "and that bright one, that's the Pole Star. And over there's the Great Bear and the Plough. There's Gemini, Dorado and Hercules . . ." I fade off, lulled to sleep by his lilting voice, and when I wake up I am still lying on the blanket outside.

It strikes me, as I turn to see the boy and girl asleep in each other's arms, that I shouldn't be here any more. Tom's grubby toes are poking out from their open sleeping bag, and a flatbread with some kind of oily filling has been trampled into the ground close to the girl's head. The scene is utterly romantic, and now I know, with absolute certainty, where I need to be.

Hugo doesn't exactly seem disappointed that I am leaving early. The fact that he trotted off to fetch us coffee and cartons of steaming hot porridge suggests that there's no bad feeling between us. He is, however, worried about me.

"Why did you sleep outside, Audrey? Was it my snoring?"

"No, it wasn't that," I say, picking out a clump of dirt from between my toes. "I could still hear you outside. Tents are very thin, you know."

"No, really?" He looks aghast.

"It wasn't your snoring," I say, laughing. "I just went outside because . . ." I tail off. "I sort of had an urge to be under the stars. It was such a beautiful night."

He nods and smiles. "So, you're still keen to head home?"

"Yes, if that's okay."

"Worried about Morgan being alone?"

"Not exactly," I say. "There are just . . . things I should see to at home. I hope you understand." He nods, and sees me off to my car.

"Let's stay in touch, Audrey," he says. "Last night was lovely."

"It really was," I say, squeezing his hand.

"And Lottie and Tamara have been in contact," he adds. "Maybe we could all get together?"

"Yes, I'd love that. Count me in." We hug tightly, and I climb into my car, registering my mud-streaked shins and realising I haven't so much as glanced in a mirror since I left home yesterday. Still, I probably look the part — grubby, dishevelled — as if I do this kind of thing all the time . . . Yeah, I think as I drive north, radio blaring now, I really can fit in anywhere. Maybe Morgan, Jenna and I could go to a festival together? There were tons of children there, and I could look after the baby while the two of them wander off to festivally things . . . Being a grandmother needn't mean quietly knitting, or disappearing into a world of beige. It'll suit me, I decide, not because I need to feel needed exactly — but because I need to be *useful*. And this is my family now, about to grow before my very eyes: not just Morgan and me, our tiny unit of two, but Morgan, Jenna and my grandchild. And maybe — just maybe — someone else will be in my life too . . .

After an hour or so I pull up at a service station, fetch a coffee and something vaguely resembling a madeleine from the café. Back in my car, I call Morgan's mobile. "You're coming home now?" he gasps. "But you said you'd be home this evening, that's what you told me—"

I frown and sip my Americano. "I've just changed my plans, okay? Is that a problem, love?"

"No, no, it's *fine* . . ."

"Morgan, why are you freaking out about me coming home early? What's going on?"

"I'm not freaking out!" Christ, he's had a party. The place is covered in broken glass and puke.

"What on earth's happened?" I exclaim.

"Nothing," he snaps. "Nothing's happened at all."

My heart feels leaden as I turn off the motorway. Perhaps something really is broken this time and he's embarking on an emergency fixing mission. At least there'll be no startling pregnancy discovery. Jenna cannot be any more pregnant than she already is.

It's just gone eleven when I pull up outside out house. I let myself in — the door is unlocked, come on in, burglars, help yourselves! — and there's no sign of life, despite Morgan having answered my call earlier. He must have sloped back to bed. On the plus side, nor are there signs of party-inflicted damage, or any hungover teenagers lying about. "Morgan?" I call upstairs. "You okay, love?"

No response. I pick up the scattering of mail that's obviously been lying behind the door since yesterday, and take it through to the kitchen. It's clean and tidy — suspiciously so. The sink is empty of dishes and the work surfaces are gleaming. I lower myself onto a chair and flip through the mail: phone bill, junk mail, a leaflet detailing up and coming events at the community centre. And a letter, the white envelope handwritten.

A Welsh postmark. I tear it open.

Dear Audrey,

How lovely to hear from you, and what a surprise. About Morgan, I mean. I'm delighted, I really am. I'm sure he'll be a wonderful father. Do you think I could help?

I stare at her words. Help, with the baby? And how does she know what kind of father Morgan will be?

Things haven't worked out with Brian, she continues. *I'm sorry, a long time ago I made a mistake . . .*

I blink at the page. It has a ragged edge; looks as if she tore it out of a jotter.

If it's not too late, she has written in her very best handwriting, *I'd really like to make things right.*

Love, Mum xxx

"Mum?" I look up to see Morgan, fully dressed in jeans and T-shirt, despite it not yet being midday.

"Hi, darling." I fold the letter in two.

"What's that?" He narrows his dark eyes.

"Um, just a letter from Mum."

"What, from *your* mum?"

"Yes." I unfold it and hand it to him.

He frowns and peers at it. "She wants to *help?*"

"Yes, I know, love . . ." I shrug and busy myself by making coffee.

"But . . ." He places it on the table and exhales. "When has she ever helped? I mean, you've done everything, Mum, all by yourself . . ."

I laugh dryly, overcome by an urge to hug him which, amazingly, he allows. "I didn't think you'd noticed."

"God, 'course I have." He disentangles himself and pushes his fringe out of his eyes. "It's just . . . d'you want her getting involved, after all this time?"

"I don't see why not, do you? I mean, I think we'll need all the help we can get . . ."

"Yeah," he laughs, "I guess. Anyway, how was the festival?"

"Oh, you know. It was fun."

He grins, studying my face. "Overdo things a bit, did you? You should be careful at your age."

"Well, I did sleep under the stars," I tell him. "I even learnt the names of some constellations."

"Right, so it was *educational*, then." He barks with laughter. "Yeah, I thought you must be a bit wrecked . . ."

"Morgan, I'm not wrecked!"

". . . 'Cause you haven't noticed, have you?"

"Oh, I have, love. The place looks great. In fact, the kitchen's tidier than I left it. Thank you, love, it feels good to be back."

"I am capable of looking after things around here," he adds, perching on the edge of the table. "You, er . . . haven't noticed anything else, have you?"

"No, should I have?" He glances towards the window, and I follow his gaze. "Oh!" I gasp, registering the view. The wheelie bins have disappeared from our back yard, and the plain brick walls now bear a row of hanging baskets bursting with bright yellow flowers. "Oh, Morgan! They're lovely. Did you put those up?"

He nods, grinning, and follows me as I step out into the breezy morning. I stare, speechless for a moment. Our once unlovely yard has been filled with tubs of blooms, and a wrought iron table bears yet more pots of flowers. "My God, Morgan, this is beautiful . . ." Pale pink roses cling to a trellis. It is a perfect miniature garden. Tears spring to my eyes as I stare, taking in the muddle of colours and scents.

"Like it?"

"Yes, of course I do. But how did you—"

"Oh, I had it all planned," he says airily, "and I was right on schedule till you phoned this morning. I had to work like mental to get it finished. God, Mum, the stress you cause me sometimes!"

"I'm sorry, love," I say, laughing.

". . . So I called Paul to give me a hand . . ."

"Paul helped you with all of this? But . . . how did you manage to buy everything? It must've cost a fortune . . ."

Morgan shrugs. "It was actually his idea. He had loads of spare plants and he asked me if thought, y'know . . . you'd like them."

"Like them?" I gasp. "I love them, thank you."

". . . and I picked up the table yesterday. There was a card in a newsagent's window, an old man was selling it. Paul took me over in his van." He pauses. "I felt a bit crap, to be honest, about your birthday. Jenna gave me such a hard time, y'know, about that list I gave you . . ." He rolls his eyes in a *women, what can you do?* sort of way.

"But you don't have any money, Morgan. You can't have been paid yet . . ."

"Nah, I sold my unicycle."

"Oh, darling!"

He shrugs awkwardly. "It's okay. Dan wanted it. He'd been on at me for ages. And I thought, y'know, it's a bit like the spy stuff in that box. I mean, God knows why you've kept it all . . ."

"It's just . . . I don't know. It's hard to let go sometimes."

"Yeah, but it's a bit childish, Mum. The unicycle, I mean. And I reckoned, well . . ." He beams at me, squinting in the sun. "I'm going to be a dad, aren't I? So I thought it was time I grew up."

Paul arrives to "finish off" the garden, and I'm taken aback by how thrilled I am that he's here. "It'd have looked even better if you'd come home this evening, like you'd planned," he teases, crouching as he eases delicate blue plants into the spaces in a tub.

I pour our coffees at the wrought iron table. "It couldn't look any better than this," I say truthfully. "You'd better tell me what everything is, though, and what I need to do to look after it."

He grins. "Morgan can take charge of maintenance. He's a good kid."

"Yes, I know he is." He takes the seat beside me and sips his coffee. Despite his heroic efforts on the gardening front, I am sort of relieved that Morgan decided to call Jenna when Paul showed up, and that the two of them have headed off to York for the day. "To look at baby stuff," Morgan explained. "Yeah, I know it's a bit soon but we want to be prepared, you know? Get an idea of what we'll need."

You don't need much, I wanted to say. Just each other. But I knew he'd roll his eyes, because what does a 44-year-old dinner lady know about love?

"So how was the festival?" Paul ventures.

"I loved it," I say. "The bands, the atmosphere, the amazing food . . . I really need to start cooking more interesting stuff. I have all the recipes from Wilton Grange, and I should teach Morgan to cook for himself — for his family . . ." I break off, realising I'm babbling.

"Maybe I could cook you a proper French meal?" I add, all in a rush. "To thank you for all this, I mean?" I cast my gaze at the explosion of flowers. "How are you with mussels? And poulet en cocotte bonne femme? Excuse my accent," I add. "It actually means housewife's chicken. Not very glamorous, huh?" I laugh, catching myself. Christ, will he think I'm asking him out? Maybe I am. I look at him, and my heart turns over when he smiles.

"That sounds delicious," he says. "So, um, did it work out? The date part of the festival, I mean?"

"Oh that didn't really . . ." I tail off. "It wasn't quite what I thought, what I wanted . . ." I shrug.

"Audrey," he says, "I'd really love to come to dinner but—" Ah, here we go.

"I could make us a French lemon tart," I barge on. "Everyone likes lemon tart, don't they? Mine was a bit bumpy — *frumpy* really — but I'm sure, if I tried it again and took it slowly, step by step . . ."

"You know, *I* can cook," he cuts in with another disarming smile. "What I wanted to say is, why don't you have some time off and I'll cook for you? Come over later, if you like."

"Oh! Yes, that would be lovely . . ."

"About seven okay?"

"Sounds great," I say.

"And could you remind Morgan that we've got an early start tomorrow?"

"Yes, of course," I say, smiling. *It's not a date*, I tell myself, glowing with happiness as Paul climbs into his van. *It's just dinner with a friend.*

This time, I don't stress about what to wear. I don't feel the need to dress up, to try and youth-ify myself, as I did on those motorway dates, setting off in the gravymobile in a dress, heels and stockings, for crying out loud. And nor am I compelled to pick my least sexually provocative dress — the one with the prim neckline and below-the-knee hem, as worn to dinner with Brad. No, tonight, I'm just going as me. After all, Paul has mostly seen me at work, tending to Mrs B. He won't be expecting a new-improved Audrey, dressed up to the nines. So I pull on jeans and a top patterned with tiny flowers, and when I go to sort out my hair, with the intention of possibly dabbing on some product or other of Morgan's, I realise it doesn't need any attention at all. It's fine, just as it is.

With time to spare, I flip open my laptop. Not to Google Stevie or Hugo, or even Wilton Grange, but to browse eBay. It's been so long since I've bid on anything, it takes three goes to remember my password. Now I'm logged in, not to browse the spy kits or Action Men but the woodwind section . . .

Yamaha clarinet. Some signs of cosmetic wear but fully operational, case included. I close the page and open it again. I pace around the living room and pick up a stray sock from the floor. Then I fetch my make-up bag and slick on some lipstick: the one Kim bought for me. Although it's scarily bright, I *think* I can carry it off. I pull out my hand mirror and flash myself a big cherry red smile, and place my bid.

CHAPTER
THIRTY-FIVE

Classic French Cuisine

He chops onions like a true professional, knife rapping briskly against the wooden board. I watch, sipping the chilled white wine he's handed me, wondering why, despite it only being my second visit here, I feel instantly at home. "Bit behind schedule," Paul explains. "Sorry, I planned to have everything ready, but Victoria dropped by and I needed to talk to her . . ."

I take a seat at the small pine kitchen table and glance at the jaunty crockery neatly arranged on a shelf. "It's fine, Paul. I'm not in a hurry to rush off, you know."

He catches my eye and smiles, triggering a flurry of butterflies in my stomach. "I'm very glad to hear that."

"So . . . Victoria. Don't tell me she's had an offer on the house?"

He shakes his head as he drops the onions into the pan, plus a crushed garlic clove and a generous slosh of brandy. "No, it's not even on the market yet. In fact, it's not being sold."

I stare at him, incredulous. "Has she changed her mind?"

"Not exactly," Paul says. "It's more a case of . . . well, you'll find out." He breaks off to lift a dish of chicken from the fridge, which he proceeds to toss into the pan with a sizzle.

"Paul, what's going on?"

"It's just a thing I made up," he says, stirring the pan and deliberately misunderstanding, I suspect.

"Um . . . can I help you at all?"

"No, no, it's fine. It's all under control." He laughs. "At least, I *think* it is . . ." He checks his watch, then chops a mound of tomatoes and throws them in too, plus a scattering of fresh herbs and a generous slosh of wine. "Actually," he says, "would you mind keeping an eye on this, just for a few minutes?"

"Yes, of course. But is everything okay—"

"Just keep it simmering gently," he adds.

"I'm sure I'll manage," I say with a smile.

He flushes. "Yes, of course you will." He laughs distractedly. "Look, sorry, my timings are all to pot. I need to pop out for a minute. Help yourself to more wine . . ."

"But where are you going—" I start.

"I meant to say," Paul cuts in, taking a big sip of his own wine — the way I do, when I need Dutch courage — "we have another guest joining us for dinner. I hope you don't mind." Before I can ask anything more, he's rushed out of the door. I frown, wondering who he's invited. Surely he's not planning to set me up with one of his friends? He doesn't strike me as the matchmaking sort and I absolutely don't *want* to be set up, thanks very much. I sip more wine and try to quell the disappointment that's gnawing away at me.

Trying to focus on the pot on the stove, I bestow Paul's deliciously-scented chicken concoction with the rapt care and attention I'd normally reserve for a baby — someone else's baby, that is. Always a far scarier prospect than looking after your own. Maybe I'll be like this with my grandchild, at first: over-attentive, as if handling a grenade that might blow up in my face. No, it'll be *fine*. While it's a long time since I've held a baby in my arms, how scary can the child of Morgan and Jenna actually be? As the tomatoey sauce gradually reduces, I add more wine, and *taste, taste, taste*, as per Brad's instructions. *How can you possibly create a beaudiful dish if you don't know what it needs?*

It needs more herbs. On closer investigation the little piles of chopped greenery on Paul's worktop appear to be thyme, parsley and, I think, tarragon. Home grown, obviously: more bunched herbs fill a wooden box, along with green beans and soil-speckled potatoes, on the worktop. I fill the kettle and click it on, beginning to relax again in the cosy, well-ordered kitchen. I rinse and top and tail the beans, glancing at a shelf crammed with cookbooks: well-worn, by the look of them. In a space between them sits a hand-drawn Father's Day card, its edges curling. TO THE BEST DAD IN THE WORLD! it reads, in wobbly capital letters.

The beans are simmering away now. I turn off the heat and drain them; don't want to boil them to oblivion. Then — just because it seems like a Wilton Grange thing to do — I tip them into a bowl and add a generous dollop of butter and plenty of paper and salt.

The door opens. I turn to see Paul, with a protective arm around a very smartly dressed Mrs B. "Our dinner guest," he says with a grin.

"Oh! Lovely to see you, Mrs B." I catch a hint of floral fragrance as I kiss her cheek, then stand back and look at her. I hope it doesn't seem rude; I just can't help it. The colour has returned to her cheeks, and her eyes are bright and sparkling. She looks as if she has just returned from a long holiday.

"You too, Audrey." She smiles and looks around the kitchen. "Mmm, something smells good in here."

"I think we're almost ready," I add.

"Sorry, Aud," Paul says quickly. "I know Mrs B doesn't like to eat too late, everything was a bit rushed . . ."

"It's fine, I was enjoying myself here." I turn to Mrs B. "Where would you like to sit?"

"Oh, I don't mind," she says. "It's just good to be out. I never go out to dinner these days." Either she has forgotten the fish bone incident, or conveniently shut it out of her mind. We take our seats at the table as Paul lights a candle and checks the dish on the hob.

"Good work, Audrey," he says with a teasing smile, then quickly sets the table for three. "Will you have wine, Mrs B?"

She frowns at him. "Of course I will. What did you think I'd have? Lemonade?"

"But your medication—" I start.

"Audrey," she says firmly, "you're not on duty this evening. You're not taking care of me."

"No, of course not," I say, my cheeks reddening.

"I'm sorry . . ." She frowns and touches my hand. "I was appalled, you know, when Victoria said you weren't needed any more . . ." She nods tersely as Paul serves her with a small portion from the earthenware pot.

"It's okay, Mrs B. I'll be fine, you know." I smile my thanks as Paul hands me a serving spoon, and scoop chicken, plus beans, onto my plate.

"I mean I'm sorry you don't have your job any more, Audrey," she adds.

"It's fine, honestly. I've loved working here, but I probably need to move on — from *both* jobs, I mean—"

"Really?" Paul exclaims. "But why? You're dinner lady of the year . . ."

"Yes, but ten years is long enough, I think. It's time for a change." I look at Paul, aware of those butterflies starting up again. I clear my throat and turn back to Mrs B. "Can I ask you . . . what's happening with your house?"

She chews noisily, then sips her wine. "Nothing," she says firmly.

"But, I thought, I mean, Victoria said . . ."

"We've talked it through," she interrupts. "Mmm, this really is good, Paul. Better, even, than last time . . ."

I stare at him. "You mean . . ." I start.

"Oh, yes," Mrs B says. "I've had this before. Paul often brings me these tasty things to the house, it's all very *French* around here . . ." She laughs, and it strikes me how right it feels, the three of us eating together as if we do this kind of thing all the time. "I'm not moving, Audrey," Mrs B adds.

"But I thought—"

"Yes, I know Victoria thinks she knows best, and I agreed to sign the house over to her." She pauses. Another swig of wine. Blimey, she can put it away. "It made sense, you see, and she does want what's best for me — or what she *thinks* is best . . ." Her pale grey eyes bore into mine. "But do you honestly think anyone should let their child dictate how they live their life?"

I pause, a bean speared on my fork. "No, I don't. I mean, I'd do anything for Morgan but I wouldn't let him make those choices for me, not if I could help it . . ."

"Well, I *can* help it," she exclaims, rapping the table, "and I'm staying. The only way I am leaving this house is in a coffin and, well, I have a proposition for the two of you." I swallow hard, already a little giddy from the wine, as Paul tops up our glasses. "Victoria's right," she continues as he clears our plates. "The house is too big, it's neglected, unused . . . such a terrible waste."

He sets a perfect lemon tart, its surface utterly flawless, on the table. "Ooh, this looks good," she says approvingly. "So . . . could we set up some kind of café or tearoom, do you think?"

A small silence settles over the room. "What do you mean, Mrs B?"

"I mean, I don't know . . ." She shrugs. "Somewhere people would love to go."

I pause, wondering if her thoughts are beginning to wander now. Yet she seems razor sharp. "You mean . . . somewhere in town?"

"No, here. No, not here — in *my* house, I mean. In the garden. What do you think?"

"I . . . wouldn't know what's involved," I start, glancing at Paul.

"But you could find out. You could manage this, Audrey. You're far too smart to be my carer. You shouldn't be spending your time cleaning my kitchen and washing my hair—"

"I've always been happy to wash your hair," I cut in.

She peers at me as Paul cuts her a slice of tart. "I want to see this old house brought to life again," she goes on. "That's what I've been wanting to tell you, Audrey. I don't need daytime naps, or to be fussed over all day. I want to feel part of something . . ." She breaks off and jabs a piece of tart into her mouth. "Paul," she adds, "we have a glut of herbs and vegetables here. I don't know what you do with them all—"

"Well, Audrey has some," he points out.

"Yes, but we have more than we can ever use between us."

I sip my wine, remembering Brad with his plans for the pub: okay, so maybe we're not talking cheese, bees or cider. But we could start . . . *something*. I turn to Mrs B, my heart quickening. "You know, I think you're right. I'm sure the three of us can do something amazing here . . ."

"I know we can," she asserts. "But for goodness' sake, could I ask the two of you one thing?" Her sharp tone stings us. I look at Paul, and under the table his fingers brush against mine, sending a shiver right through me. "Please stop calling me Mrs B," she says,

416

draining her glass. "It's Elizabeth, all right?" Her face softens, and she beams at the two of us. "I'd like you to call me Elizabeth from now on."

"Okay, Mrs — Elizabeth," I say with a smile.

"Thank you. I'd appreciate that." She turns to Paul, her eyes glinting mischievously in the candlelight. "Now Paul, could you stop gazing at Audrey for a moment and please refill my glass?"

Eight Months Later

Dear Mum,

Thank you so much for the beautiful baby dresses you sent for Mia. I couldn't believe you'd kept them after all this time, and had stitched in those embroidered name labels in every one. Jenna was amazed. She didn't know my maiden name. She thought they'd belonged to the real Audrey!

I'm sure they'll soon fit Mia perfectly. She is a gorgeous baby and Morgan and Jenna are doing incredibly well as new parents. They're so much more relaxed than I was. They're now living in the house in Castle Street and I have moved in with my newish boyfriend, Paul, in a cottage in the grounds of the big house where we both work. I am managing the café we've opened and sort of overseeing things with the lady who owns the place. She says I'm her right-hand woman.

To be honest, Paul has taken charge of the cooking. It's more his thing, really — he's a natural. I did a posh French cookery course, and he's just fiddled about in his kitchen, and he's far better than I am! What I am good at, though, is making things happen. I don't want to seem boastful, but I sorted out all the permissions to open the café and got the certificates we needed. I hired the staff and trained them, making sure we do things as efficiently as possible — I think being a dinner lady has been pretty useful actually. Maybe I'm not just good with children, but people generally because our customers keep coming back. We do simple lunches, and afternoon teas, and Morgan looks after the gardens. He loves it. I think he's found his niche.

Anyway, enough about us. I was delighted that you're planning to come up and stay. We have plenty of room for you here. Mrs B has a whole upper floor of her house that she doesn't even use, and I can get a room ready for you. It's wonderful seeing this old house coming alive.

Paul would love to meet you, Mum, as would Mia of course. The funny thing is, she looks a lot like you!

Much love,
Audrey

To the manager, Wilton Grange Hotel

I enclose a cheque for £434.24 in settlement of my unpaid extras bill for my stay (July 2–24). I realise this is a little late. Apologies.

With many thanks,
Audrey Pepper
(Dinner lady of the year)

Feeling inspired by Audrey's culinary adventures? Then turn the page for some of the dishes she tried her hand at.

Happy cooking!

The Highlight Recipes

Soupe à l'oignon

Everyone knows cheese and onion
are made for each other . . .

Ingredients
90g unsalted butter
8 onions, finely sliced
2 tbsp plain flour
6 tbsp red wine
150ml white wine
1 tsp sugar
4 slices baguette
2 tbsp olive oil
150g cheese, grated

Method
- Melt the butter in a saucepan and gently sauté the onions until soft and translucent.
- In a heatproof jug, mix the wines and 1.5 litres of boiling water.

- Sprinkle the onions with flour and stir, then pour the liquid over the onions and stir again.
- Simmer gently for 15–20 minutes, skimming any impurities from the surface. Add a little more boiling water if your soup is looking too thick. Add the sugar and season to taste.
- To make the croutons, rub one side of the baguette slices with olive oil and sprinkle with grated cheese. Grill until bubbling.
- Pour the soup into bowls, float the croutons on top and enjoy.

Moules Marinière

Simple but Frenchly impressive

Ingredients
2kg mussels
30g butter
6 shallots, thinly sliced
2 cloves garlic, crushed
150ml dry white wine
A handful of chopped parsley

Method
- Scrub the mussels thoroughly under running cold water. To debeard them, tug away the black threads, then tap each mussel to check that it closes. Discard any with cracked shells or that won't close when tapped.
- Melt the butter in a large saucepan, toss in the shallots, then the garlic, and sauté for a few minutes until the shallots have softened.
- Add the wine plus 100ml water and simmer gently until it has reduced in volume by roughly a half.

Now add your mussels, covering the pan and simmering for around 5 minutes until all the mussels have opened.

- Tip the pan contents into a colander, over a bowl, so you catch the mussels. Pour the wine and shallot sauce back into the saucepan and bubble for a few minutes to reduce.
- To serve, divide the mussels into bowls, pour over the sauce, sprinkle with parsley and serve with fresh crusty bread.

Poulet en Cocotte Bonne Femme

A pot of buttery loveliness

Ingredients
8 chicken thighs
4 rashers of bacon, chopped small
300g shallots, peeled
500g small new potatoes
Approx. 30g butter
2 cloves garlic
A handful of chopped fresh herbs (e.g. thyme, tarragon, parsley), or a teaspoon of dried mixed herbs

Method
- Preheat the oven to 200°C (gas mark 6). Melt a knob of butter in a heatproof casserole on the hob. Add the bacon and fry until coloured, then remove with a slotted spoon and set aside.
- Add a little more butter to the pan and allow it to sizzle, then add the chicken. Brown in batches until well coloured on all sides. Remove from pan and set aside.

- Drop the shallots into a pan of boiling water. Simmer for 5 minutes, then drain.
- Drop the potatoes into a pan of water, bring to the boil and simmer until just tender, then drain. Add the shallots and potatoes to the casserole in which you browned your chicken, adding a little more butter if needed. Swoosh them around so they brown nicely.
- Sprinkle a little salt and the dried herbs (if using) over the chicken and place them in the casserole along with the potatoes and onions. Add the bacon and chopped herbs and turn up the heat, stirring so everything is sizzling gently.
- Place the casserole in the oven, with a lid or covered in foil, and roast for 45 minutes, basting the chicken with the buttery juices from time to time. Do keep an eye to check it isn't looking too dry, and add a little more butter if necessary. Enjoy with a leafy green salad (or leeks vinaigrette, below) and a glass of chilled white wine.

Leeks Vinaigrette

Delicious with just about anything — especially your rustic poulet, above — or enjoy on its own for lunch with crusty bread

Ingredients
6 leeks
Bouquet garni
2 large tomatoes
6 spring onions, finely chopped
A small bunch of chives, chopped
3 tbsp olive oil
1 tbsp balsamic vinegar
1 tbsp mustard

Method
- Trim both ends of the leeks, leaving just the tender white parts. Chop each leek into three or four pieces and drop into a pan of boiling water with the bouquet garni.
- Simmer for around 20 minutes until tender. Remove

the leeks with a slotted spoon and set aside — but don't discard the water in the pan.

- Drop the tomatoes into the still bubbling water for a few seconds, then lift out carefully with a slotted spoon. Allow the tomatoes to cool a little and strip off their skins — they should come away easily. Meanwhile, keep the pan of water (your leek stock) bubbling away until it has reduced by a third.

- Chop the tomatoes into small pieces and combine with the chopped spring onions and chives.

- To make your vinaigrette dressing, combine the olive oil, vinegar, mustard and 3 tablespoons of leek stock from the pan until it forms a smooth emulsion. Season well and add the tomato and spring onion mixture.

- Place your leeks in a shallow serving bowl and dress with the tomatoey vinaigrette, finishing with a few grinds of black pepper.

Crème Brûlée

A super-easy take on the classic posh custard

Audrey cooked her custard on the hob, with curdling consequences. This method — gently baked in the oven — is an altogether less nerve-racking prospect. As the brûlées should be chilled overnight, it's best to make these the day before you serve them.

Ingredients
4 large egg yolks
4 tbsp caster sugar, plus extra for dusting the tops
500ml double cream
1 vanilla pod or a few drops of quality vanilla essence
For individual brûlées you will need four ramekins

Method
- Pre-heat your oven at 110°C, gas mark 1/4. Whisk together the egg yolks and sugar in a heatproof bowl until pale and fluffy.
- Heat the cream in a pan until just below boiling point. Pour the cream into the bowl, stirring as you

do so. Slit the vanilla pod if using, scrape out the seeds and add to the bowl, or add the vanilla essence. If you have used a vanilla pod, sieve your mixture to remove the seeds.

- Place four ramekins in a deep roasting tin and divide your mixture between them. Boil a kettle, and carefully pour the water into the tin until it reaches halfway up the ramekins. Take care not to slosh water onto your brûlées. Bake for 45 minutes, then allow to cool and chill in the fridge overnight.

- For the topping, sprinkle each brûlée with caster sugar to around the depth of a pound coin. If you're being fancy, use a blowtorch to caramelise the tops. Otherwise, set your grill as hot as it can go and place your brûlées underneath until the sugary tops are golden and bubbling. Allow to cool and tuck in.

Madeleines

Buttery, lemony, light-as-a-feather cakes

Makes 12

Ingredients
2 eggs
100g caster sugar
100g plain flour
1 lemon, juice squeezed and zest finely grated
3/4 teaspoon baking powder
100g butter, melted and cooled
You'll need a shell-shaped madeleine tin for this

Method
- Brush your tray with melted butter, then shake in a little flour through a sieve, brushing off any excess. This will ensure your madeleines easily slip out of the tin.
- Whisk the eggs and sugar until lightly foamed, then whisk in the flour, melted butter, baking powder and lemon juice and zest. Leave to stand for 20 minutes.

- Pour into the madeleine tray and bake for 8–10 minutes until risen, lightly golden and springy to touch. Cool on a wire rack and enjoy with a cuppa.

AS GOOD AS IT GETS?

Fiona Gibson

Charlotte Bristow is worried about her husband Will. With her sixteen-year-old daughter Rosie newly signed to a top modelling agency, and Will recently out of a job, things are changing in their household. As Will dusts down his old leather trousers and starts partying with their new "fun" neighbours, Charlotte begins to wonder what on earth is going on. So when Fraser, Charlotte's ex — and father of Rosie — suddenly arrives back on the scene, she starts to imagine what might have been . . .

LUCKY GIRL

Fiona Gibson

Everyone always told Stella Moon how lucky she was to have a famous dad. But when her mum died, and he withdrew to his allotment leaving Stella and her brother alone to play in rusty cars and exist for a whole week on Black Forest gateaux, she didn't feel lucky at all.

Now in her thirties Stella has made sure she has a strict routine as a music teacher and a peaceful, tidy home. Until two noisy little girls move in next door.

At first, she feels besieged. The girls hound her, bearing sticky gifts of edible jewellery and firing personal questions. But it's their friendship that helps her to confront the truth about her own childhood and start living life to the full.